BALTIMORE

Empty Graves

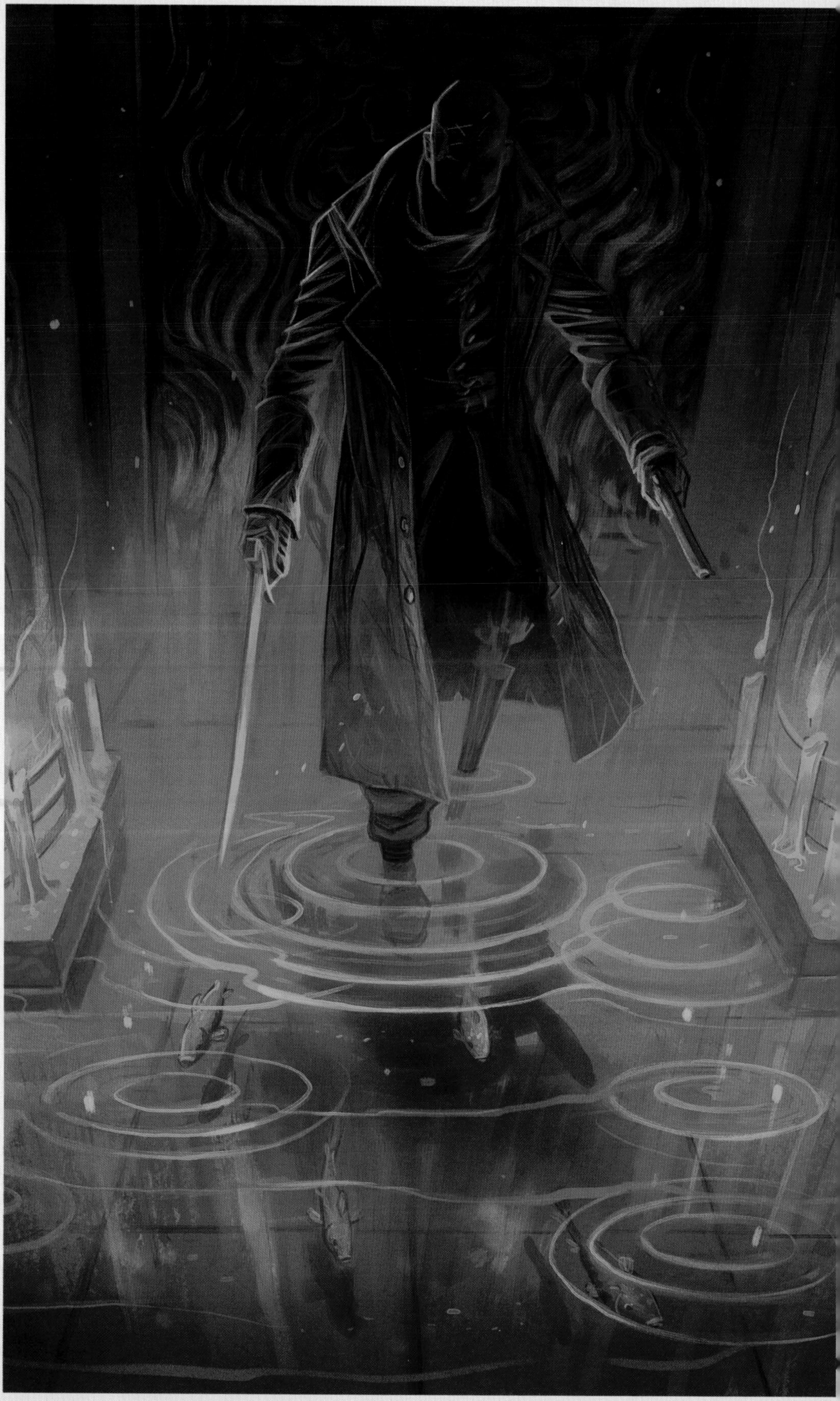

BALTIMORE™
EMPTY GRAVES

VOLUME SEVEN

Story by
MIKE MIGNOLA
CHRISTOPHER GOLDEN

Art by
PETER BERGTING

Colors by
MICHELLE MADSEN

Letters by
CLEM ROBINS

Cover Art by
MIKE MIGNOLA with **DAVE STEWART**

Chapter Break Art by
BEN STENBECK with **DAVE STEWART**

Publisher **MIKE RICHARDSON**

Editor **SCOTT ALLIE**

Associate Editor **HANNAH MEANS-SHANNON**

Assistant Editor **KATII O'BRIEN**

Collection Designer **CINDY CACEREZ-SPRAGUE**

Digital Art Technician **CHRISTINA MCKENZIE**

DARK HORSE BOOKS

Neil Hankerson *Executive Vice President* • Tom Weddle *Chief Financial Officer* • Randy Stradley *Vice President of Publishing* • Michael Martens *Vice President of Book Trade Sales* • Matt Parkinson Vice President of Marketing • David Scroggy *Vice President of Product Development* • Dale LaFountain *Vice President of Information Technology* • Cara Niece *Vice President of Production and Scheduling* • Nick McWhorter *Vice President of Media Licensing* • Ken Lizzi *General Counsel* • Dave Marshall *Editor in Chief* • Davey Estrada *Editorial Director* • Scott Allie *Executive Senior Editor* • Chris Warner *Senior Books Editor* • Cary Grazzini *Director of Specialty Projects* • Lia Ribacchi *Art Director* • Vanessa Todd *Director of Print Purchasing* • Matt Dryer *Director of Digital Art and Prepress* • Mark Bernardi *Director of Digital Publishing* • Sarah Robertson *Director of Product Sales* • Michael Gombos *Director of International Publishing and Licensing*

DarkHorse.com

Published by Dark Horse Books
A division of Dark Horse Comics, Inc.
10956 SE Main Street
Milwaukie, OR 97222

International Licensing: (503) 905-2377
Comic Shop Locator Service: (888) 266-4226

First edition: December 2016
ISBN 978-1-50670-042-7

1 3 5 7 9 10 8 6 4 2

Printed in China

This volume collects *Baltimore: Empty Graves* #1–#5, published by Dark Horse Comics.

Library of Congress Cataloging-in-Publication Data

Names: Mignola, Michael, author. | Golden, Christopher, author. | Bergting,
  Peter, artist. | Madsen, Michelle (Illustrator), artist. | Robins, Clem,
  1955- letterer. | Stenbeck, Ben, artist. | Stewart, Dave, artist.
Title: Baltimore. Volume 7, Empty graves / story by Mike Mignola, Christopher
  Golden ; art by Peter Bergting ; colors by Michelle Madsen ; letters by
  Clem Robins ; cover art by Mike Mignola with Dave Stewart ; chapter break
  art by Ben Stenbeck with Dave Stewart.
Other titles: Empty graves
Description: Milwaukie, OR : Dark Horse Books, 2016.
Identifiers: LCCN 2016031768 | ISBN 9781506700427 (hardback)
Subjects: LCSH: Comic books, strips, etc. | BISAC: COMICS & GRAPHIC NOVELS /
  Horror.
Classification: LCC PN6727.M53 B38 2016 | DDC 741.5/973--dc23
LC record available at https://lccn.loc.gov/2016031768

CHAPTER ONE

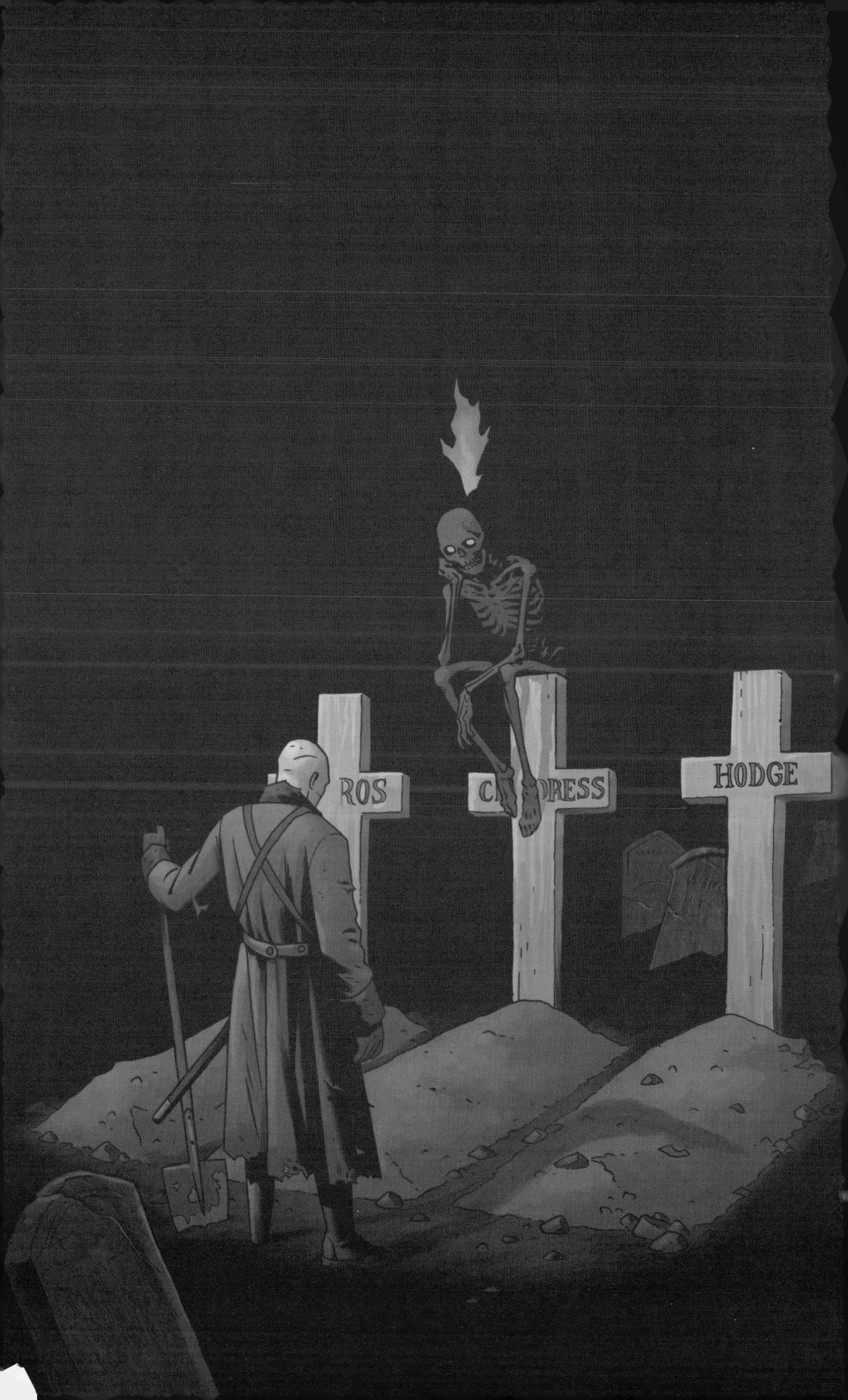
ROS
HODGE

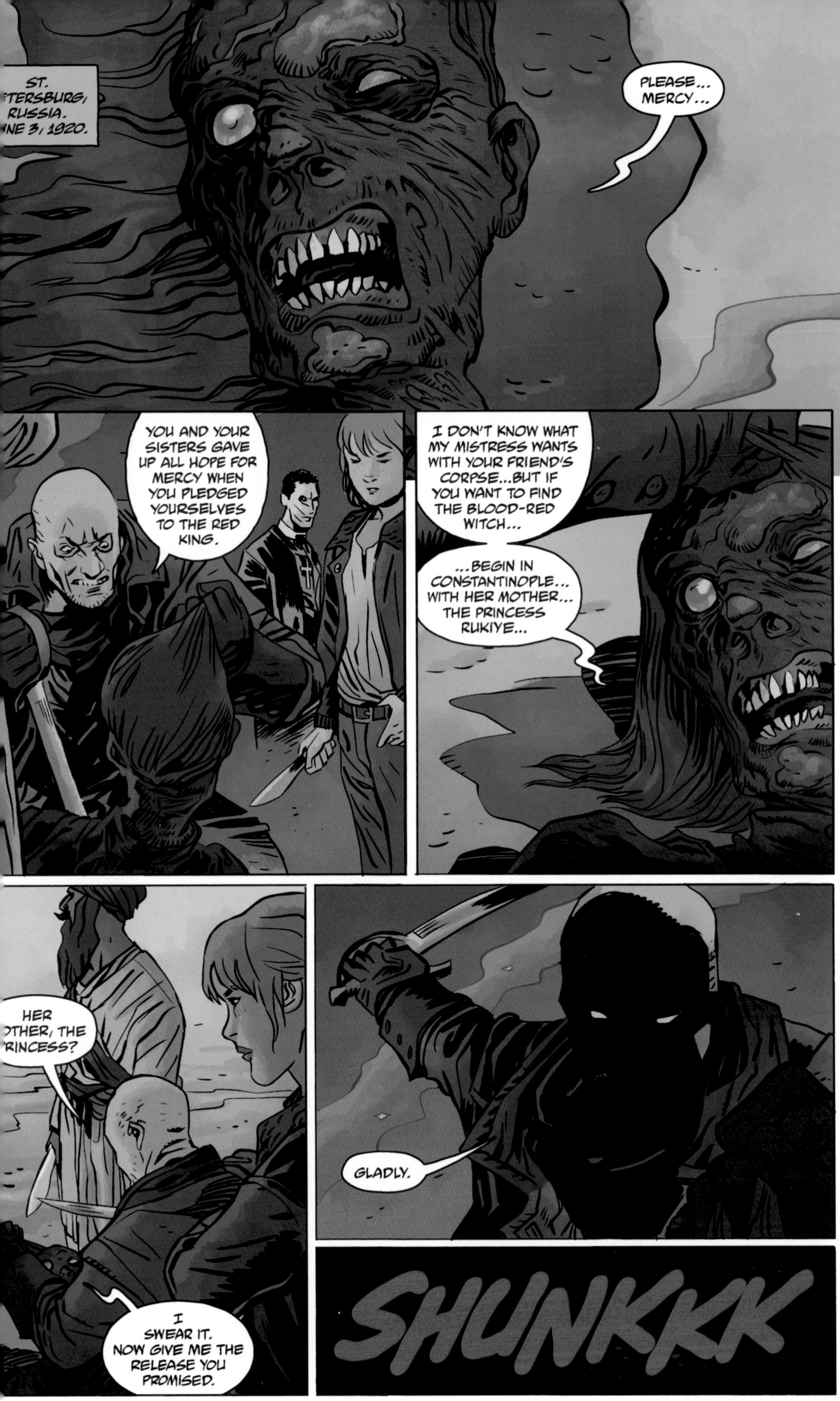
ST. ETERSBURG, RUSSIA. NE 3, 1920.
PLEASE... MERCY...
YOU AND YOUR SISTERS GAVE UP ALL HOPE FOR MERCY WHEN YOU PLEDGED YOURSELVES TO THE RED KING.
I DON'T KNOW WHAT MY MISTRESS WANTS WITH YOUR FRIEND'S CORPSE...BUT IF YOU WANT TO FIND THE BLOOD-RED WITCH...
...BEGIN IN CONSTANTINOPLE... WITH HER MOTHER... THE PRINCESS RUKIYE...
HER OTHER, THE RINCESS?
I SWEAR IT. NOW GIVE ME THE RELEASE YOU PROMISED.
GLADLY.
SHUNKKK

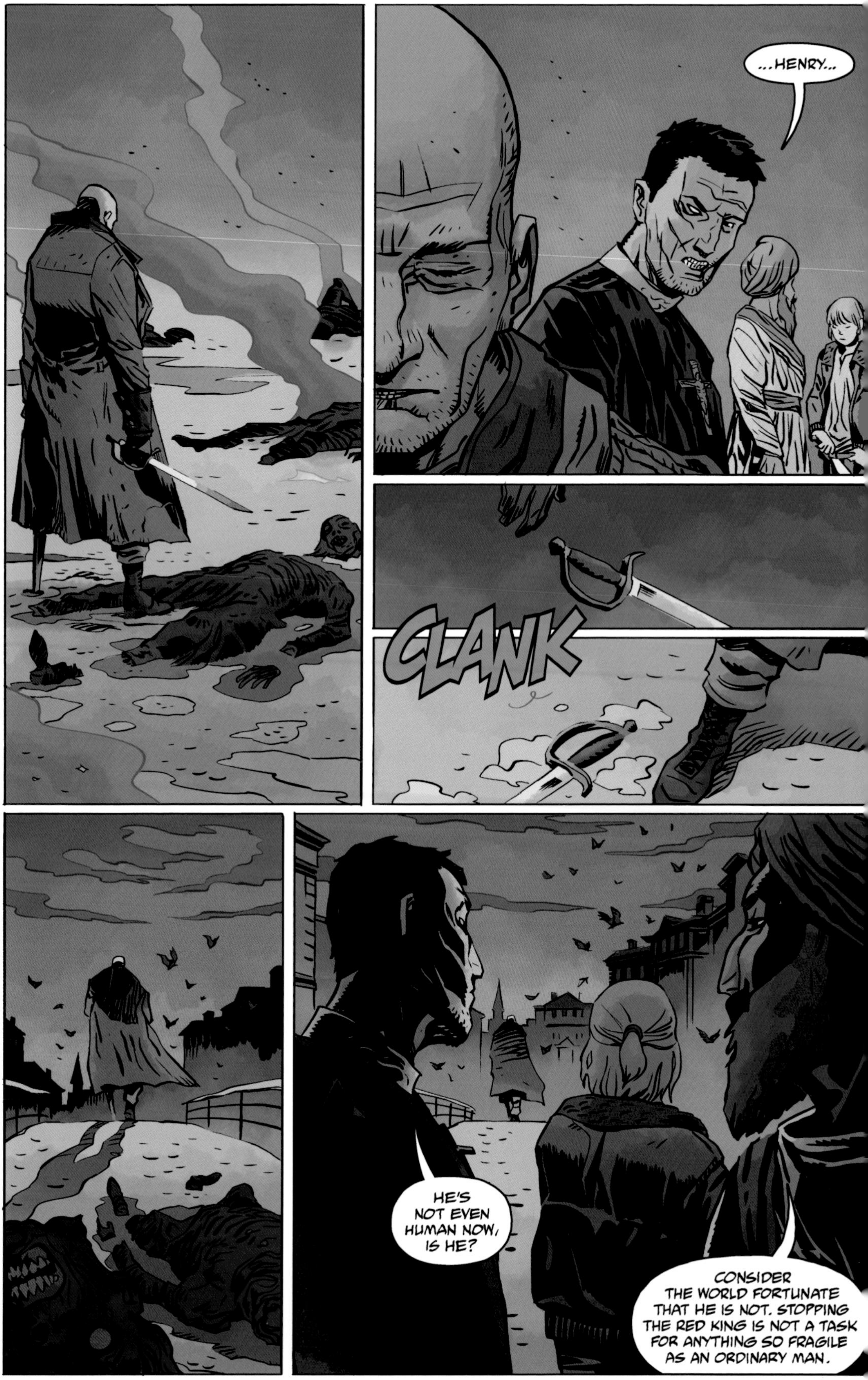
...HENRY...
CLANK
HE'S NOT EVEN HUMAN NOW, IS HE?
CONSIDER THE WORLD FORTUNATE THAT HE IS NOT. STOPPING THE RED KING IS NOT A TASK FOR ANYTHING SO FRAGILE AS AN ORDINARY MAN.

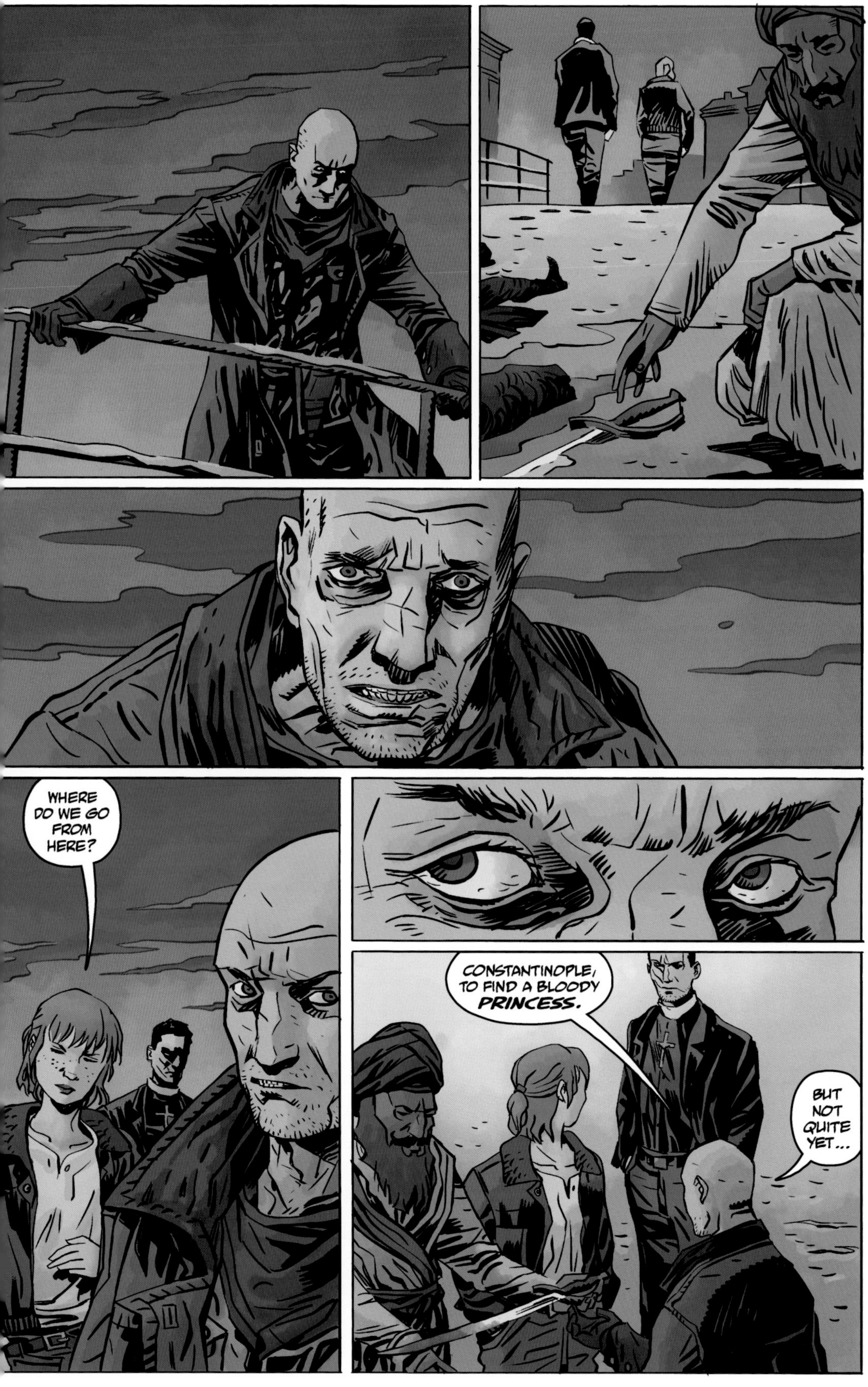
WHERE DO WE GO FROM HERE?
CONSTANTINOPLE, TO FIND A BLOODY PRINCESS.
BUT NOT QUITE YET...

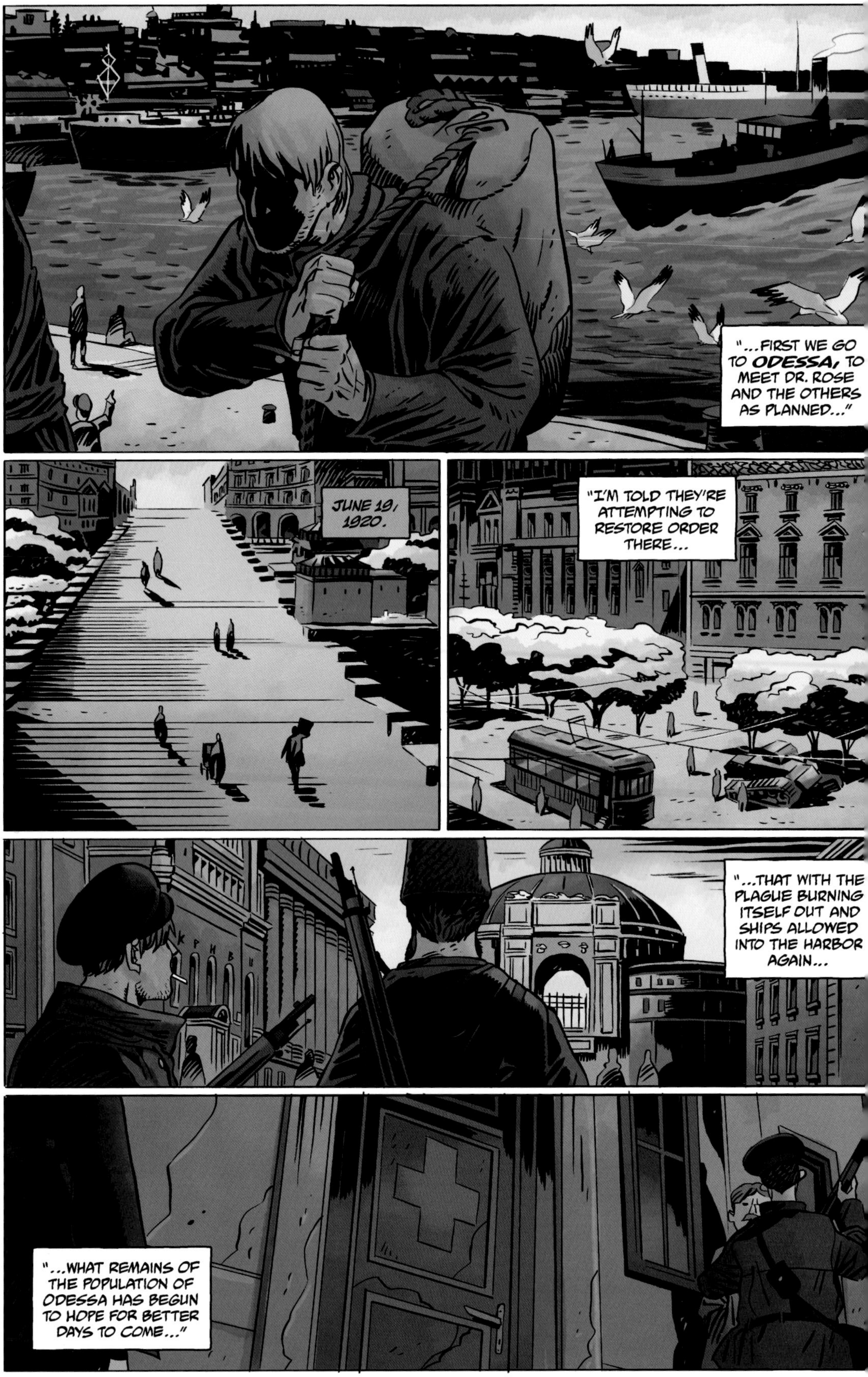
"...FIRST WE GO TO ODESSA, TO MEET DR. ROSE AND THE OTHERS AS PLANNED..."
JUNE 19, 1920.
"I'M TOLD THEY'RE ATTEMPTING TO RESTORE ORDER THERE...
"...THAT WITH THE PLAGUE BURNING ITSELF OUT AND SHIPS ALLOWED INTO THE HARBOR AGAIN...
"...WHAT REMAINS OF THE POPULATION OF ODESSA HAS BEGUN TO HOPE FOR BETTER DAYS TO COME..."

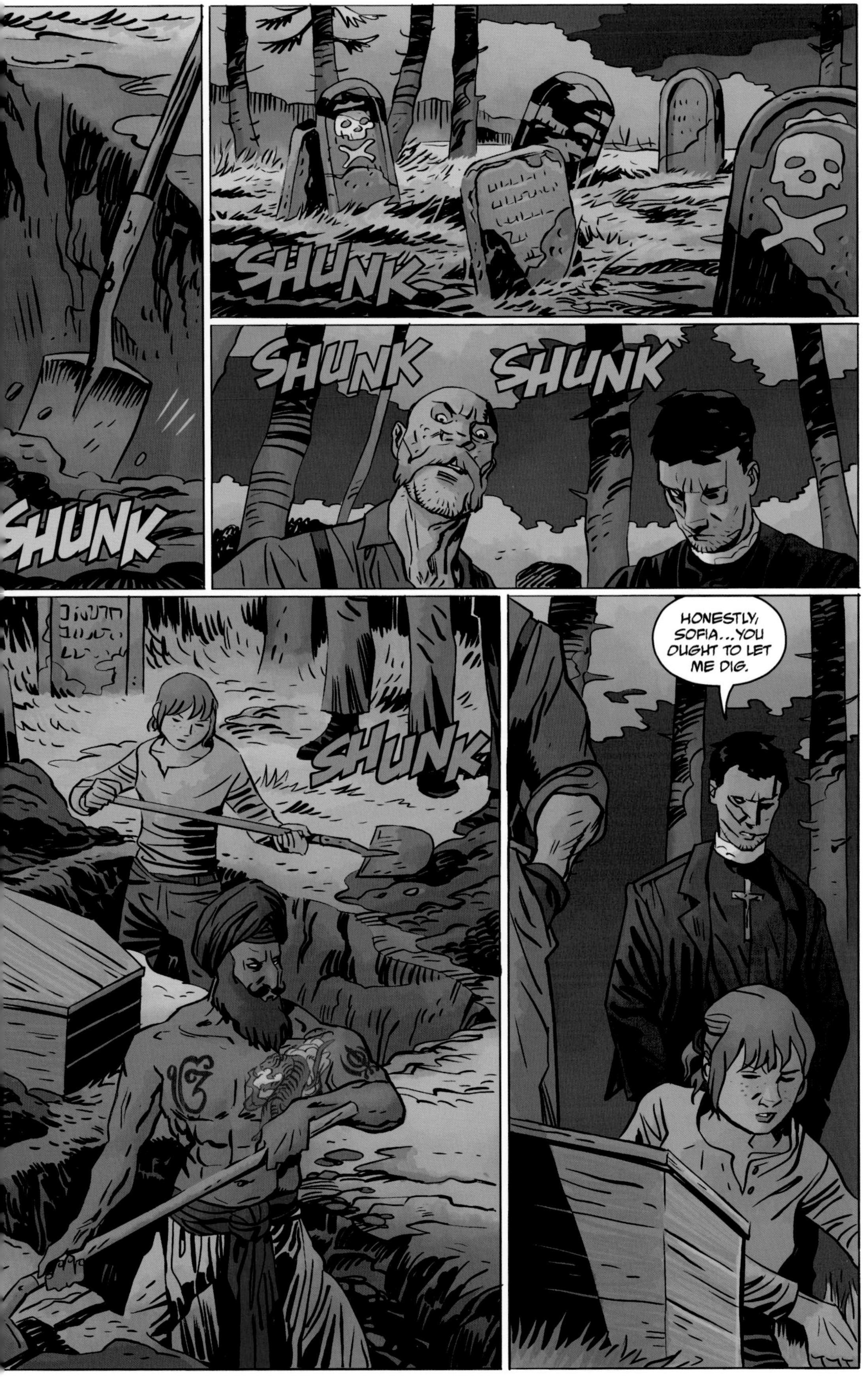
SHUNK
SHUNK
SHUNK
SHUNK
SHUNK
HONESTLY, SOFIA...YOU OUGHT TO LET ME DIG.

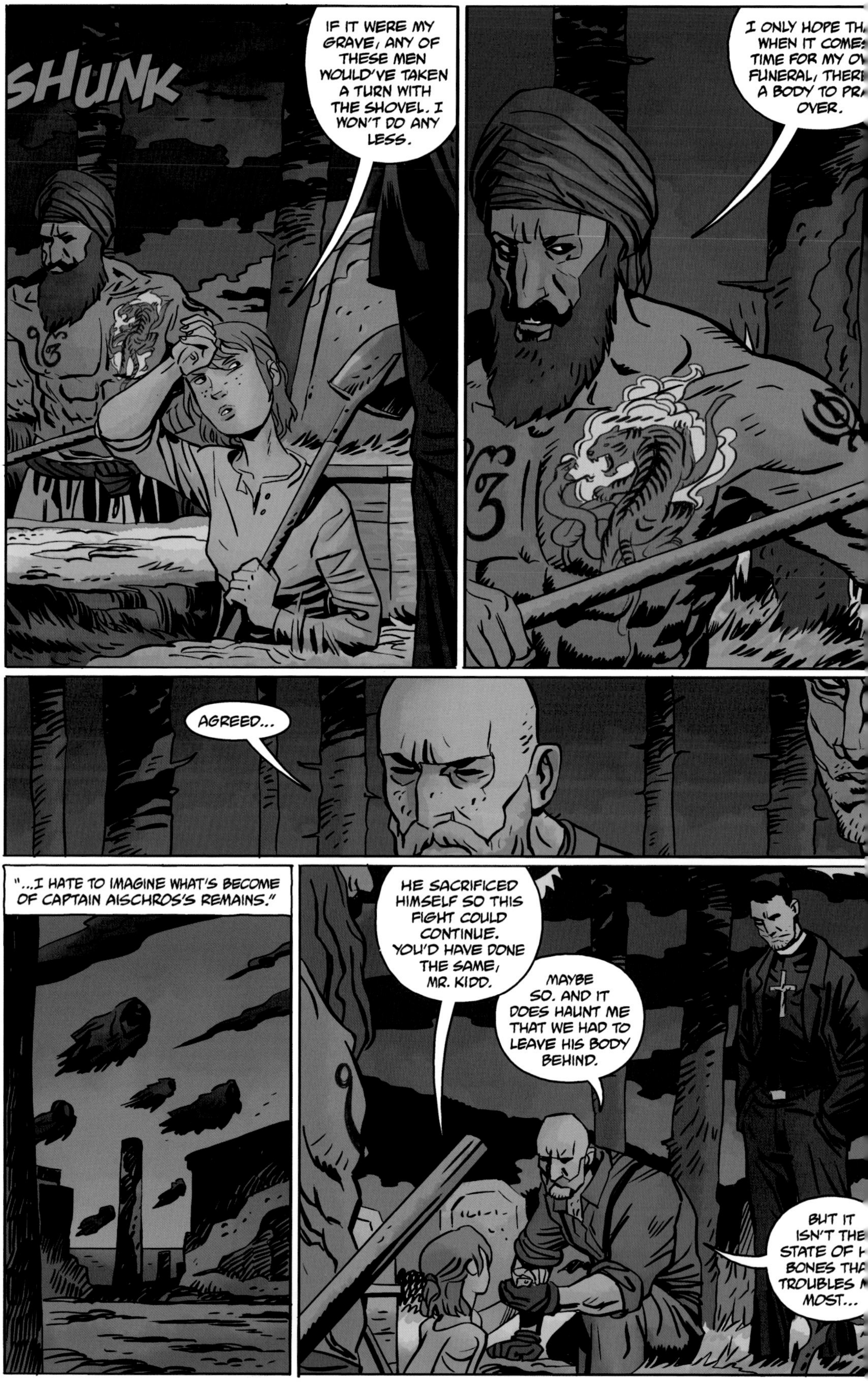
SHUNK
IF IT WERE MY GRAVE, ANY OF THESE MEN WOULD'VE TAKEN A TURN WITH THE SHOVEL. I WON'T DO ANY LESS.
I ONLY HOPE TH WHEN IT COME TIME FOR MY O FUNERAL, THER A BODY TO PR OVER.
AGREED...
"...I HATE TO IMAGINE WHAT'S BECOME OF CAPTAIN AISCHROS'S REMAINS."
HE SACRIFICED HIMSELF SO THIS FIGHT COULD CONTINUE. YOU'D HAVE DONE THE SAME, MR. KIDD.
MAYBE SO. AND IT DOES HAUNT ME THAT WE HAD TO LEAVE HIS BODY BEHIND.
BUT IT ISN'T THE STATE OF H BONES THA TROUBLES M MOST...

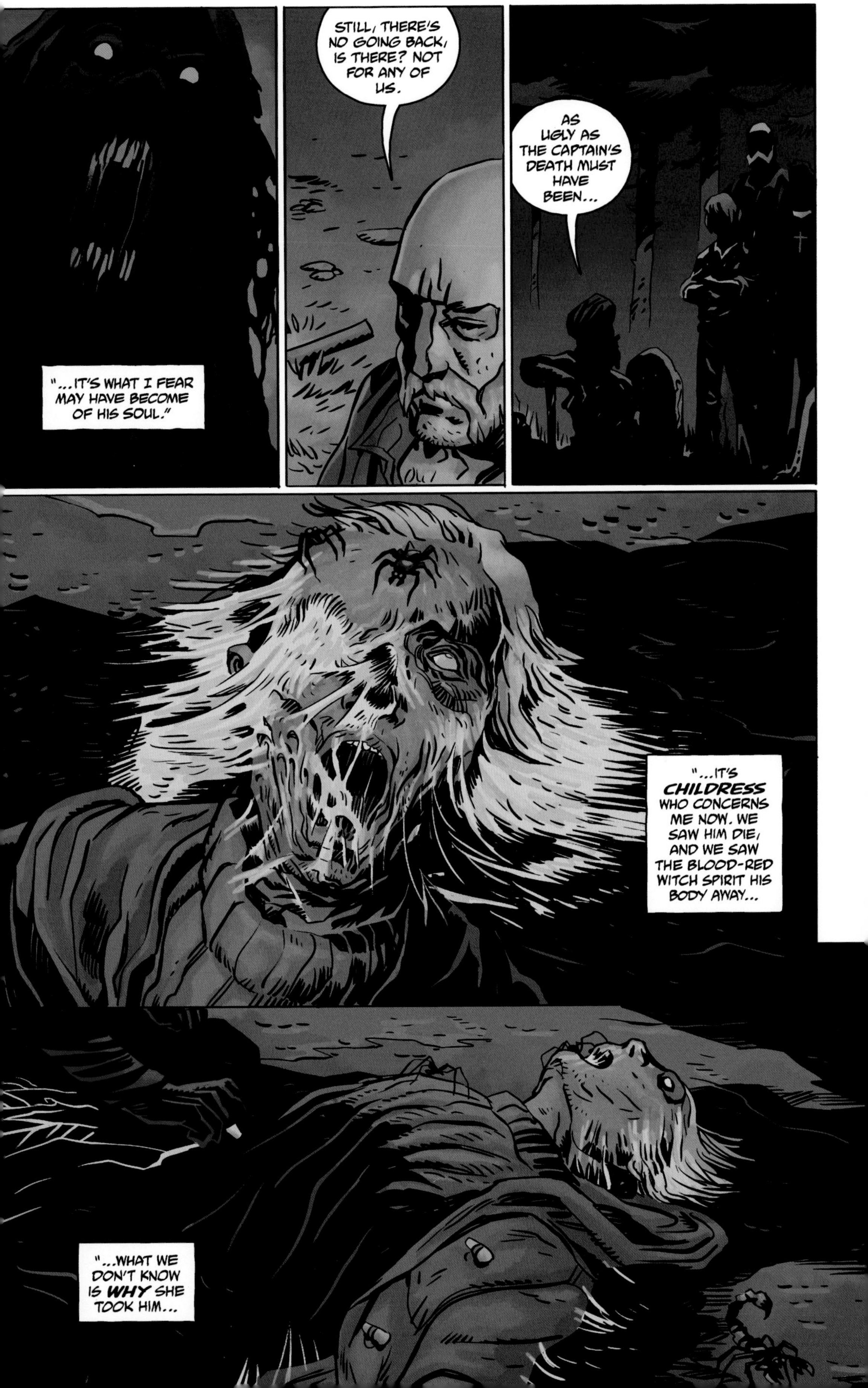
"...IT'S WHAT I FEAR MAY HAVE BECOME OF HIS SOUL."
STILL, THERE'S NO GOING BACK, IS THERE? NOT FOR ANY OF US.
AS UGLY AS THE CAPTAIN'S DEATH MUST HAVE BEEN...
"...IT'S CHILDRESS WHO CONCERNS ME NOW. WE SAW HIM DIE, AND WE SAW THE BLOOD-RED WITCH SPIRIT HIS BODY AWAY...
"...WHAT WE DON'T KNOW IS WHY SHE TOOK HIM...

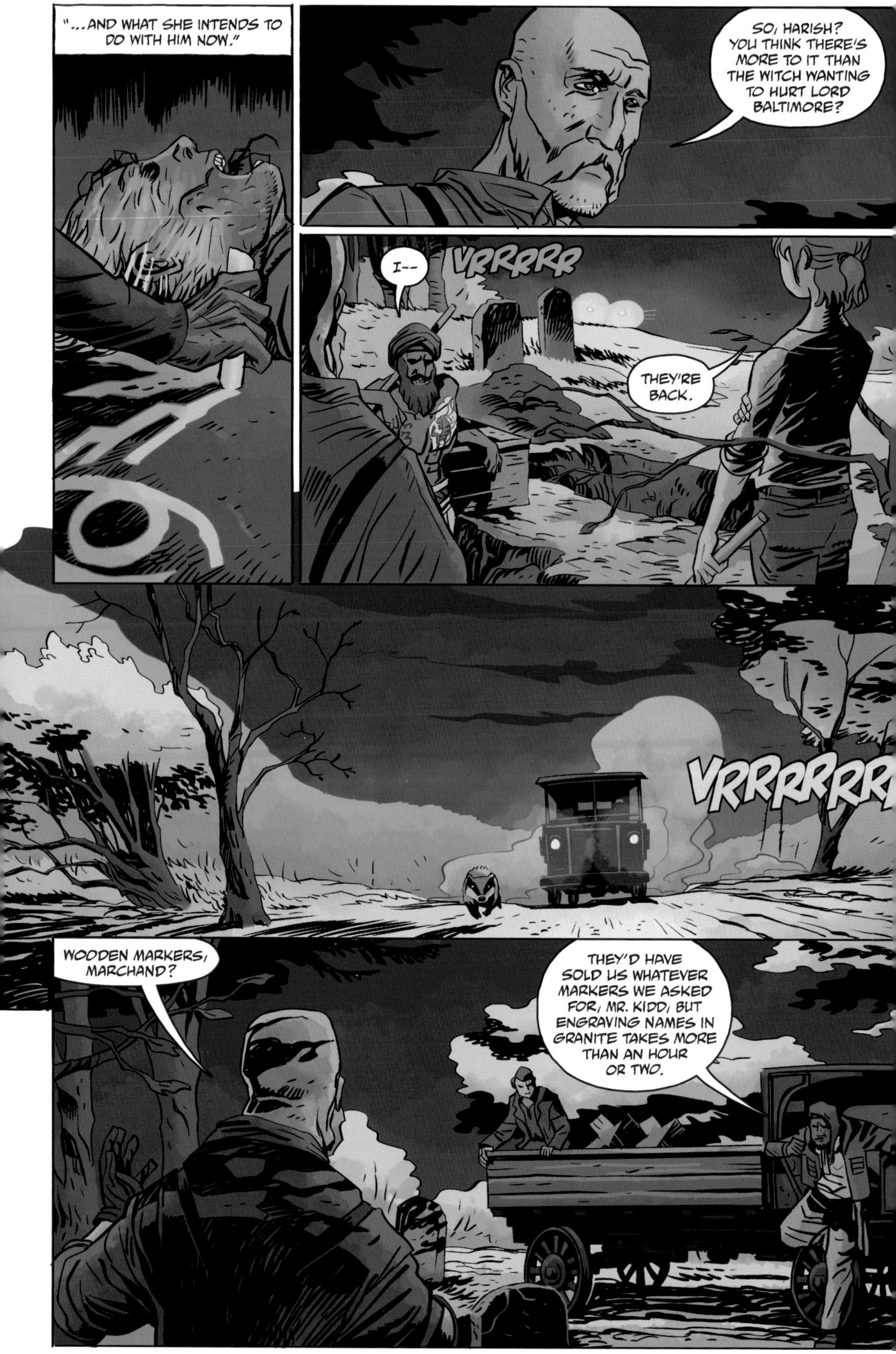
"...AND WHAT SHE INTENDS TO DO WITH HIM NOW."
SO, HARISH? YOU THINK THERE'S MORE TO IT THAN THE WITCH WANTING TO HURT LORD BALTIMORE?
I--
VRRRRR
THEY'RE BACK.
VRRRRRR
WOODEN MARKERS, MARCHAND?
THEY'D HAVE SOLD US WHATEVER MARKERS WE ASKED FOR, MR. KIDD, BUT ENGRAVING NAMES IN GRANITE TAKES MORE THAN AN HOUR OR TWO.

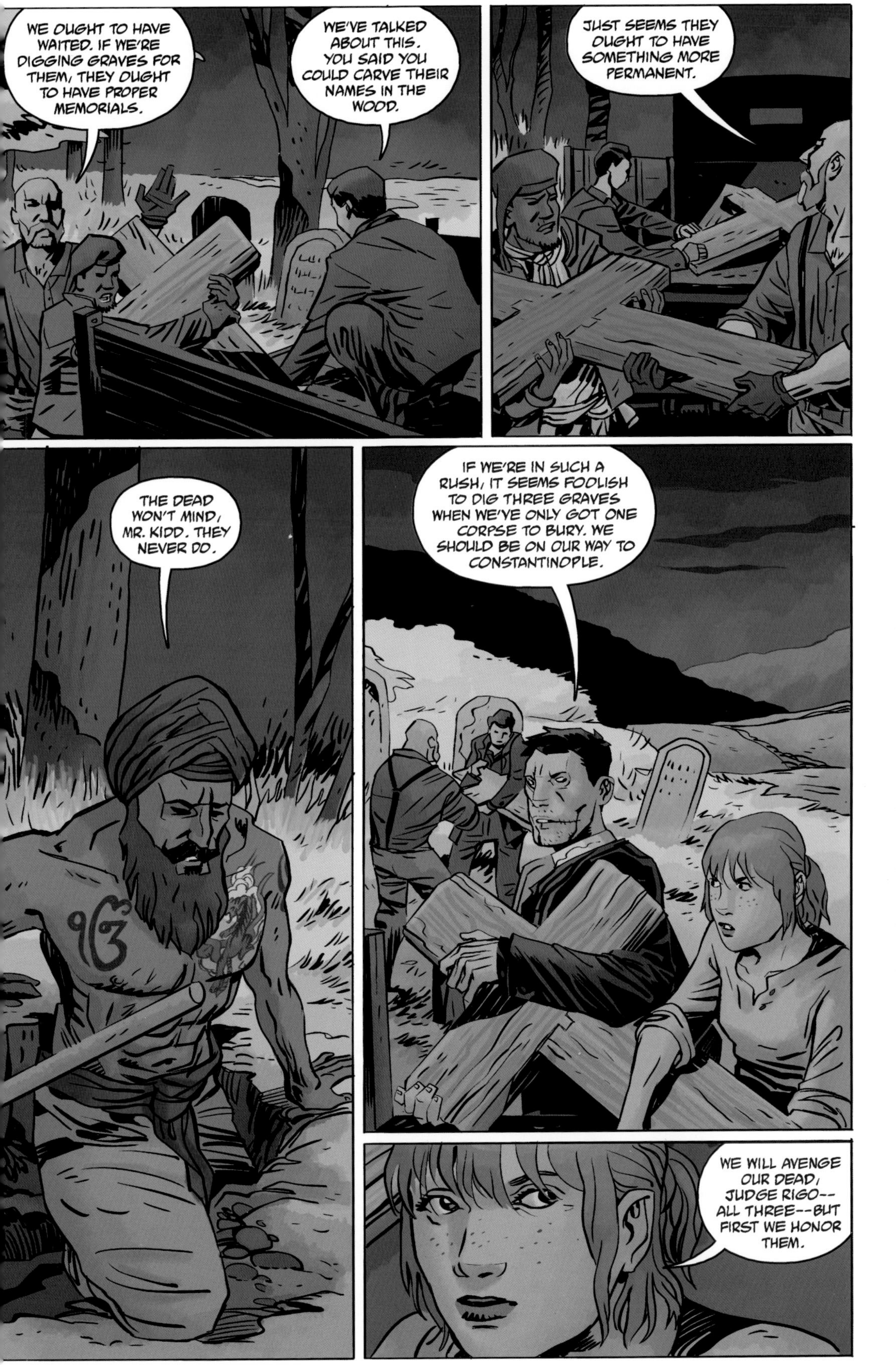
WE OUGHT TO HAVE WAITED. IF WE'RE DIGGING GRAVES FOR THEM, THEY OUGHT TO HAVE PROPER MEMORIALS.
WE'VE TALKED ABOUT THIS. YOU SAID YOU COULD CARVE THEIR NAMES IN THE WOOD.
JUST SEEMS THEY OUGHT TO HAVE SOMETHING MORE PERMANENT.
THE DEAD WON'T MIND, MR. KIDD. THEY NEVER DO.
IF WE'RE IN SUCH A RUSH, IT SEEMS FOOLISH TO DIG THREE GRAVES WHEN WE'VE ONLY GOT ONE CORPSE TO BURY. WE SHOULD BE ON OUR WAY TO CONSTANTINOPLE.
WE WILL AVENGE OUR DEAD, JUDGE RIGO-- ALL THREE--BUT FIRST WE HONOR THEM.

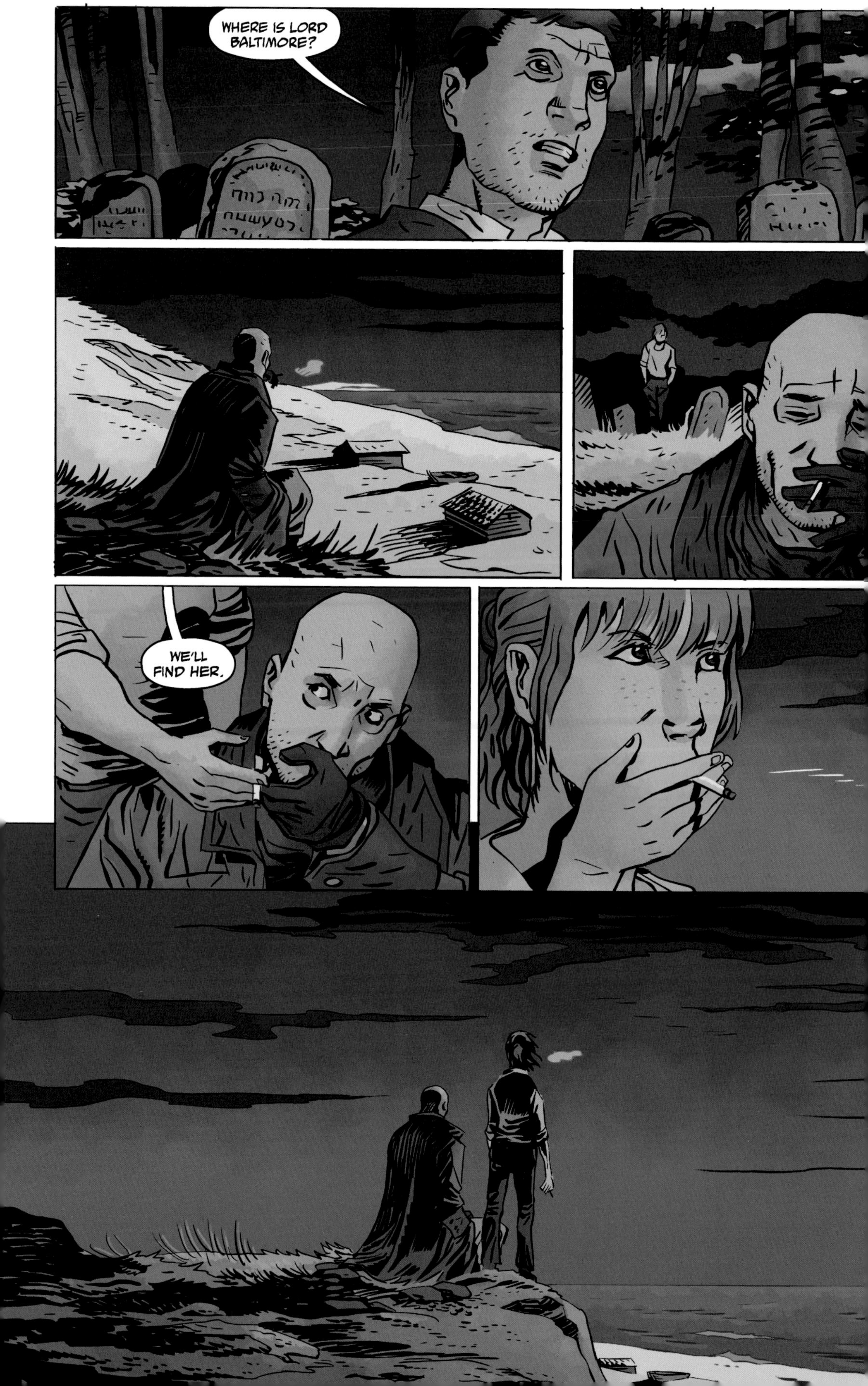
WHERE IS LORD BALTIMORE?
WE'LL FIND HER.

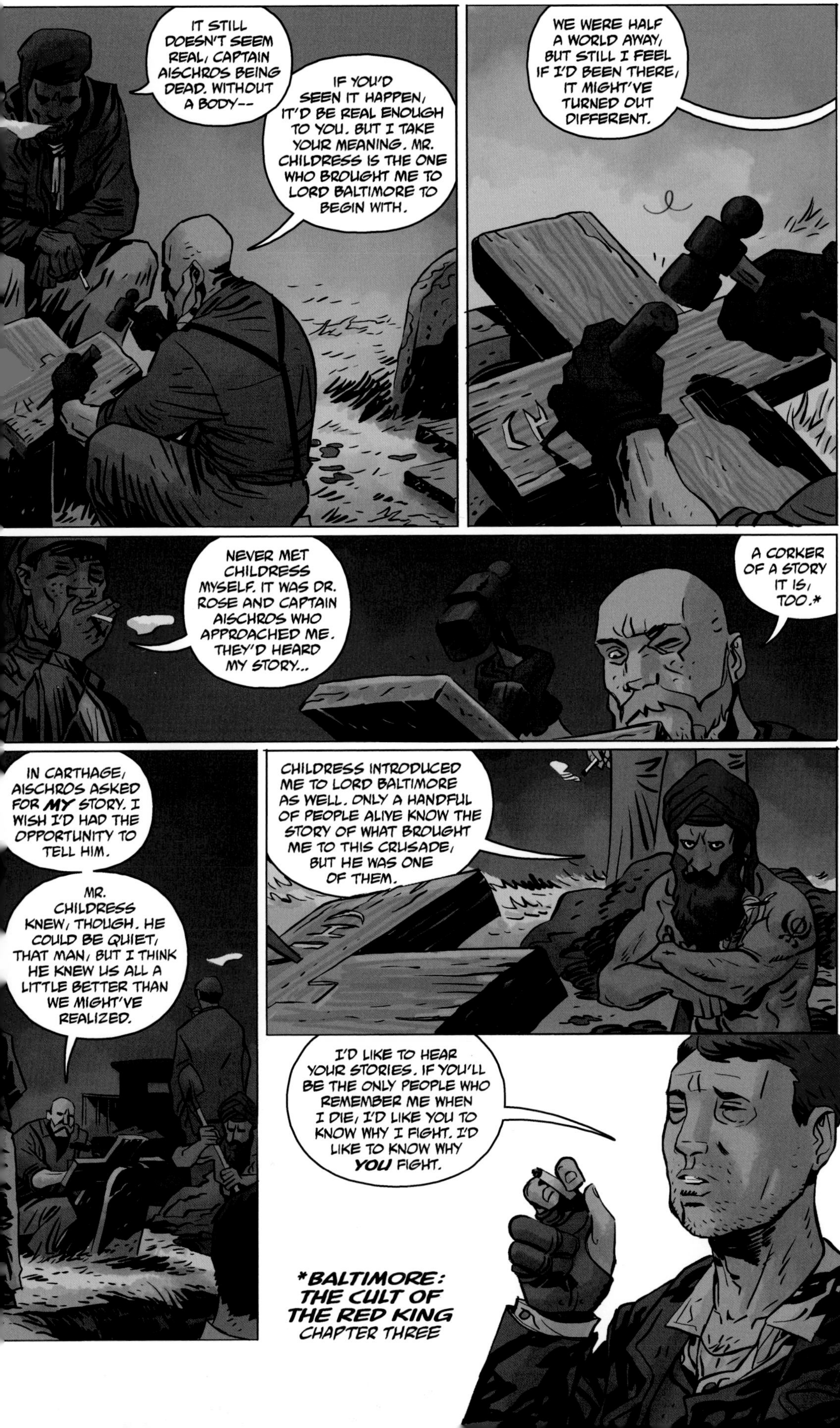

IT STILL DOESN'T SEEM REAL, CAPTAIN AISCHROS BEING DEAD. WITHOUT A BODY--
IF YOU'D SEEN IT HAPPEN, IT'D BE REAL ENOUGH TO YOU. BUT I TAKE YOUR MEANING. MR. CHILDRESS IS THE ONE WHO BROUGHT ME TO LORD BALTIMORE TO BEGIN WITH.
WE WERE HALF A WORLD AWAY, BUT STILL I FEEL IF I'D BEEN THERE, IT MIGHT'VE TURNED OUT DIFFERENT.
NEVER MET CHILDRESS MYSELF. IT WAS DR. ROSE AND CAPTAIN AISCHROS WHO APPROACHED ME. THEY'D HEARD MY STORY...
A CORKER OF A STORY IT IS, TOO.*
IN CARTHAGE, AISCHROS ASKED FOR **MY** STORY. I WISH I'D HAD THE OPPORTUNITY TO TELL HIM.
MR. CHILDRESS KNEW, THOUGH. HE COULD BE QUIET, THAT MAN, BUT I THINK HE KNEW US ALL A LITTLE BETTER THAN WE MIGHT'VE REALIZED.
CHILDRESS INTRODUCED ME TO LORD BALTIMORE AS WELL. ONLY A HANDFUL OF PEOPLE ALIVE KNOW THE STORY OF WHAT BROUGHT ME TO THIS CRUSADE, BUT HE WAS ONE OF THEM.
I'D LIKE TO HEAR YOUR STORIES. IF YOU'LL BE THE ONLY PEOPLE WHO REMEMBER ME WHEN I DIE, I'D LIKE YOU TO KNOW WHY I FIGHT. I'D LIKE TO KNOW WHY **YOU** FIGHT.
*BALTIMORE: THE CULT OF THE RED KING CHAPTER THREE

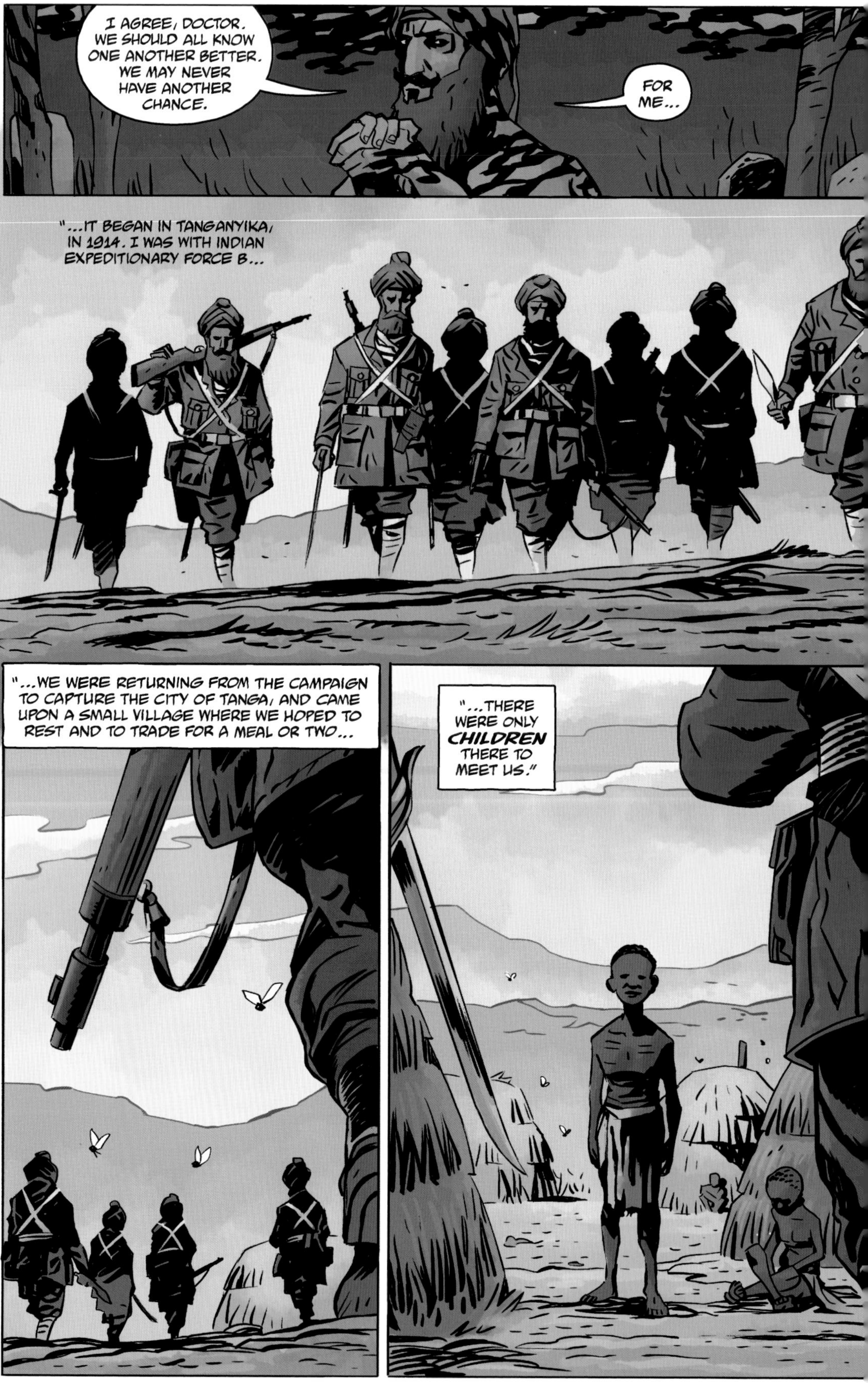
I AGREE, DOCTOR. WE SHOULD ALL KNOW ONE ANOTHER BETTER. WE MAY NEVER HAVE ANOTHER CHANCE.
FOR ME...
"...IT BEGAN IN TANGANYIKA, IN 1914. I WAS WITH INDIAN EXPEDITIONARY FORCE B...
"...WE WERE RETURNING FROM THE CAMPAIGN TO CAPTURE THE CITY OF TANGA, AND CAME UPON A SMALL VILLAGE WHERE WE HOPED TO REST AND TO TRADE FOR A MEAL OR TWO...
"...THERE WERE ONLY CHILDREN THERE TO MEET US."

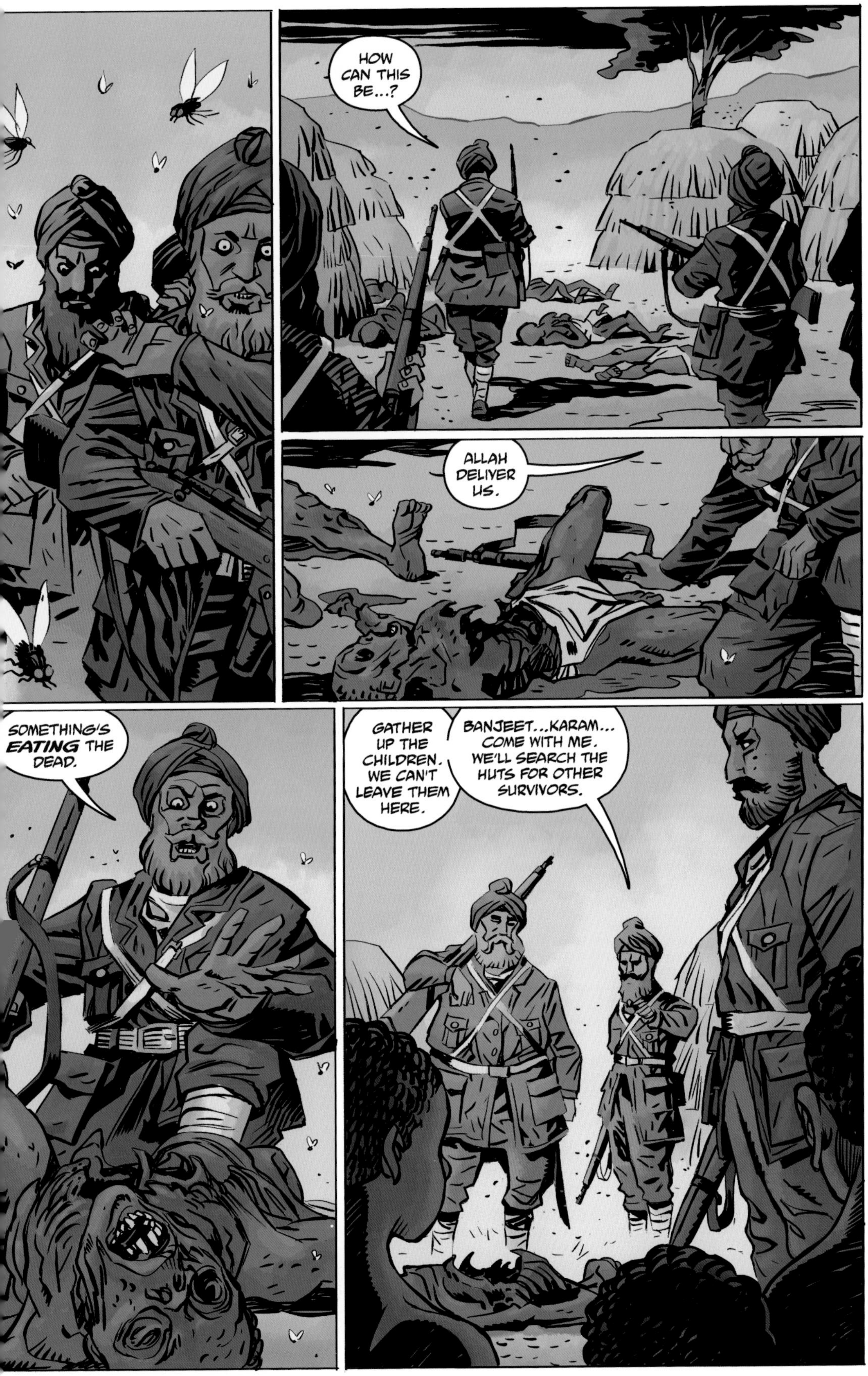
HOW CAN THIS BE...?
ALLAH DELIVER US.
SOMETHING'S **EATING** THE DEAD.
GATHER UP THE CHILDREN. WE CAN'T LEAVE THEM HERE.
BANJEET...KARAM... COME WITH ME. WE'LL SEARCH THE HUTS FOR OTHER SURVIVORS.

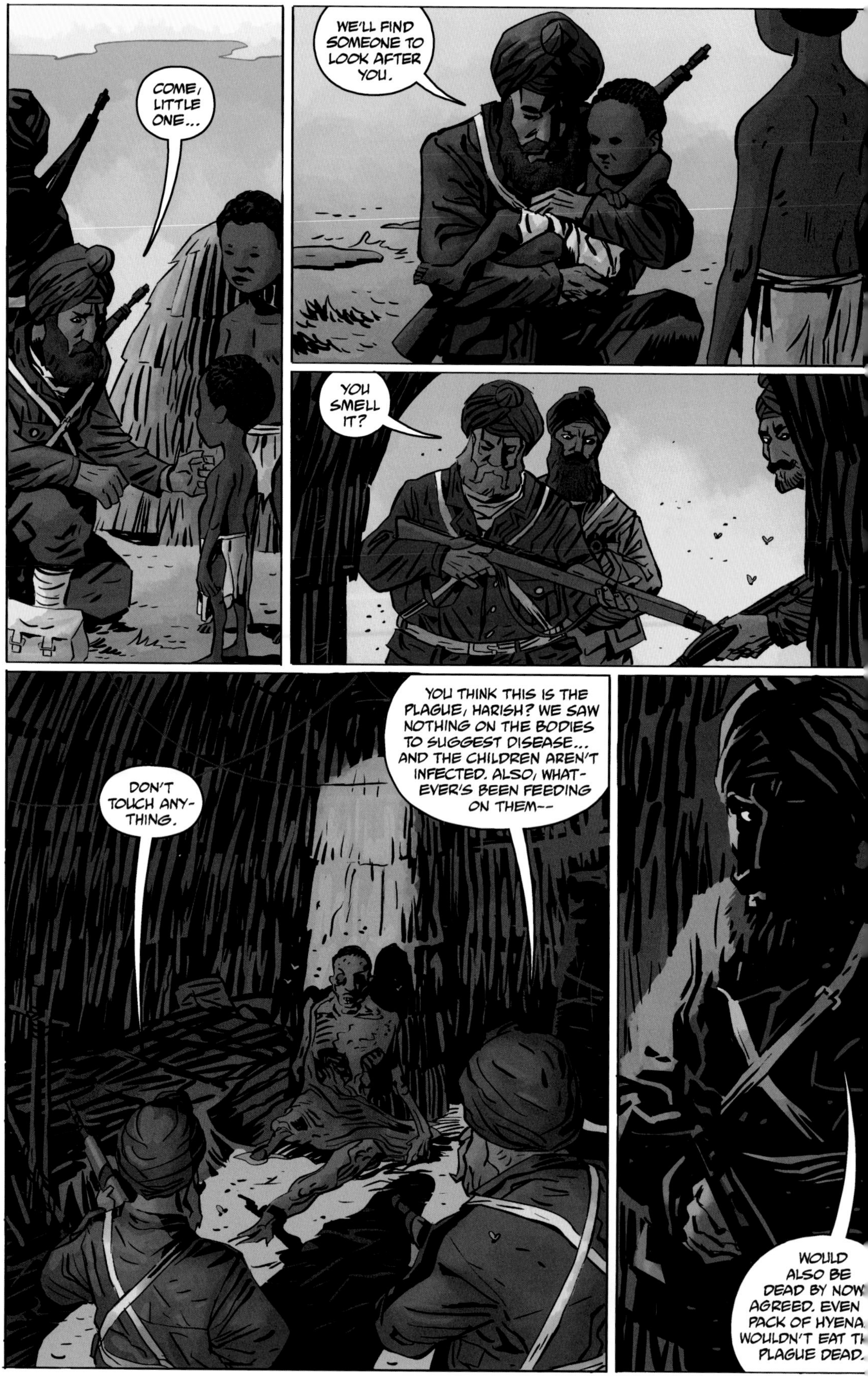
COME, LITTLE ONE...
WE'LL FIND SOMEONE TO LOOK AFTER YOU.
YOU SMELL IT?
DON'T TOUCH ANYTHING.
YOU THINK THIS IS THE PLAGUE, HARISH? WE SAW NOTHING ON THE BODIES TO SUGGEST DISEASE... AND THE CHILDREN AREN'T INFECTED. ALSO, WHATEVER'S BEEN FEEDING ON THEM--
WOULD ALSO BE DEAD BY NOW
AGREED. EVEN PACK OF HYENA WOULDN'T EAT TH PLAGUE DEAD.

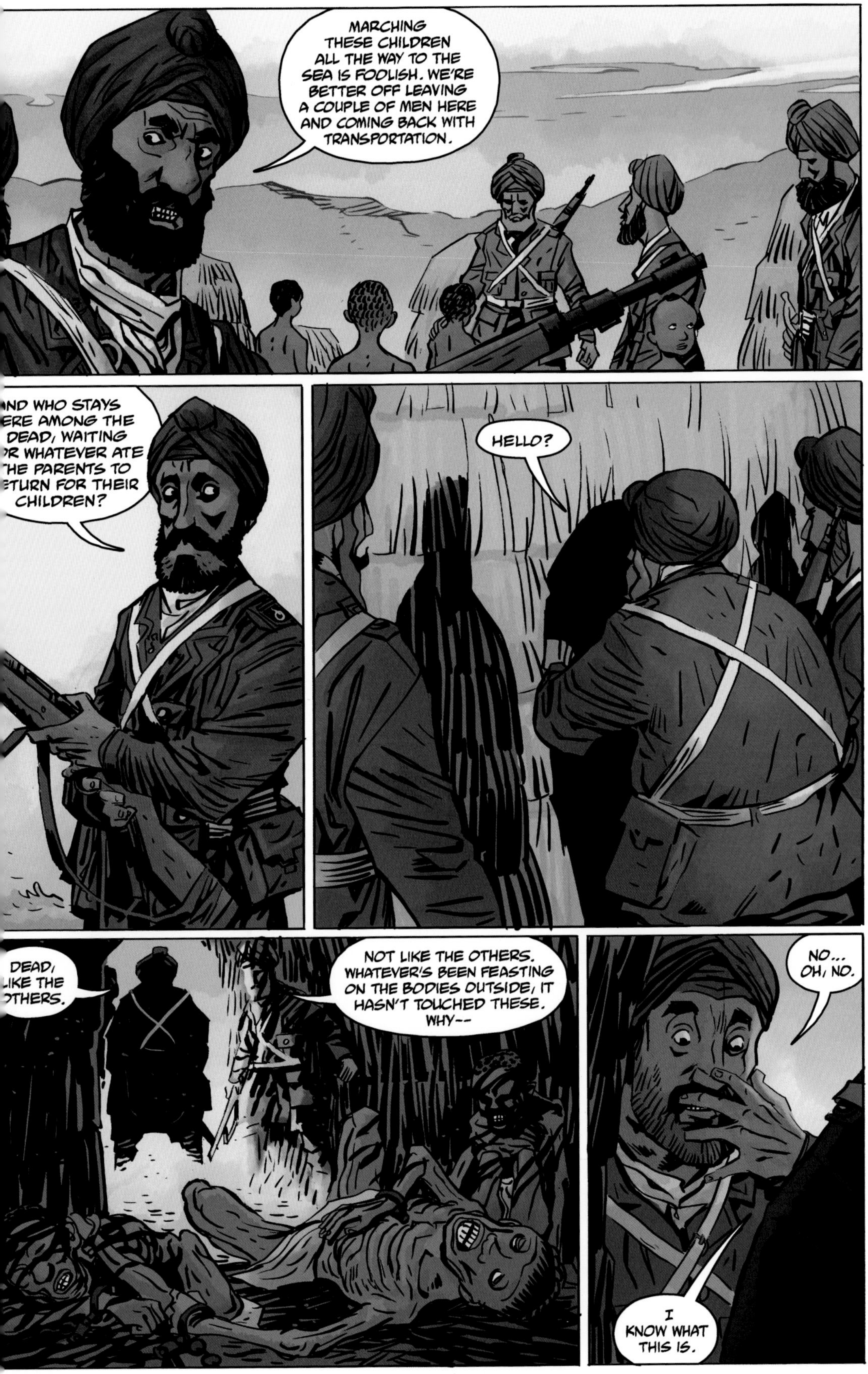
MARCHING THESE CHILDREN ALL THE WAY TO THE SEA IS FOOLISH. WE'RE BETTER OFF LEAVING A COUPLE OF MEN HERE AND COMING BACK WITH TRANSPORTATION.
ND WHO STAYS ERE AMONG THE DEAD, WAITING R WHATEVER ATE THE PARENTS TO ETURN FOR THEIR CHILDREN?
HELLO?
DEAD, IKE THE THERS.
NOT LIKE THE OTHERS. WHATEVER'S BEEN FEASTING ON THE BODIES OUTSIDE, IT HASN'T TOUCHED THESE. WHY--
NO... OH, NO.
I KNOW WHAT THIS IS.

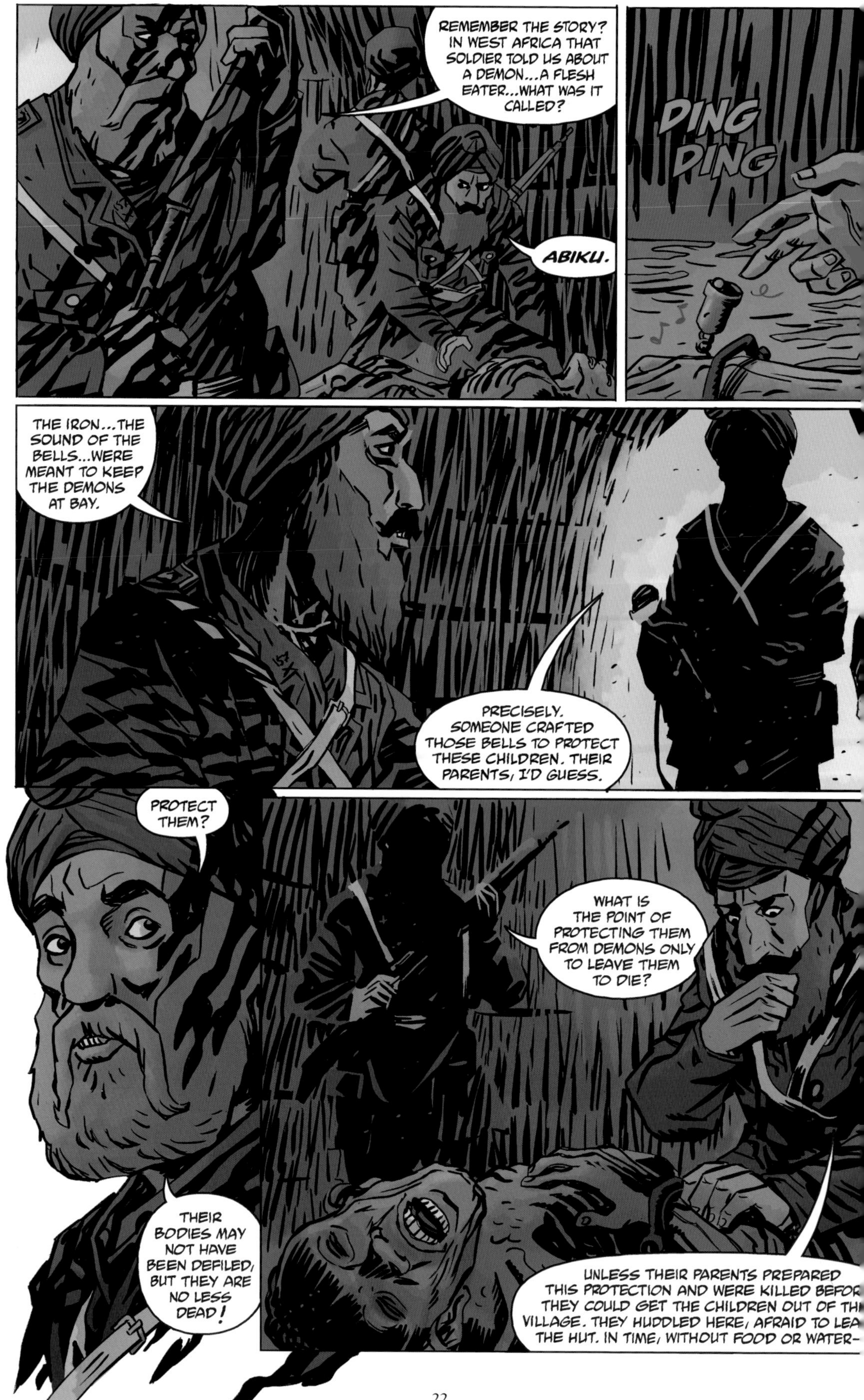
REMEMBER THE STORY? IN WEST AFRICA THAT SOLDIER TOLD US ABOUT A DEMON...A FLESH EATER...WHAT WAS IT CALLED?
ABIKU.
DING DING
THE IRON...THE SOUND OF THE BELLS...WERE MEANT TO KEEP THE DEMONS AT BAY.
PRECISELY. SOMEONE CRAFTED THOSE BELLS TO PROTECT THESE CHILDREN. THEIR PARENTS, I'D GUESS.
PROTECT THEM?
WHAT IS THE POINT OF PROTECTING THEM FROM DEMONS ONLY TO LEAVE THEM TO DIE?
THEIR BODIES MAY NOT HAVE BEEN DEFILED, BUT THEY ARE NO LESS DEAD!
UNLESS THEIR PARENTS PREPARED THIS PROTECTION AND WERE KILLED BEFOR
THEY COULD GET THE CHILDREN OUT OF TH
VILLAGE. THEY HUDDLED HERE, AFRAID TO LEA
THE HUT. IN TIME, WITHOUT FOOD OR WATER-

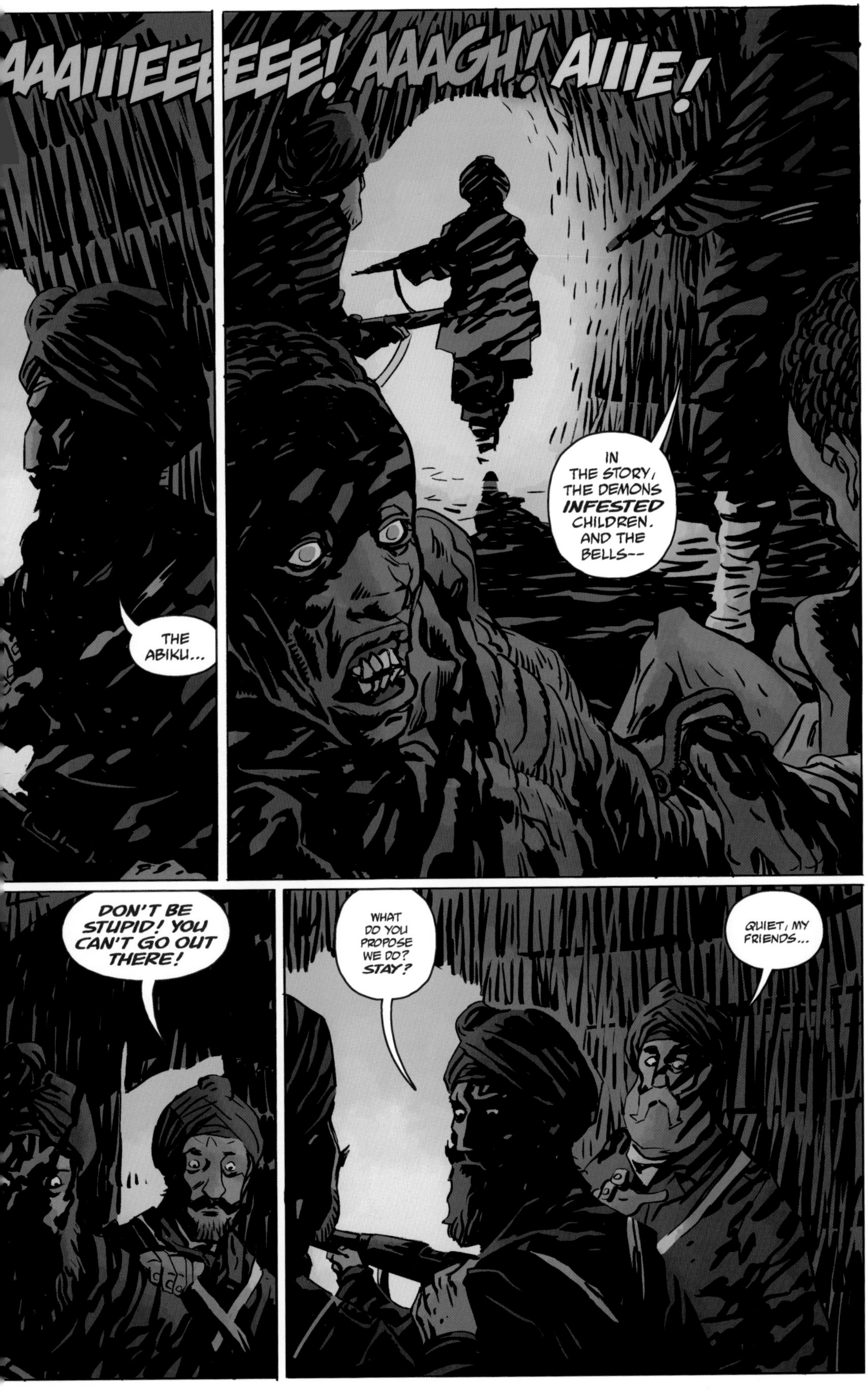
AAAIIIEEEEEEE! AAAGH! AIIIE!
IN THE STORY, THE DEMONS INFESTED CHILDREN. AND THE BELLS--
THE ABIKU...
DON'T BE STUPID! YOU CAN'T GO OUT THERE!
WHAT DO YOU PROPOSE WE DO? STAY?
QUIET, MY FRIENDS...

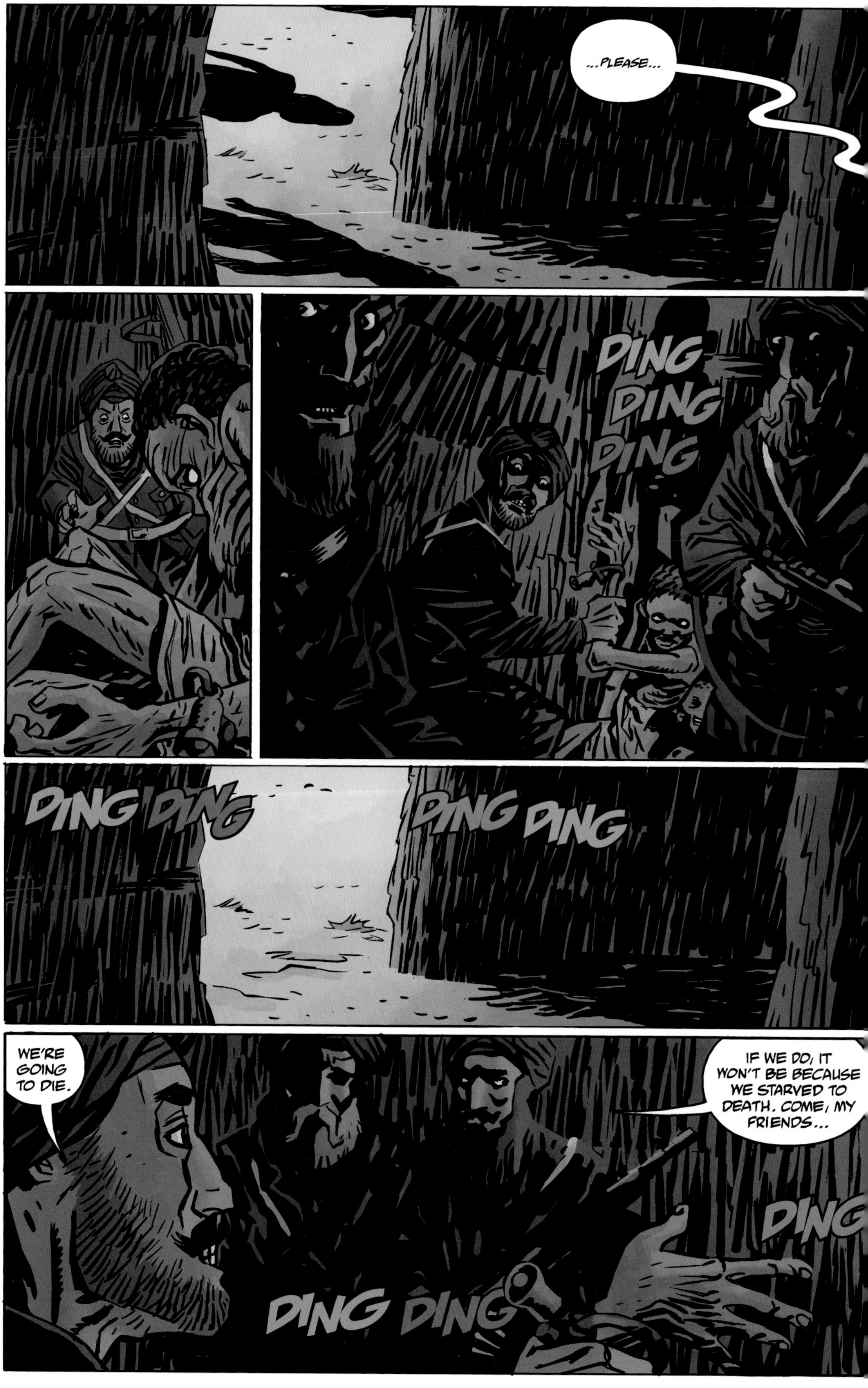
...PLEASE...
DING
DING
DING
DING DING
DING DING
WE'RE GOING TO DIE.
IF WE DO, IT WON'T BE BECAUSE WE STARVED TO DEATH. COME, MY FRIENDS...
DING
DING DING

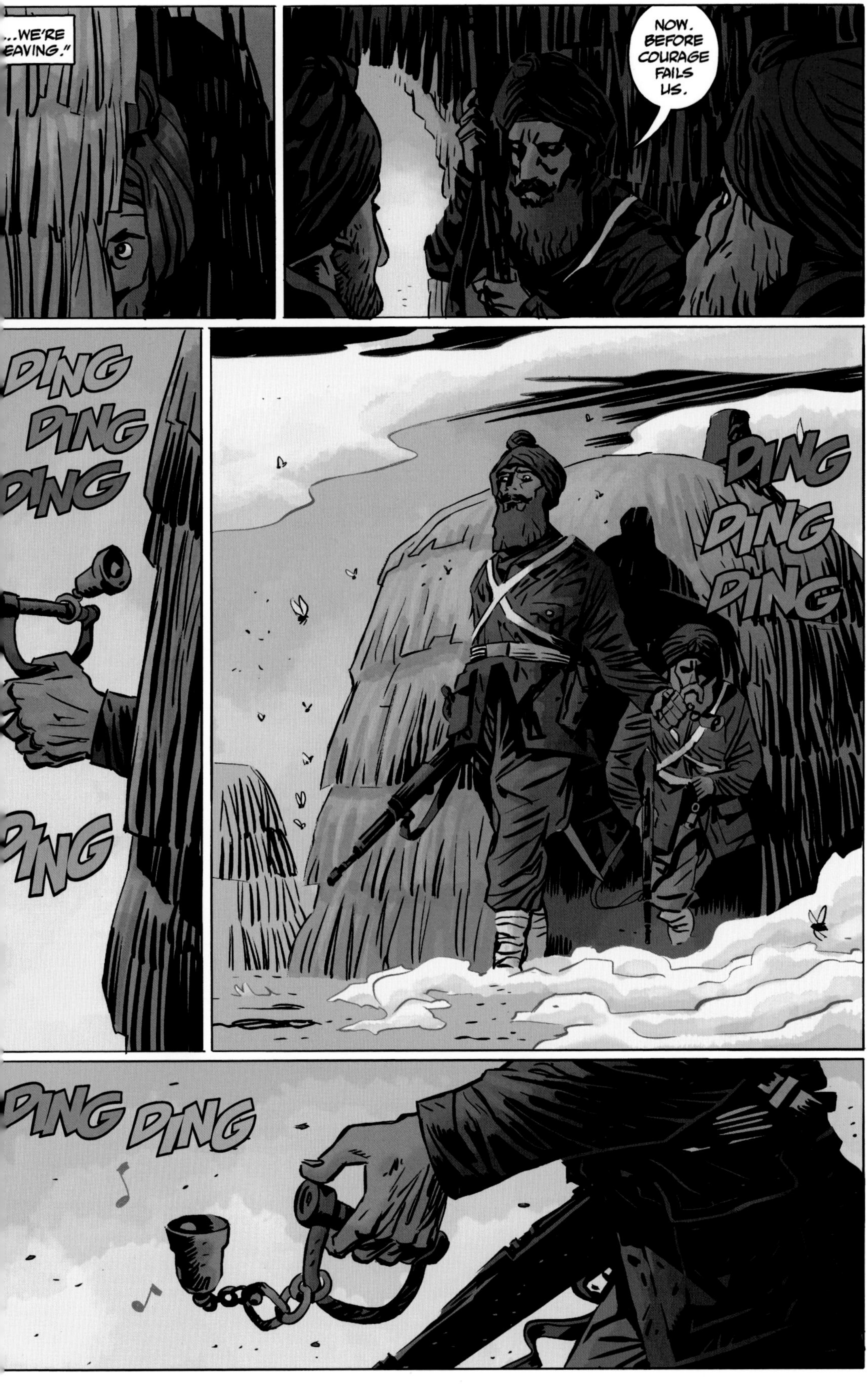
...WE'RE
EAVING."
NOW. BEFORE COURAGE FAILS US.
DING
DING
DING
DING
DING
DING
DING
DING
DING DING

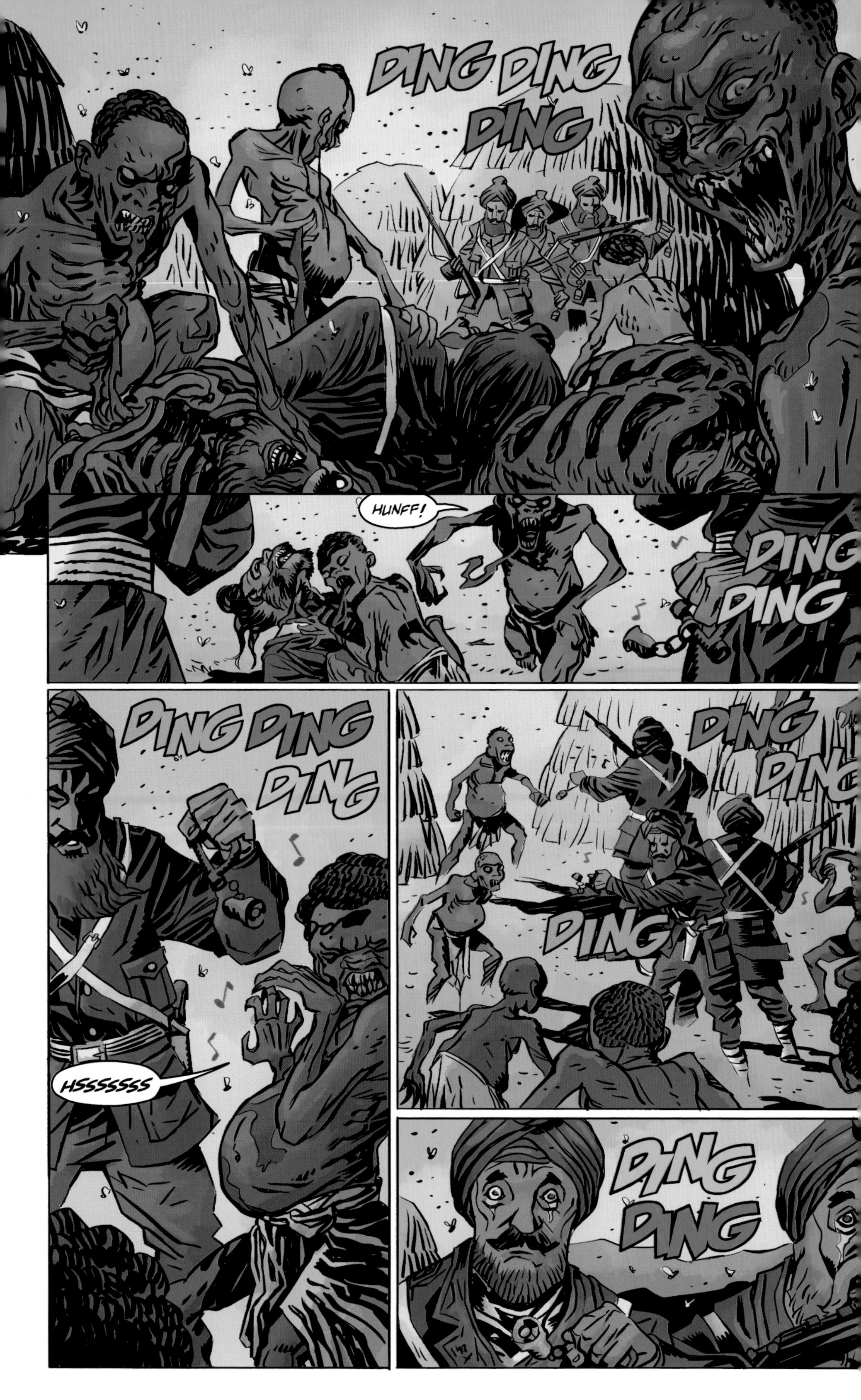
DING DING
DING
HUNFF!
DING
DING
DING DING
DING
HSSSSSSS
DING
DING
DING
DING
DING

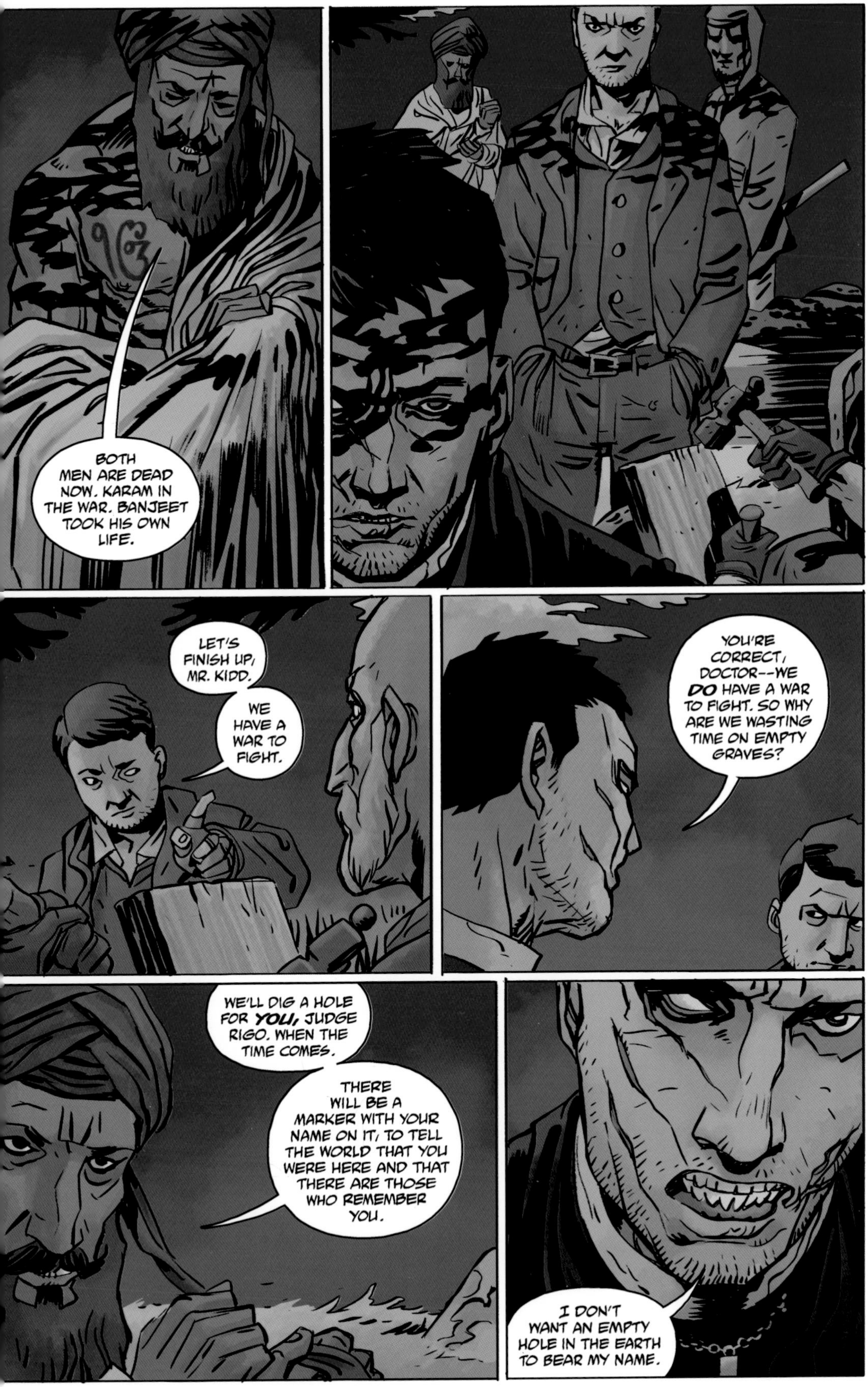
BOTH MEN ARE DEAD NOW. KARAM IN THE WAR. BANJEET TOOK HIS OWN LIFE.
LET'S FINISH UP, MR. KIDD.
WE HAVE A WAR TO FIGHT.
YOU'RE CORRECT, DOCTOR--WE DO HAVE A WAR TO FIGHT. SO WHY ARE WE WASTING TIME ON EMPTY GRAVES?
WE'LL DIG A HOLE FOR YOU, JUDGE RIGO. WHEN THE TIME COMES.
THERE WILL BE A MARKER WITH YOUR NAME ON IT, TO TELL THE WORLD THAT YOU WERE HERE AND THAT THERE ARE THOSE WHO REMEMBER YOU.
I DON'T WANT AN EMPTY HOLE IN THE EARTH TO BEAR MY NAME.

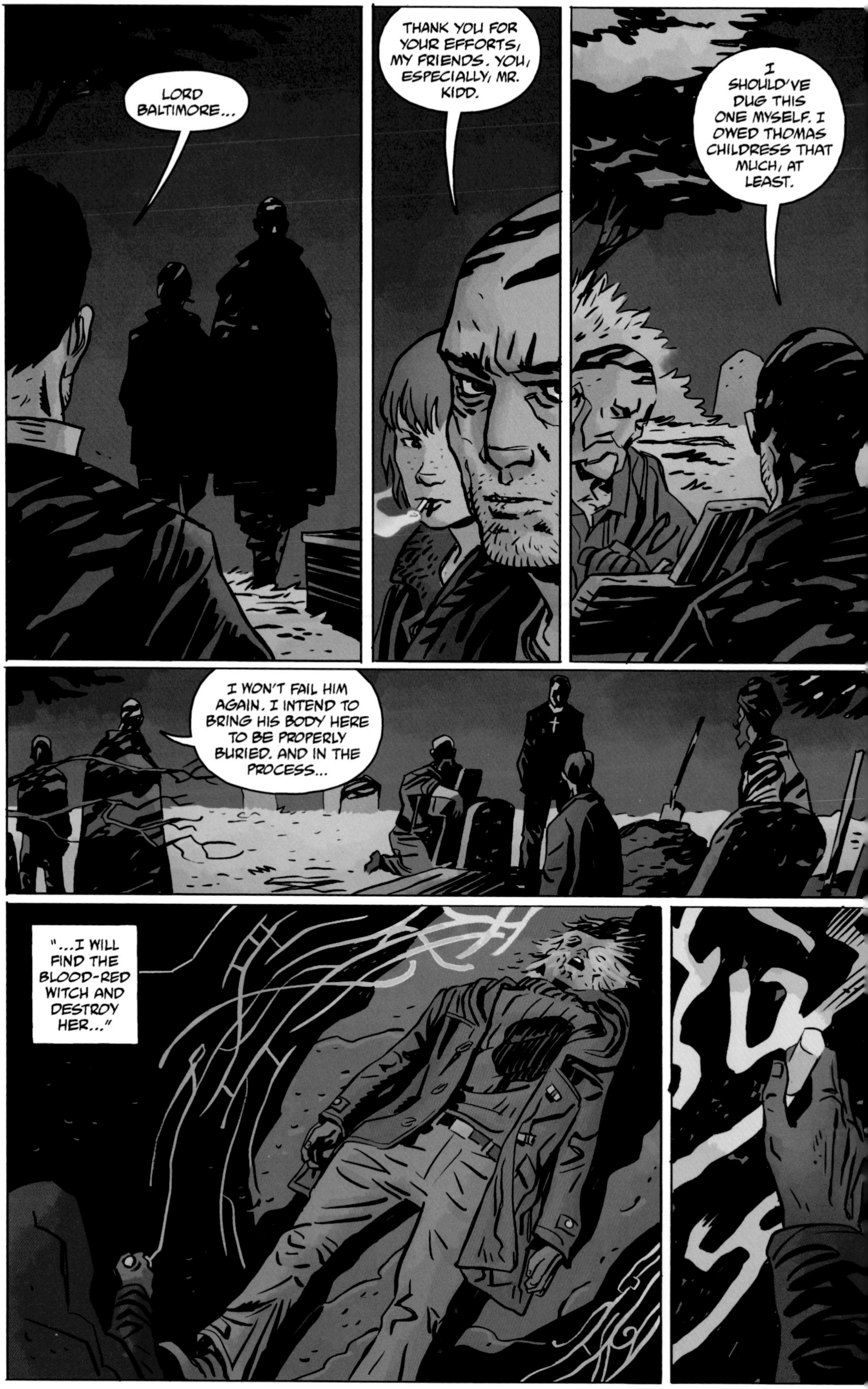
LORD BALTIMORE...
THANK YOU FOR YOUR EFFORTS, MY FRIENDS. YOU, ESPECIALLY, MR. KIDD.
I SHOULD'VE DUG THIS ONE MYSELF. I OWED THOMAS CHILDRESS THAT MUCH, AT LEAST.
I WON'T FAIL HIM AGAIN. I INTEND TO BRING HIS BODY HERE TO BE PROPERLY BURIED. AND IN THE PROCESS...
"...I WILL FIND THE BLOOD-RED WITCH AND DESTROY HER..."

CHAPTER TWO

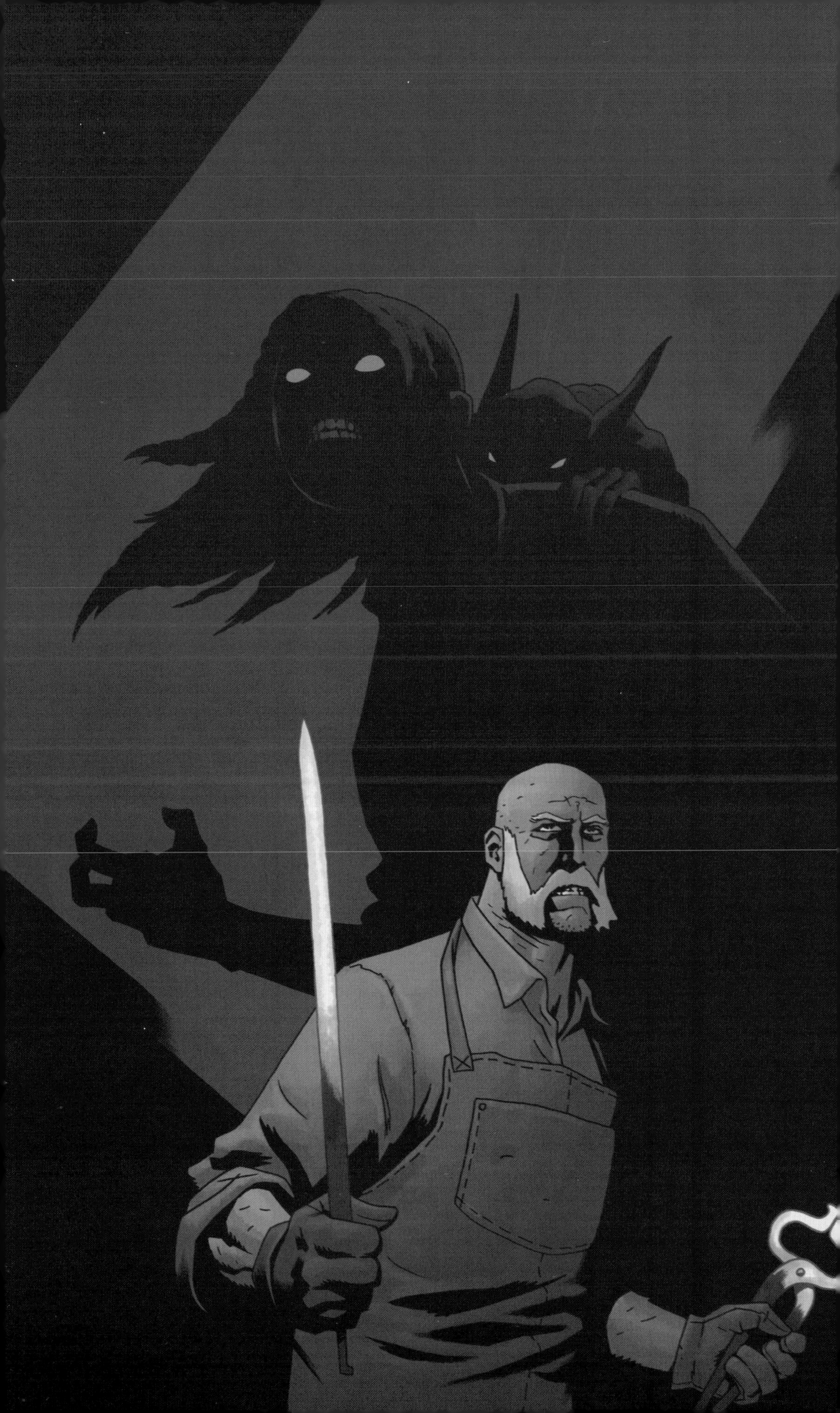

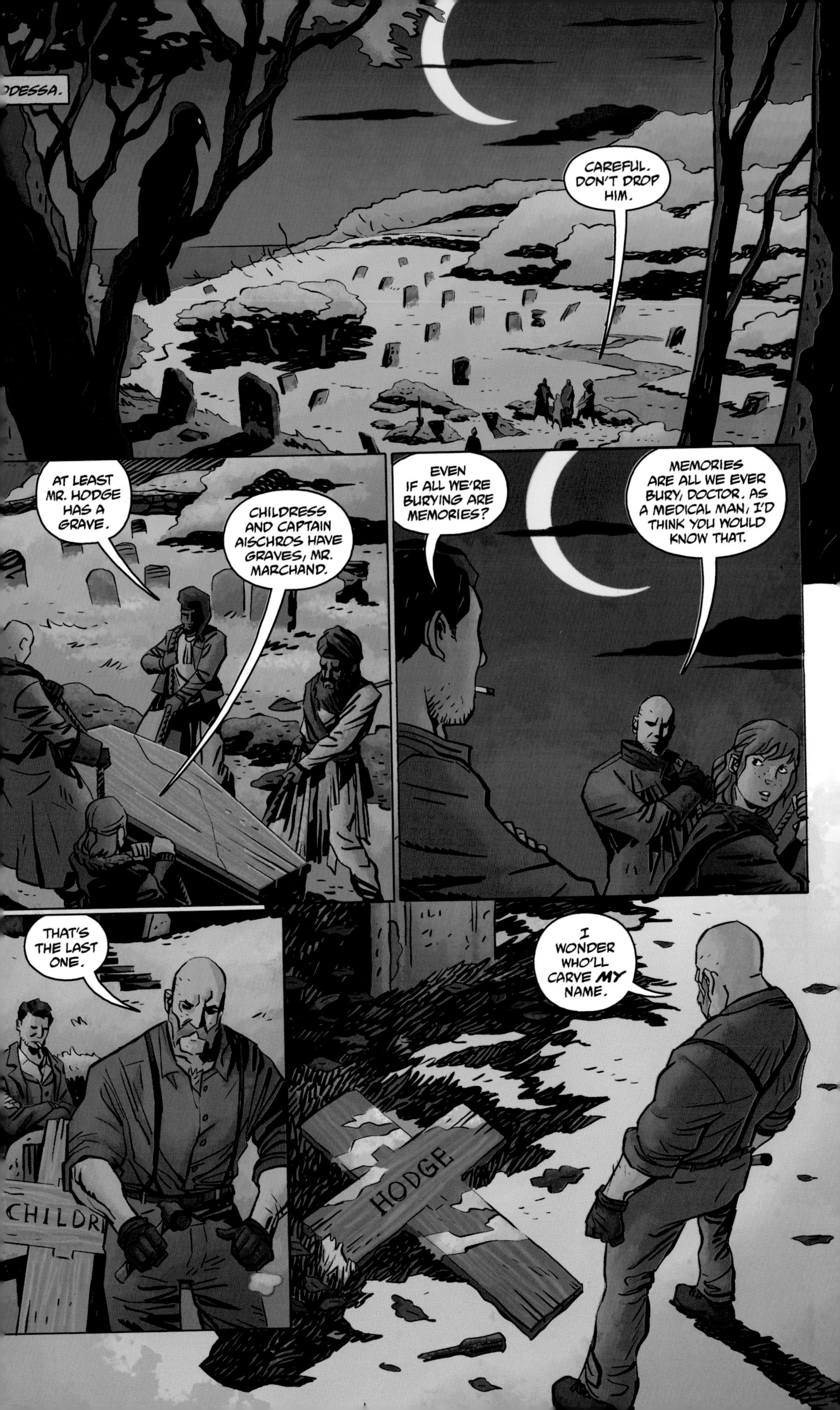

ODESSA.
CAREFUL. DON'T DROP HIM.
AT LEAST MR. HODGE HAS A GRAVE.
CHILDRESS AND CAPTAIN AISCHROS HAVE GRAVES, MR. MARCHAND.
EVEN IF ALL WE'RE BURYING ARE MEMORIES?
MEMORIES ARE ALL WE EVER BURY, DOCTOR. AS A MEDICAL MAN, I'D THINK YOU WOULD KNOW THAT.
THAT'S THE LAST ONE.
CHILDR
HODGE
I WONDER WHO'LL CARVE ***MY*** NAME.

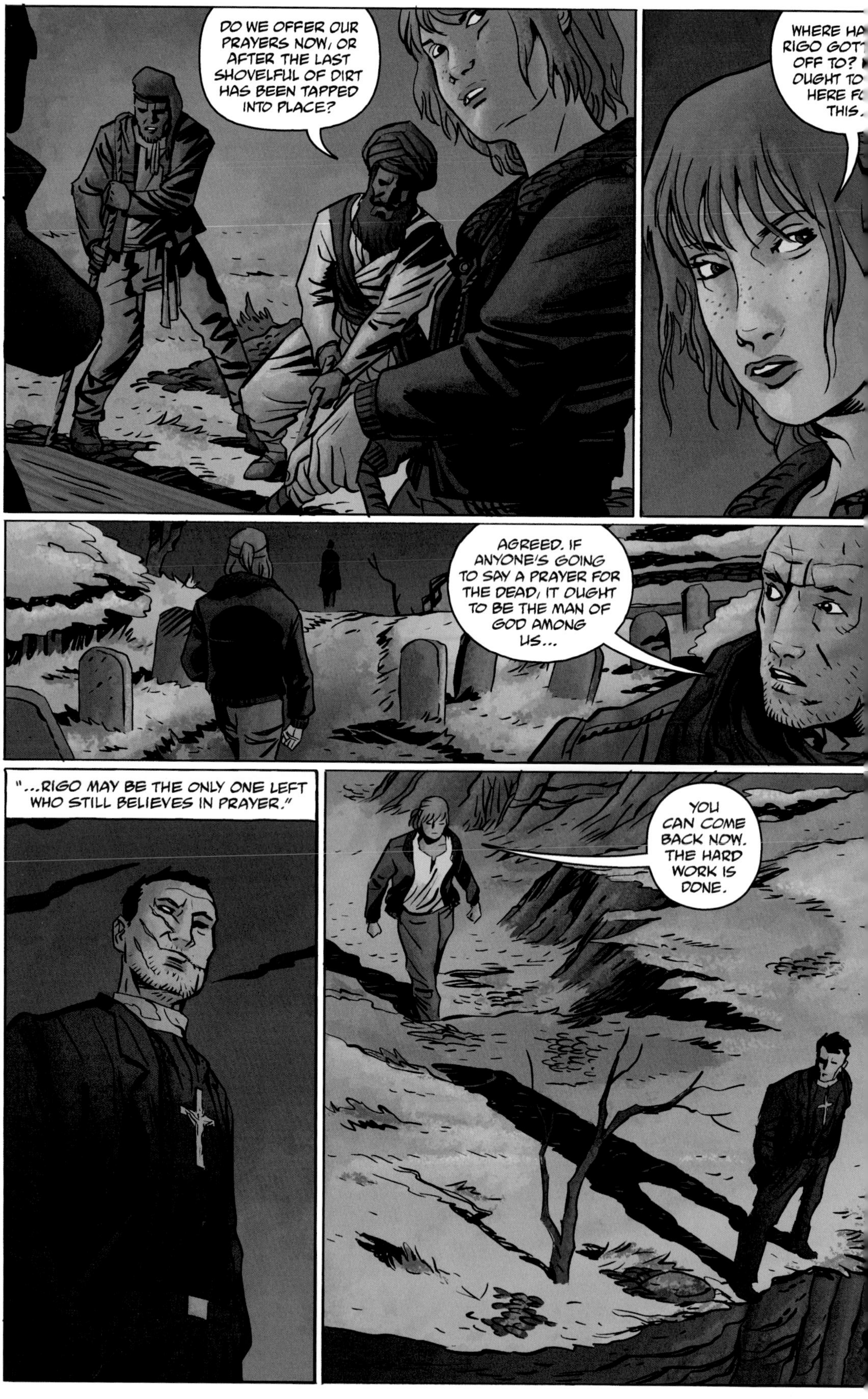
DO WE OFFER OUR PRAYERS NOW, OR AFTER THE LAST SHOVELFUL OF DIRT HAS BEEN TAPPED INTO PLACE?
WHERE HA RIGO GOTT OFF TO? OUGHT TO HERE F THIS.
AGREED. IF ANYONE'S GOING TO SAY A PRAYER FOR THE DEAD, IT OUGHT TO BE THE MAN OF GOD AMONG US...
"...RIGO MAY BE THE ONLY ONE LEFT WHO STILL BELIEVES IN PRAYER."
YOU CAN COME BACK NOW. THE HARD WORK IS DONE.

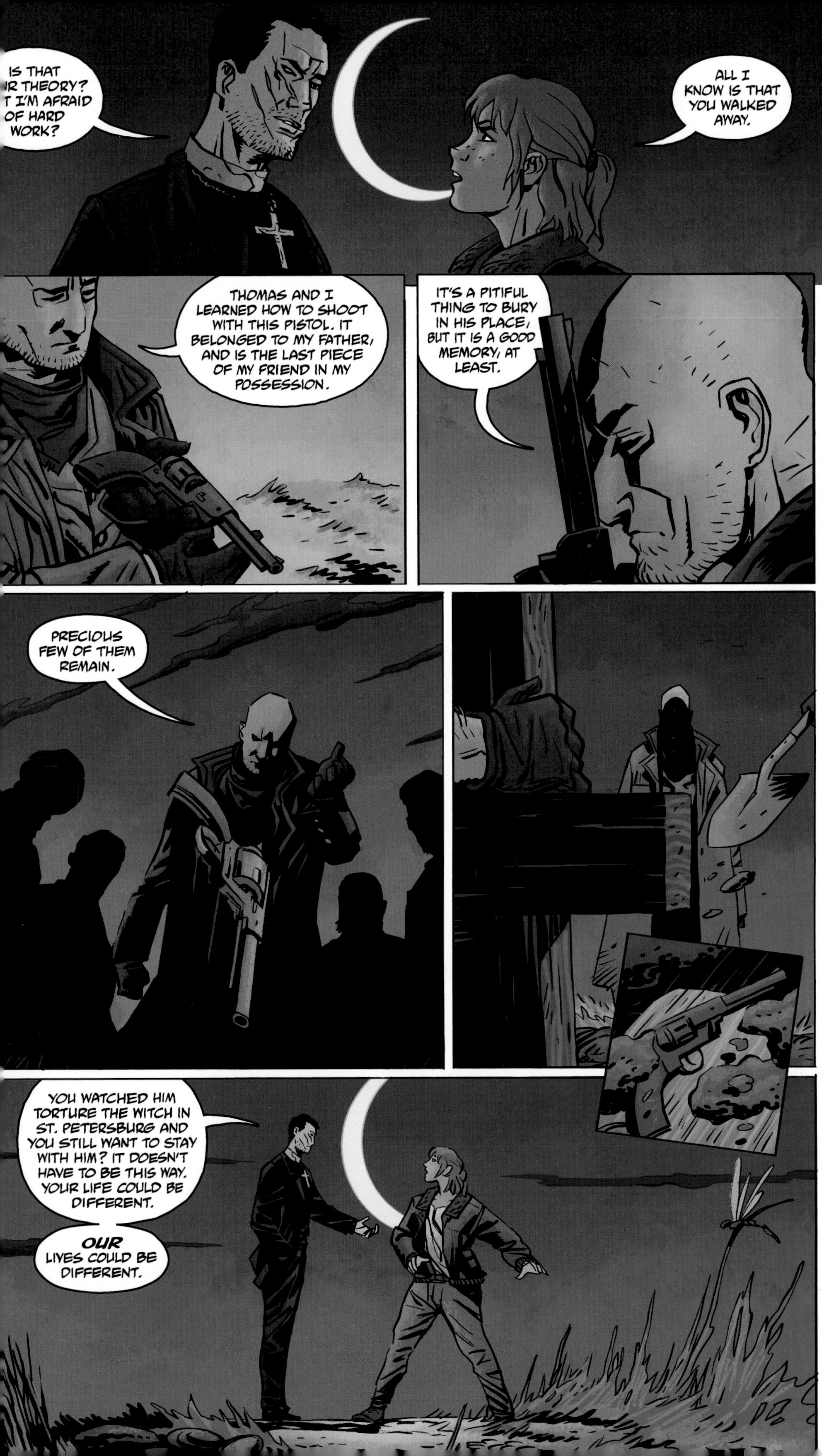
IS THAT
R THEORY?
T I'M AFRAID
OF HARD
WORK?
ALL I KNOW IS THAT YOU WALKED AWAY.
THOMAS AND I LEARNED HOW TO SHOOT WITH THIS PISTOL. IT BELONGED TO MY FATHER, AND IS THE LAST PIECE OF MY FRIEND IN MY POSSESSION.
IT'S A PITIFUL THING TO BURY IN HIS PLACE, BUT IT IS A GOOD MEMORY, AT LEAST.
PRECIOUS FEW OF THEM REMAIN.
YOU WATCHED HIM TORTURE THE WITCH IN ST. PETERSBURG AND YOU STILL WANT TO STAY WITH HIM? IT DOESN'T HAVE TO BE THIS WAY. YOUR LIFE COULD BE DIFFERENT.
OUR LIVES COULD BE DIFFERENT.

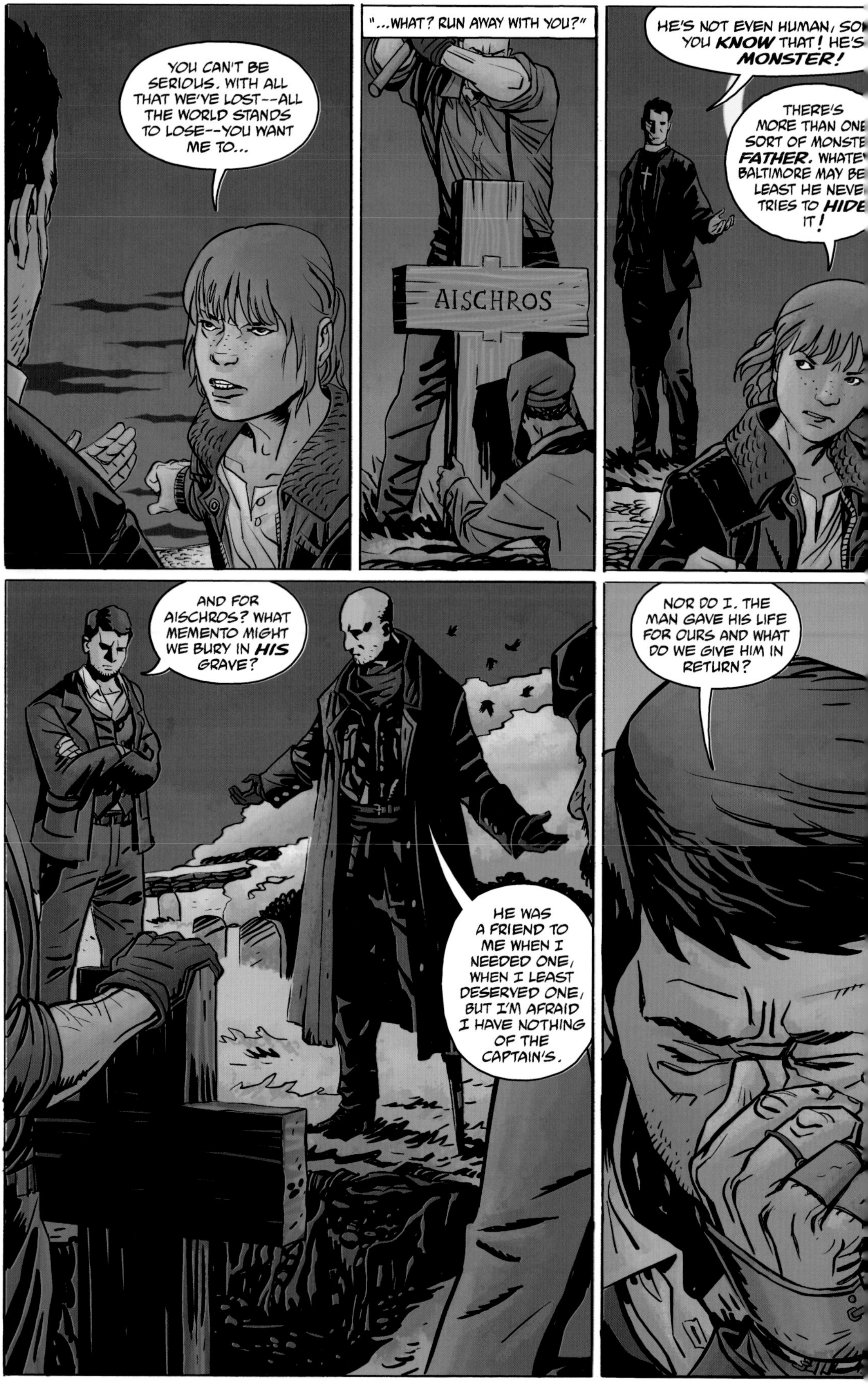

YOU CAN'T BE SERIOUS. WITH ALL THAT WE'VE LOST--ALL THE WORLD STANDS TO LOSE--YOU WANT ME TO...
"...WHAT? RUN AWAY WITH YOU?"
AISCHROS
HE'S NOT EVEN HUMAN, SO YOU KNOW THAT! HE'S MONSTER!
THERE'S MORE THAN ONE SORT OF MONSTE FATHER. WHATE BALTIMORE MAY BE LEAST HE NEVE TRIES TO HIDE IT!
AND FOR AISCHROS? WHAT MEMENTO MIGHT WE BURY IN HIS GRAVE?
HE WAS A FRIEND TO ME WHEN I NEEDED ONE, WHEN I LEAST DESERVED ONE, BUT I'M AFRAID I HAVE NOTHING OF THE CAPTAIN'S.
NOR DO I. THE MAN GAVE HIS LIFE FOR OURS AND WHAT DO WE GIVE HIM IN RETURN?

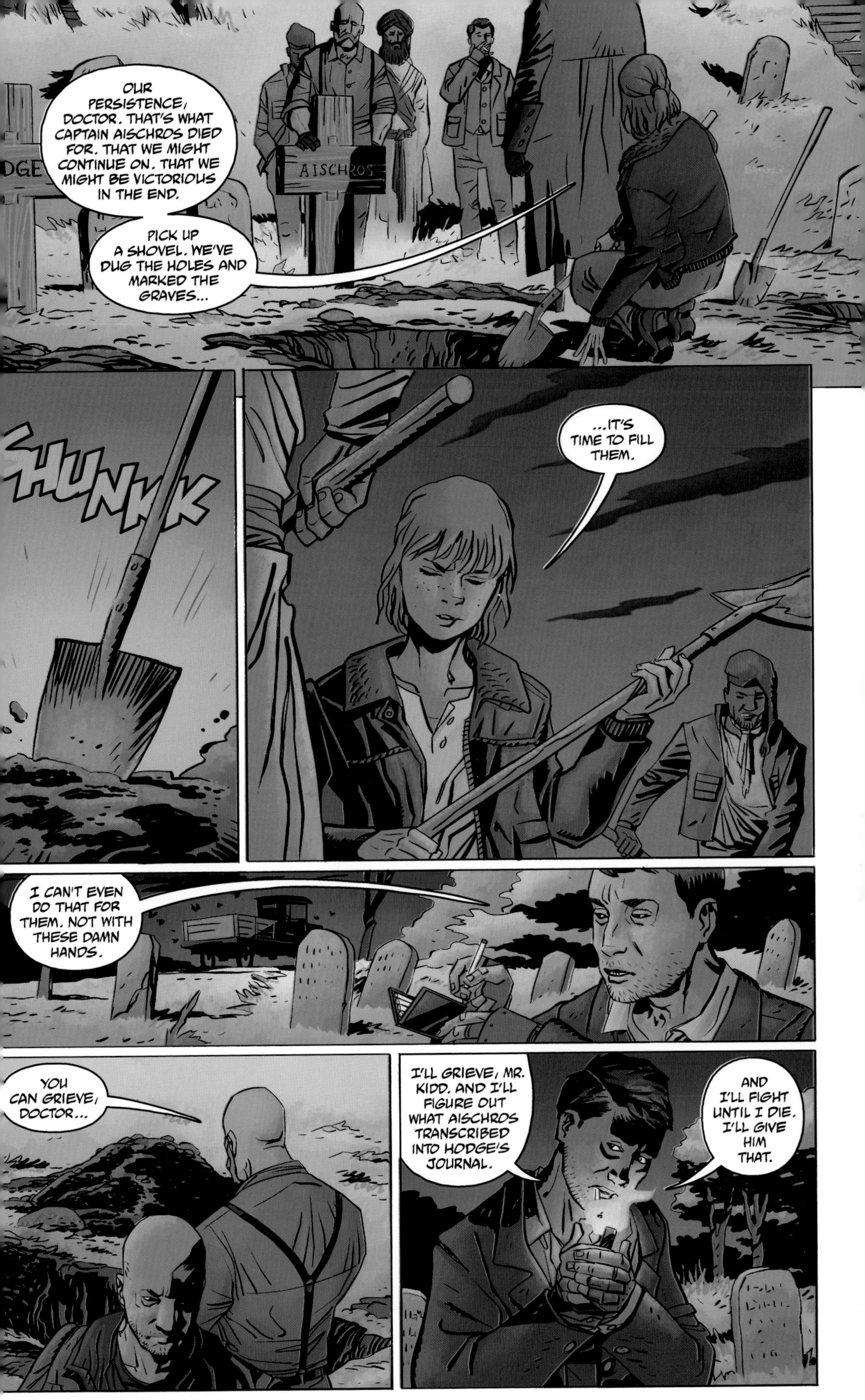
DGE
AISCHROS
OUR PERSISTENCE, DOCTOR. THAT'S WHAT CAPTAIN AISCHROS DIED FOR. THAT WE MIGHT CONTINUE ON. THAT WE MIGHT BE VICTORIOUS IN THE END.
PICK UP A SHOVEL. WE'VE DUG THE HOLES AND MARKED THE GRAVES...
SHUNKK
...IT'S TIME TO FILL THEM.
I CAN'T EVEN DO THAT FOR THEM. NOT WITH THESE DAMN HANDS.
YOU CAN GRIEVE, DOCTOR...
I'LL GRIEVE, MR. KIDD. AND I'LL FIGURE OUT WHAT AISCHROS TRANSCRIBED INTO HODGE'S JOURNAL.
AND I'LL FIGHT UNTIL I DIE. I'LL GIVE HIM THAT.

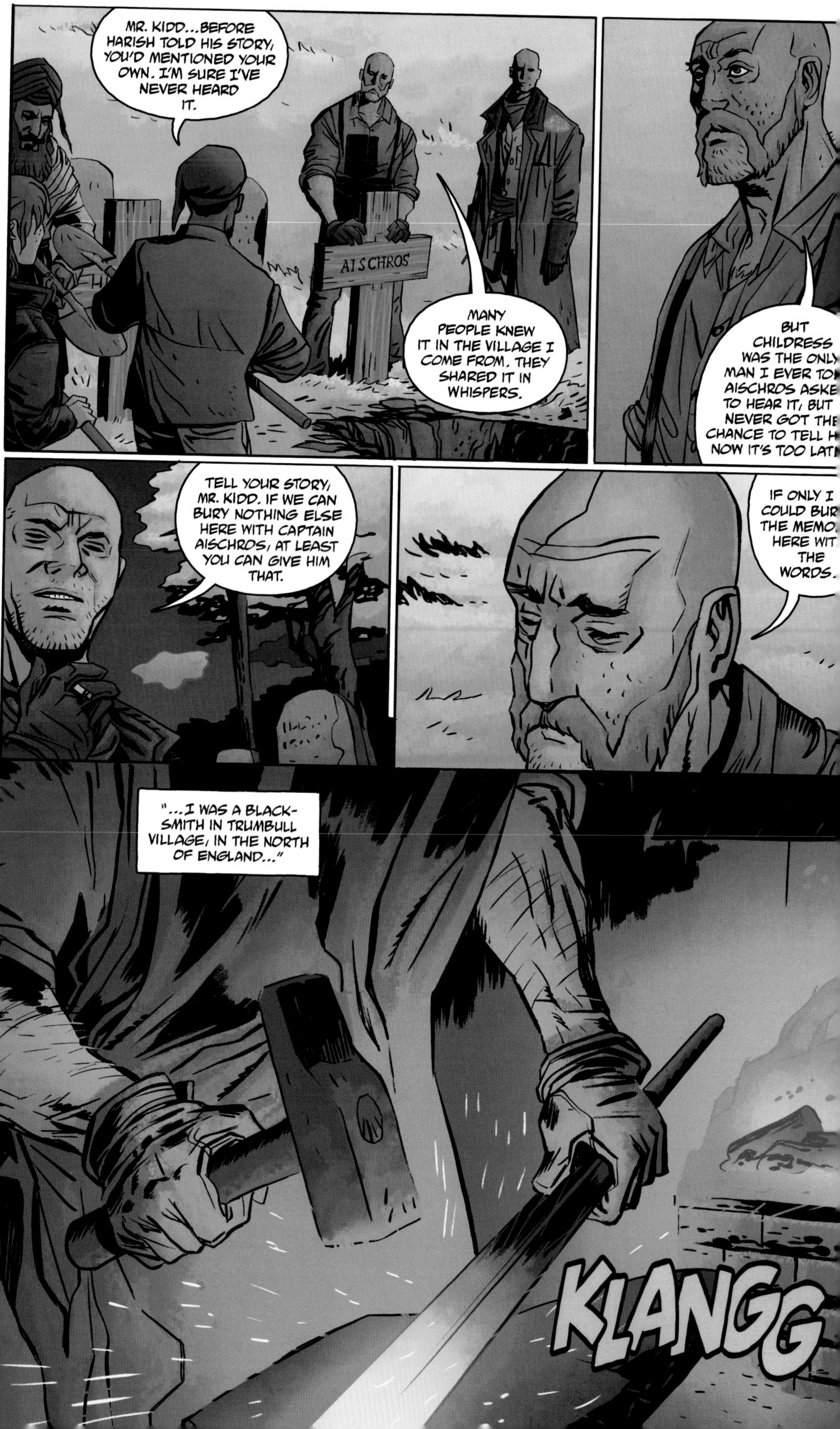
MR. KIDD...BEFORE HARISH TOLD HIS STORY, YOU'D MENTIONED YOUR OWN. I'M SURE I'VE NEVER HEARD IT.
AISCHROS
MANY PEOPLE KNEW IT IN THE VILLAGE I COME FROM. THEY SHARED IT IN WHISPERS.
BUT CHILDRESS WAS THE ONL MAN I EVER TO AISCHROS ASKE TO HEAR IT, BUT NEVER GOT THE CHANCE TO TELL H NOW IT'S TOO LAT
TELL YOUR STORY, MR. KIDD. IF WE CAN BURY NOTHING ELSE HERE WITH CAPTAIN AISCHROS, AT LEAST YOU CAN GIVE HIM THAT.
IF ONLY I COULD BUR THE MEMO HERE WIT THE WORDS.
"...I WAS A BLACK-SMITH IN TRUMBULL VILLAGE, IN THE NORTH OF ENGLAND..."
KLANGG

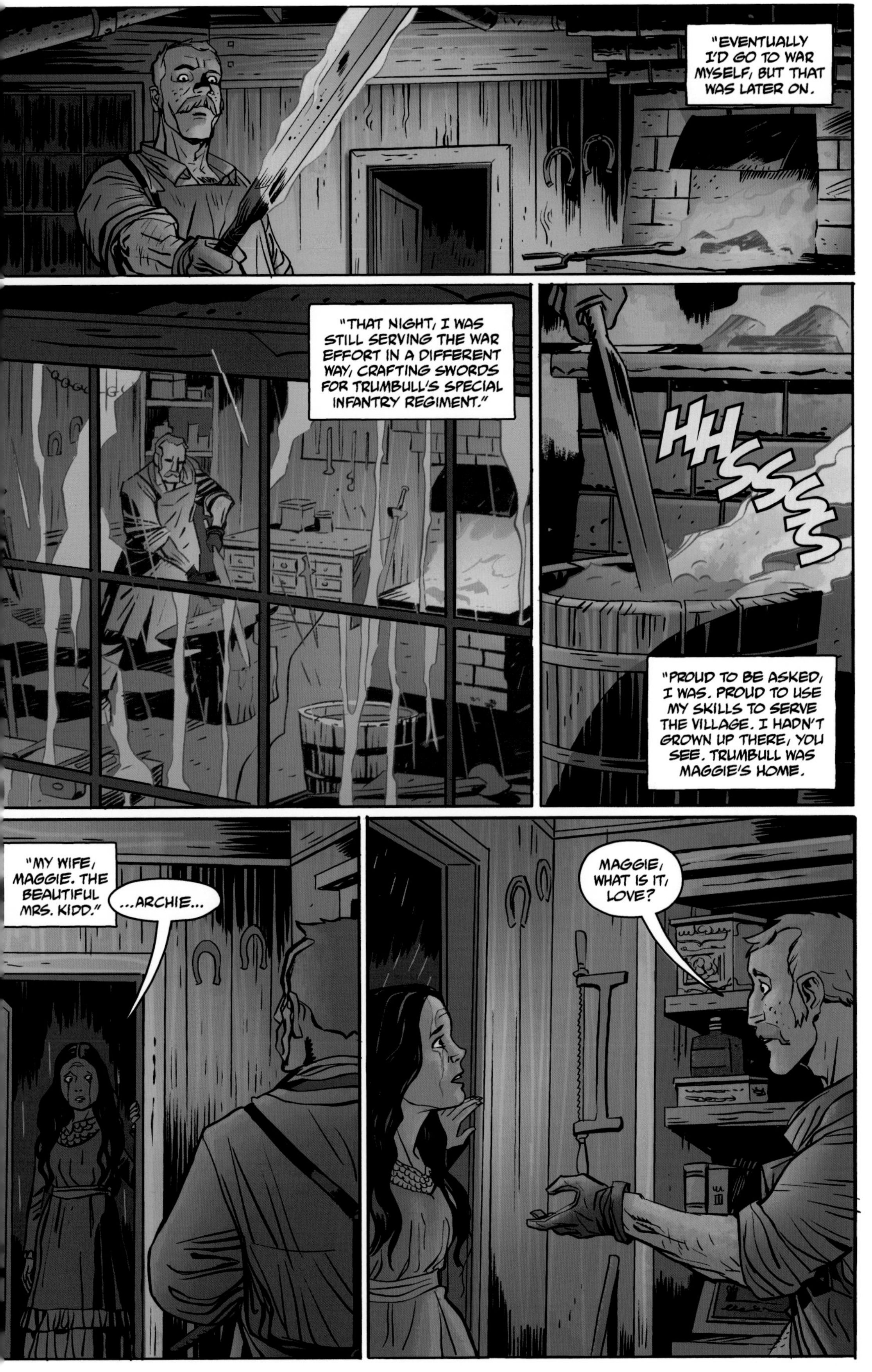
"EVENTUALLY I'D GO TO WAR MYSELF, BUT THAT WAS LATER ON.
"THAT NIGHT, I WAS STILL SERVING THE WAR EFFORT IN A DIFFERENT WAY, CRAFTING SWORDS FOR TRUMBULL'S SPECIAL INFANTRY REGIMENT."
HHSSSSS
"PROUD TO BE ASKED, I WAS. PROUD TO USE MY SKILLS TO SERVE THE VILLAGE. I HADN'T GROWN UP THERE, YOU SEE. TRUMBULL WAS MAGGIE'S HOME.
"MY WIFE, MAGGIE. THE BEAUTIFUL MRS. KIDD."
...ARCHIE...
MAGGIE, WHAT IS IT, LOVE?

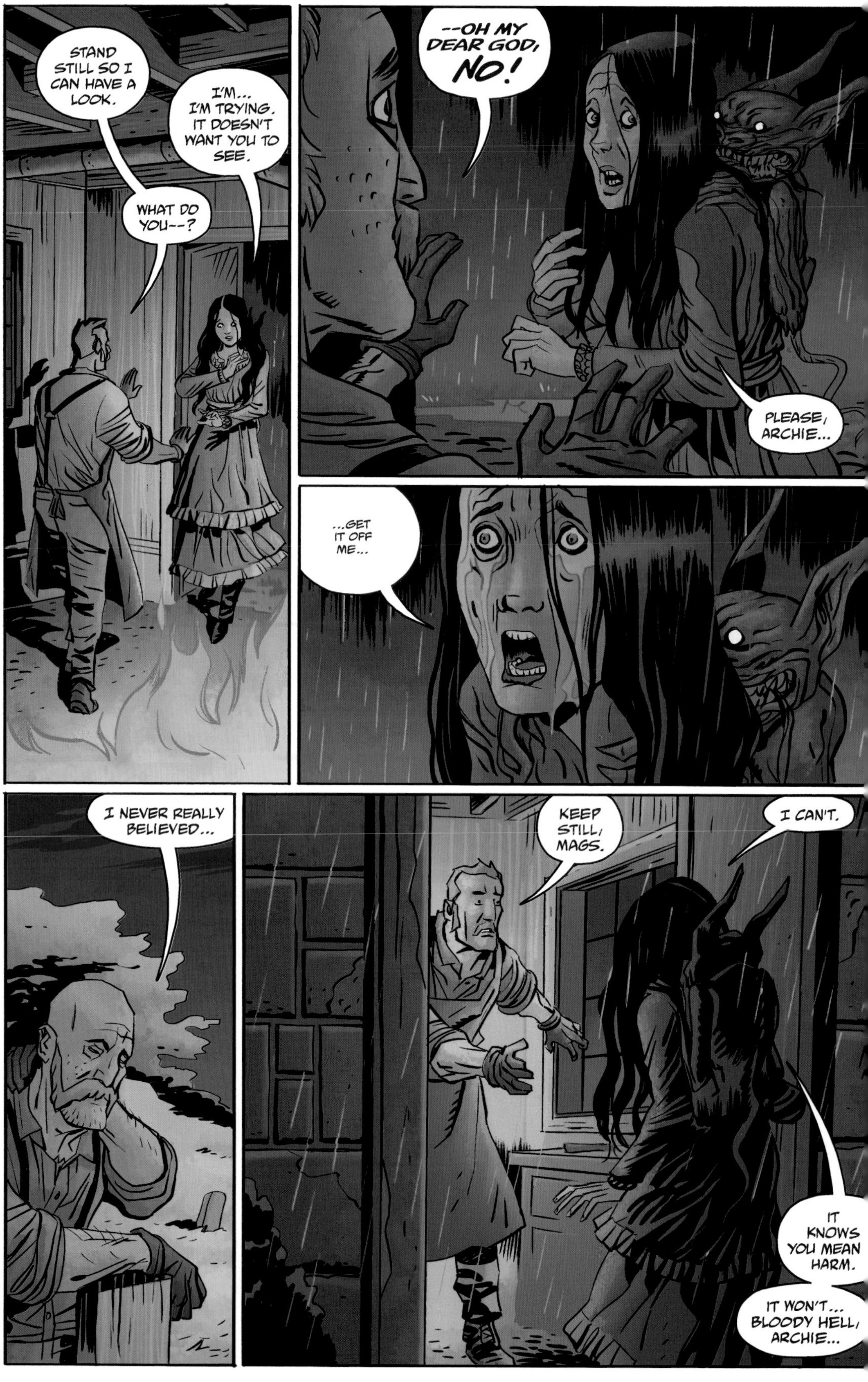
STAND STILL SO I CAN HAVE A LOOK.
I'M... I'M TRYING. IT DOESN'T WANT YOU TO SEE.
WHAT DO YOU--?
--OH MY DEAR GOD, NO!
PLEASE, ARCHIE...
...GET IT OFF ME...
I NEVER REALLY BELIEVED...
KEEP STILL, MAGS.
I CAN'T.
IT KNOWS YOU MEAN HARM.
IT WON'T... BLOODY HELL, ARCHIE...

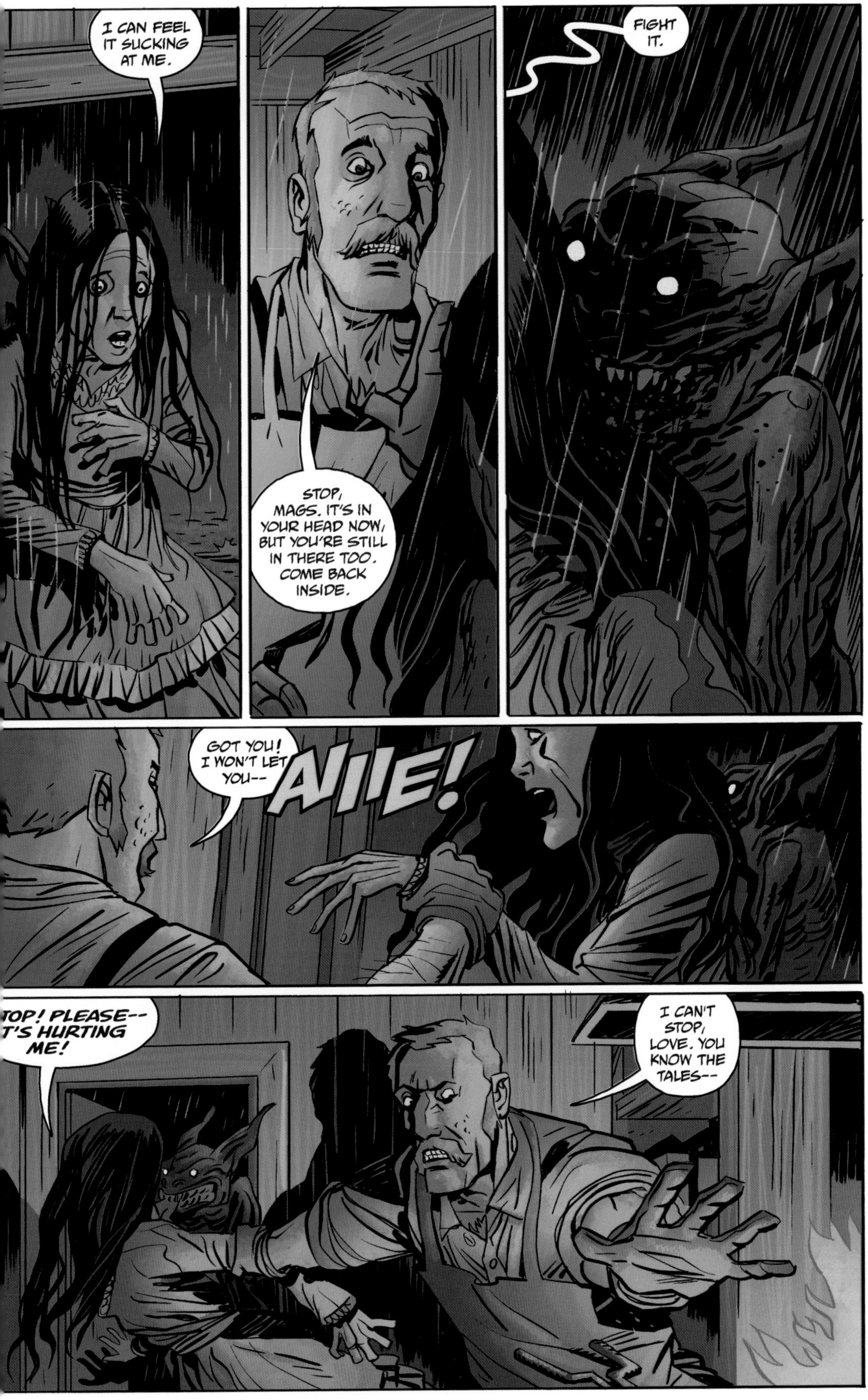
I CAN FEEL IT SUCKING AT ME.
STOP, MAGS. IT'S IN YOUR HEAD NOW, BUT YOU'RE STILL IN THERE TOO. COME BACK INSIDE.
FIGHT IT.
GOT YOU! I WON'T LET YOU--
AIIE!
TOP! PLEASE-- T'S HURTING ME!
I CAN'T STOP, LOVE. YOU KNOW THE TALES--

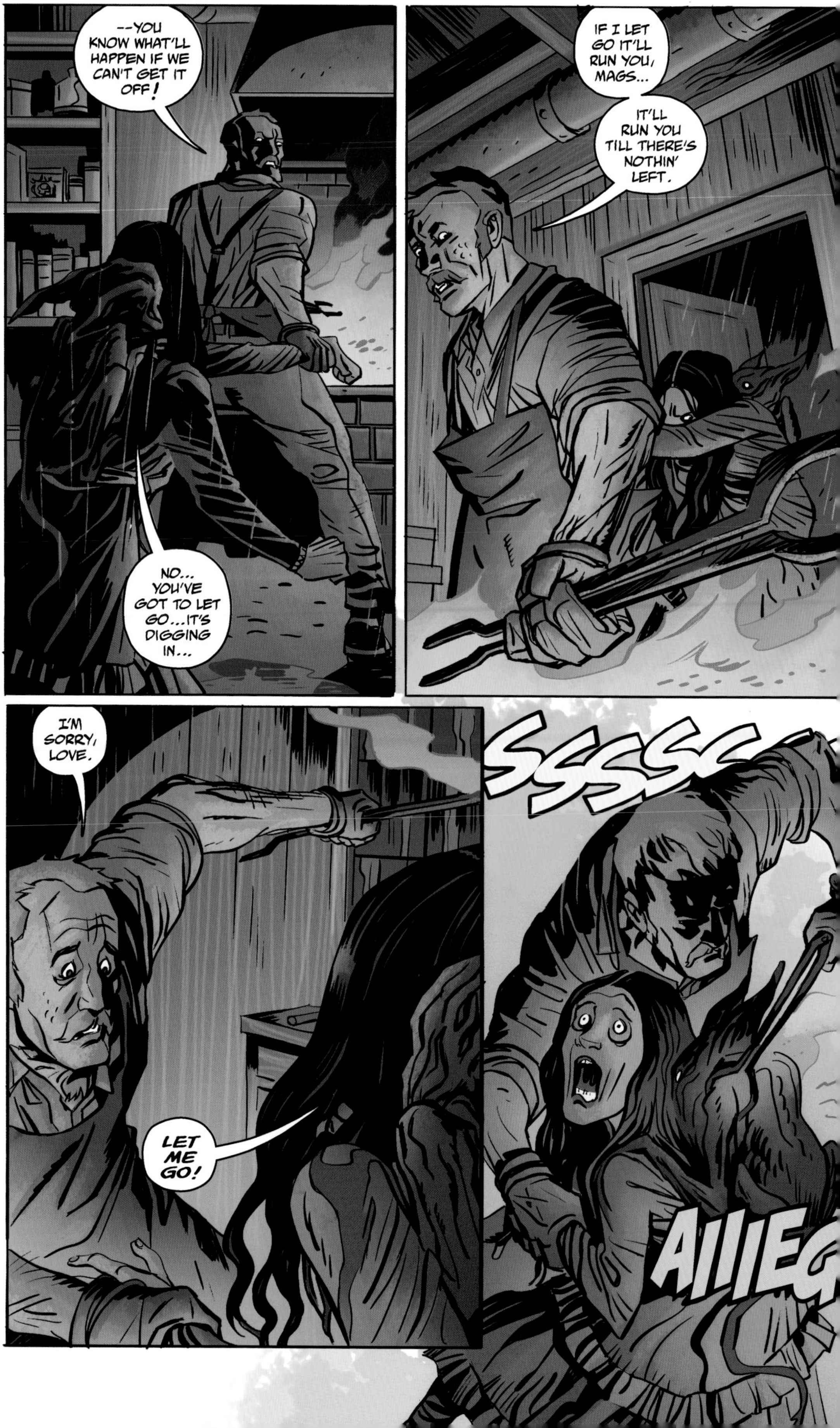
--YOU KNOW WHAT'LL HAPPEN IF WE CAN'T GET IT OFF!
NO... YOU'VE GOT TO LET GO...IT'S DIGGING IN...
IF I LET GO IT'LL RUN YOU, MAGS...
IT'LL RUN YOU TILL THERE'S NOTHIN' LEFT.
I'M SORRY, LOVE.
LET ME GO!
SSSSS
AIIEG

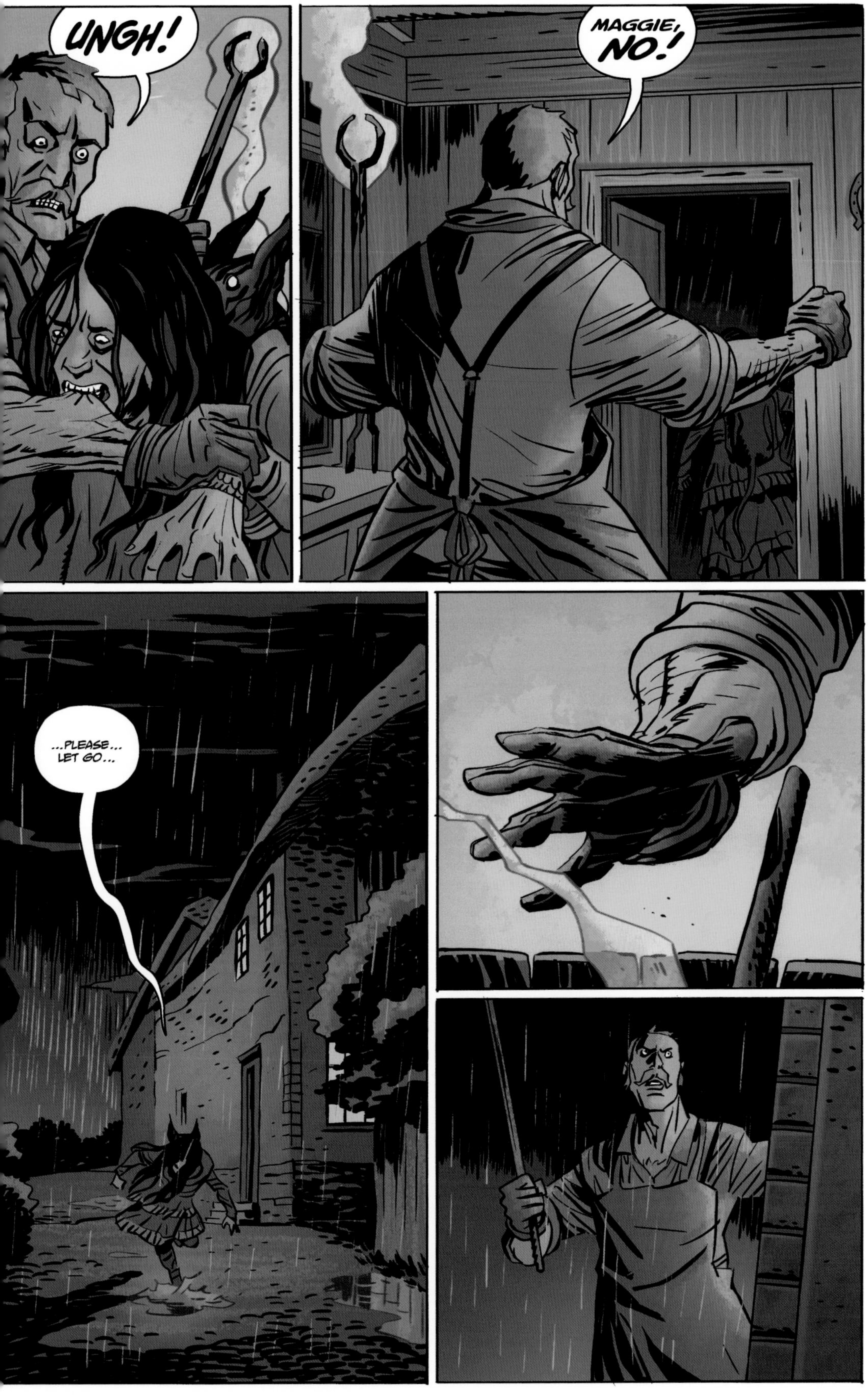
UNGH!
MAGGIE, NO!
...PLEASE... LET GO...

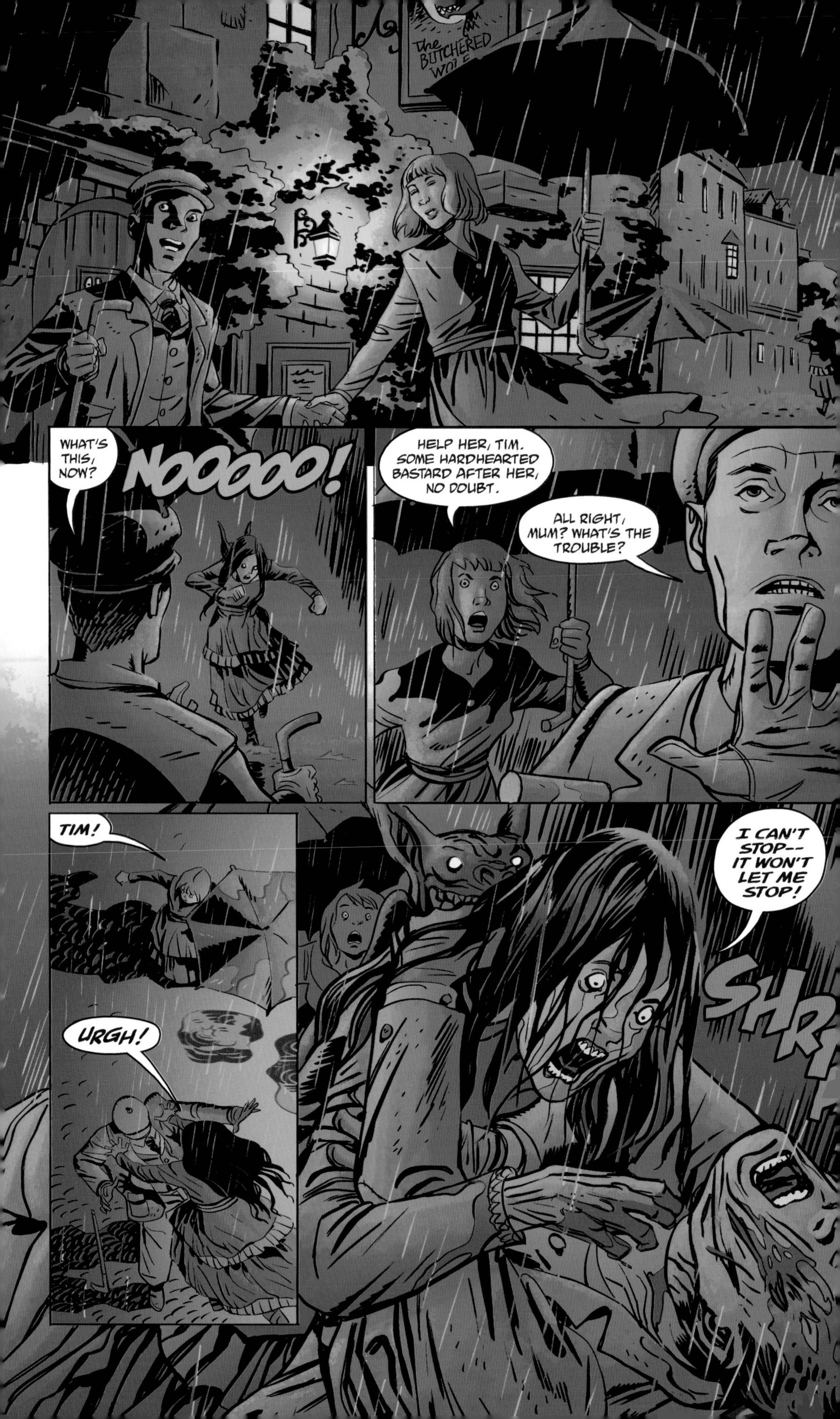
The BUTCHERED WOLF
WHAT'S THIS, NOW?
NOOOOO!
HELP HER, TIM. SOME HARDHEARTED BASTARD AFTER HER, NO DOUBT.
ALL RIGHT, MUM? WHAT'S THE TROUBLE?
TIM!
URGH!
I CAN'T STOP-- IT WON'T LET ME STOP!
SHR

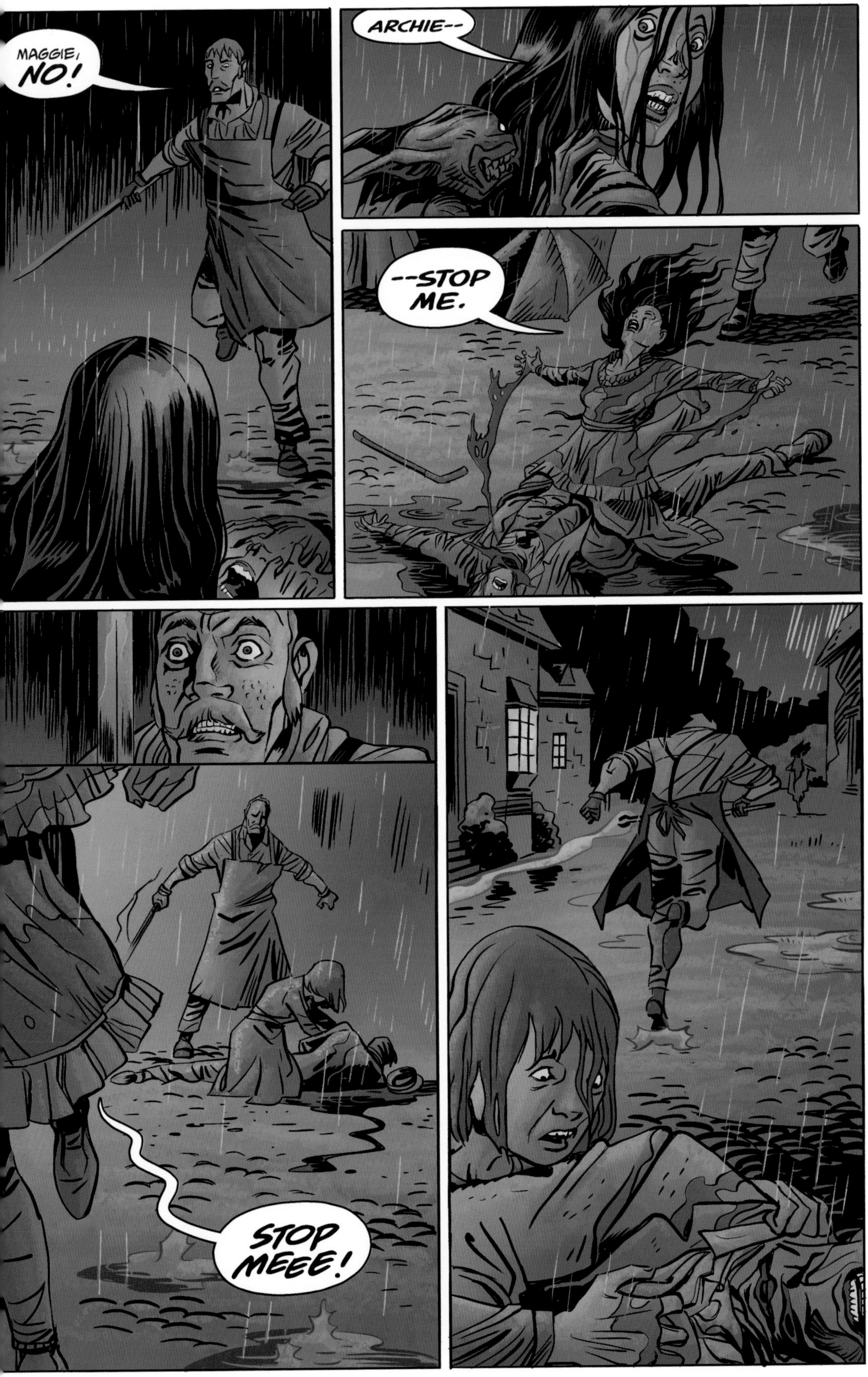
MAGGIE, NO!
ARCHIE--
--STOP ME.
STOP MEEE!

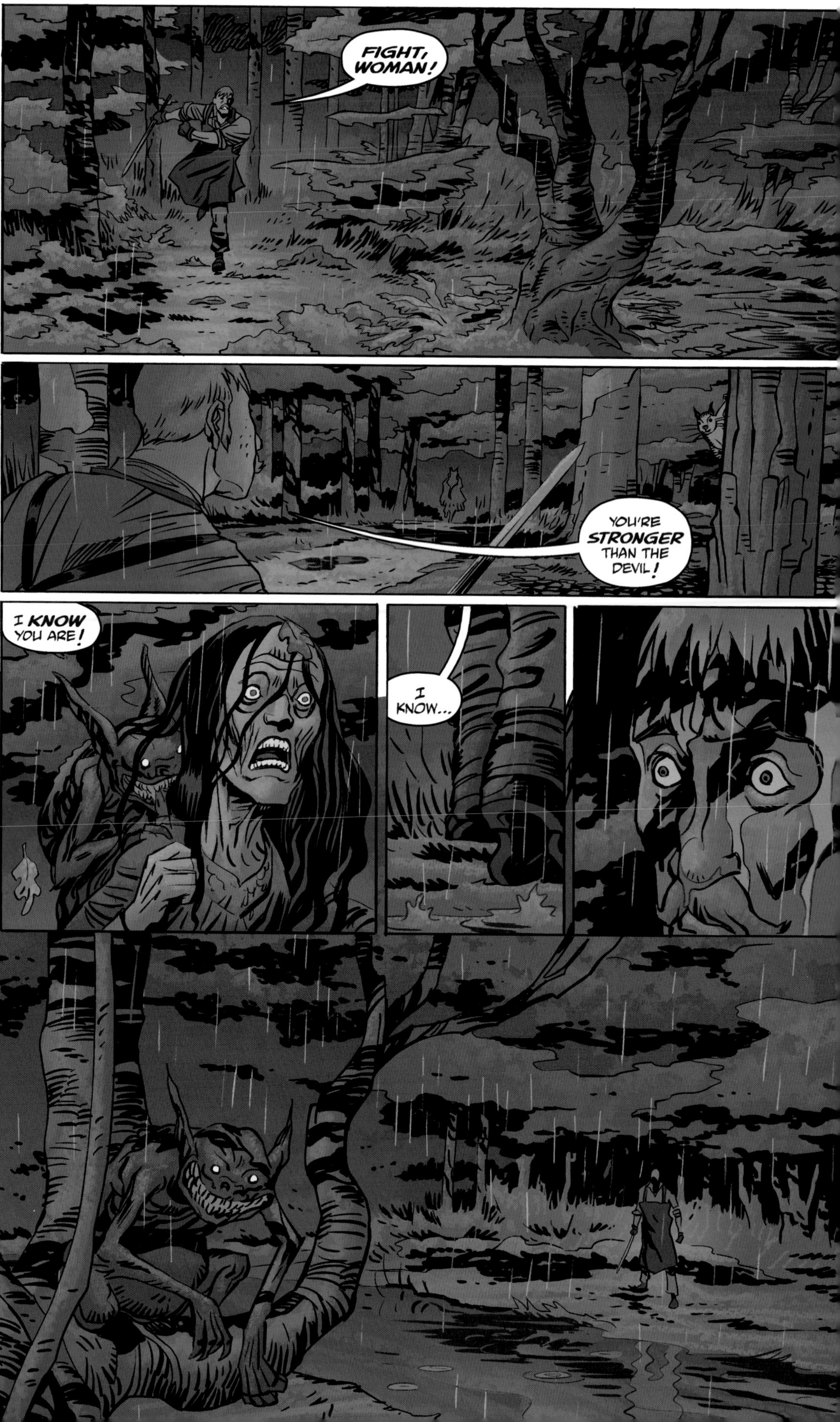
FIGHT, WOMAN!
YOU'RE STRONGER THAN THE DEVIL!
I KNOW YOU ARE!
I KNOW...

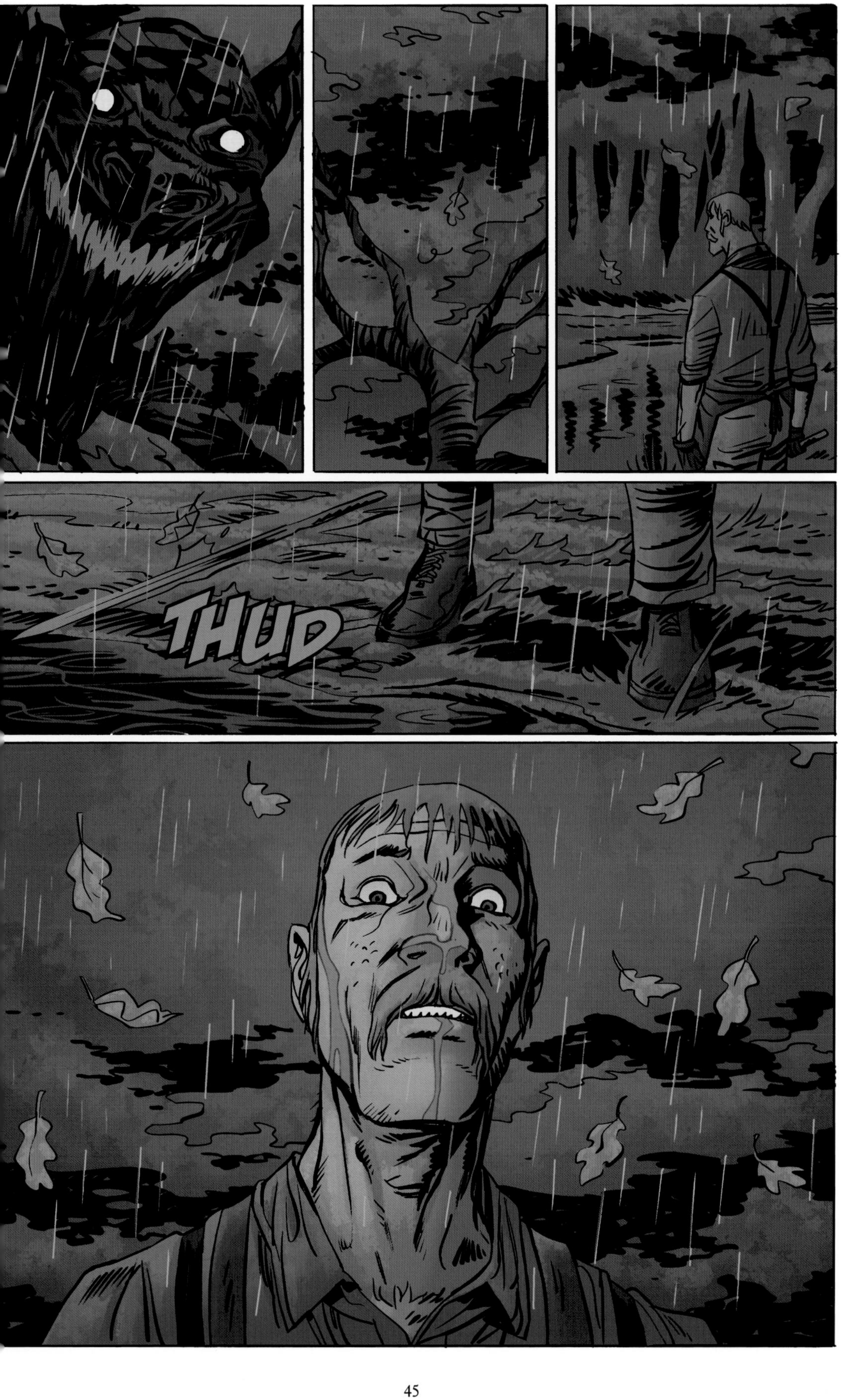
THUD

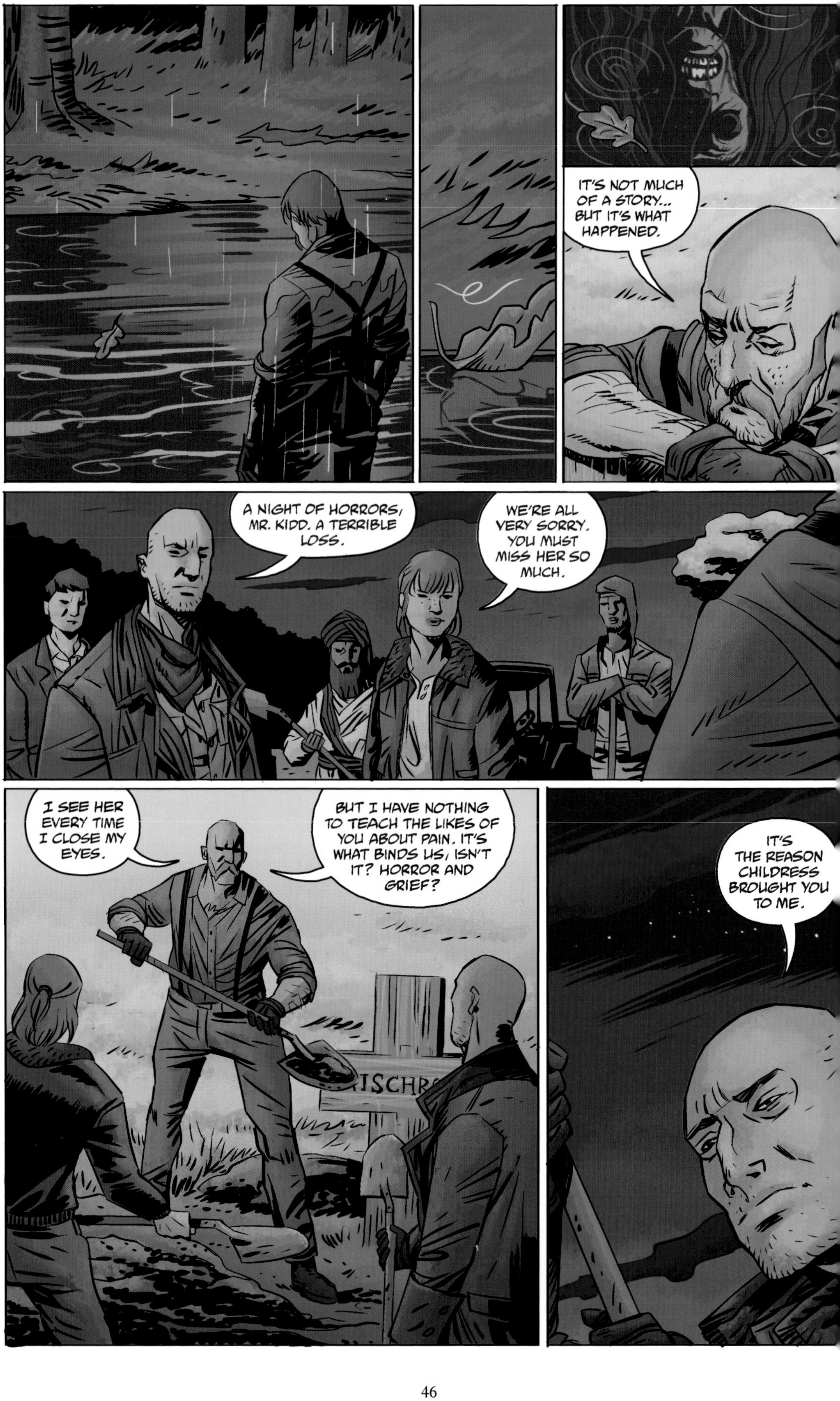
IT'S NOT MUCH OF A STORY... BUT IT'S WHAT HAPPENED.
A NIGHT OF HORRORS, MR. KIDD. A TERRIBLE LOSS.
WE'RE ALL VERY SORRY. YOU MUST MISS HER SO MUCH.
I SEE HER EVERY TIME I CLOSE MY EYES.
BUT I HAVE NOTHING TO TEACH THE LIKES OF YOU ABOUT PAIN. IT'S WHAT BINDS US, ISN'T IT? HORROR AND GRIEF?
IT'S THE REASON CHILDRESS BROUGHT YOU TO ME.

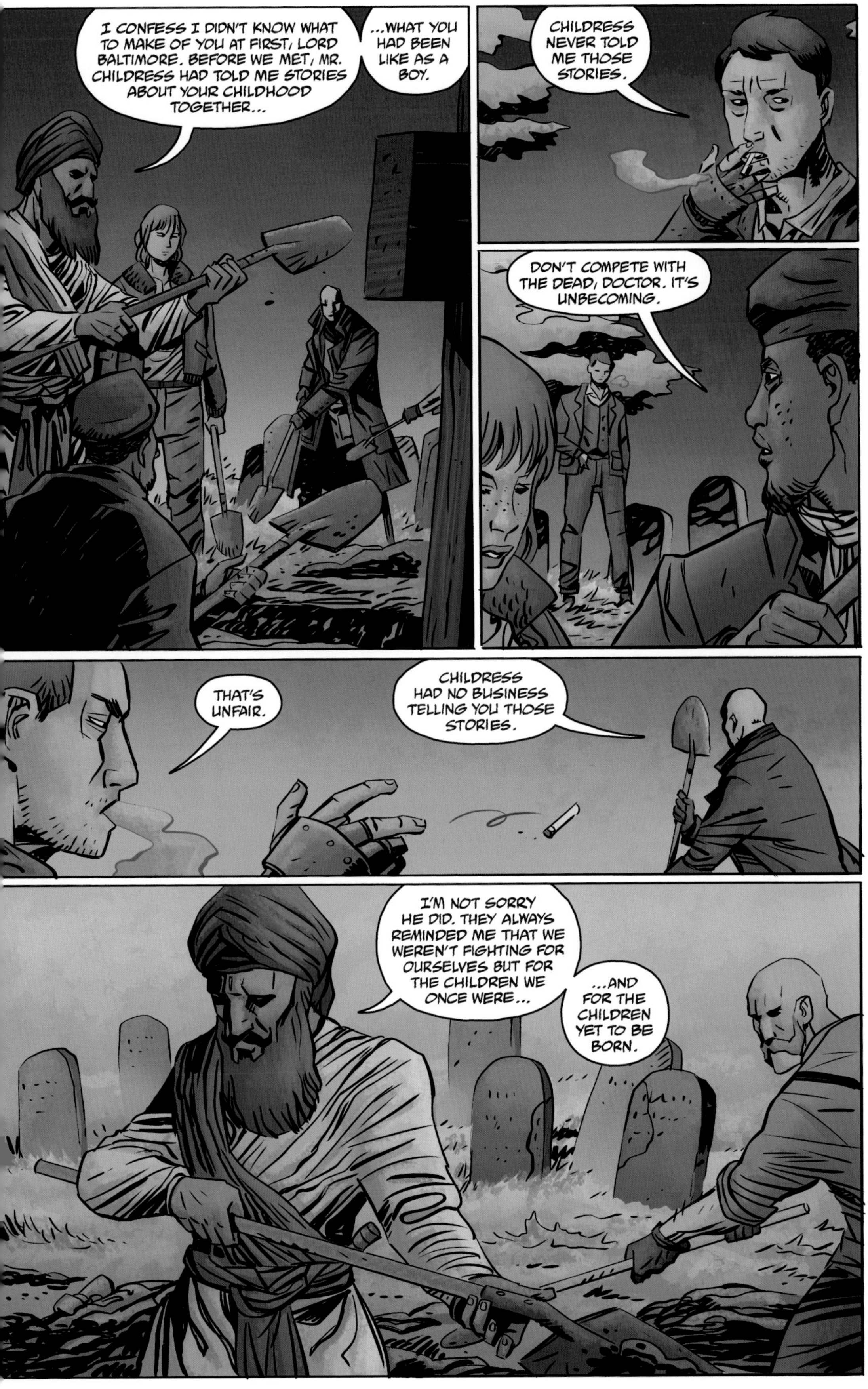
I CONFESS I DIDN'T KNOW WHAT TO MAKE OF YOU AT FIRST, LORD BALTIMORE. BEFORE WE MET, MR. CHILDRESS HAD TOLD ME STORIES ABOUT YOUR CHILDHOOD TOGETHER...
...WHAT YOU HAD BEEN LIKE AS A BOY.
CHILDRESS NEVER TOLD ME THOSE STORIES.
DON'T COMPETE WITH THE DEAD, DOCTOR. IT'S UNBECOMING.
THAT'S UNFAIR.
CHILDRESS HAD NO BUSINESS TELLING YOU THOSE STORIES.
I'M NOT SORRY HE DID. THEY ALWAYS REMINDED ME THAT WE WEREN'T FIGHTING FOR OURSELVES BUT FOR THE CHILDREN WE ONCE WERE...
...AND FOR THE CHILDREN YET TO BE BORN.

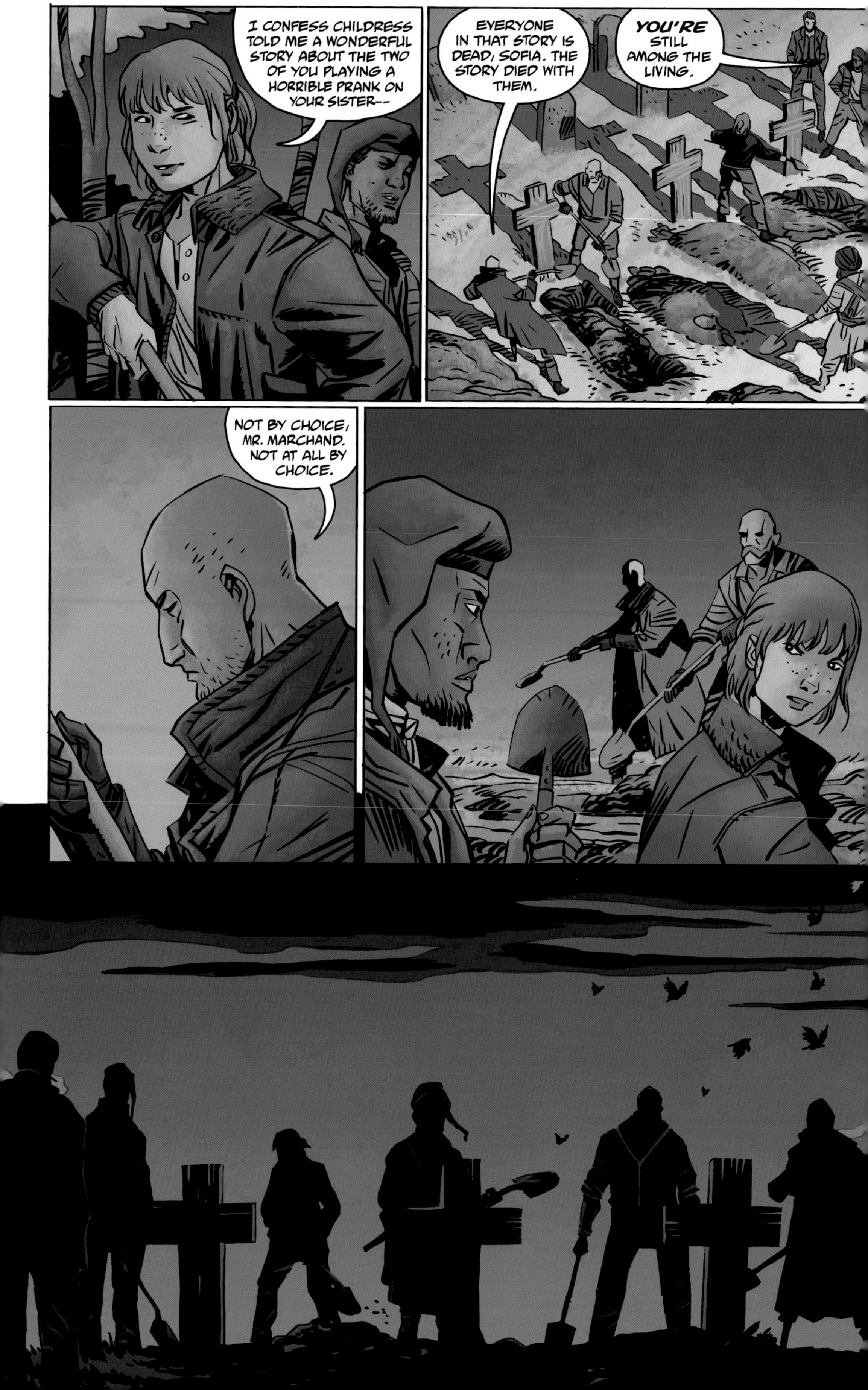
I CONFESS CHILDRESS TOLD ME A WONDERFUL STORY ABOUT THE TWO OF YOU PLAYING A HORRIBLE PRANK ON YOUR SISTER--
EVERYONE IN THAT STORY IS DEAD, SOFIA. THE STORY DIED WITH THEM.
YOU'RE STILL AMONG THE LIVING.
NOT BY CHOICE, MR. MARCHAND. NOT AT ALL BY CHOICE.

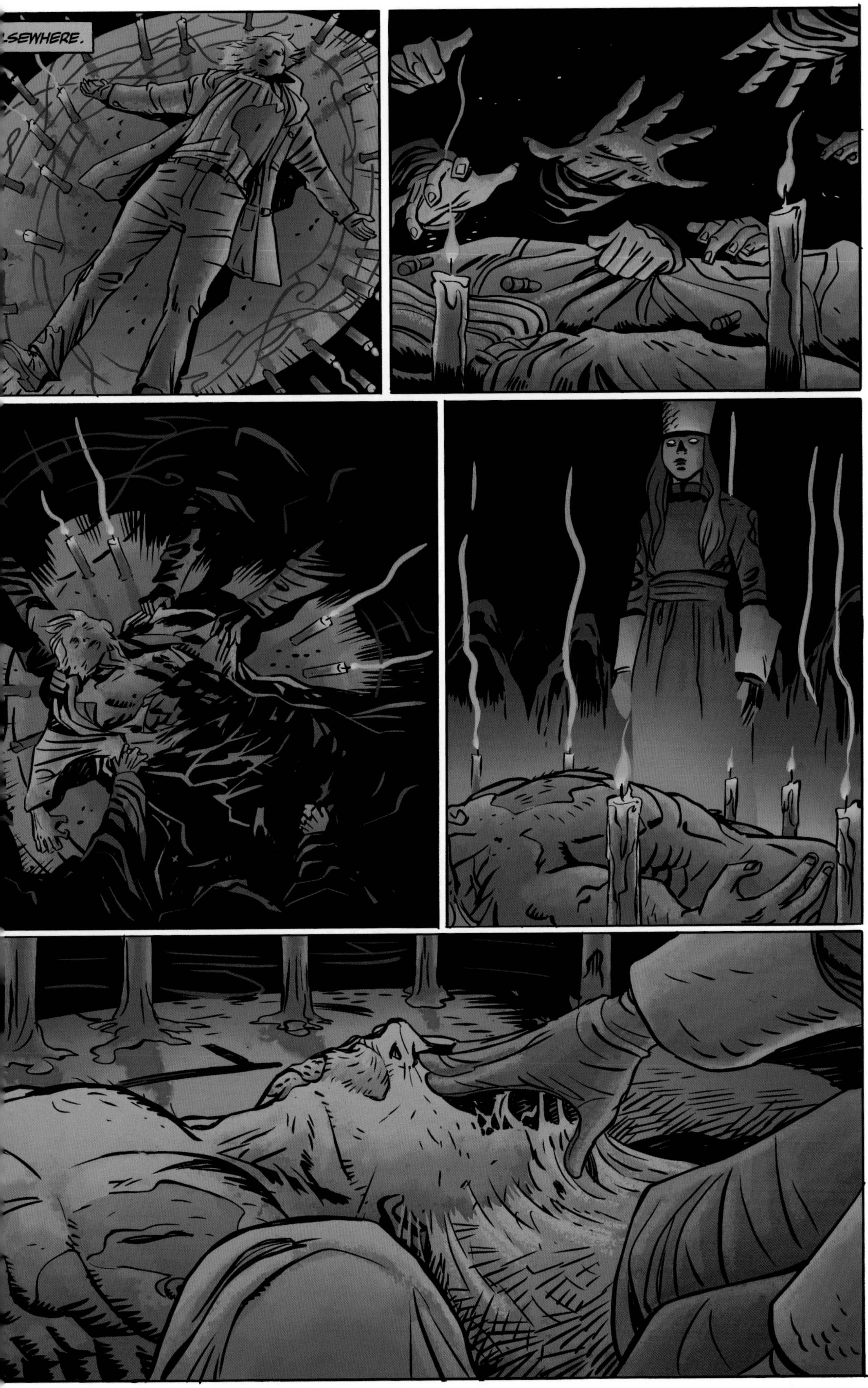
-SEWHERE.

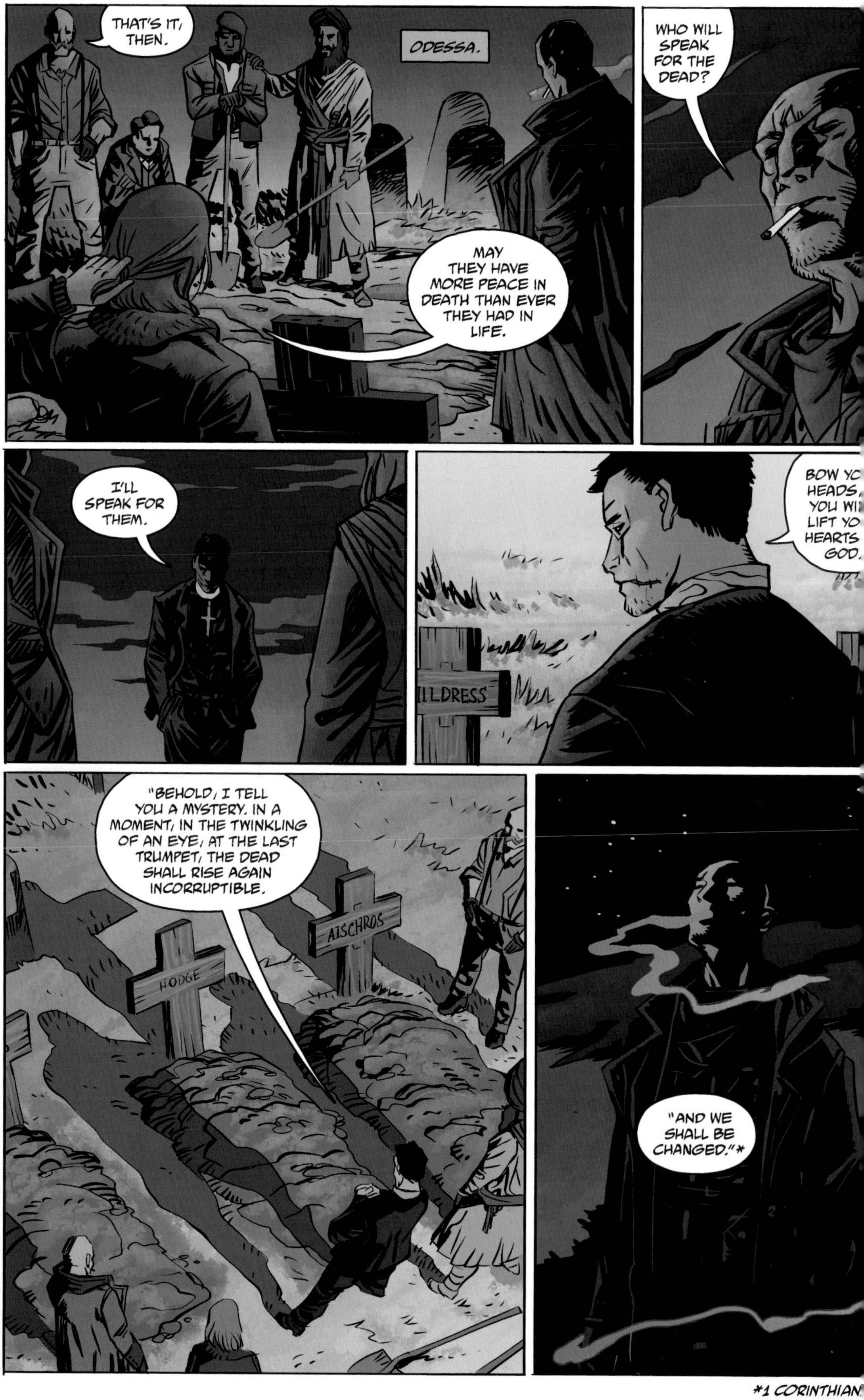
ODESSA.
THAT'S IT, THEN.
MAY THEY HAVE MORE PEACE IN DEATH THAN EVER THEY HAD IN LIFE.
WHO WILL SPEAK FOR THE DEAD?
I'LL SPEAK FOR THEM.
BOW YC HEADS, YOU WI LIFT YO HEARTS GOD.
ILDRESS
"BEHOLD, I TELL YOU A MYSTERY. IN A MOMENT, IN THE TWINKLING OF AN EYE, AT THE LAST TRUMPET, THE DEAD SHALL RISE AGAIN INCORRUPTIBLE.
HODGE
AISCHROS
"AND WE SHALL BE CHANGED."*

*1 CORINTHIAN

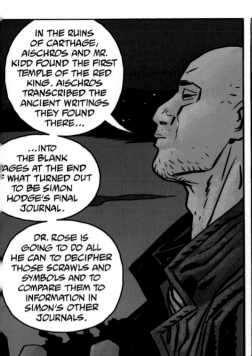

IN THE RUINS OF CARTHAGE, AISCHROS AND MR. KIDD FOUND THE FIRST TEMPLE OF THE RED KING. AISCHROS TRANSCRIBED THE ANCIENT WRITINGS THEY FOUND THERE...

...INTO THE BLANK PAGES AT THE END OF WHAT TURNED OUT TO BE SIMON HODGE'S FINAL JOURNAL.

DR. ROSE IS GOING TO DO ALL HE CAN TO DECIPHER THOSE SCRAWLS AND SYMBOLS AND TO COMPARE THEM TO INFORMATION IN SIMON'S OTHER JOURNALS.

UNTIL THEN, OUR BEST HOPE IS TO FIND THE BLOOD-RED WITCH, WHO STOLE CHILDRESS'S REMAINS.

HER TRAIL LEADS TO CONSTANTINOPLE, AND I INTEND TO FOLLOW. BEFORE YOU DECIDE IF YOU WILL COME ALONG, THERE IS SOMETHING I MUST SAY.

I BELIEVED THAT WHEN I FINALLY TOOK VENGEANCE ON THE MONSTER THAT MURDERED MY FAMILY, I WOULD DIE WITH HIM.

I DID NOT. IT SEEMS I *CANNOT*.

MY FONDEST WISH NOW IS THAT WHEN I DESTROY THE RED KING, I WILL FINALLY BE ALLOWED MY OWN DEATH.

TO LIVE BEYOND THAT WOULD BE THE ULTIMATE INJUSTICE. THE TRUE HELL.

I UNDER-STAND THAT NONE OF YOU FEELS AS I DO.

THESE GRAVES, BOTH HODGE'S AND THE EMPTY GRAVES OF AISCHROS AND CHILDRESS, ARE YET ANOTHER REMINDER THAT TO FALL IN WITH ME IS TO COURT YOUR OWN DEATH.

IF YOU CONTINUE ON WITH ME, YOU WILL SURELY DIE. IF YOU WANT TO BREAK OFF, TO RETURN TO WHAT PASSES FOR ORDINARY LIFE IN THIS CHANGED WORLD, NOW IS THE TIME.

GO AND LIVE...

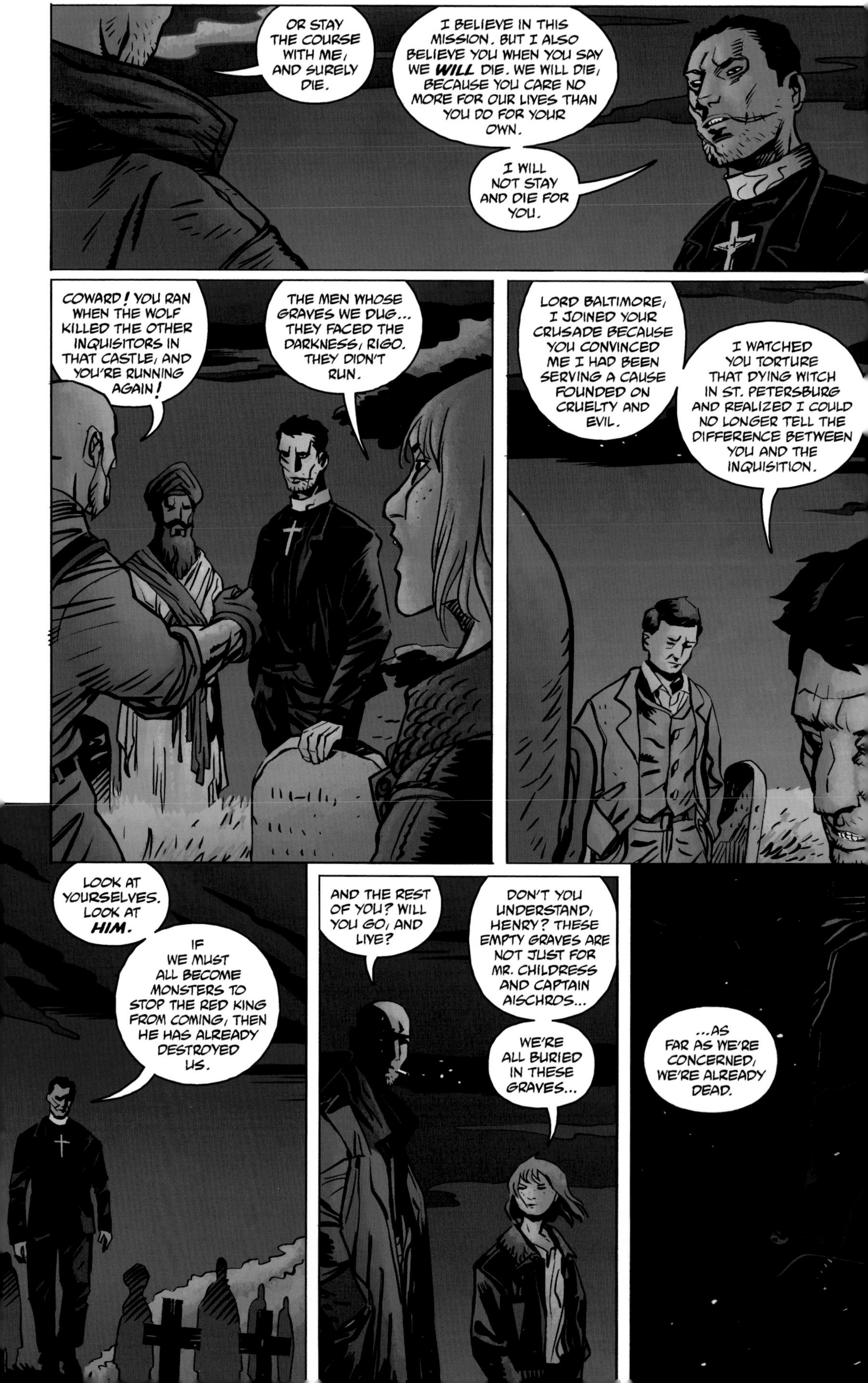
OR STAY THE COURSE WITH ME, AND SURELY DIE.
I BELIEVE IN THIS MISSION. BUT I ALSO BELIEVE YOU WHEN YOU SAY WE *WILL* DIE. WE WILL DIE, BECAUSE YOU CARE NO MORE FOR OUR LIVES THAN YOU DO FOR YOUR OWN.
I WILL NOT STAY AND DIE FOR YOU.
COWARD! YOU RAN WHEN THE WOLF KILLED THE OTHER INQUISITORS IN THAT CASTLE, AND YOU'RE RUNNING AGAIN!
THE MEN WHOSE GRAVES WE DUG... THEY FACED THE DARKNESS, RIGO. THEY DIDN'T RUN.
LORD BALTIMORE, I JOINED YOUR CRUSADE BECAUSE YOU CONVINCED ME I HAD BEEN SERVING A CAUSE FOUNDED ON CRUELTY AND EVIL.
I WATCHED YOU TORTURE THAT DYING WITCH IN ST. PETERSBURG AND REALIZED I COULD NO LONGER TELL THE DIFFERENCE BETWEEN YOU AND THE INQUISITION.
LOOK AT YOURSELVES. LOOK AT *HIM*.
IF WE MUST ALL BECOME MONSTERS TO STOP THE RED KING FROM COMING, THEN HE HAS ALREADY DESTROYED US.
AND THE REST OF YOU? WILL YOU GO, AND LIVE?
DON'T YOU UNDERSTAND, HENRY? THESE EMPTY GRAVES ARE NOT JUST FOR MR. CHILDRESS AND CAPTAIN AISCHROS...
WE'RE ALL BURIED IN THESE GRAVES...
...AS FAR AS WE'RE CONCERNED, WE'RE ALREADY DEAD.

CHAPTER THREE

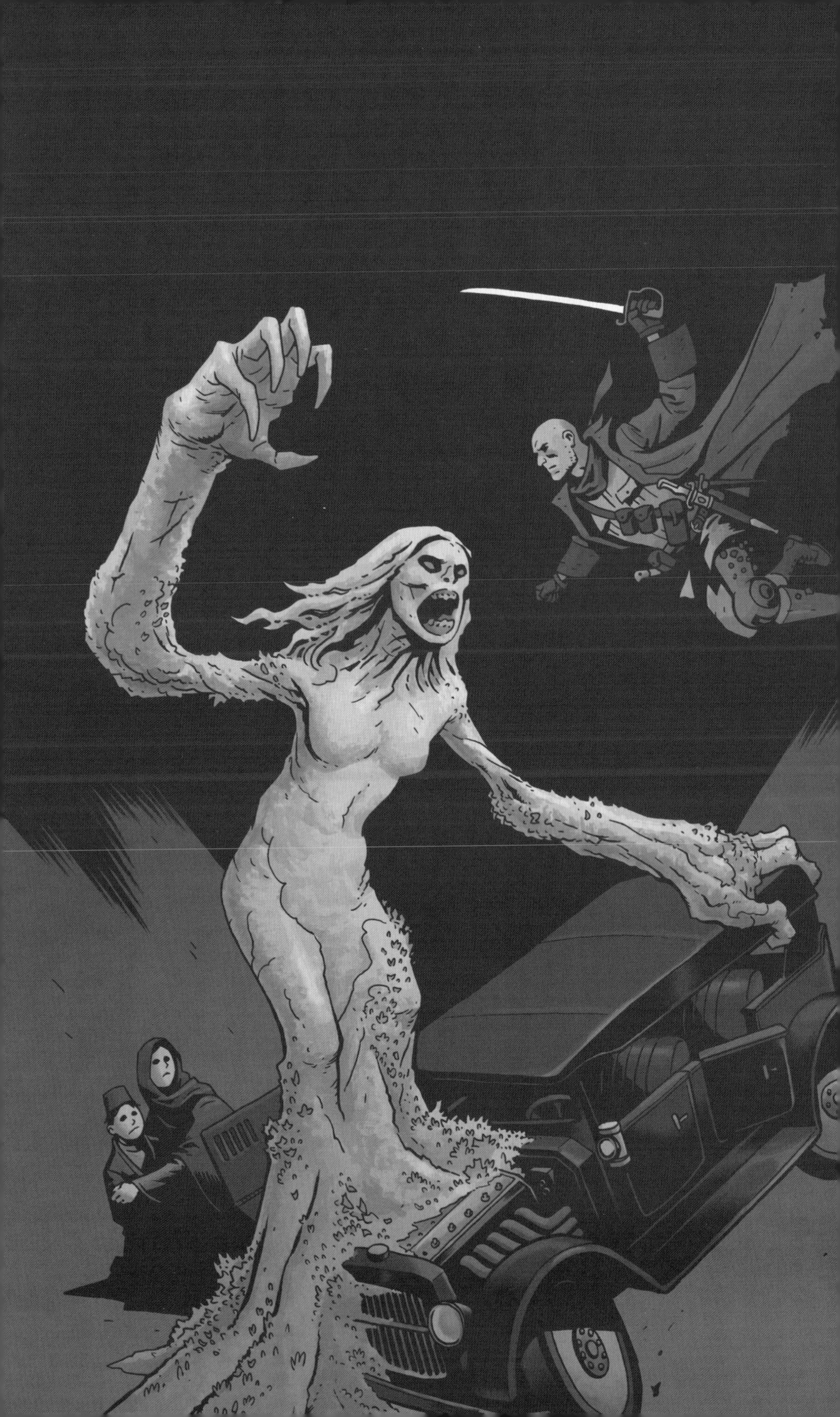

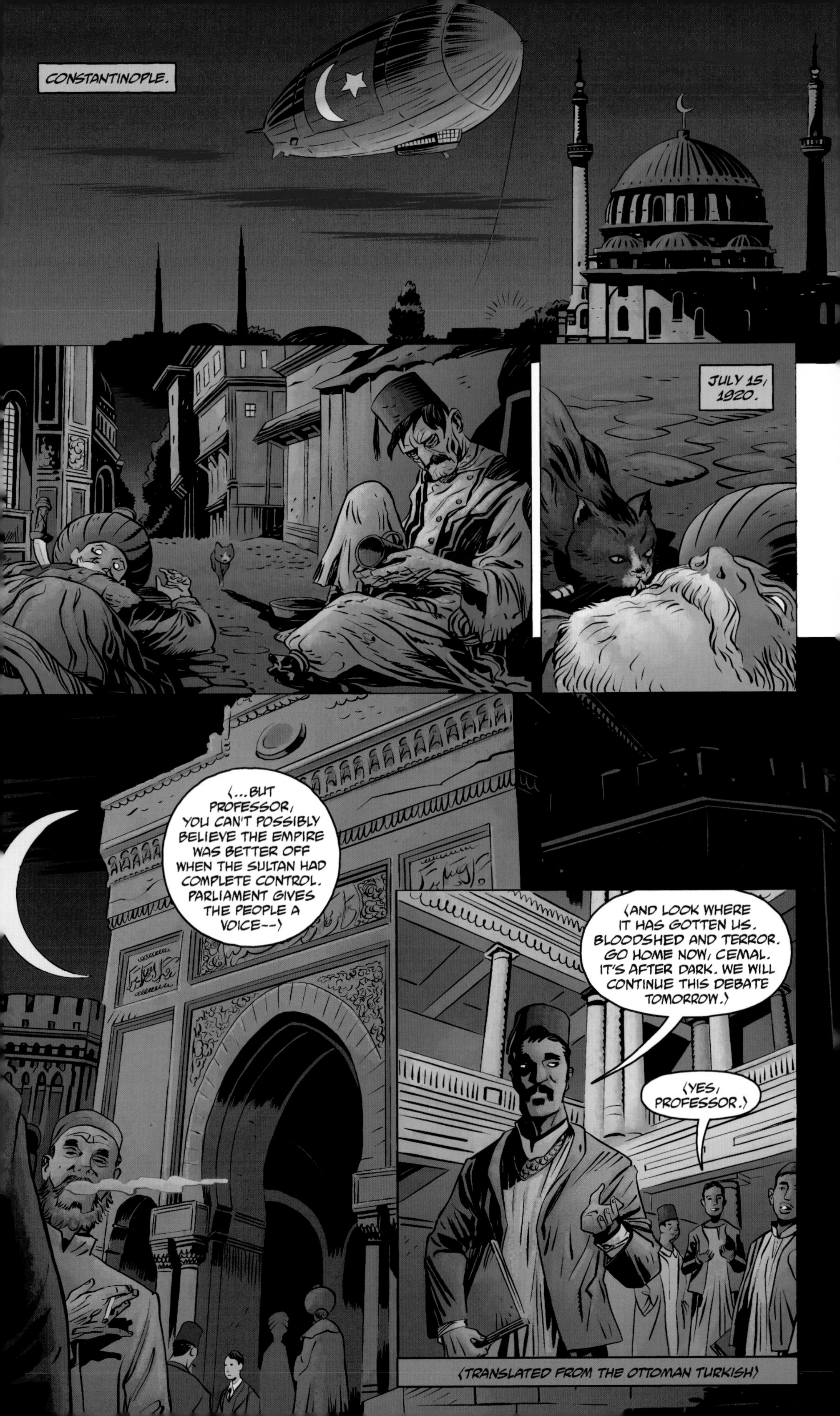
CONSTANTINOPLE.
JULY 15, 1920.
⟨...BUT PROFESSOR, YOU CAN'T POSSIBLY BELIEVE THE EMPIRE WAS BETTER OFF WHEN THE SULTAN HAD COMPLETE CONTROL. PARLIAMENT GIVES THE PEOPLE A VOICE--⟩
⟨AND LOOK WHERE IT HAS GOTTEN US. BLOODSHED AND TERROR. GO HOME NOW, CEMAL. IT'S AFTER DARK. WE WILL CONTINUE THIS DEBATE TOMORROW.⟩
⟨YES, PROFESSOR.⟩
⟨TRANSLATED FROM THE OTTOMAN TURKISH⟩

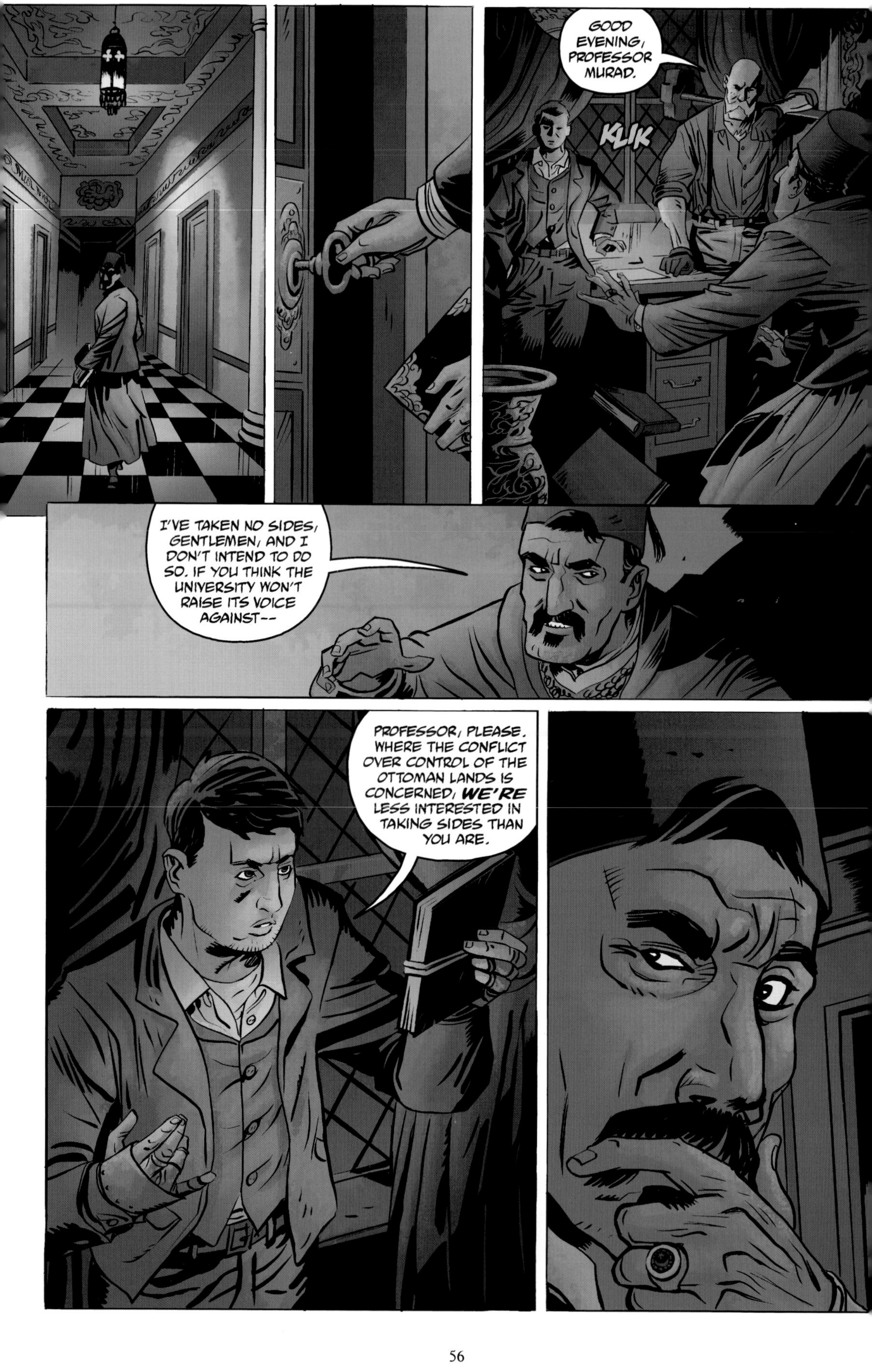
GOOD EVENING, PROFESSOR MURAD.
KLIK
I'VE TAKEN NO SIDES, GENTLEMEN, AND I DON'T INTEND TO DO SO. IF YOU THINK THE UNIVERSITY WON'T RAISE ITS VOICE AGAINST--
PROFESSOR, PLEASE. WHERE THE CONFLICT OVER CONTROL OF THE OTTOMAN LANDS IS CONCERNED, WE'RE LESS INTERESTED IN TAKING SIDES THAN YOU ARE.

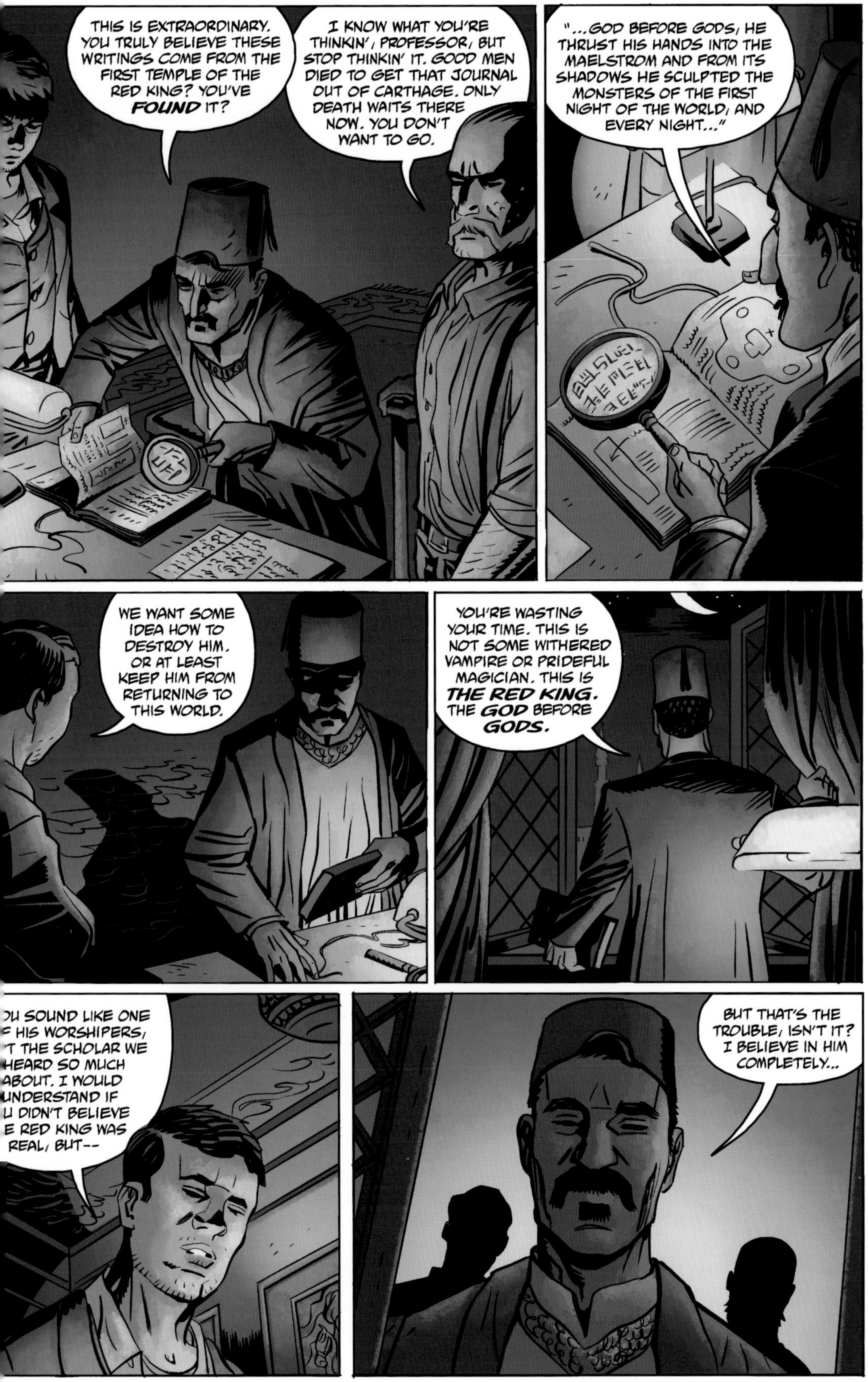
THIS IS EXTRAORDINARY. YOU TRULY BELIEVE THESE WRITINGS COME FROM THE FIRST TEMPLE OF THE RED KING? YOU'VE FOUND IT?
I KNOW WHAT YOU'RE THINKIN', PROFESSOR, BUT STOP THINKIN' IT. GOOD MEN DIED TO GET THAT JOURNAL OUT OF CARTHAGE. ONLY DEATH WAITS THERE NOW. YOU DON'T WANT TO GO.
"...GOD BEFORE GODS, HE THRUST HIS HANDS INTO THE MAELSTROM AND FROM ITS SHADOWS HE SCULPTED THE MONSTERS OF THE FIRST NIGHT OF THE WORLD, AND EVERY NIGHT..."
WE WANT SOME IDEA HOW TO DESTROY HIM. OR AT LEAST KEEP HIM FROM RETURNING TO THIS WORLD.
YOU'RE WASTING YOUR TIME. THIS IS NOT SOME WITHERED VAMPIRE OR PRIDEFUL MAGICIAN. THIS IS THE RED KING. THE GOD BEFORE GODS.
OU SOUND LIKE ONE F HIS WORSHIPERS, T THE SCHOLAR WE HEARD SO MUCH ABOUT. I WOULD UNDERSTAND IF U DIDN'T BELIEVE E RED KING WAS REAL, BUT--
BUT THAT'S THE TROUBLE, ISN'T IT? I BELIEVE IN HIM COMPLETELY...

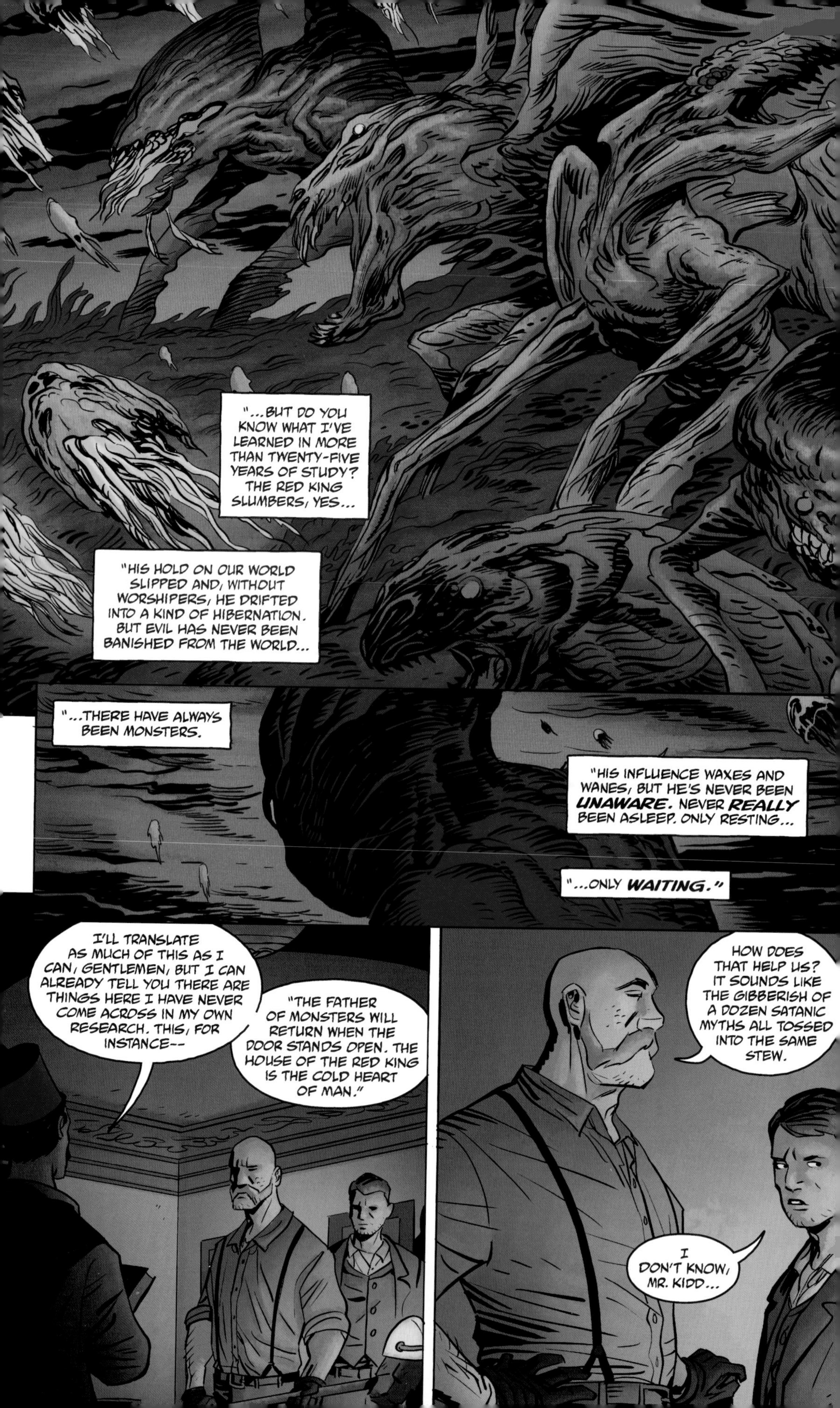
"...BUT DO YOU KNOW WHAT I'VE LEARNED IN MORE THAN TWENTY-FIVE YEARS OF STUDY? THE RED KING SLUMBERS, YES...
"HIS HOLD ON OUR WORLD SLIPPED AND, WITHOUT WORSHIPERS, HE DRIFTED INTO A KIND OF HIBERNATION. BUT EVIL HAS NEVER BEEN BANISHED FROM THE WORLD...
"...THERE HAVE ALWAYS BEEN MONSTERS.
"HIS INFLUENCE WAXES AND WANES, BUT HE'S NEVER BEEN UNAWARE. NEVER REALLY BEEN ASLEEP. ONLY RESTING...
"...ONLY WAITING."
I'LL TRANSLATE AS MUCH OF THIS AS I CAN, GENTLEMEN, BUT I CAN ALREADY TELL YOU THERE ARE THINGS HERE I HAVE NEVER COME ACROSS IN MY OWN RESEARCH. THIS, FOR INSTANCE--
"THE FATHER OF MONSTERS WILL RETURN WHEN THE DOOR STANDS OPEN. THE HOUSE OF THE RED KING IS THE COLD HEART OF MAN."
HOW DOES THAT HELP US? IT SOUNDS LIKE THE GIBBERISH OF A DOZEN SATANIC MYTHS ALL TOSSED INTO THE SAME STEW.
I DON'T KNOW, MR. KIDD...

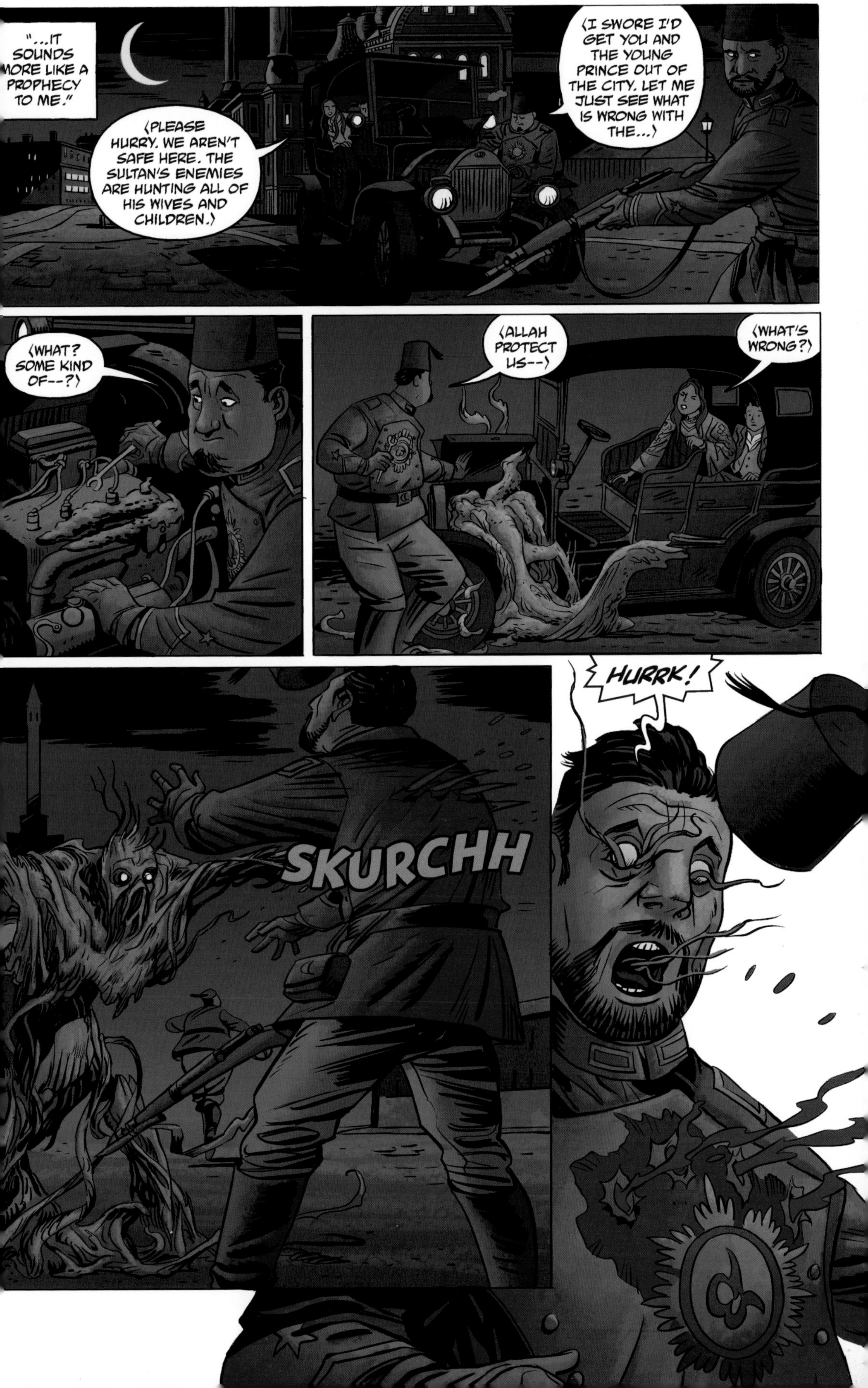
"...IT SOUNDS MORE LIKE A PROPHECY TO ME."
⟨PLEASE HURRY. WE AREN'T SAFE HERE. THE SULTAN'S ENEMIES ARE HUNTING ALL OF HIS WIVES AND CHILDREN.⟩
⟨I SWORE I'D GET YOU AND THE YOUNG PRINCE OUT OF THE CITY. LET ME JUST SEE WHAT IS WRONG WITH THE...⟩
⟨WHAT? SOME KIND OF--?⟩
⟨ALLAH PROTECT US--⟩
⟨WHAT'S WRONG?⟩
SKURCHH
HURRK!

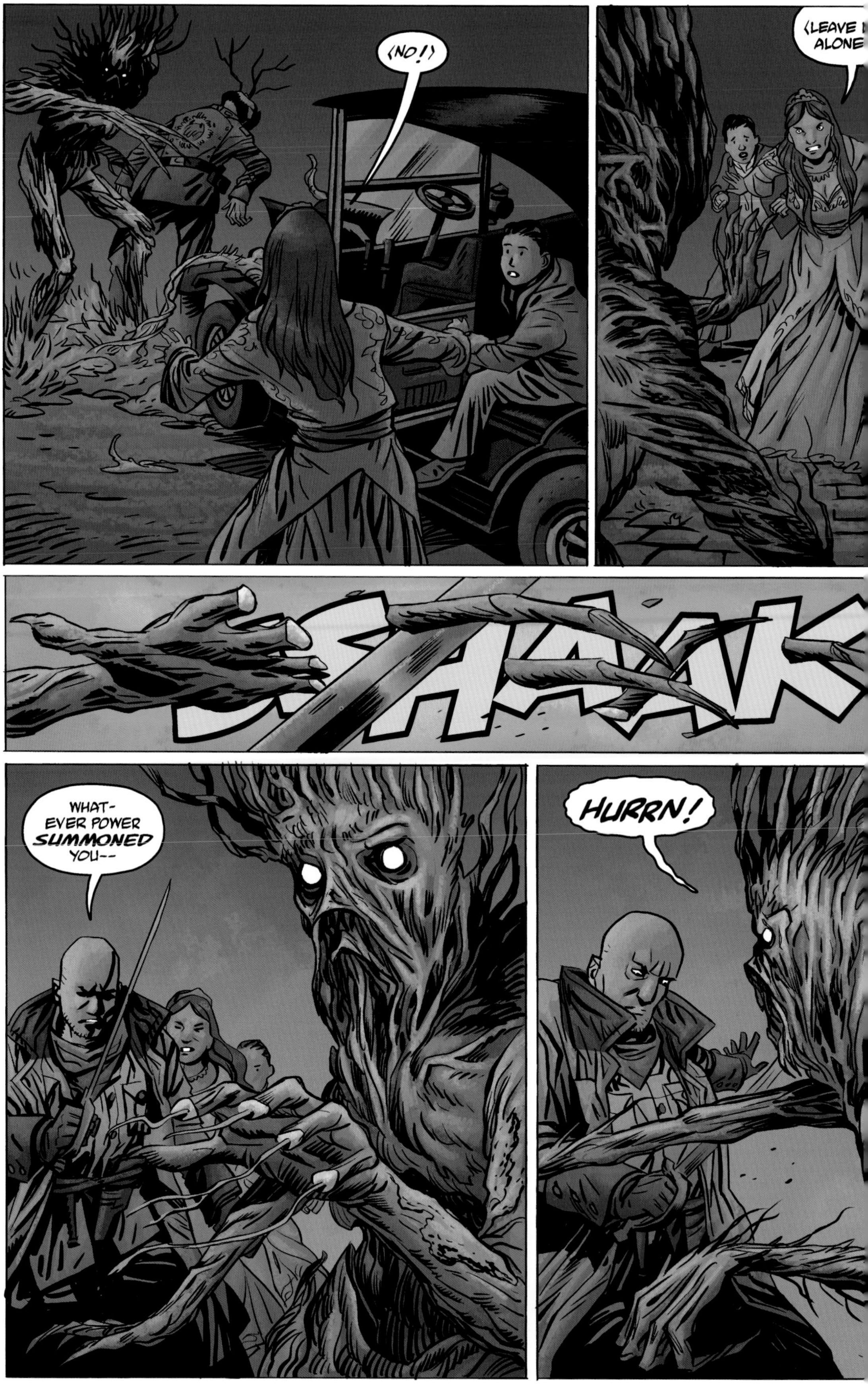
⟨NO!⟩
⟨LEAVE ALONE
SHAAK
WHAT-EVER POWER SUMMONED YOU--
HURRN!

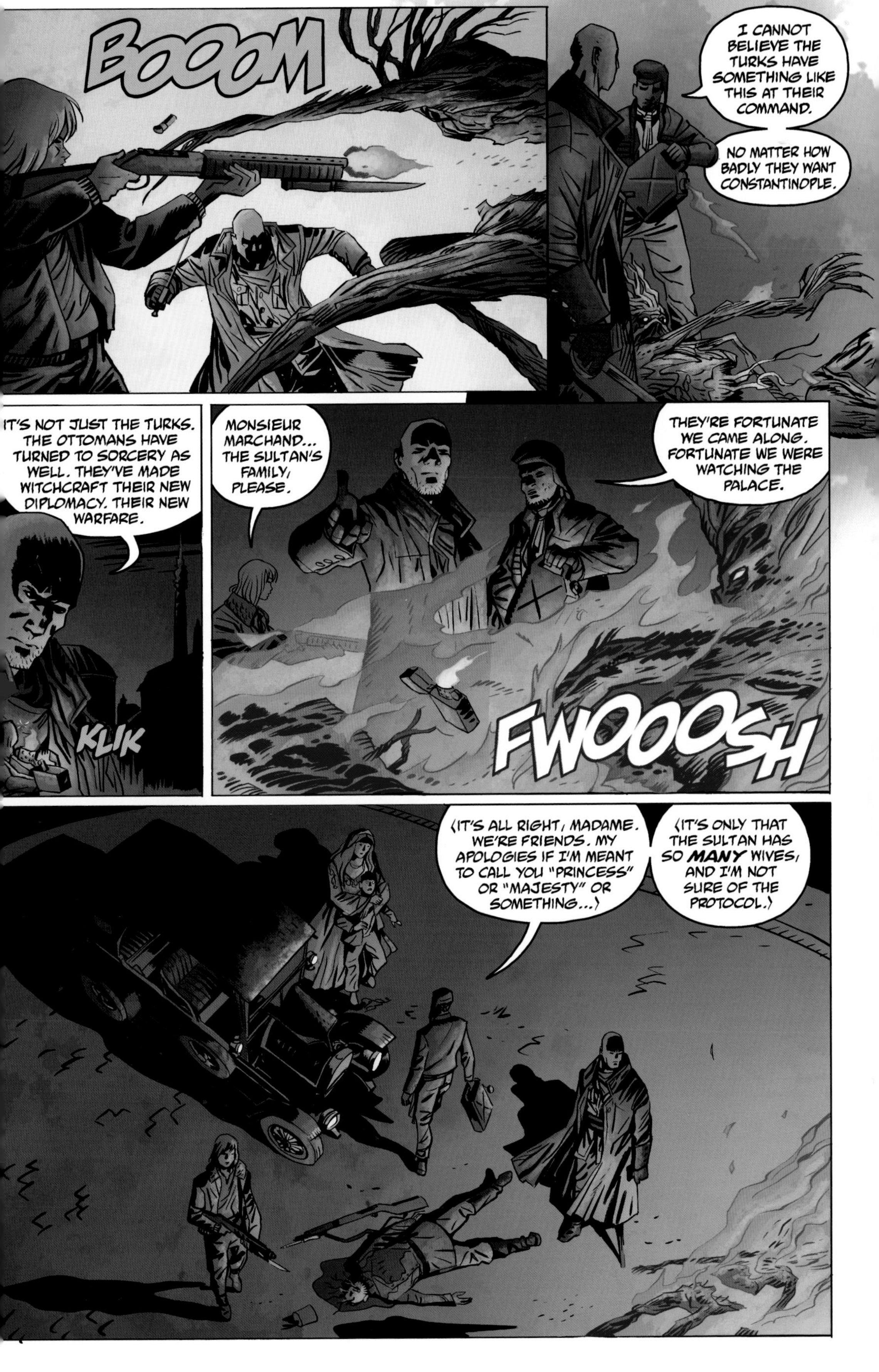
BOOOM
I CANNOT BELIEVE THE TURKS HAVE SOMETHING LIKE THIS AT THEIR COMMAND.
NO MATTER HOW BADLY THEY WANT CONSTANTINOPLE.
IT'S NOT JUST THE TURKS. THE OTTOMANS HAVE TURNED TO SORCERY AS WELL. THEY'VE MADE WITCHCRAFT THEIR NEW DIPLOMACY. THEIR NEW WARFARE.
KLIK
MONSIEUR MARCHAND... THE SULTAN'S FAMILY, PLEASE.
THEY'RE FORTUNATE WE CAME ALONG. FORTUNATE WE WERE WATCHING THE PALACE.
FWOOOSH
‹IT'S ALL RIGHT, MADAME. WE'RE FRIENDS. MY APOLOGIES IF I'M MEANT TO CALL YOU "PRINCESS" OR "MAJESTY" OR SOMETHING...›
‹IT'S ONLY THAT THE SULTAN HAS SO **MANY** WIVES, AND I'M NOT SURE OF THE PROTOCOL.›

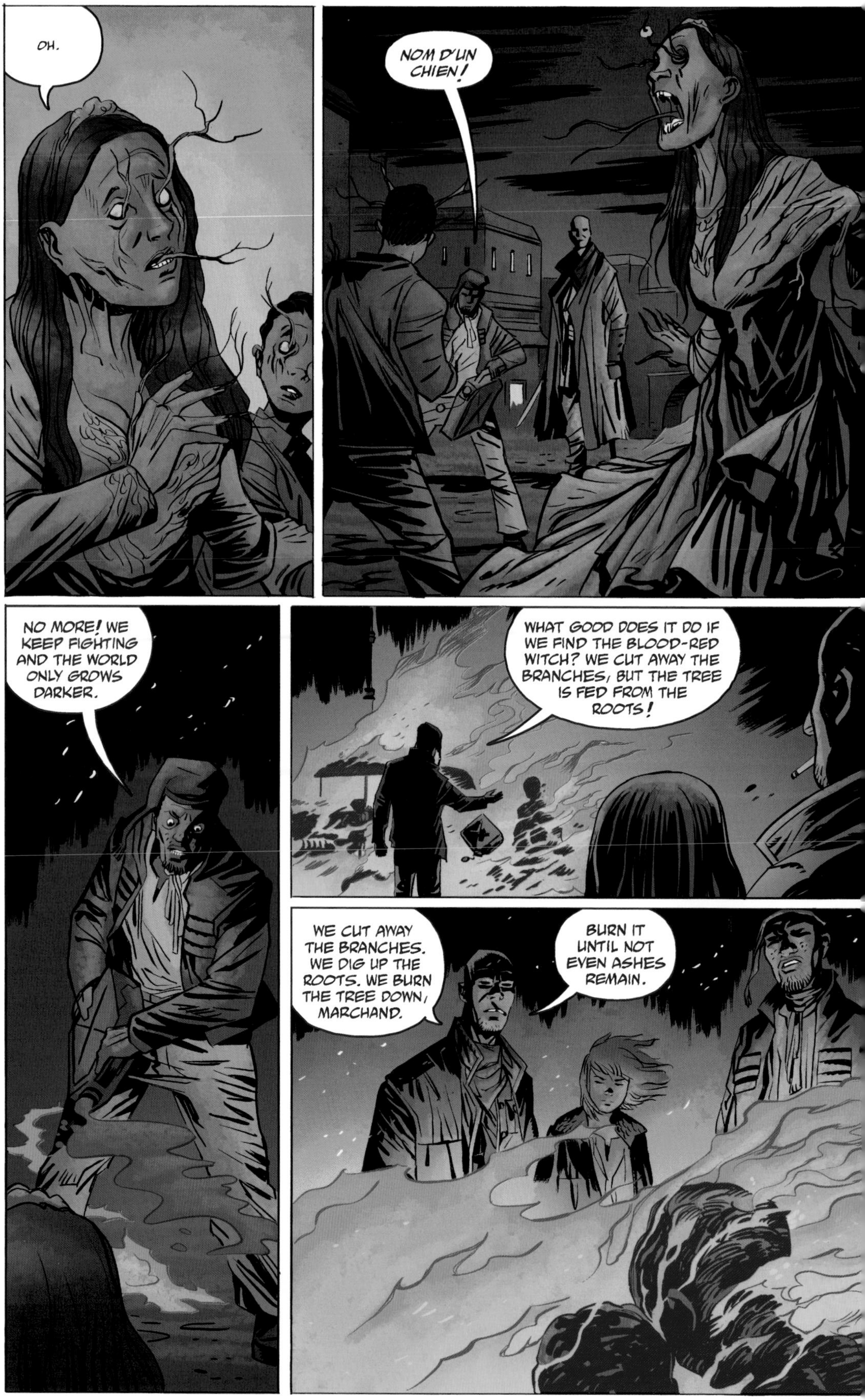
OH.
NOM D'UN CHIEN!
NO MORE! WE KEEP FIGHTING AND THE WORLD ONLY GROWS DARKER.
WHAT GOOD DOES IT DO IF WE FIND THE BLOOD-RED WITCH? WE CUT AWAY THE BRANCHES, BUT THE TREE IS FED FROM THE ROOTS!
WE CUT AWAY THE BRANCHES. WE DIG UP THE ROOTS. WE BURN THE TREE DOWN, MARCHAND.
BURN IT UNTIL NOT EVEN ASHES REMAIN.

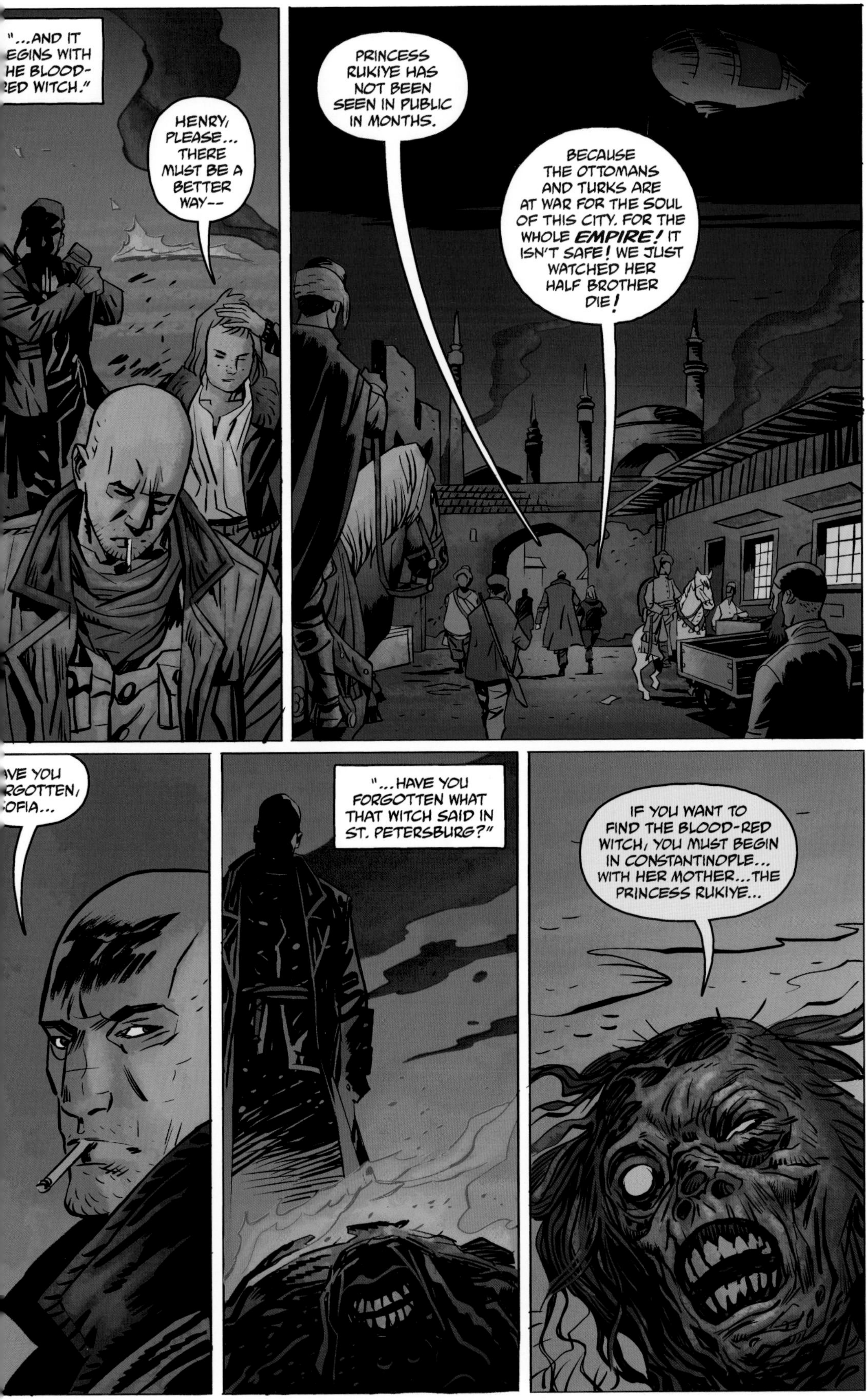
"...AND IT
EGINS WITH
HE BLOOD-
ED WITCH."
HENRY, PLEASE... THERE MUST BE A BETTER WAY--
PRINCESS RUKIYE HAS NOT BEEN SEEN IN PUBLIC IN MONTHS.
BECAUSE THE OTTOMANS AND TURKS ARE AT WAR FOR THE SOUL OF THIS CITY. FOR THE WHOLE EMPIRE! IT ISN'T SAFE! WE JUST WATCHED HER HALF BROTHER DIE!
AVE YOU
RGOTTEN,
OFIA...
"...HAVE YOU FORGOTTEN WHAT THAT WITCH SAID IN ST. PETERSBURG?"
IF YOU WANT TO FIND THE BLOOD-RED WITCH, YOU MUST BEGIN IN CONSTANTINOPLE... WITH HER MOTHER...THE PRINCESS RUKIYE...

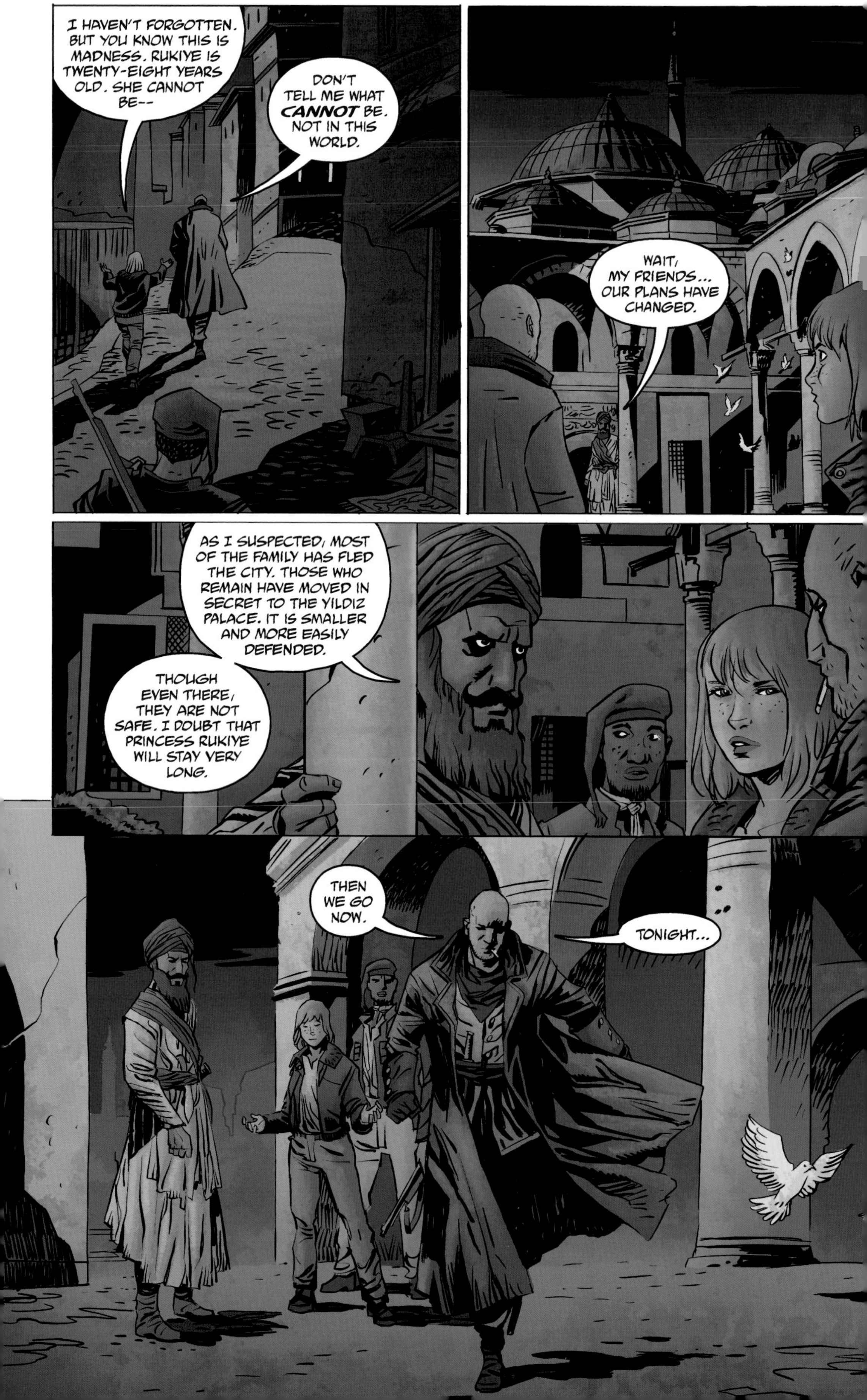
I HAVEN'T FORGOTTEN. BUT YOU KNOW THIS IS MADNESS. RUKIYE IS TWENTY-EIGHT YEARS OLD. SHE CANNOT BE--
DON'T TELL ME WHAT **CANNOT** BE. NOT IN THIS WORLD.
WAIT, MY FRIENDS... OUR PLANS HAVE CHANGED.
AS I SUSPECTED, MOST OF THE FAMILY HAS FLED THE CITY. THOSE WHO REMAIN HAVE MOVED IN SECRET TO THE YILDIZ PALACE. IT IS SMALLER AND MORE EASILY DEFENDED.
THOUGH EVEN THERE, THEY ARE NOT SAFE. I DOUBT THAT PRINCESS RUKIYE WILL STAY VERY LONG.
THEN WE GO NOW.
TONIGHT...

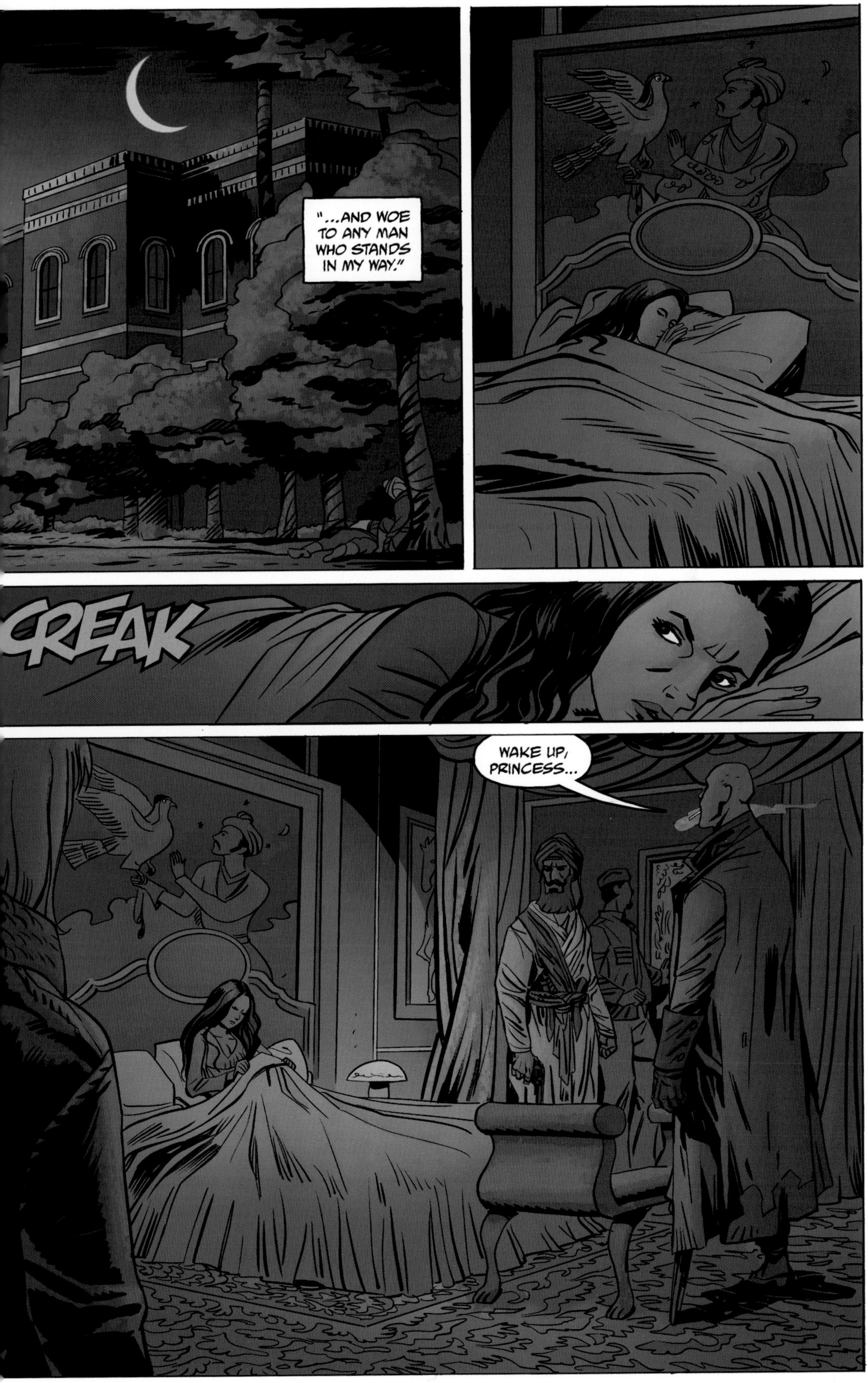
"...AND WOE TO ANY MAN WHO STANDS IN MY WAY."
CREAK
WAKE UP, PRINCESS...

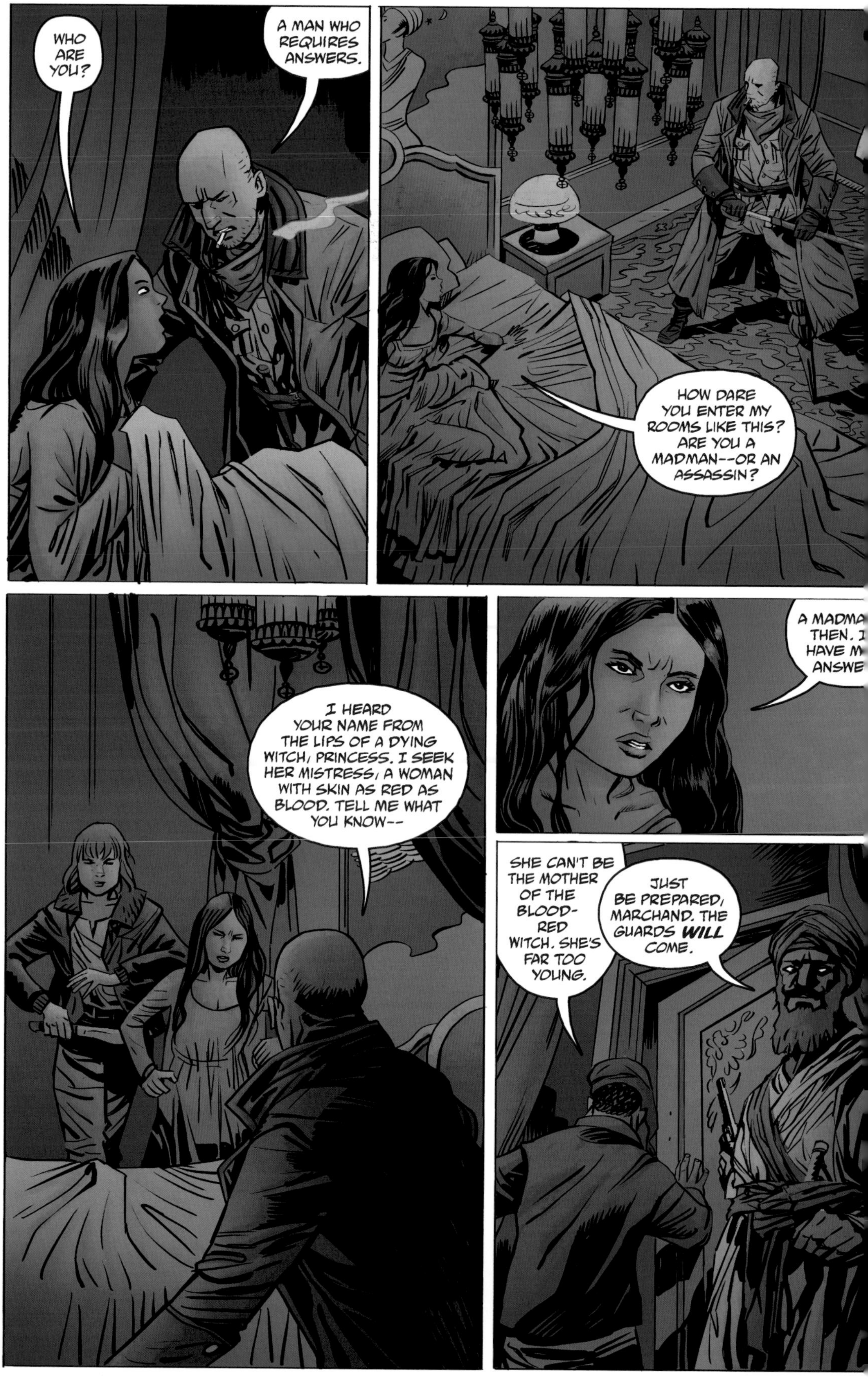
WHO ARE YOU?
A MAN WHO REQUIRES ANSWERS.
HOW DARE YOU ENTER MY ROOMS LIKE THIS? ARE YOU A MADMAN--OR AN ASSASSIN?
I HEARD YOUR NAME FROM THE LIPS OF A DYING WITCH, PRINCESS. I SEEK HER MISTRESS, A WOMAN WITH SKIN AS RED AS BLOOD. TELL ME WHAT YOU KNOW--
A MADMA THEN. I HAVE M ANSWE
SHE CAN'T BE THE MOTHER OF THE BLOOD-RED WITCH. SHE'S FAR TOO YOUNG.
JUST BE PREPARED, MARCHAND. THE GUARDS *WILL* COME.

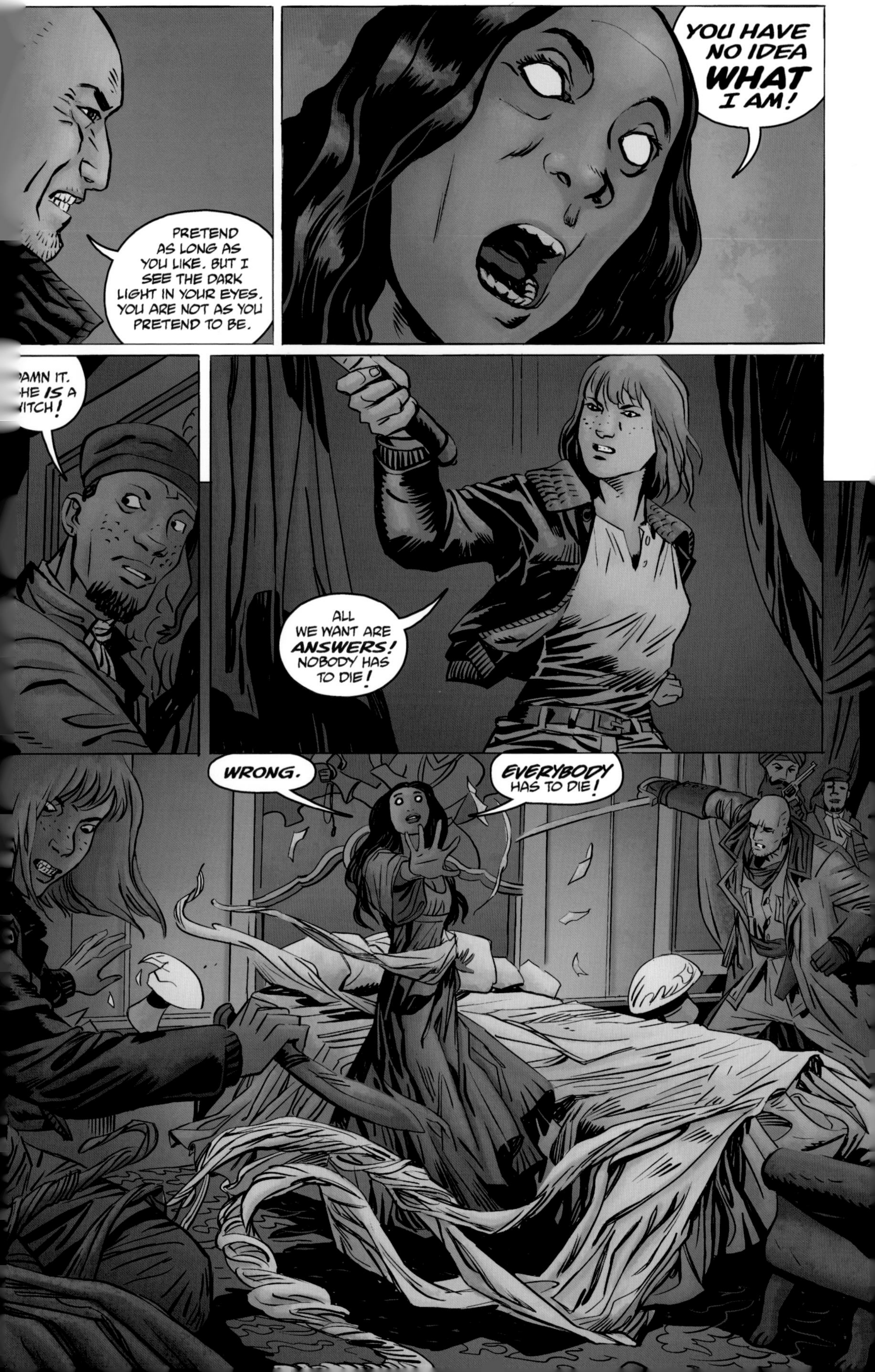
PRETEND AS LONG AS YOU LIKE. BUT I SEE THE DARK LIGHT IN YOUR EYES. YOU ARE NOT AS YOU PRETEND TO BE.
YOU HAVE NO IDEA WHAT I AM!
DAMN IT. HE IS A ITCH!
ALL WE WANT ARE ANSWERS! NOBODY HAS TO DIE!
WRONG.
EVERYBODY HAS TO DIE!

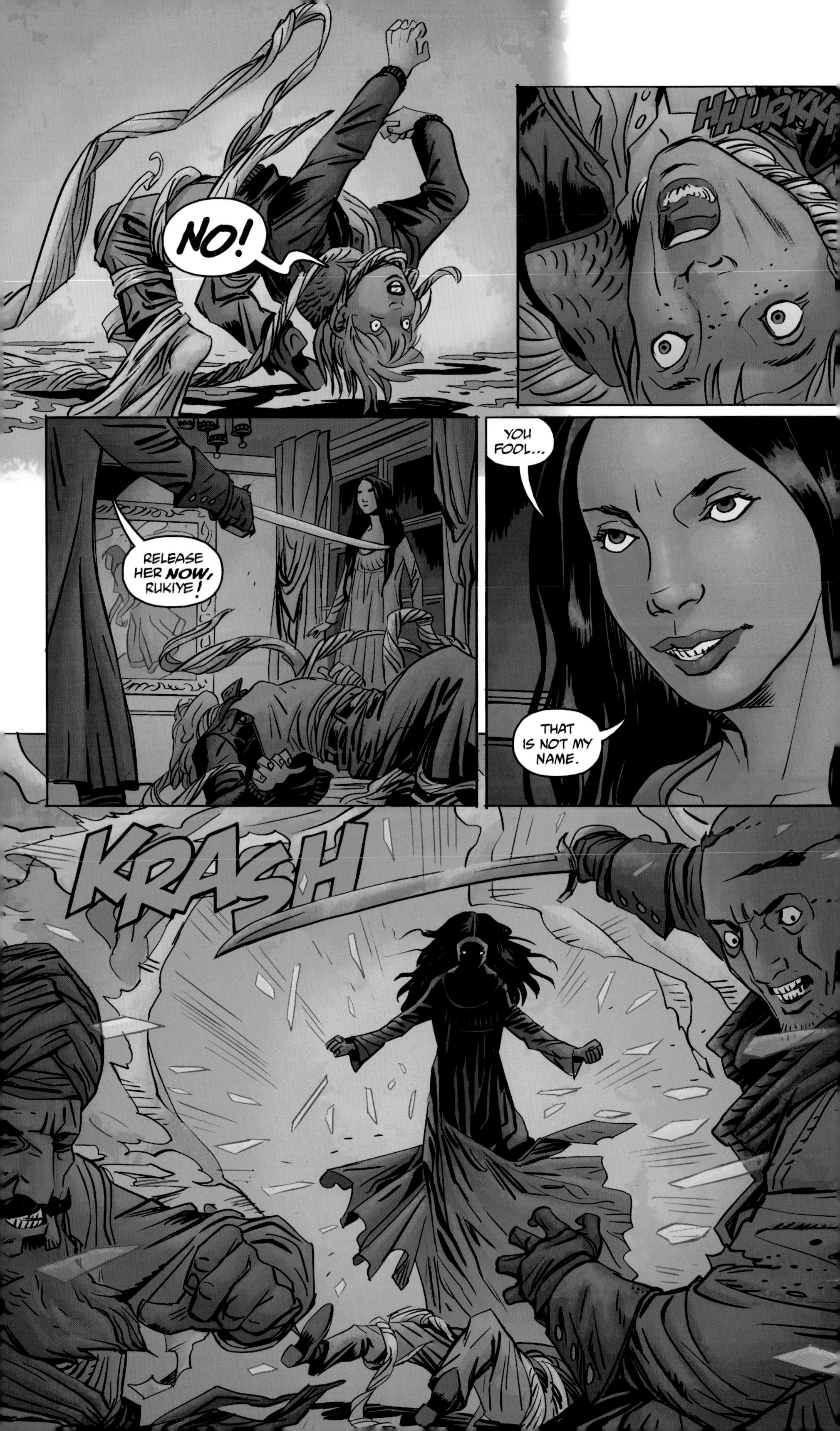
NO!
HHURKK
RELEASE HER NOW, RUKIYE!
YOU FOOL...
THAT IS NOT MY NAME.
KRASH

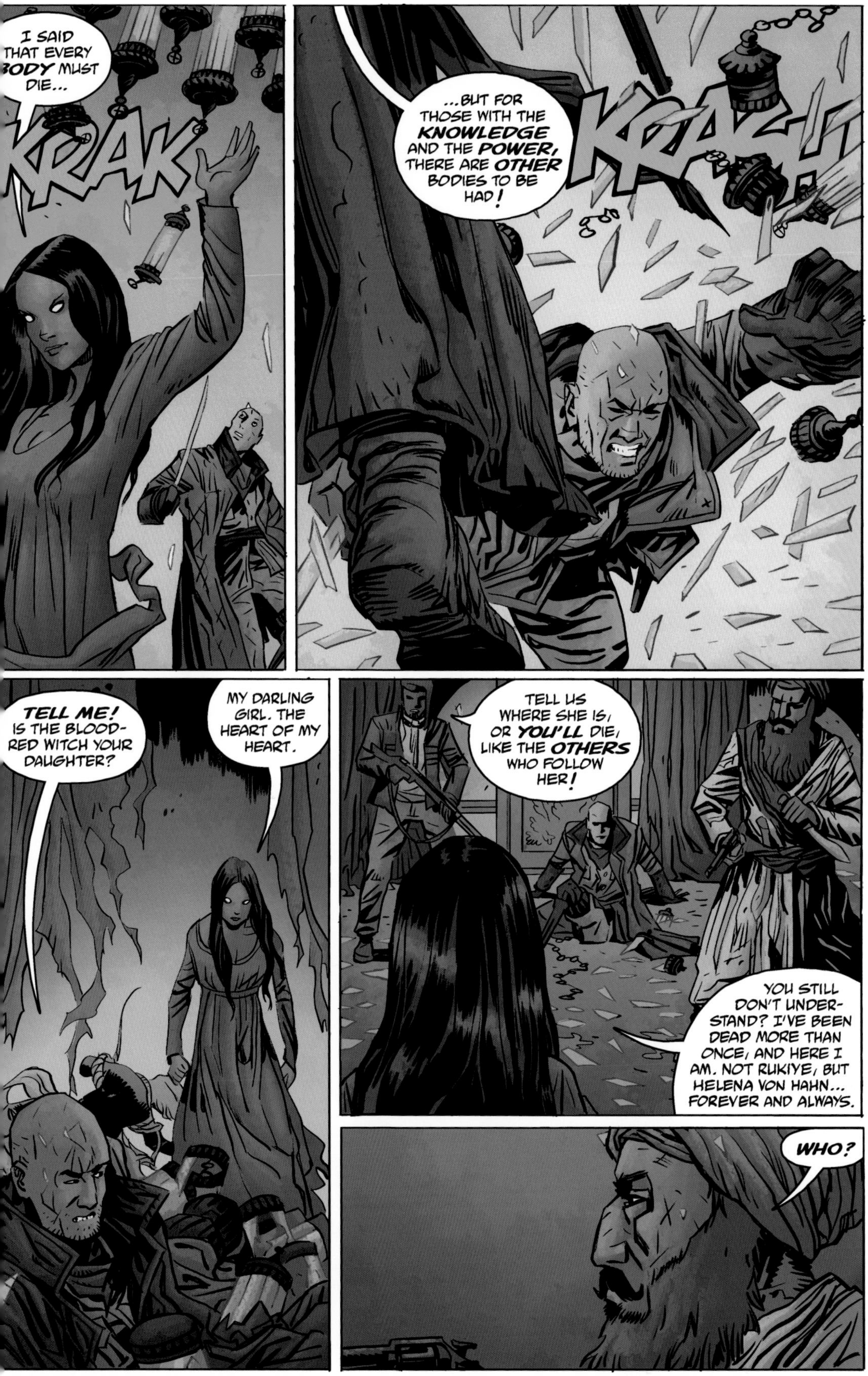
I SAID THAT EVERY BODY MUST DIE...
KRAK
...BUT FOR THOSE WITH THE KNOWLEDGE AND THE POWER, THERE ARE OTHER BODIES TO BE HAD!
KRAK
TELL ME! IS THE BLOOD-RED WITCH YOUR DAUGHTER?
MY DARLING GIRL. THE HEART OF MY HEART.
TELL US WHERE SHE IS, OR YOU'LL DIE, LIKE THE OTHERS WHO FOLLOW HER!
YOU STILL DON'T UNDER-STAND? I'VE BEEN DEAD MORE THAN ONCE, AND HERE I AM. NOT RUKIYE, BUT HELENA VON HAHN... FOREVER AND ALWAYS.
WHO?

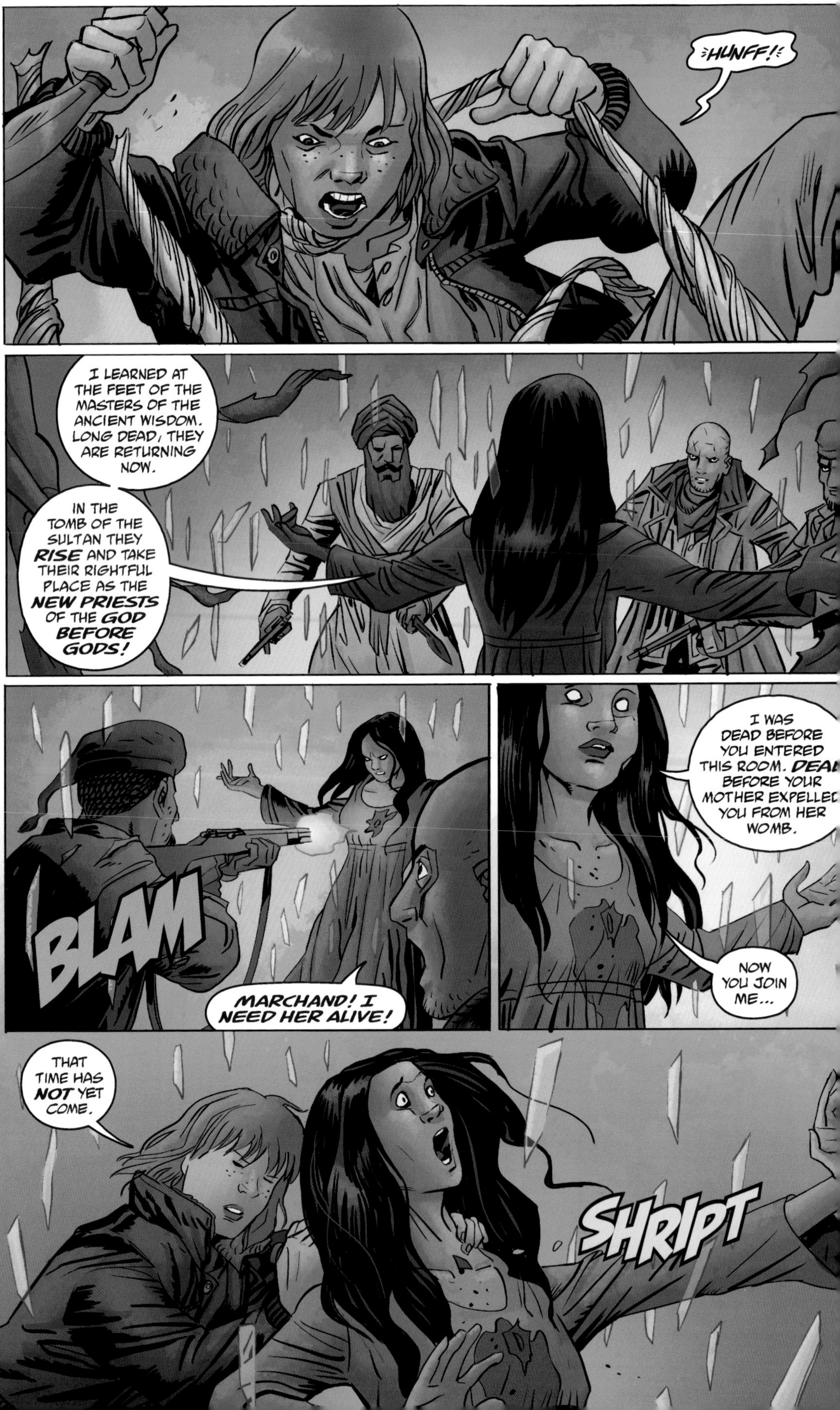

HUNFF!
I LEARNED AT THE FEET OF THE MASTERS OF THE ANCIENT WISDOM. LONG DEAD, THEY ARE RETURNING NOW.
IN THE TOMB OF THE SULTAN THEY RISE AND TAKE THEIR RIGHTFUL PLACE AS THE NEW PRIESTS OF THE GOD BEFORE GODS!
BLAM
MARCHAND! I NEED HER ALIVE!
I WAS DEAD BEFORE YOU ENTERED THIS ROOM. DEAD BEFORE YOUR MOTHER EXPELLED YOU FROM HER WOMB.
NOW YOU JOIN ME...
THAT TIME HAS NOT YET COME.
SHRIPT

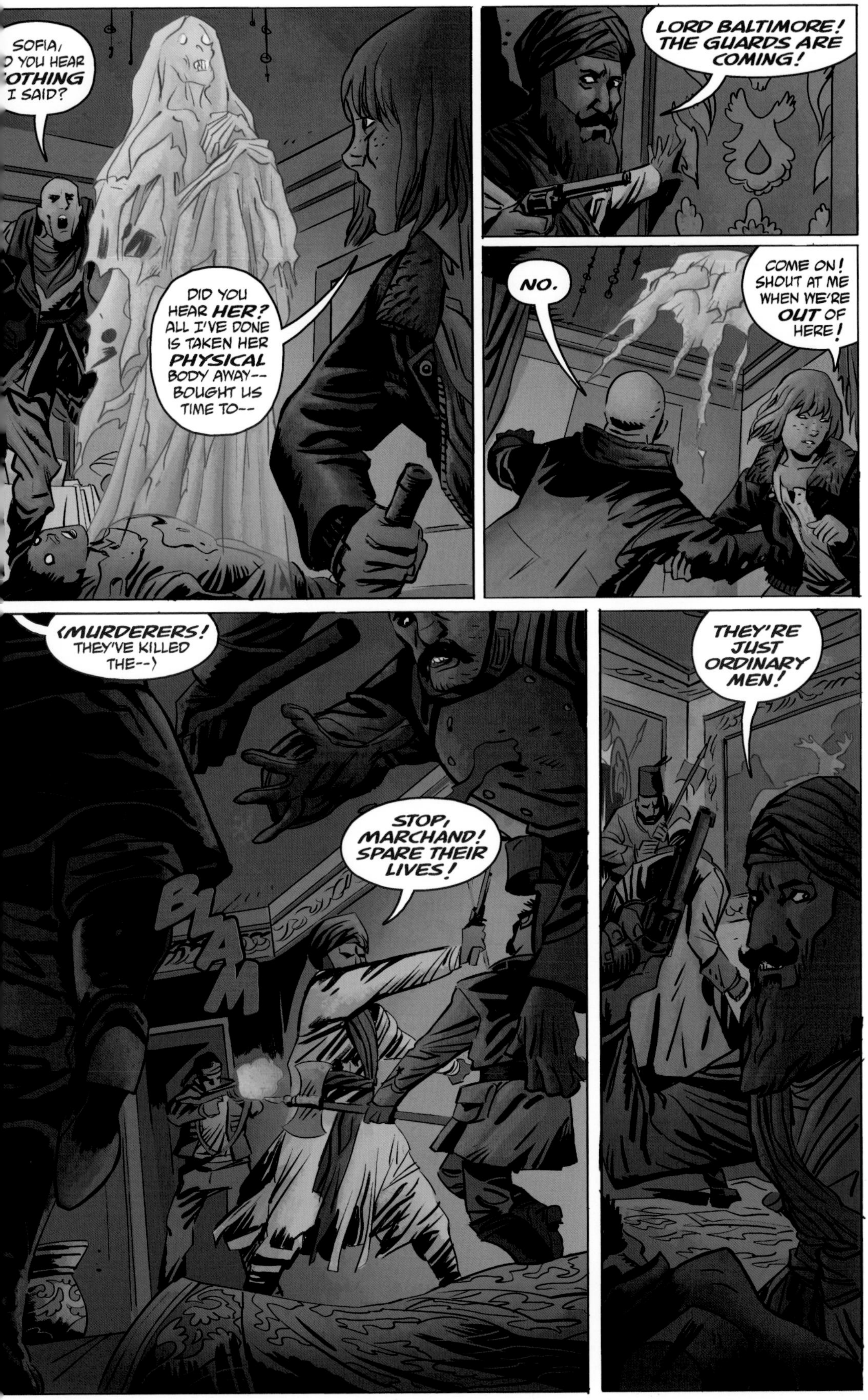
SOFIA, DO YOU HEAR NOTHING I SAID?
DID YOU HEAR HER? ALL I'VE DONE IS TAKEN HER PHYSICAL BODY AWAY-- BOUGHT US TIME TO--
LORD BALTIMORE! THE GUARDS ARE COMING!
NO.
COME ON! SHOUT AT ME WHEN WE'RE OUT OF HERE!
‹MURDERERS! THEY'VE KILLED THE--›
STOP, MARCHAND! SPARE THEIR LIVES!
BLAM
THEY'RE JUST ORDINARY MEN!

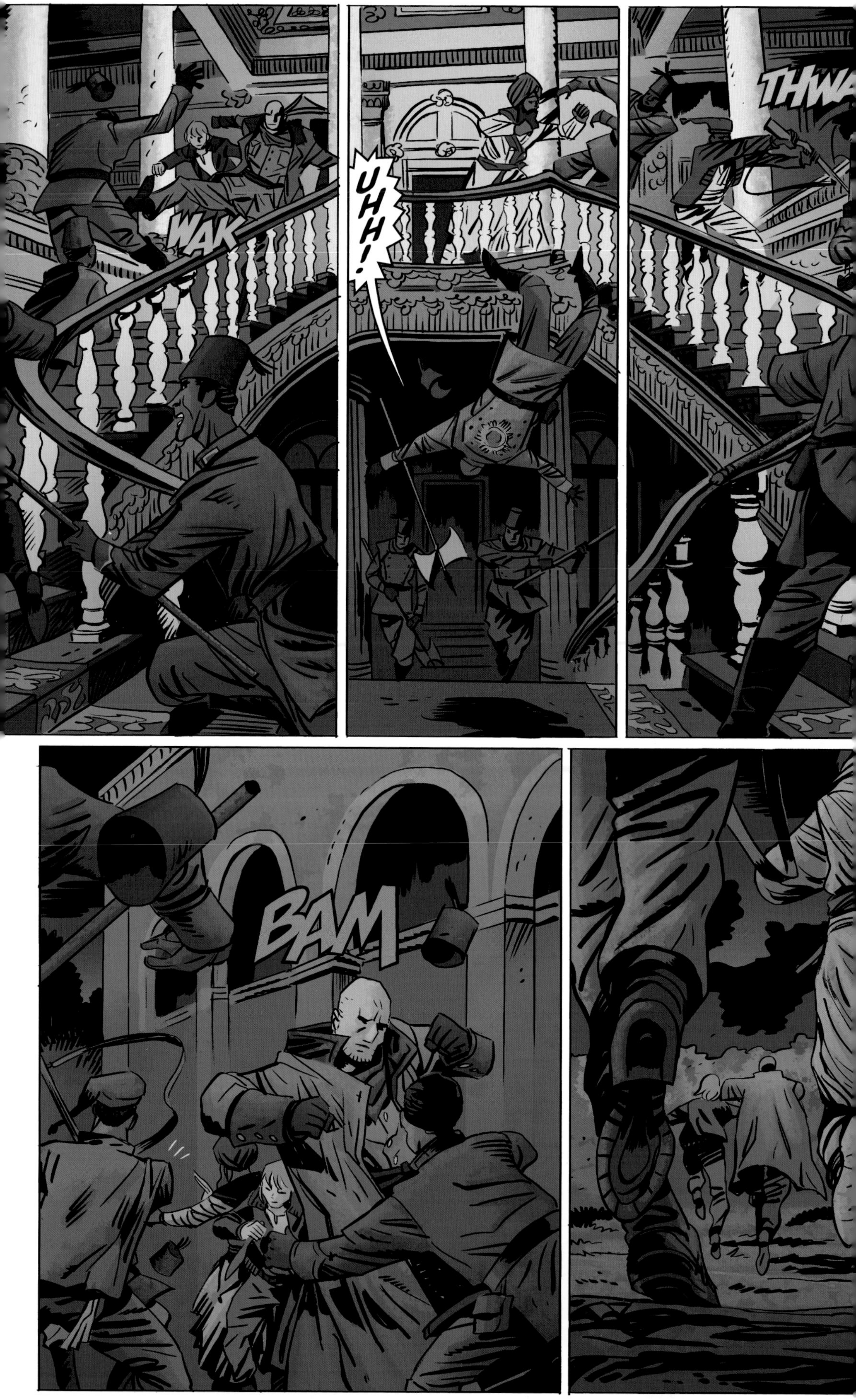
WAK
UHHH!
THWA
BAM

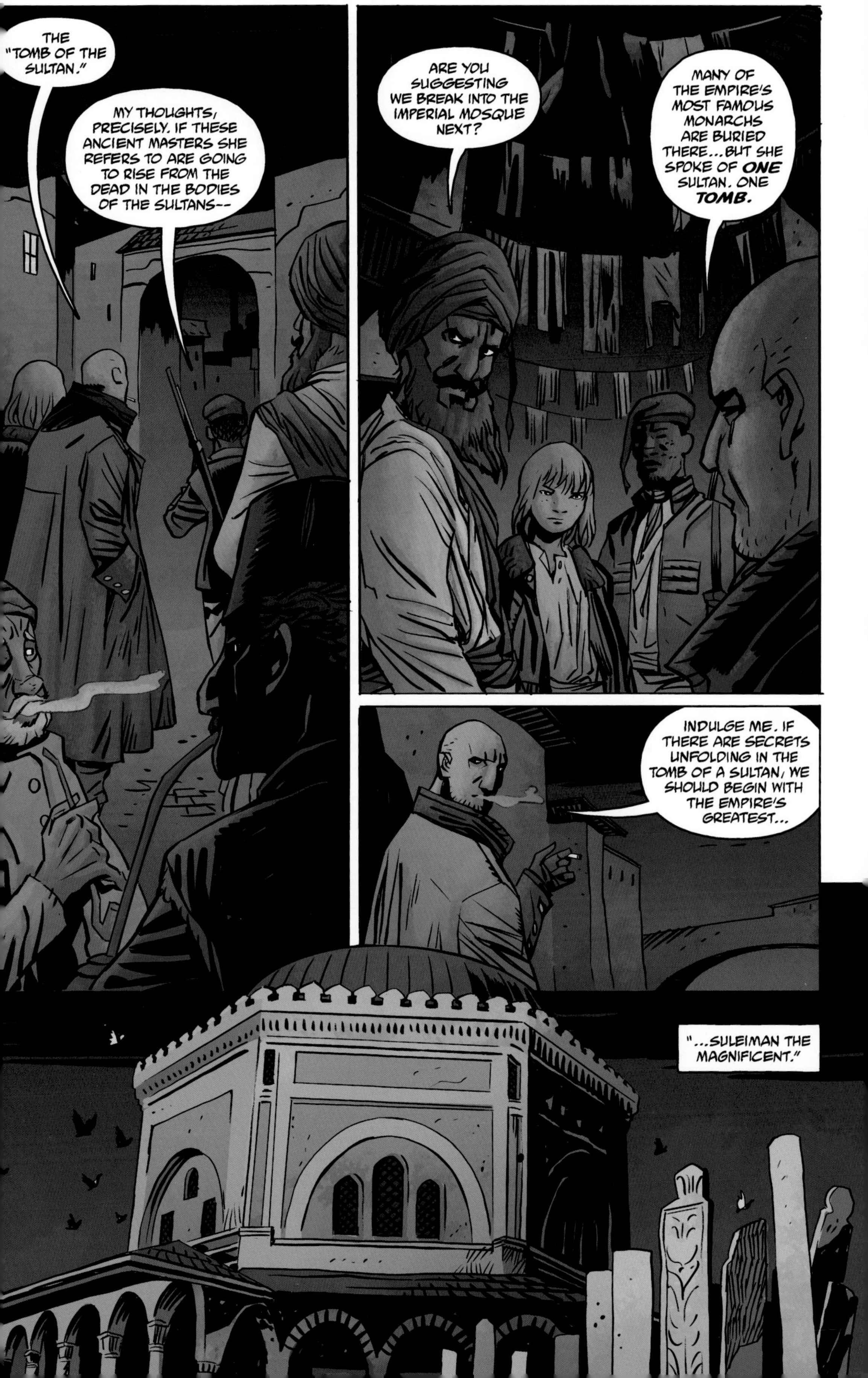
THE "TOMB OF THE SULTAN."
MY THOUGHTS, PRECISELY. IF THESE ANCIENT MASTERS SHE REFERS TO ARE GOING TO RISE FROM THE DEAD IN THE BODIES OF THE SULTANS--
ARE YOU SUGGESTING WE BREAK INTO THE IMPERIAL MOSQUE NEXT?
MANY OF THE EMPIRE'S MOST FAMOUS MONARCHS ARE BURIED THERE... BUT SHE SPOKE OF ONE SULTAN. ONE TOMB.
INDULGE ME. IF THERE ARE SECRETS UNFOLDING IN THE TOMB OF A SULTAN, WE SHOULD BEGIN WITH THE EMPIRE'S GREATEST...
"...SULEIMAN THE MAGNIFICENT."

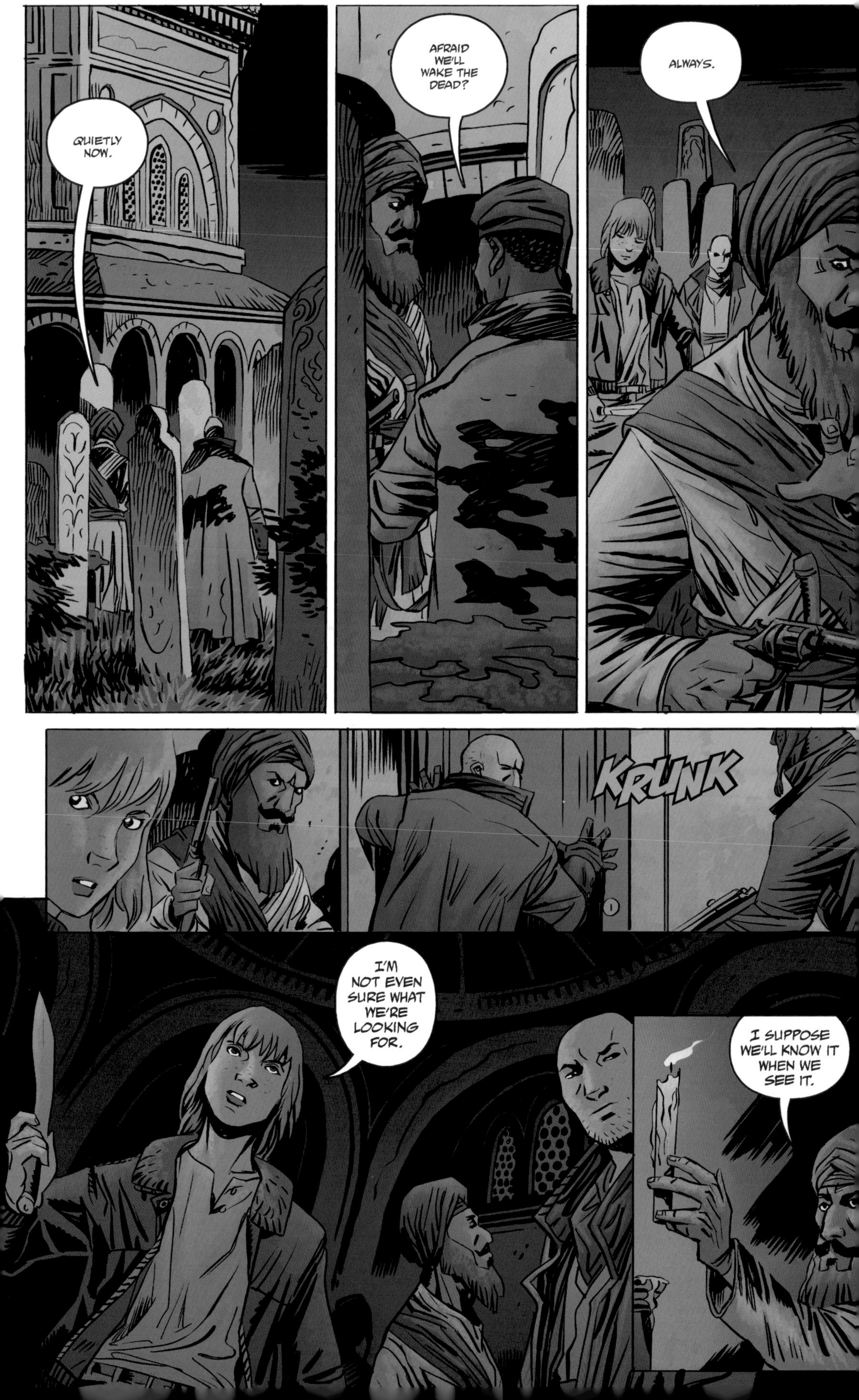
QUIETLY NOW.
AFRAID WE'LL WAKE THE DEAD?
ALWAYS.
KRUNK
I'M NOT EVEN SURE WHAT WE'RE LOOKING FOR.
I SUPPOSE WE'LL KNOW IT WHEN WE SEE IT.

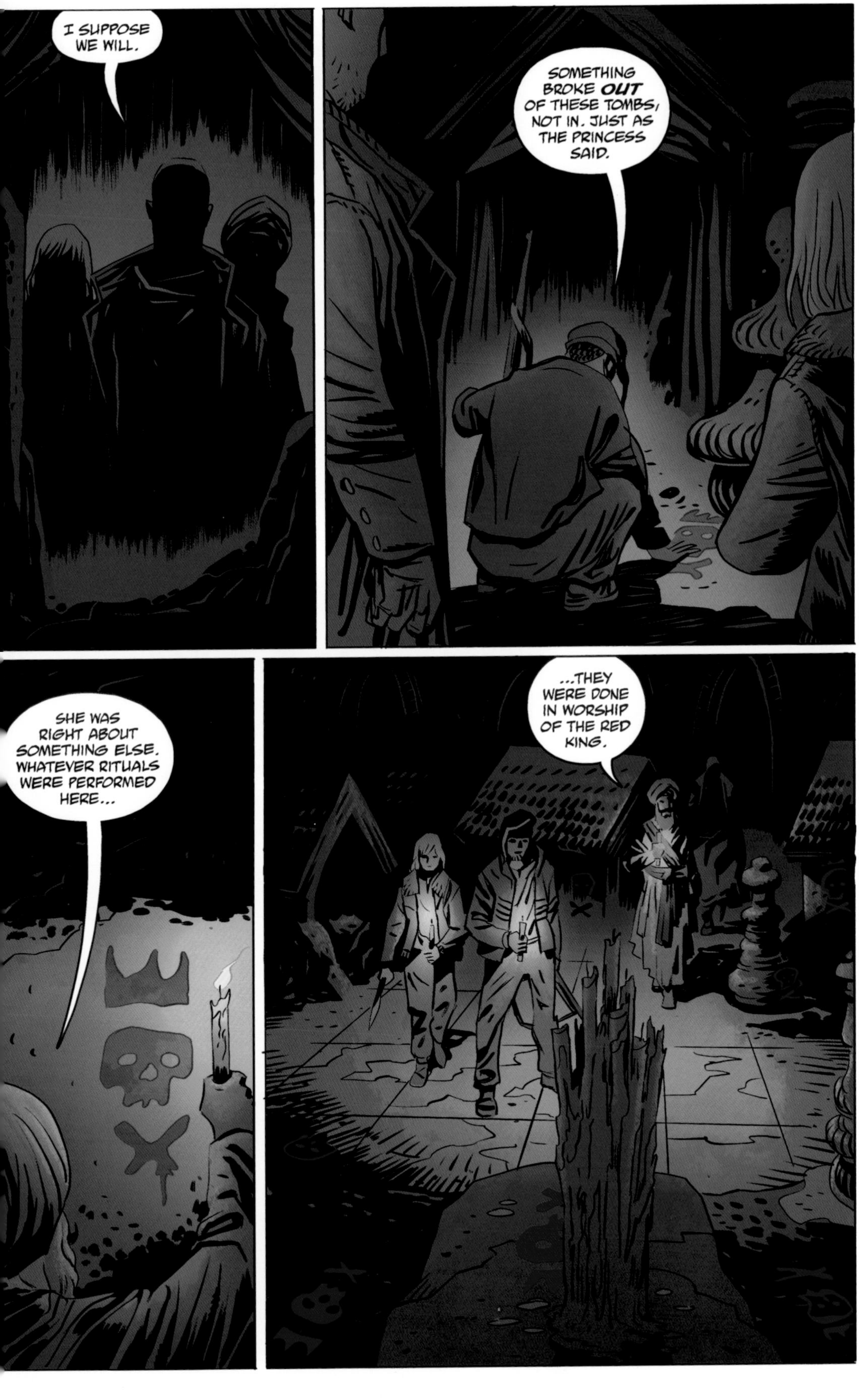
I SUPPOSE WE WILL.
SOMETHING BROKE OUT OF THESE TOMBS, NOT IN. JUST AS THE PRINCESS SAID.
SHE WAS RIGHT ABOUT SOMETHING ELSE. WHATEVER RITUALS WERE PERFORMED HERE...
...THEY WERE DONE IN WORSHIP OF THE RED KING.

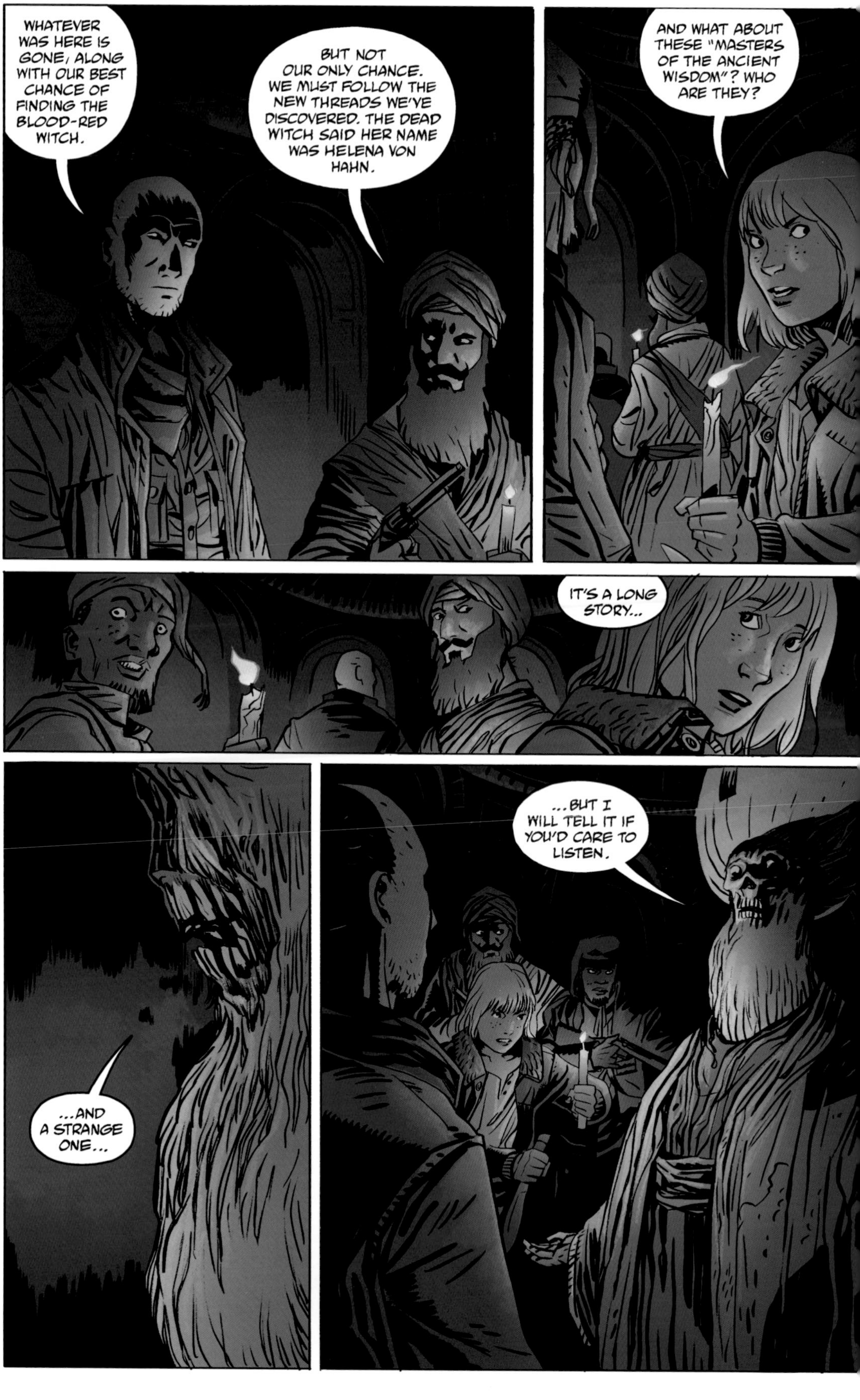
WHATEVER WAS HERE IS GONE, ALONG WITH OUR BEST CHANCE OF FINDING THE BLOOD-RED WITCH.
BUT NOT OUR ONLY CHANCE. WE MUST FOLLOW THE NEW THREADS WE'VE DISCOVERED. THE DEAD WITCH SAID HER NAME WAS HELENA VON HAHN.
AND WHAT ABOUT THESE "MASTERS OF THE ANCIENT WISDOM"? WHO ARE THEY?
IT'S A LONG STORY...
...AND A STRANGE ONE...
...BUT I WILL TELL IT IF YOU'D CARE TO LISTEN.

CHAPTER FOUR

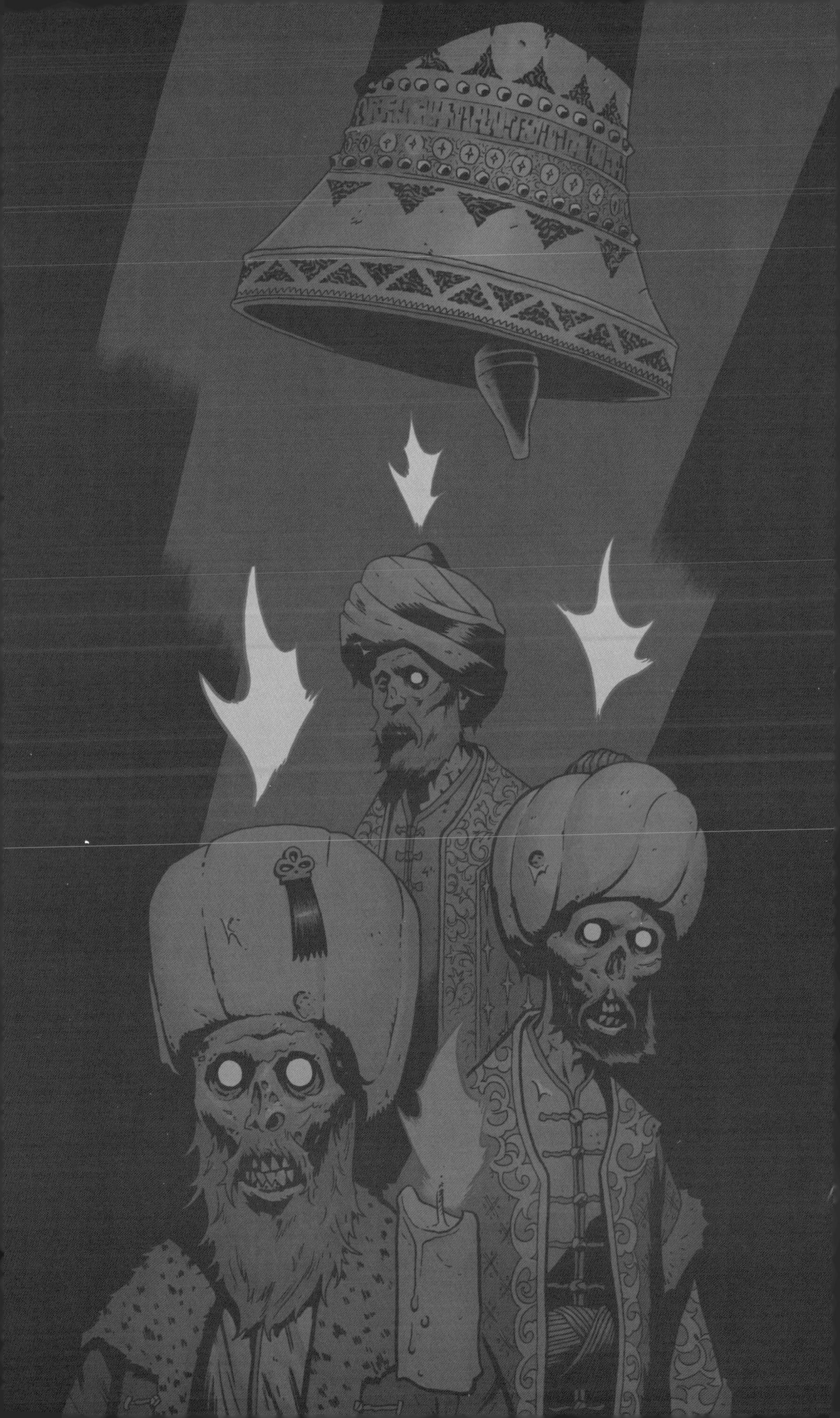

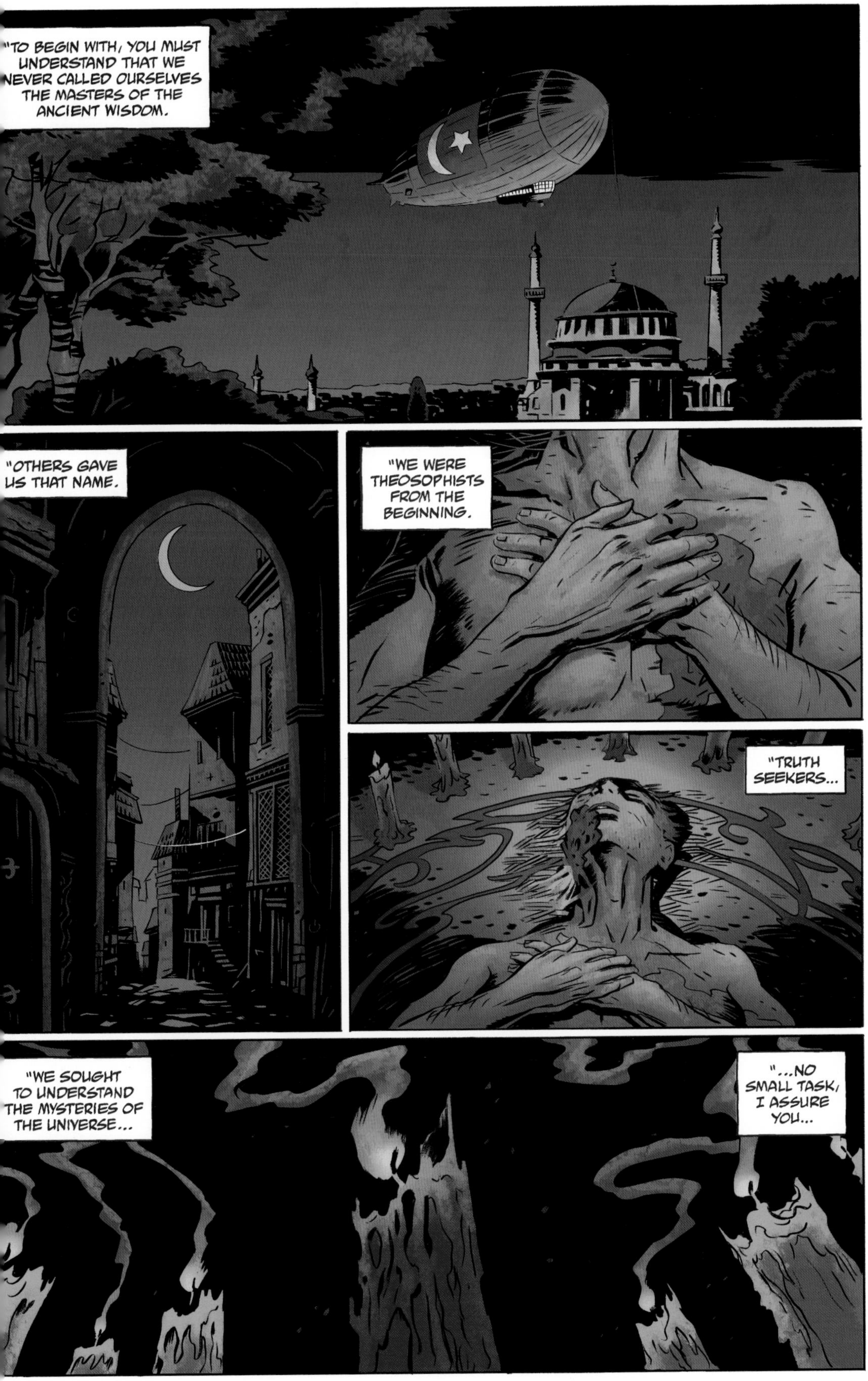
"TO BEGIN WITH, YOU MUST UNDERSTAND THAT WE NEVER CALLED OURSELVES THE MASTERS OF THE ANCIENT WISDOM.
"OTHERS GAVE US THAT NAME.
"WE WERE THEOSOPHISTS FROM THE BEGINNING.
"TRUTH SEEKERS...
"WE SOUGHT TO UNDERSTAND THE MYSTERIES OF THE UNIVERSE...
"...NO SMALL TASK, I ASSURE YOU...

"WE SEARCHED FOR THE THREADS THAT BOUND HUMANITY TO DIVINITY..."

...EARTH TO THE COSMOS...

...AND WE FOUND THEM.

WE BECAME THE ELDER BROTHERS OF THE HUMAN RACE. SOME ACCUSED US OF SORCERY, BUT WE WERE NEVER MAGICIANS.

WE WERE MERELY WISE.

IT MAY ASTONISH YOU TO HEAR IT, BUT I DON'T CARE WHAT YOU ARE.

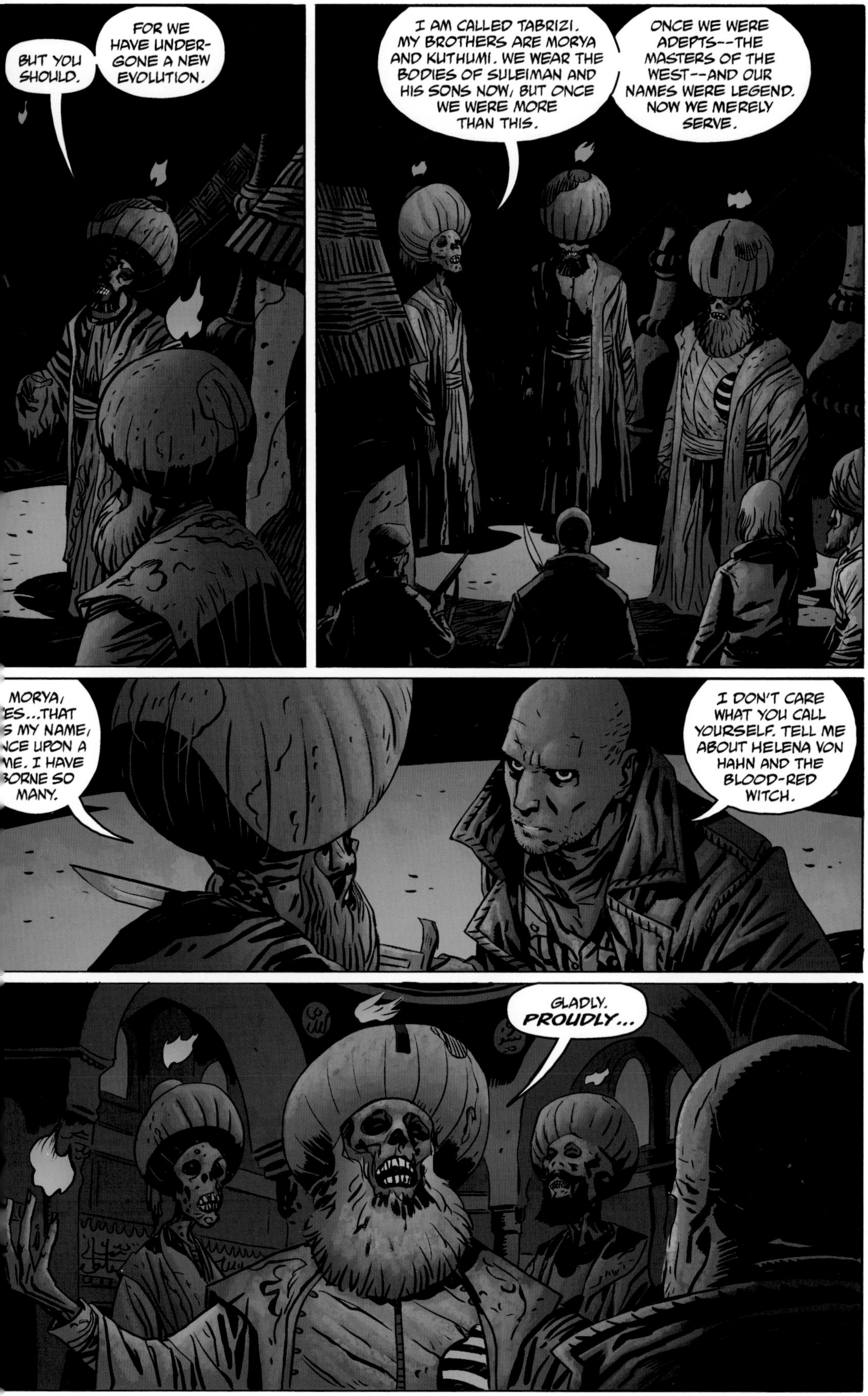
BUT YOU SHOULD.
FOR WE HAVE UNDER-GONE A NEW EVOLUTION.
I AM CALLED TABRIZI. MY BROTHERS ARE MORYA AND KUTHUMI. WE WEAR THE BODIES OF SULEIMAN AND HIS SONS NOW, BUT ONCE WE WERE MORE THAN THIS.
ONCE WE WERE ADEPTS--THE MASTERS OF THE WEST--AND OUR NAMES WERE LEGEND. NOW WE MERELY SERVE.
MORYA, ES...THAT S MY NAME, NCE UPON A ME. I HAVE ORNE SO MANY.
I DON'T CARE WHAT YOU CALL YOURSELF. TELL ME ABOUT HELENA VON HAHN AND THE BLOOD-RED WITCH.
GLADLY. PROUDLY...

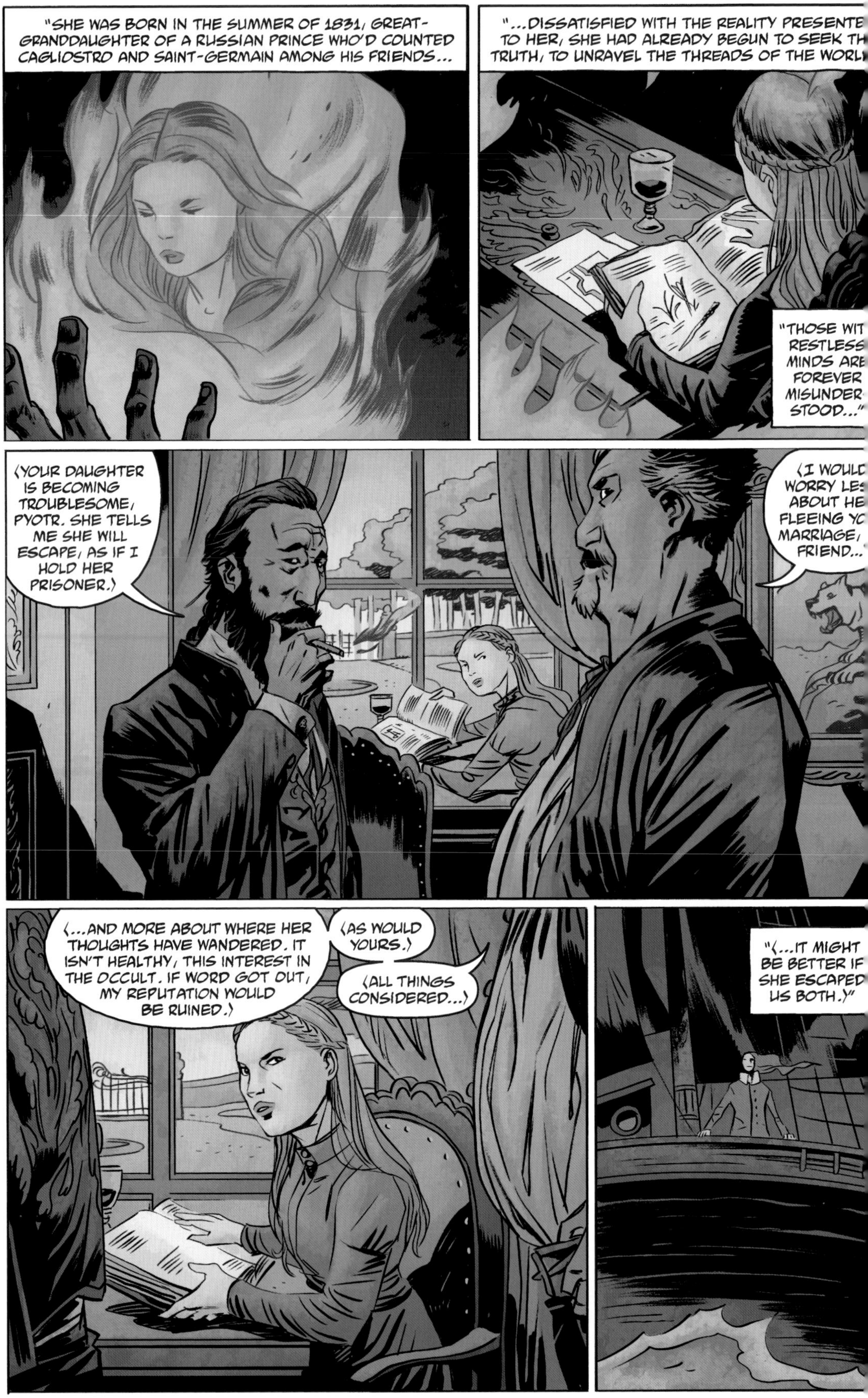
"SHE WAS BORN IN THE SUMMER OF 1831, GREAT-GRANDDAUGHTER OF A RUSSIAN PRINCE WHO'D COUNTED CAGLIOSTRO AND SAINT-GERMAIN AMONG HIS FRIENDS...
"...DISSATISFIED WITH THE REALITY PRESENTE TO HER, SHE HAD ALREADY BEGUN TO SEEK TH TRUTH, TO UNRAVEL THE THREADS OF THE WORL
"THOSE WIT RESTLESS MINDS ARE FOREVER MISUNDER-STOOD..."
⟨YOUR DAUGHTER IS BECOMING TROUBLESOME, PYOTR. SHE TELLS ME SHE WILL ESCAPE, AS IF I HOLD HER PRISONER.⟩
⟨I WOULD WORRY LES ABOUT HE FLEEING YO MARRIAGE, FRIEND...
⟨...AND MORE ABOUT WHERE HER THOUGHTS HAVE WANDERED. IT ISN'T HEALTHY, THIS INTEREST IN THE OCCULT. IF WORD GOT OUT, MY REPUTATION WOULD BE RUINED.⟩
⟨AS WOULD YOURS.⟩
⟨ALL THINGS CONSIDERED...⟩
"⟨...IT MIGHT BE BETTER IF SHE ESCAPED US BOTH.⟩"

⟨TRANSLATED FROM THE RUS

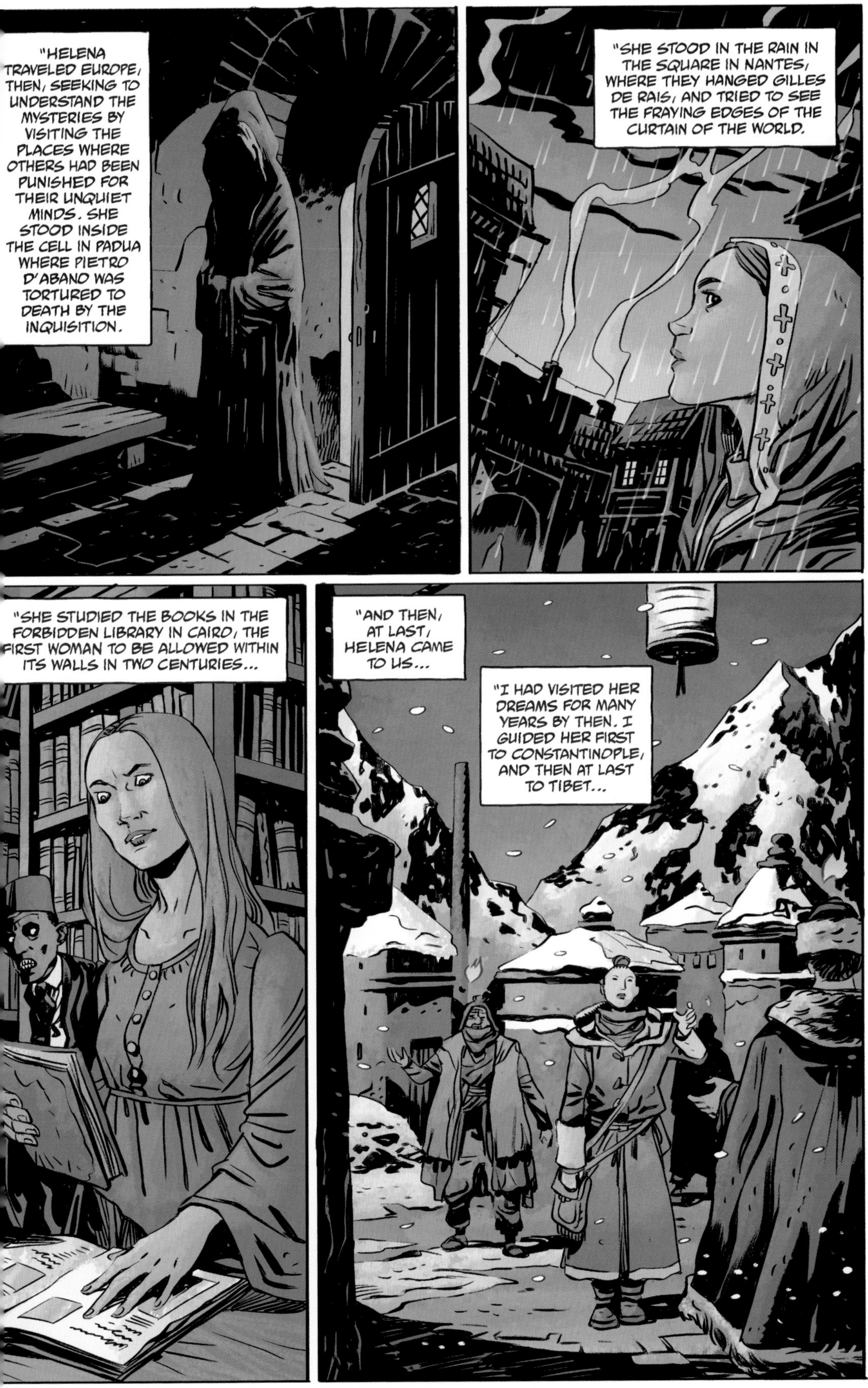
"HELENA TRAVELED EUROPE, THEN, SEEKING TO UNDERSTAND THE MYSTERIES BY VISITING THE PLACES WHERE OTHERS HAD BEEN PUNISHED FOR THEIR UNQUIET MINDS. SHE STOOD INSIDE THE CELL IN PADUA WHERE PIETRO D'ABANO WAS TORTURED TO DEATH BY THE INQUISITION.
"SHE STOOD IN THE RAIN IN THE SQUARE IN NANTES, WHERE THEY HANGED GILLES DE RAIS, AND TRIED TO SEE THE FRAYING EDGES OF THE CURTAIN OF THE WORLD.
"SHE STUDIED THE BOOKS IN THE FORBIDDEN LIBRARY IN CAIRO, THE FIRST WOMAN TO BE ALLOWED WITHIN ITS WALLS IN TWO CENTURIES...
"AND THEN, AT LAST, HELENA CAME TO US...
"I HAD VISITED HER DREAMS FOR MANY YEARS BY THEN. I GUIDED HER FIRST TO CONSTANTINOPLE, AND THEN AT LAST TO TIBET...

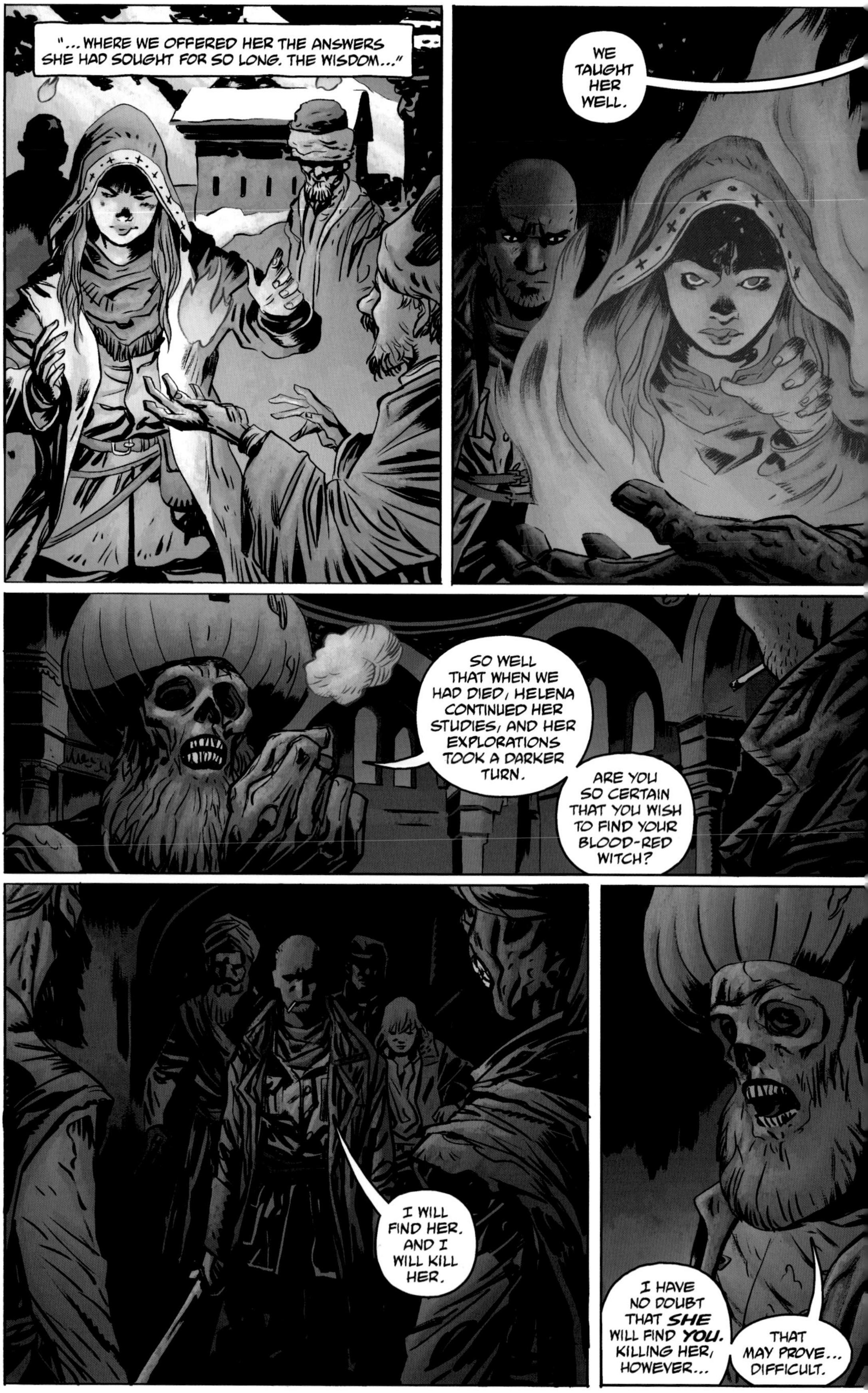
"...WHERE WE OFFERED HER THE ANSWERS SHE HAD SOUGHT FOR SO LONG. THE WISDOM..."
WE TAUGHT HER WELL.
SO WELL THAT WHEN WE HAD DIED, HELENA CONTINUED HER STUDIES, AND HER EXPLORATIONS TOOK A DARKER TURN.
ARE YOU SO CERTAIN THAT YOU WISH TO FIND YOUR BLOOD-RED WITCH?
I WILL FIND HER. AND I WILL KILL HER.
I HAVE NO DOUBT THAT SHE WILL FIND YOU. KILLING HER, HOWEVER...
THAT MAY PROVE... DIFFICULT.

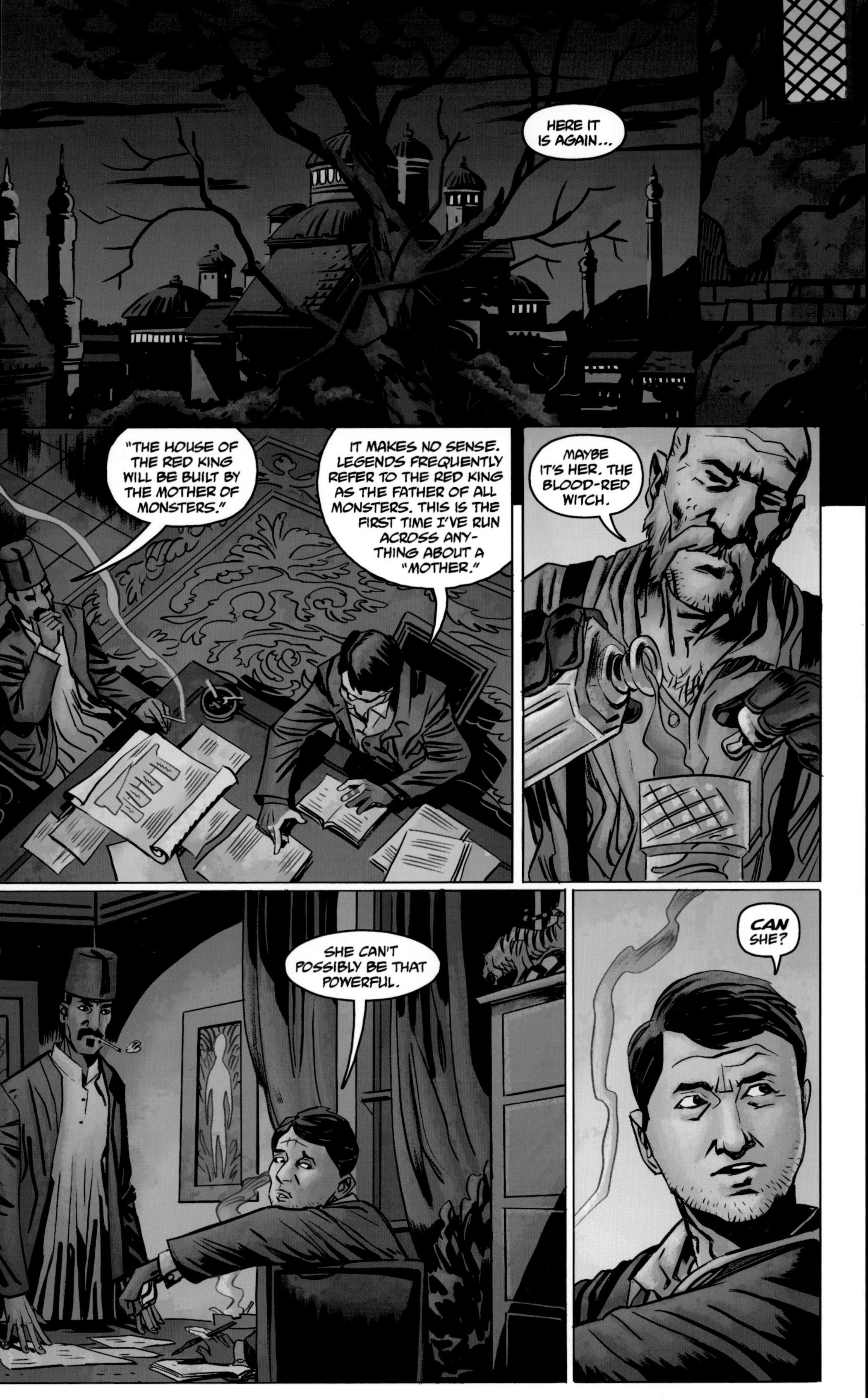
HERE IT IS AGAIN...
"THE HOUSE OF THE RED KING WILL BE BUILT BY THE MOTHER OF MONSTERS."
IT MAKES NO SENSE. LEGENDS FREQUENTLY REFER TO THE RED KING AS THE FATHER OF ALL MONSTERS. THIS IS THE FIRST TIME I'VE RUN ACROSS ANYTHING ABOUT A "MOTHER."
MAYBE IT'S HER. THE BLOOD-RED WITCH.
SHE CAN'T POSSIBLY BE THAT POWERFUL.
CAN SHE?

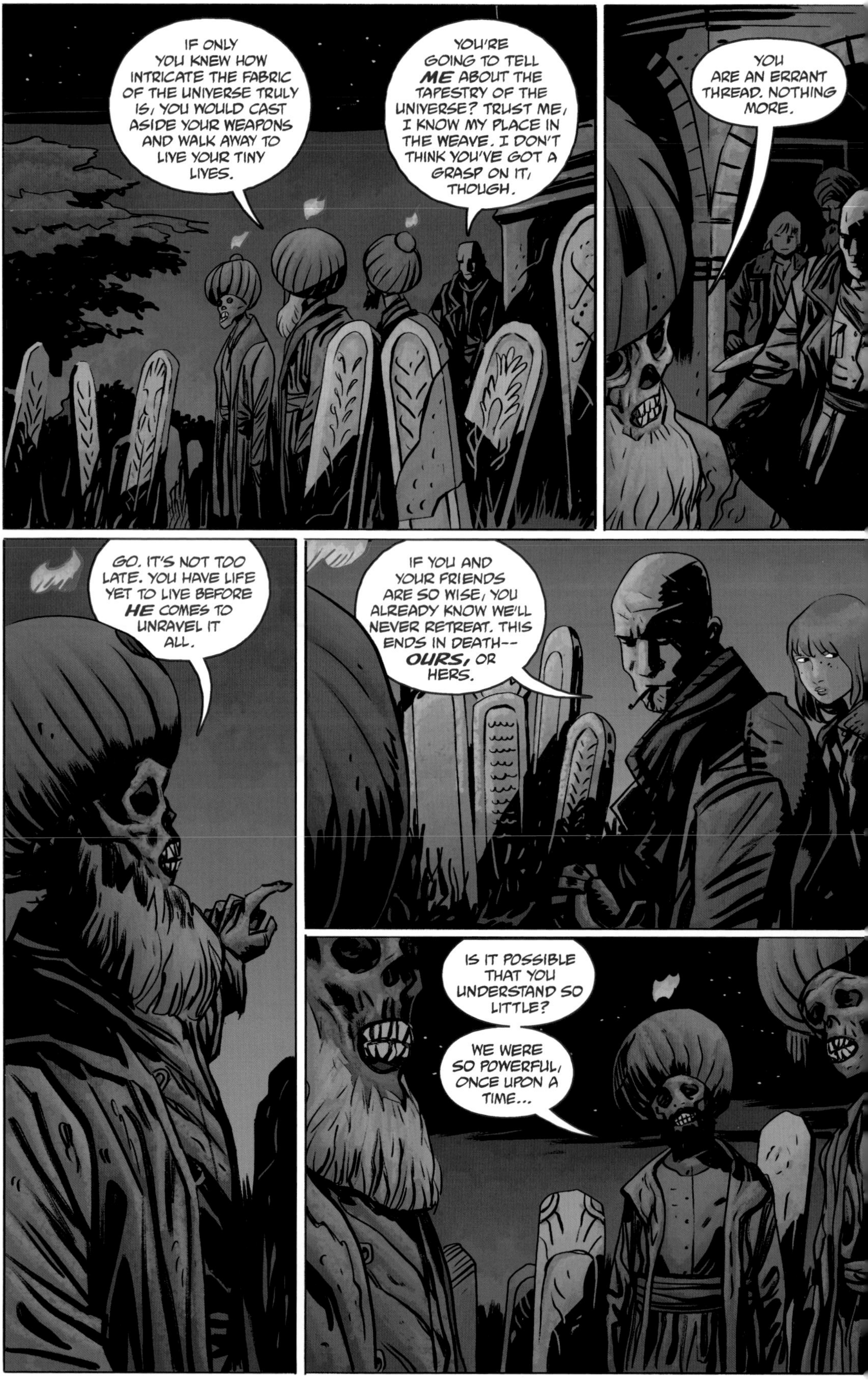
IF ONLY YOU KNEW HOW INTRICATE THE FABRIC OF THE UNIVERSE TRULY IS, YOU WOULD CAST ASIDE YOUR WEAPONS AND WALK AWAY TO LIVE YOUR TINY LIVES.
YOU'RE GOING TO TELL ME ABOUT THE TAPESTRY OF THE UNIVERSE? TRUST ME, I KNOW MY PLACE IN THE WEAVE. I DON'T THINK YOU'VE GOT A GRASP ON IT, THOUGH.
YOU ARE AN ERRANT THREAD. NOTHING MORE.
GO. IT'S NOT TOO LATE. YOU HAVE LIFE YET TO LIVE BEFORE HE COMES TO UNRAVEL IT ALL.
IF YOU AND YOUR FRIENDS ARE SO WISE, YOU ALREADY KNOW WE'LL NEVER RETREAT. THIS ENDS IN DEATH-- OURS, OR HERS.
IS IT POSSIBLE THAT YOU UNDERSTAND SO LITTLE?
WE WERE SO POWERFUL, ONCE UPON A TIME...

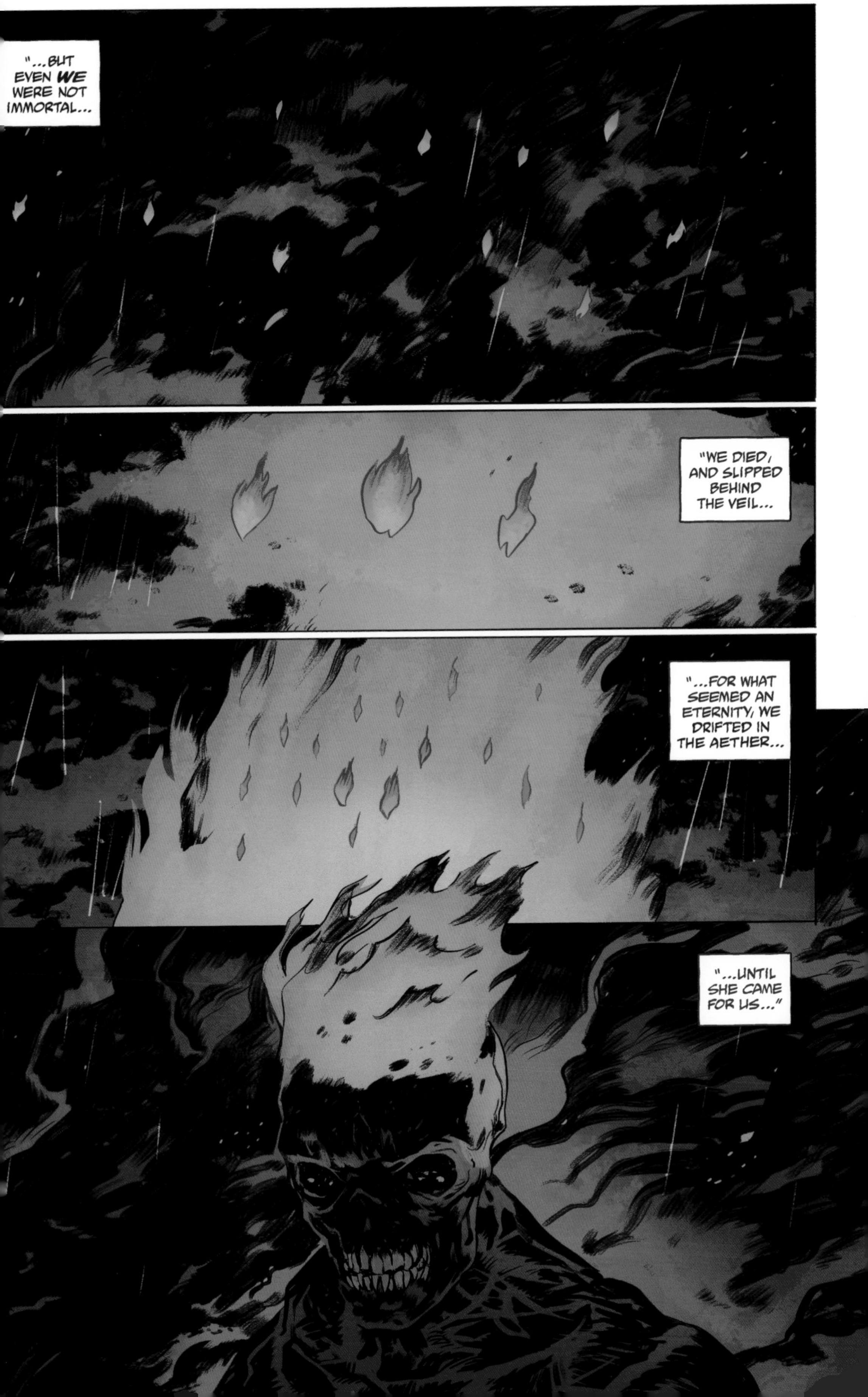
"...BUT EVEN WE WERE NOT IMMORTAL...
"WE DIED, AND SLIPPED BEHIND THE VEIL...
"...FOR WHAT SEEMED AN ETERNITY, WE DRIFTED IN THE AETHER...
"...UNTIL SHE CAME FOR US..."

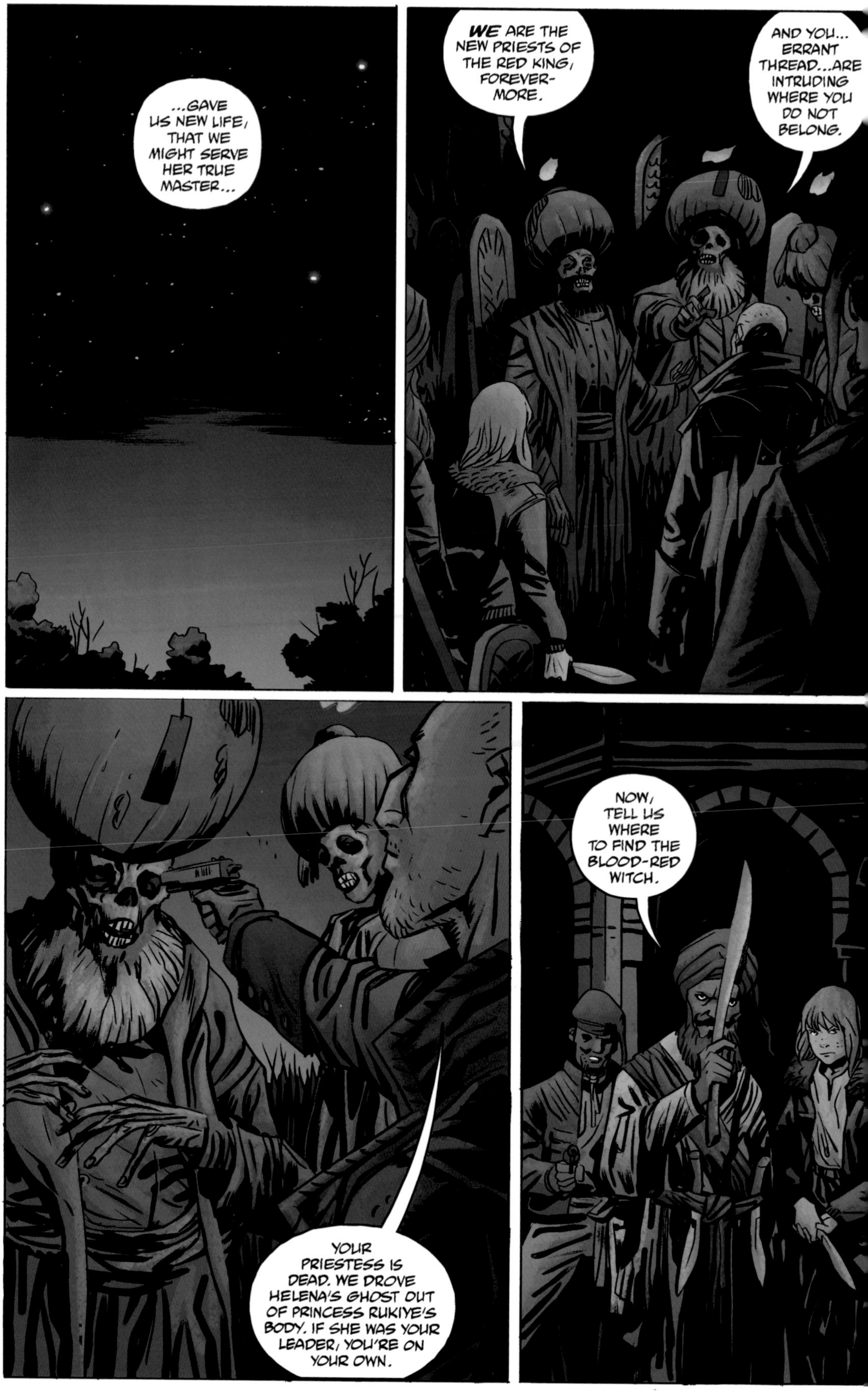
...GAVE US NEW LIFE, THAT WE MIGHT SERVE HER TRUE MASTER...
WE ARE THE NEW PRIESTS OF THE RED KING, FOREVER-MORE.
AND YOU... ERRANT THREAD...ARE INTRUDING WHERE YOU DO NOT BELONG.
YOUR PRIESTESS IS DEAD. WE DROVE HELENA'S GHOST OUT OF PRINCESS RUKIYE'S BODY. IF SHE WAS YOUR LEADER, YOU'RE ON YOUR OWN.
NOW, TELL US WHERE TO FIND THE BLOOD-RED WITCH.

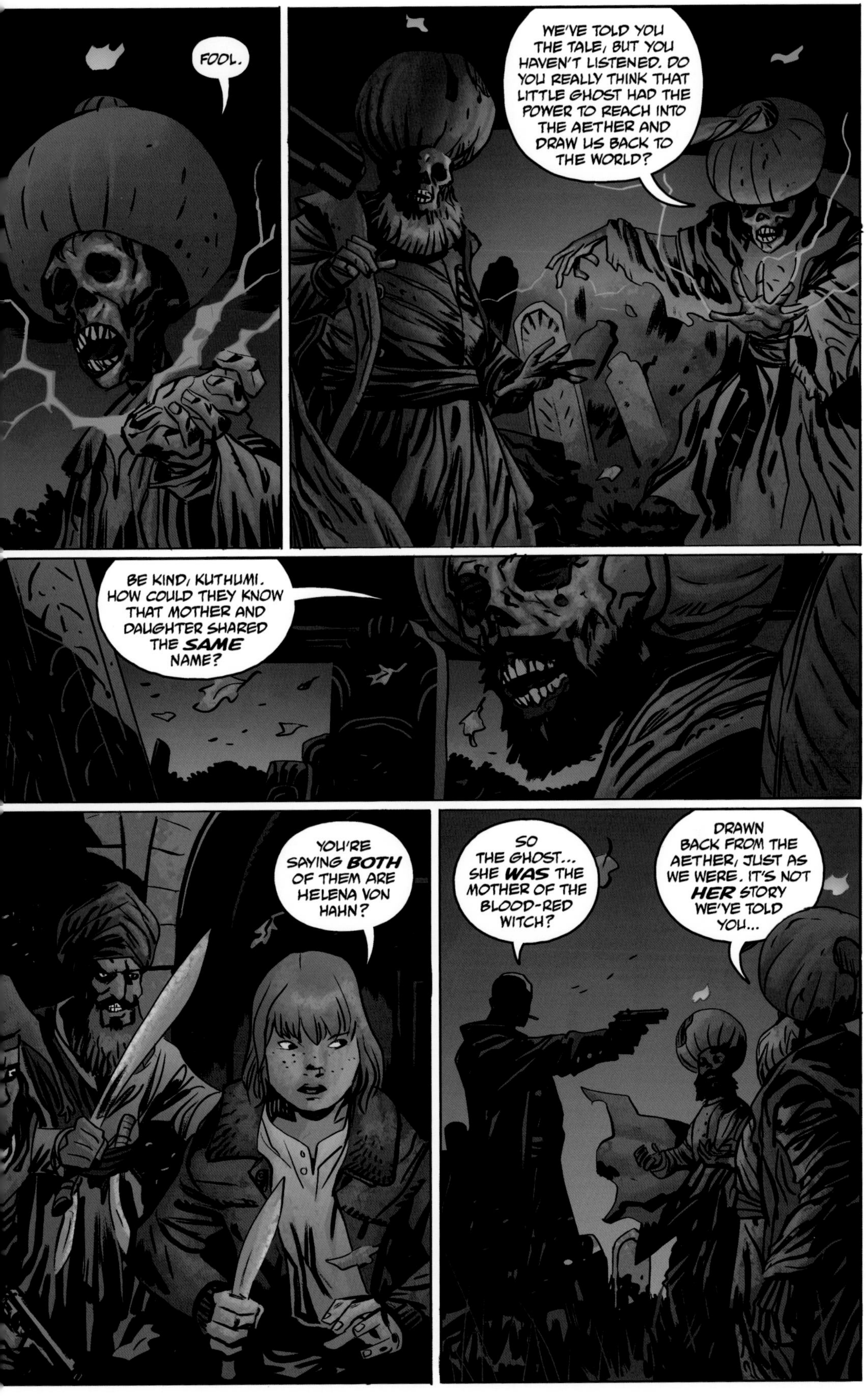
FOOL.
WE'VE TOLD YOU THE TALE, BUT YOU HAVEN'T LISTENED. DO YOU REALLY THINK THAT LITTLE GHOST HAD THE POWER TO REACH INTO THE AETHER AND DRAW US BACK TO THE WORLD?
BE KIND, KUTHUMI. HOW COULD THEY KNOW THAT MOTHER AND DAUGHTER SHARED THE SAME NAME?
YOU'RE SAYING BOTH OF THEM ARE HELENA VON HAHN?
SO THE GHOST... SHE WAS THE MOTHER OF THE BLOOD-RED WITCH?
DRAWN BACK FROM THE AETHER, JUST AS WE WERE. IT'S NOT HER STORY WE'VE TOLD YOU...

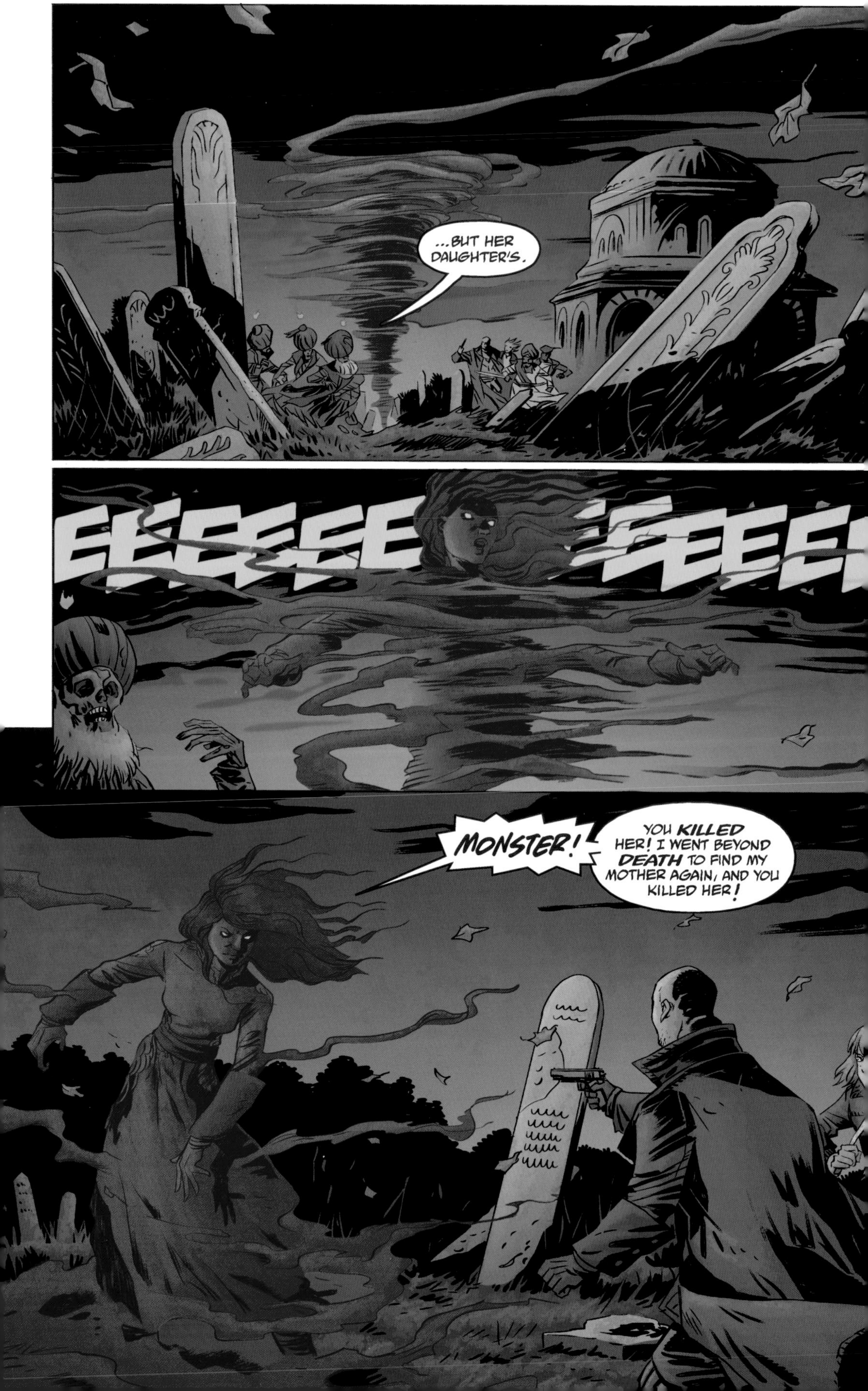
...BUT HER DAUGHTER'S.
EEEEEEEEEEE
MONSTER!
YOU KILLED HER! I WENT BEYOND DEATH TO FIND MY MOTHER AGAIN, AND YOU KILLED HER!

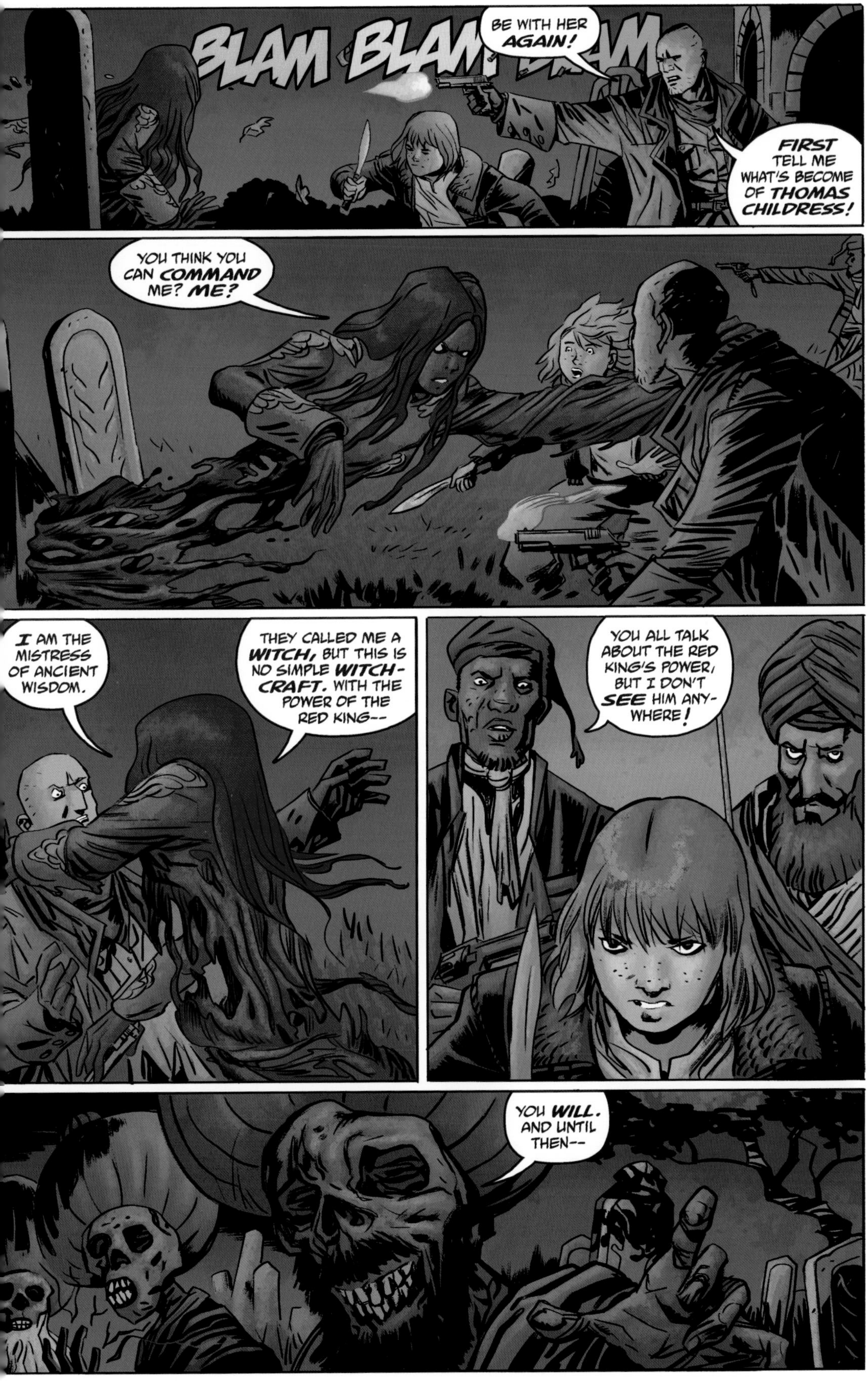
BLAM BLAM BLAM
BE WITH HER AGAIN!
FIRST TELL ME WHAT'S BECOME OF THOMAS CHILDRESS!
YOU THINK YOU CAN COMMAND ME? ME?
I AM THE MISTRESS OF ANCIENT WISDOM.
THEY CALLED ME A WITCH, BUT THIS IS NO SIMPLE WITCH-CRAFT. WITH THE POWER OF THE RED KING--
YOU ALL TALK ABOUT THE RED KING'S POWER, BUT I DON'T SEE HIM ANY-WHERE!
YOU WILL. AND UNTIL THEN--

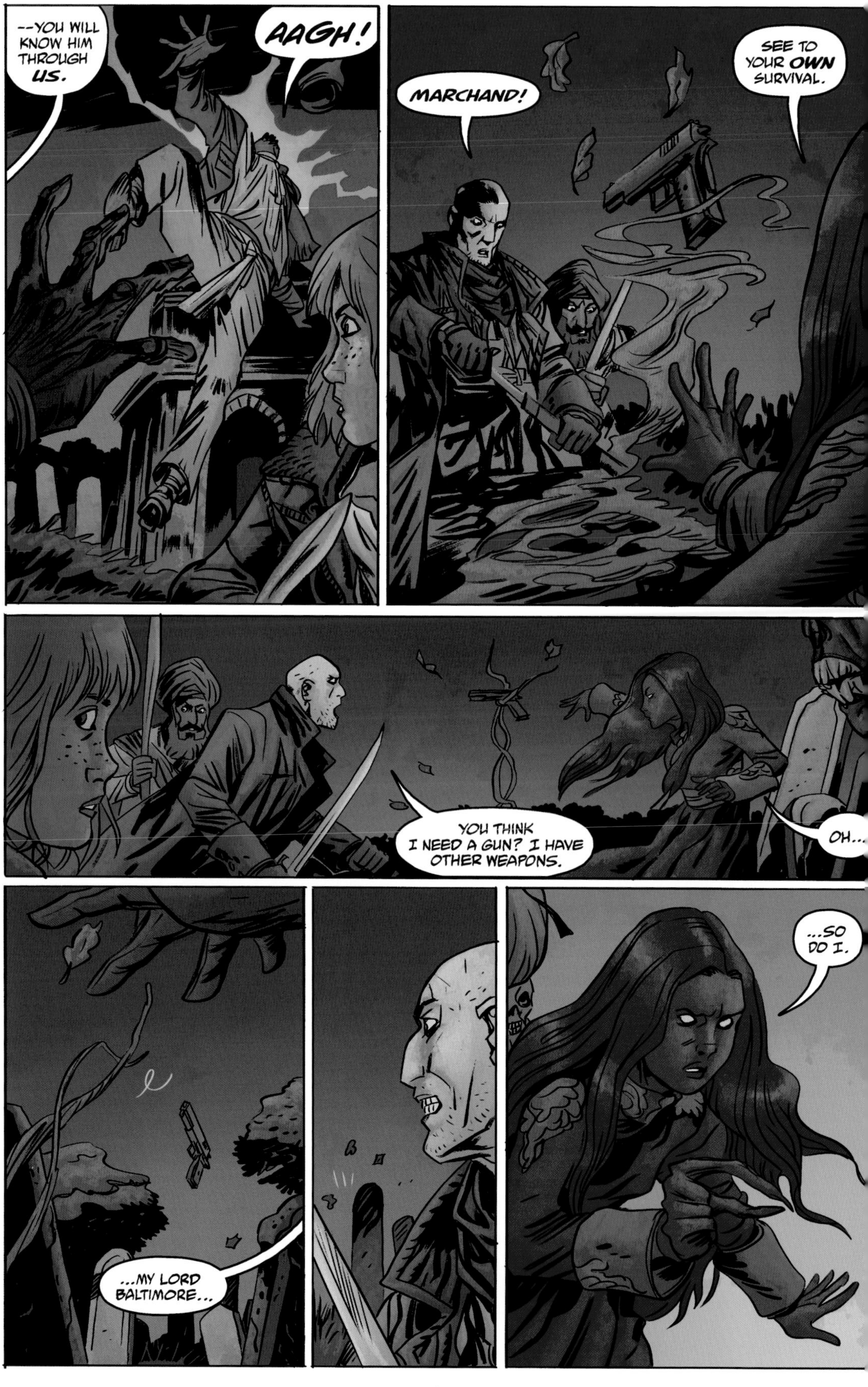
--YOU WILL KNOW HIM THROUGH US.
AAGH!
MARCHAND!
SEE TO YOUR OWN SURVIVAL.
YOU THINK I NEED A GUN? I HAVE OTHER WEAPONS.
OH...
...MY LORD BALTIMORE...
...SO DO I.

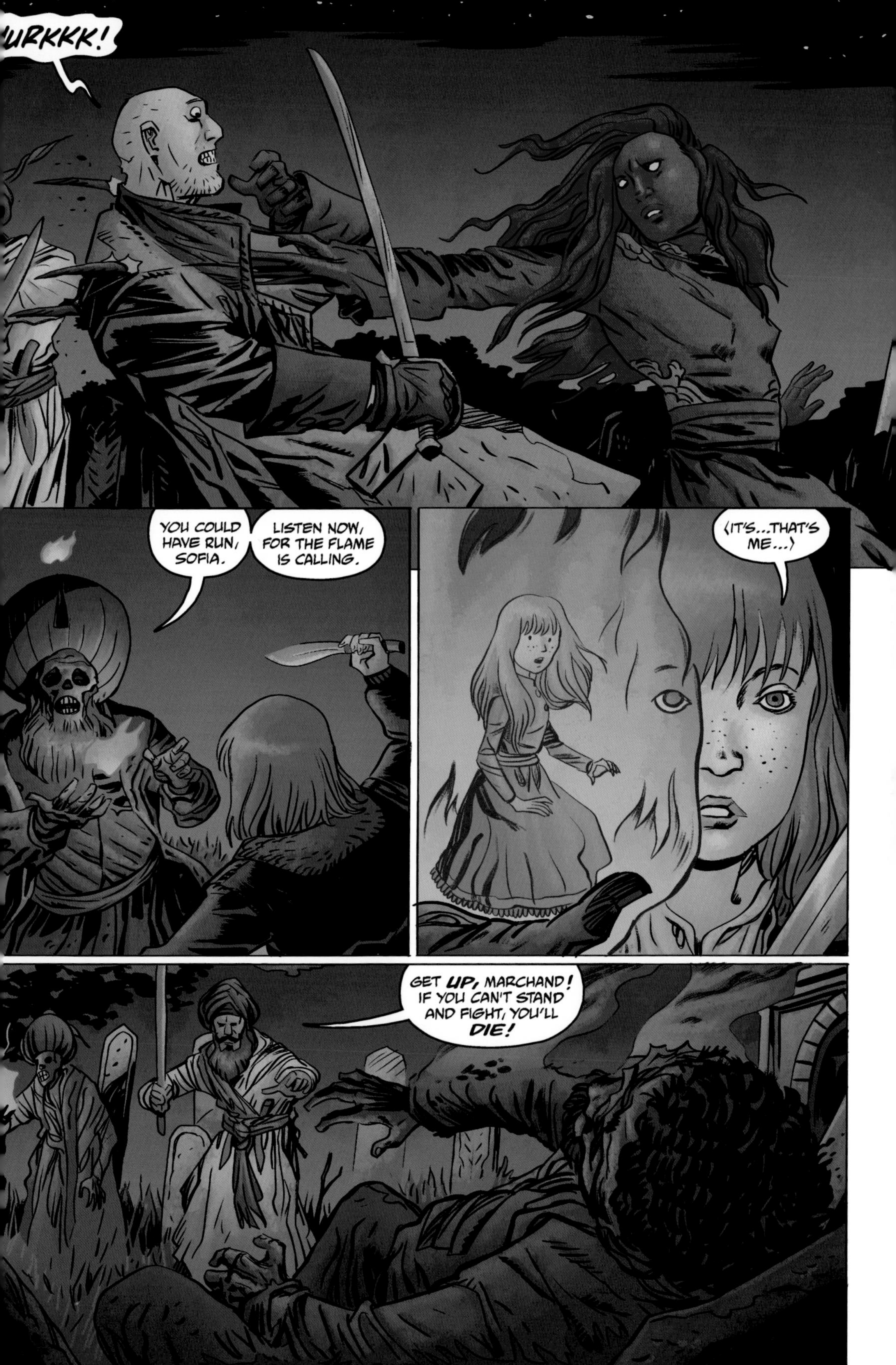
URKKK!
YOU COULD HAVE RUN, SOFIA.
LISTEN NOW, FOR THE FLAME IS CALLING.
‹IT'S...THAT'S ME...›
GET UP, MARCHAND! IF YOU CAN'T STAND AND FIGHT, YOU'LL DIE!

NSLATED FROM THE ESTONIAN›

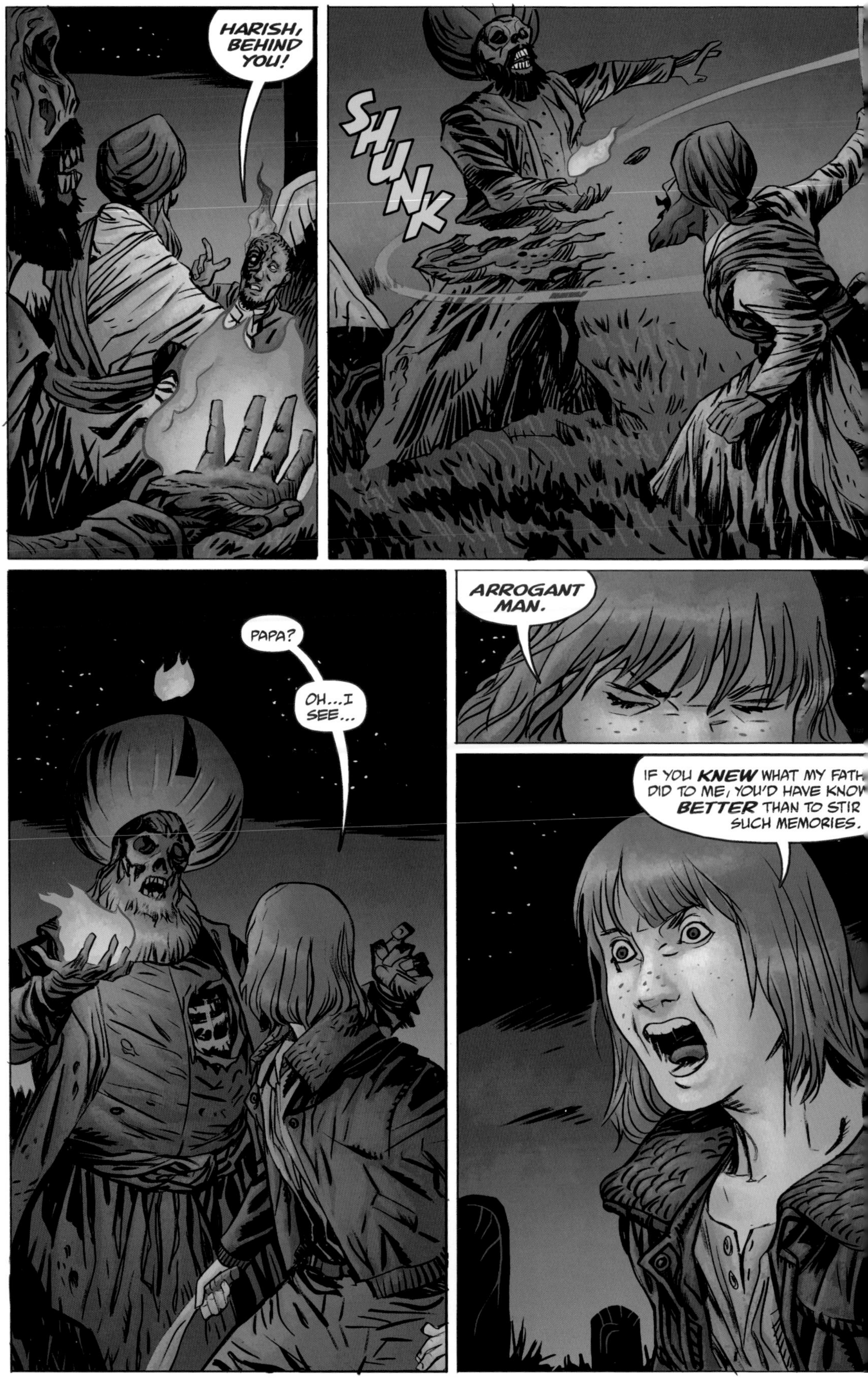
HARISH, BEHIND YOU!
SHUNK
PAPA?
OH...I SEE...
ARROGANT MAN.
IF YOU KNEW WHAT MY FATH
DID TO ME, YOU'D HAVE KNOV
BETTER THAN TO STIR
SUCH MEMORIES.

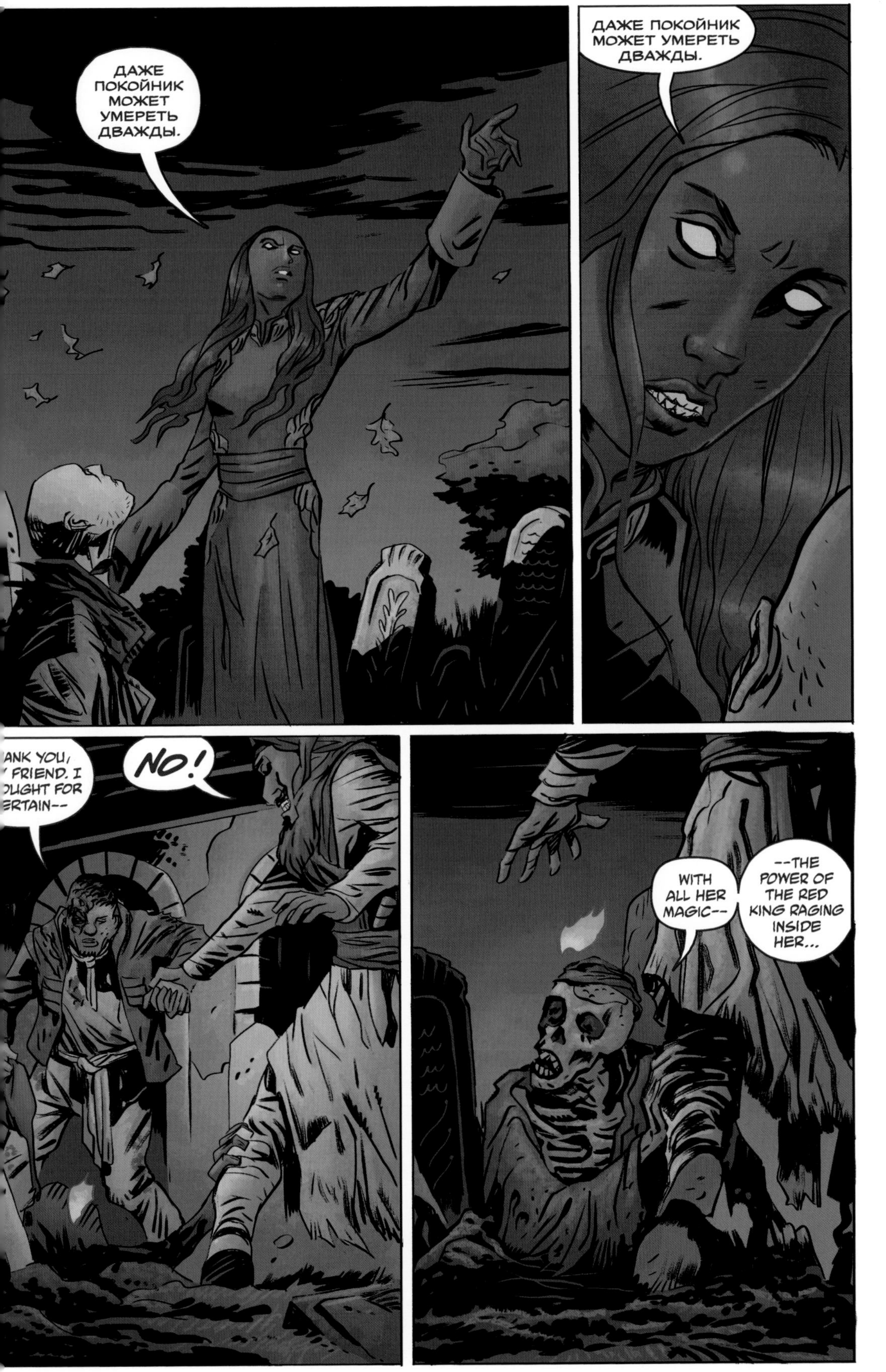
ДАЖЕ ПОКОЙНИК МОЖЕТ УМЕРЕТЬ ДВАЖДЫ.
ДАЖЕ ПОКОЙНИК МОЖЕТ УМЕРЕТЬ ДВАЖДЫ.
ANK YOU, FRIEND. I OUGHT FOR ERTAIN--
NO!
WITH ALL HER MAGIC--
--THE POWER OF THE RED KING RAGING INSIDE HER...

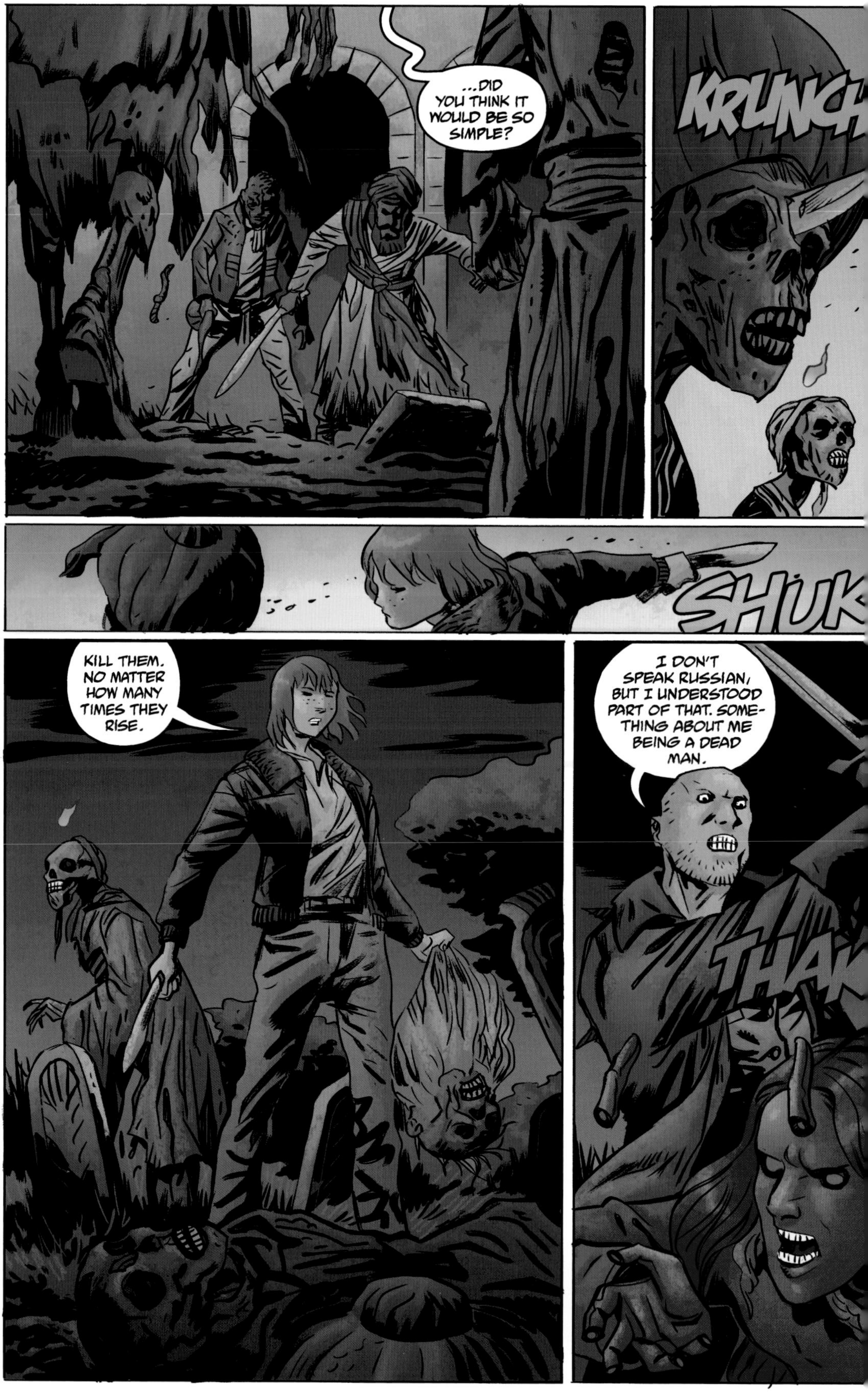
...DID YOU THINK IT WOULD BE SO SIMPLE?
KRUNCH
SHUK
KILL THEM. NO MATTER HOW MANY TIMES THEY RISE.
I DON'T SPEAK RUSSIAN, BUT I UNDERSTOOD PART OF THAT. SOMETHING ABOUT ME BEING A DEAD MAN.
THAK

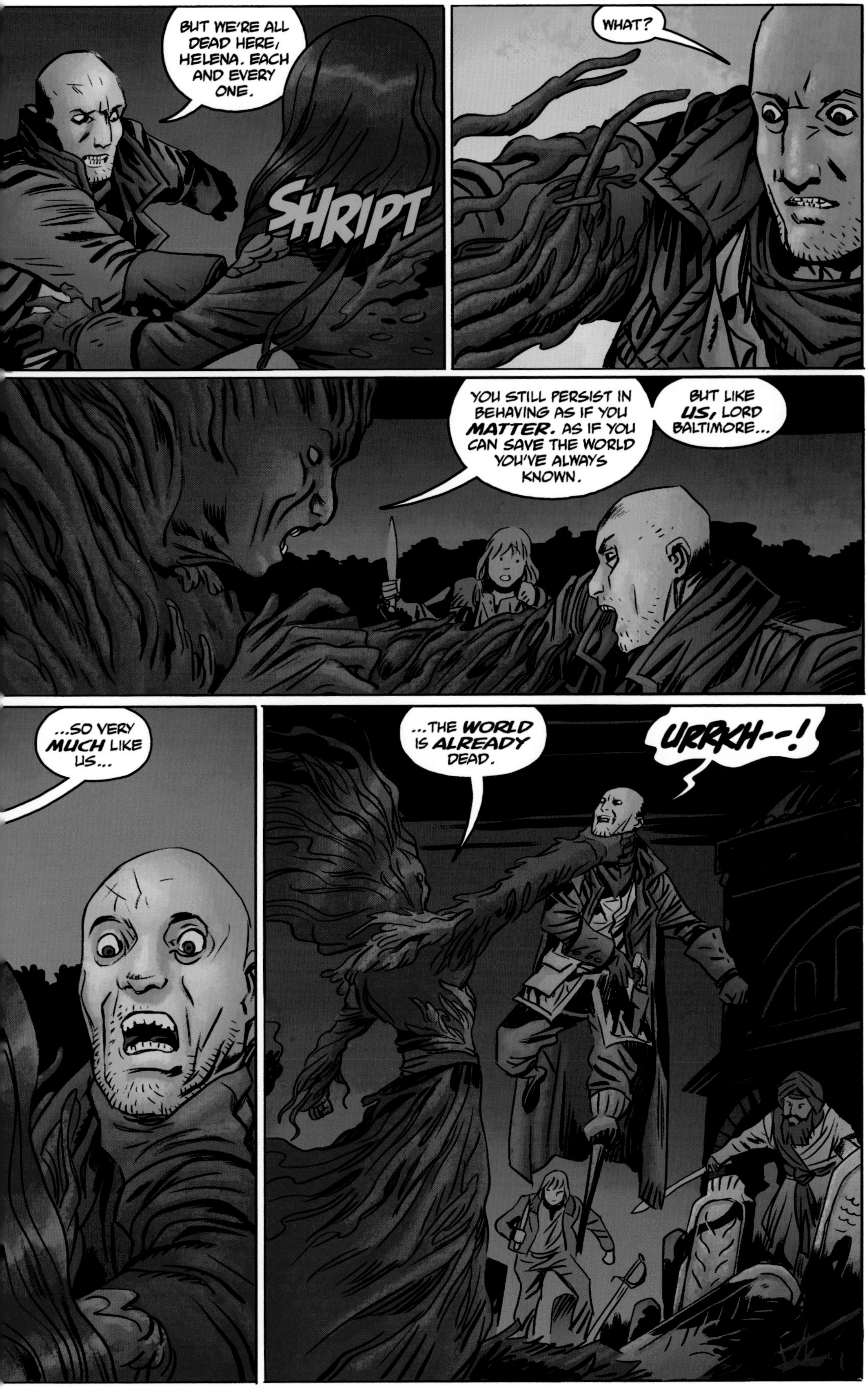
BUT WE'RE ALL DEAD HERE, HELENA. EACH AND EVERY ONE.
SHRIPT
WHAT?
YOU STILL PERSIST IN BEHAVING AS IF YOU MATTER. AS IF YOU CAN SAVE THE WORLD YOU'VE ALWAYS KNOWN.
BUT LIKE US, LORD BALTIMORE...
...SO VERY MUCH LIKE US...
...THE WORLD IS ALREADY DEAD.
URRKH--!

BLAM
BLAM
BLAM

NO.

WAIT...VON HAHN...

IS IT POSSIBLE...

THAT'S NOT HER NAME.

YOU *KNOW* HER, LORD BALTIMORE! *BACK AWAY!*

WHAT ARE YOU TALKING ABOUT?

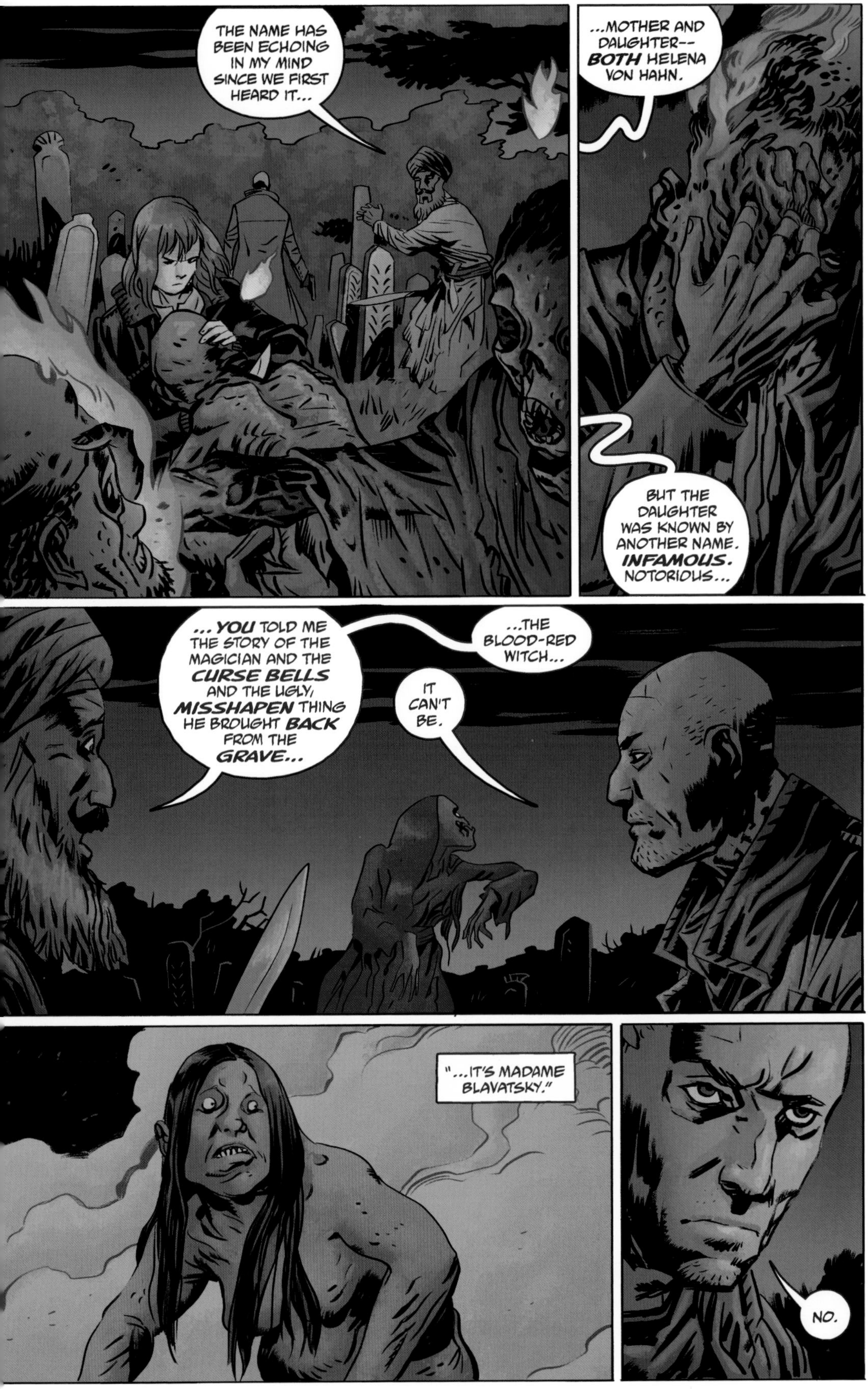
THE NAME HAS BEEN ECHOING IN MY MIND SINCE WE FIRST HEARD IT...
...MOTHER AND DAUGHTER-- BOTH HELENA VON HAHN.
BUT THE DAUGHTER WAS KNOWN BY ANOTHER NAME. INFAMOUS. NOTORIOUS...
...YOU TOLD ME THE STORY OF THE MAGICIAN AND THE CURSE BELLS AND THE UGLY, MISSHAPEN THING HE BROUGHT BACK FROM THE GRAVE...
...THE BLOOD-RED WITCH...
IT CAN'T BE.
"...IT'S MADAME BLAVATSKY."
NO.

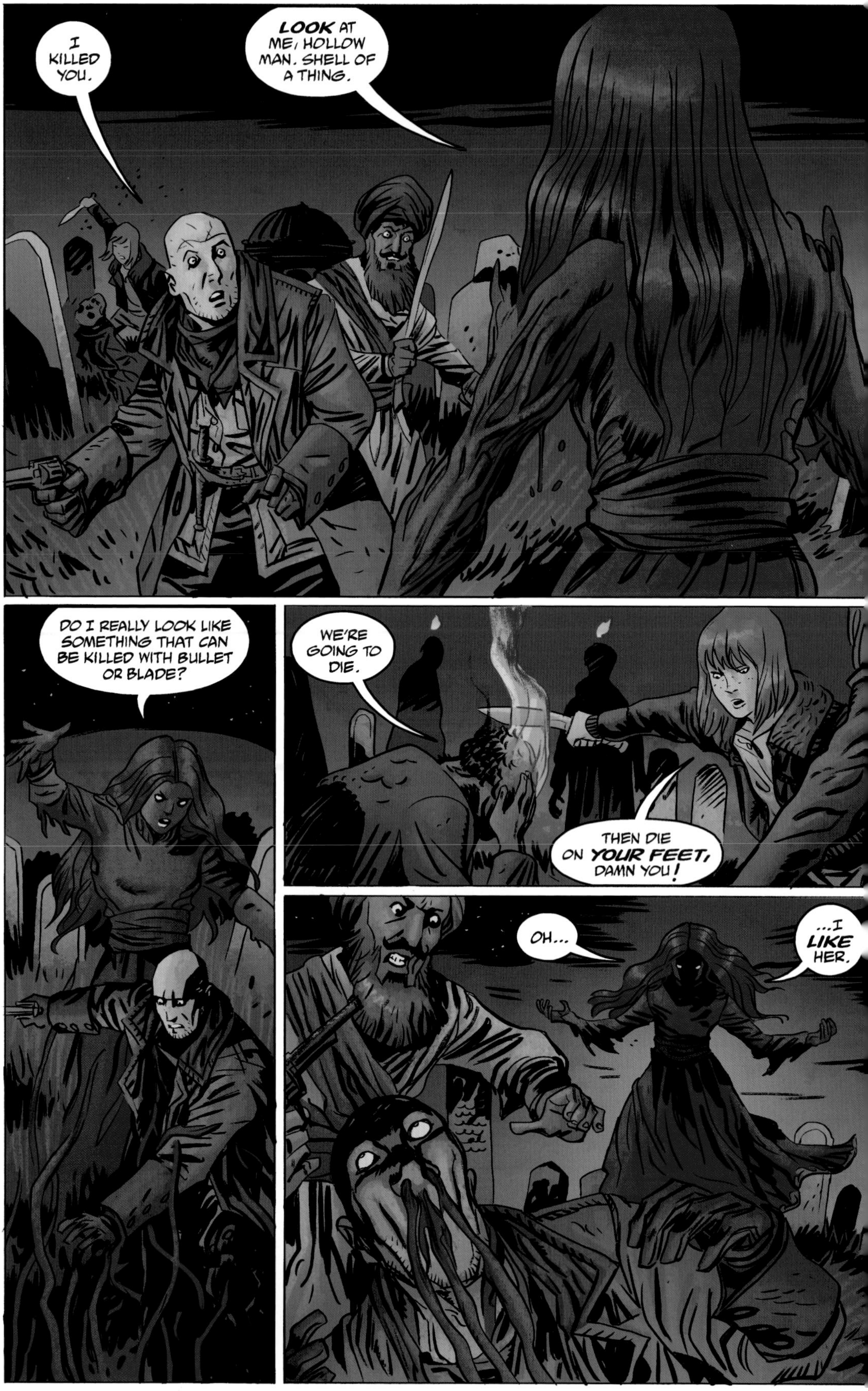
I KILLED YOU.
LOOK AT ME, HOLLOW MAN. SHELL OF A THING.
DO I REALLY LOOK LIKE SOMETHING THAT CAN BE KILLED WITH BULLET OR BLADE?
WE'RE GOING TO DIE.
THEN DIE ON **YOUR FEET,** DAMN YOU!
OH...
...I **LIKE** HER.

CHAPTER FIVE

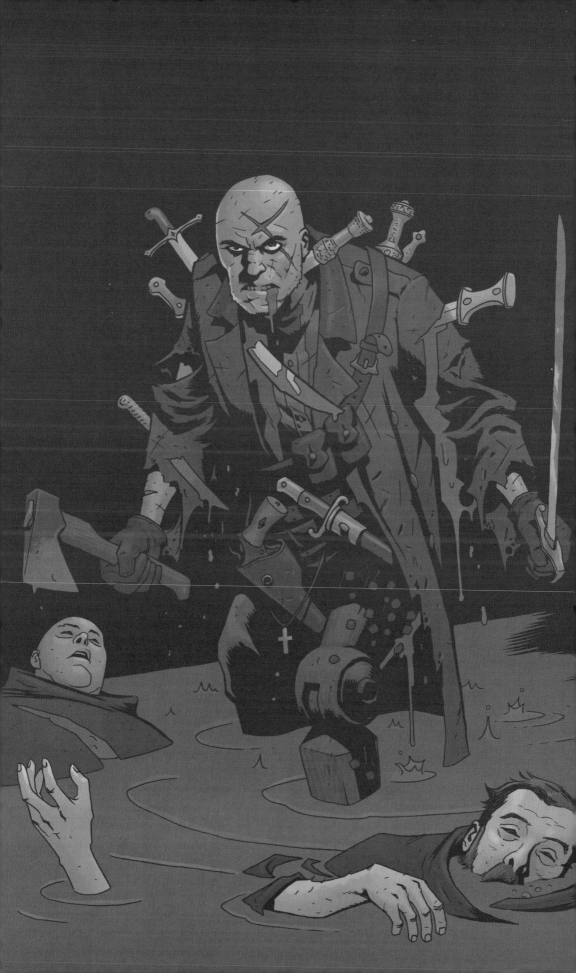

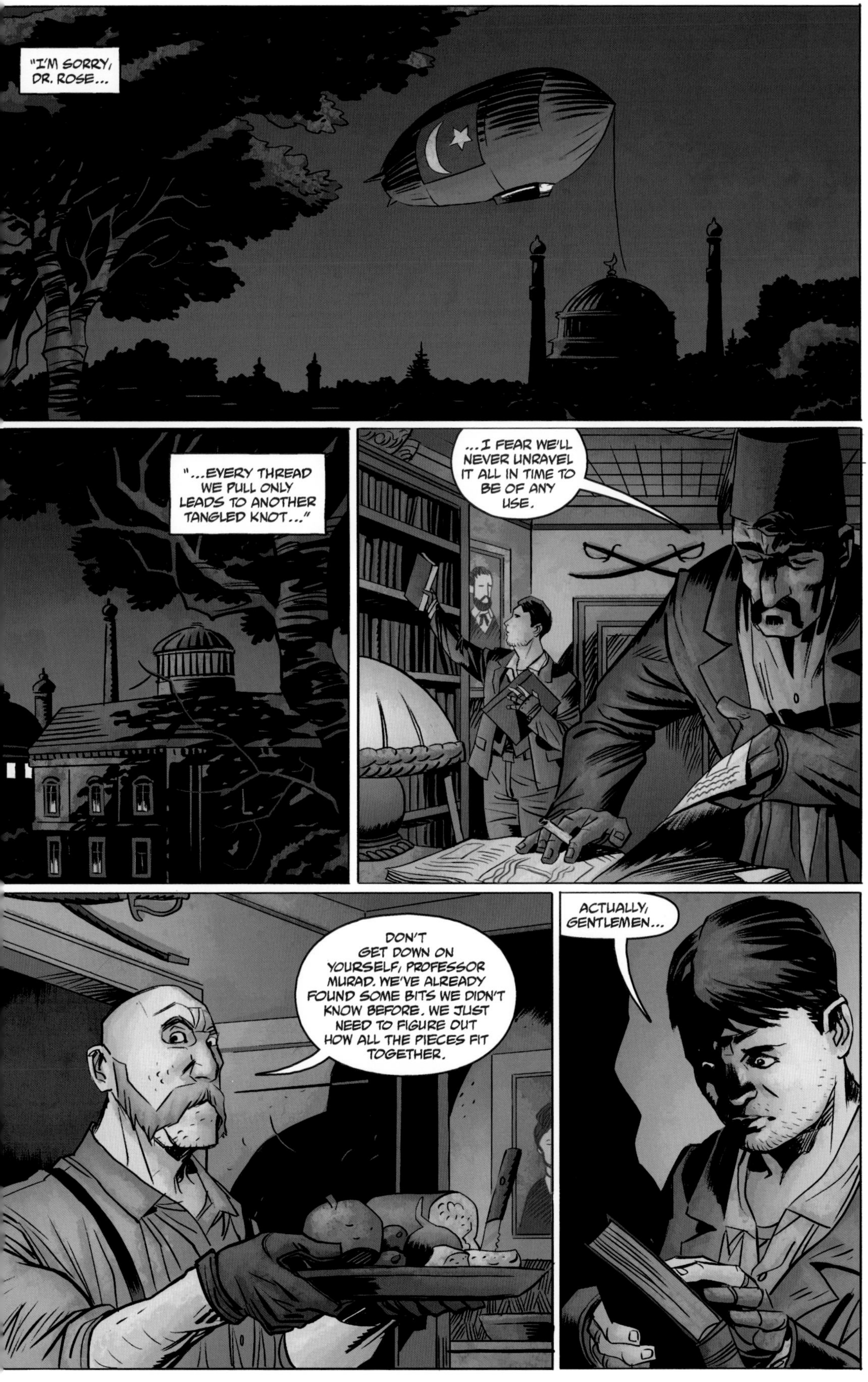
"I'M SORRY, DR. ROSE...
"...EVERY THREAD WE PULL ONLY LEADS TO ANOTHER TANGLED KNOT..."
...I FEAR WE'LL NEVER UNRAVEL IT ALL IN TIME TO BE OF ANY USE.
DON'T GET DOWN ON YOURSELF, PROFESSOR MURAD. WE'VE ALREADY FOUND SOME BITS WE DIDN'T KNOW BEFORE. WE JUST NEED TO FIGURE OUT HOW ALL THE PIECES FIT TOGETHER.
ACTUALLY, GENTLEMEN...

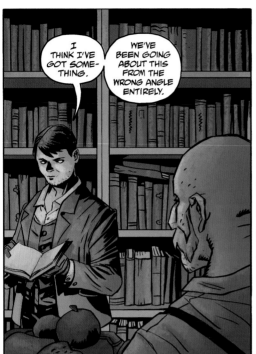

I THINK I'VE GOT SOMETHING.

WE'VE BEEN GOING ABOUT THIS FROM THE WRONG ANGLE ENTIRELY.

WHAT IS IT THAT YOU THINK YOU'VE GOT?

THE "MOTHER OF MONSTERS." WE'VE BEEN SO FOCUSED ON THAT PHRASE.

BUT THERE'S A WORD IN THIS GERMANIC TEXT...IT COULD BE TRANSLATED AS "WOMB"...

BUT IT COULD ALSO MEAN "NEST."

AND THIS IS YOUR BIG BREAKTHROUGH? THE MOTHER OF MONSTERS MAY HAVE A NEST SOMEWHERE?

WHAT IF THE MOTHER OF MONSTERS ISN'T THE BLOOD-RED WITCH?

WHAT IF IT'S NOT A FLESH-AND-BLOOD **MOTHER** AT ALL?

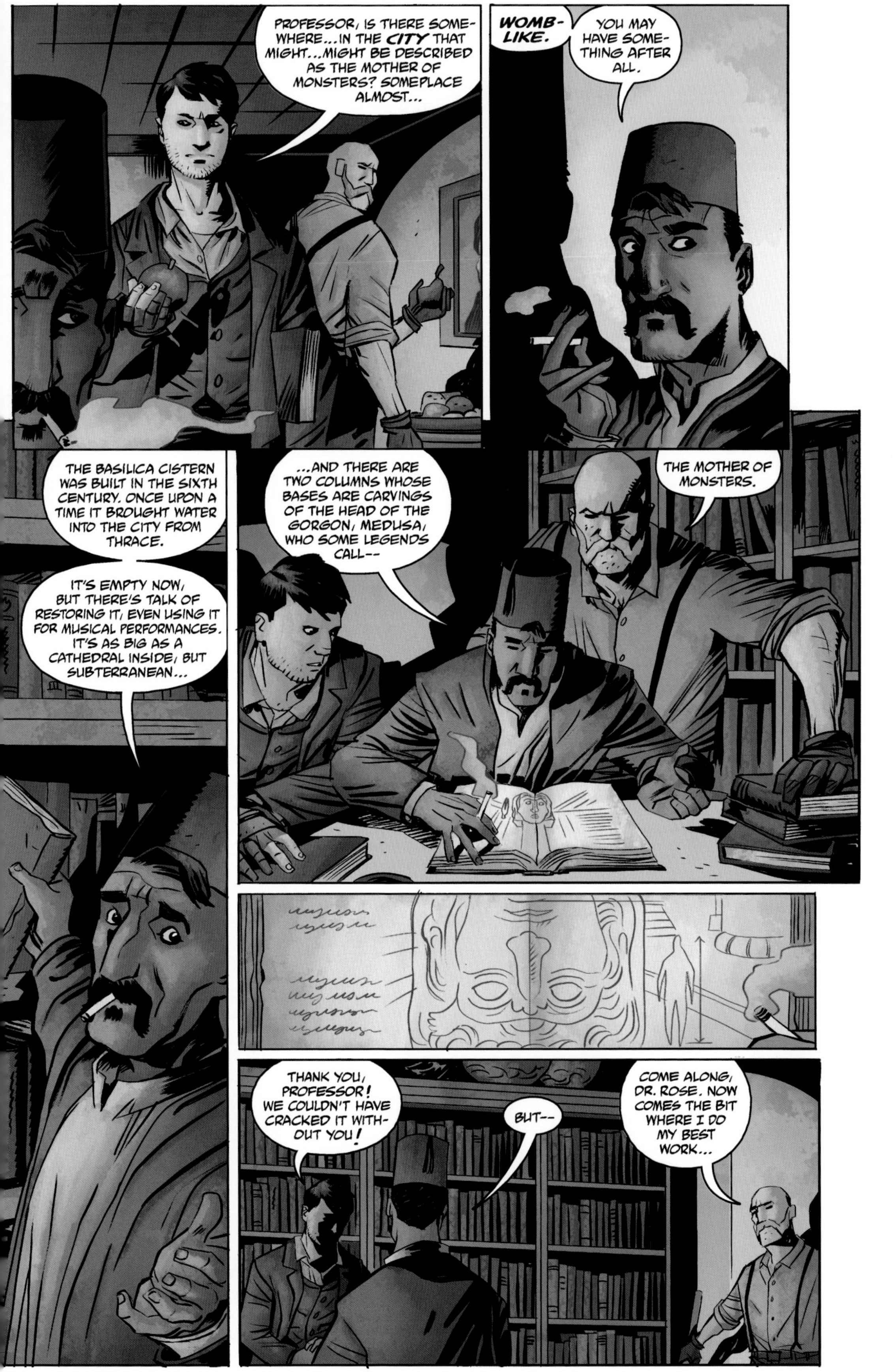
PROFESSOR, IS THERE SOMEWHERE...IN THE CITY THAT MIGHT...MIGHT BE DESCRIBED AS THE MOTHER OF MONSTERS? SOMEPLACE ALMOST...
WOMB-LIKE.
YOU MAY HAVE SOMETHING AFTER ALL.
THE BASILICA CISTERN WAS BUILT IN THE SIXTH CENTURY. ONCE UPON A TIME IT BROUGHT WATER INTO THE CITY FROM THRACE.
IT'S EMPTY NOW, BUT THERE'S TALK OF RESTORING IT, EVEN USING IT FOR MUSICAL PERFORMANCES. IT'S AS BIG AS A CATHEDRAL INSIDE, BUT SUBTERRANEAN...
...AND THERE ARE TWO COLUMNS WHOSE BASES ARE CARVINGS OF THE HEAD OF THE GORGON, MEDUSA, WHO SOME LEGENDS CALL--
THE MOTHER OF MONSTERS.
THANK YOU, PROFESSOR! WE COULDN'T HAVE CRACKED IT WITHOUT YOU!
BUT--
COME ALONG, DR. ROSE. NOW COMES THE BIT WHERE I DO MY BEST WORK...

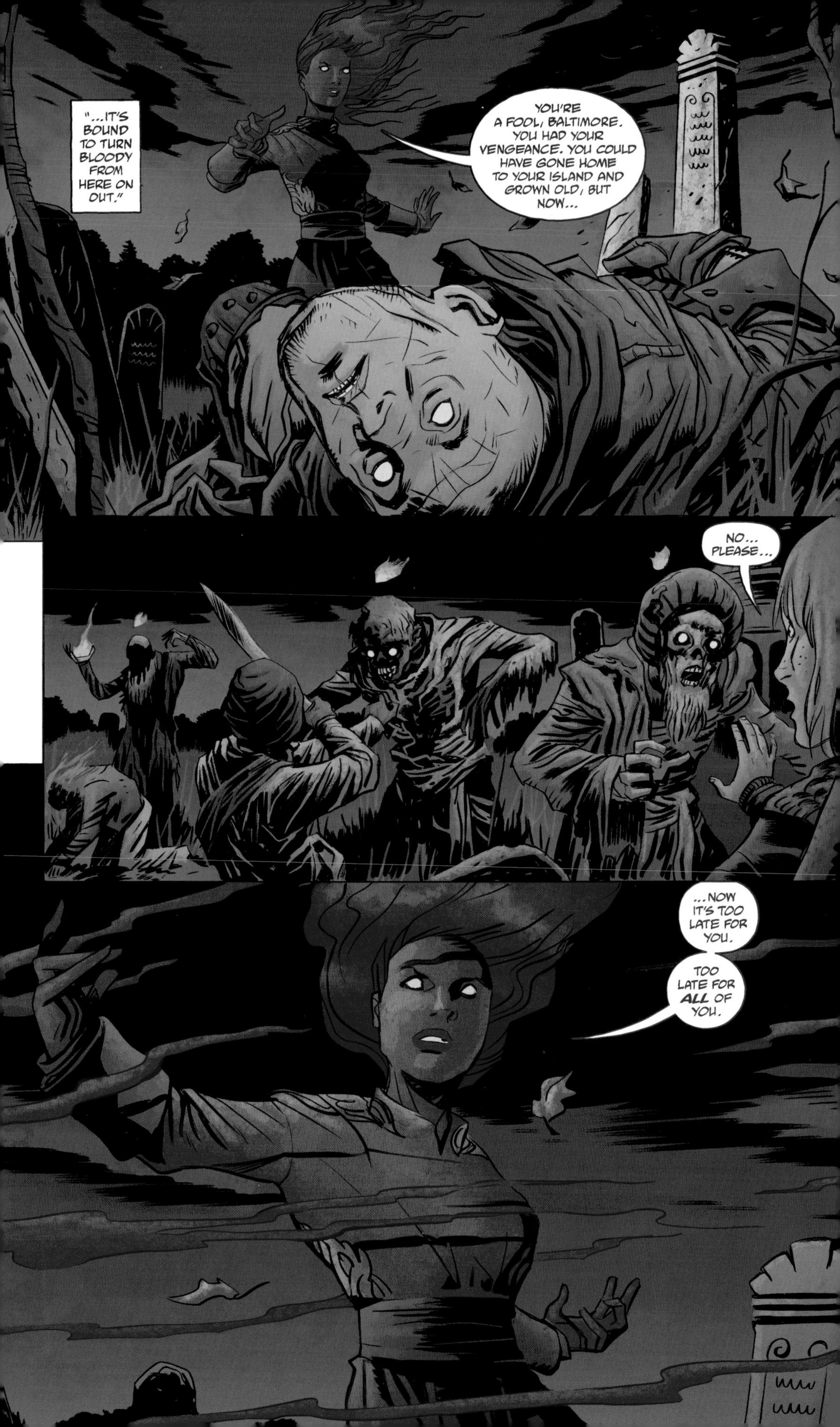
"...IT'S BOUND TO TURN BLOODY FROM HERE ON OUT."
YOU'RE A FOOL, BALTIMORE. YOU HAD YOUR VENGEANCE. YOU COULD HAVE GONE HOME TO YOUR ISLAND AND GROWN OLD, BUT NOW...
NO... PLEASE...
...NOW IT'S TOO LATE FOR YOU.
TOO LATE FOR **ALL** OF YOU.

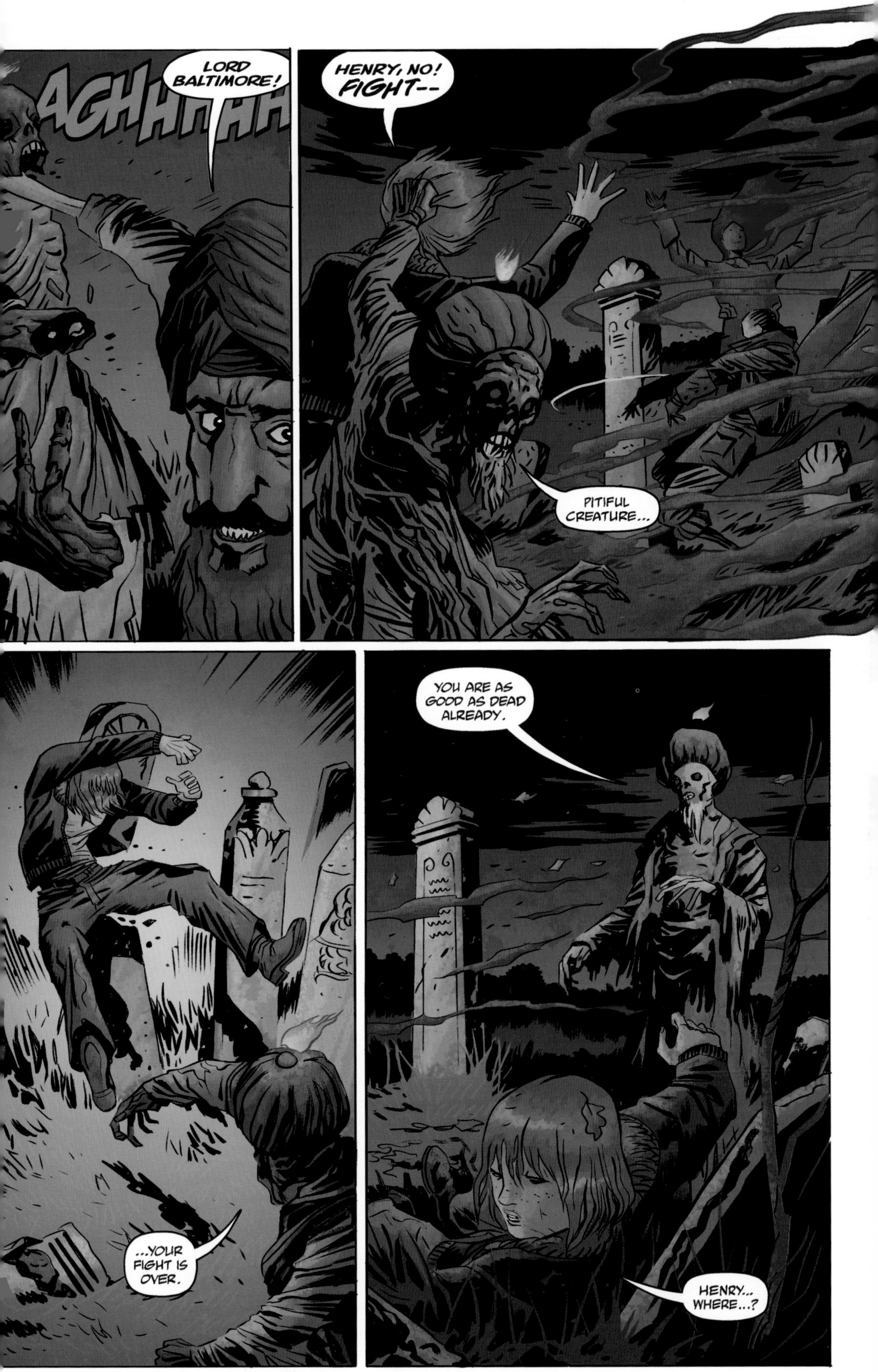
AGHHHHH
LORD BALTIMORE!
HENRY, NO! FIGHT--
PITIFUL CREATURE...
...YOUR FIGHT IS OVER.
YOU ARE AS GOOD AS DEAD ALREADY.
HENRY... WHERE...?

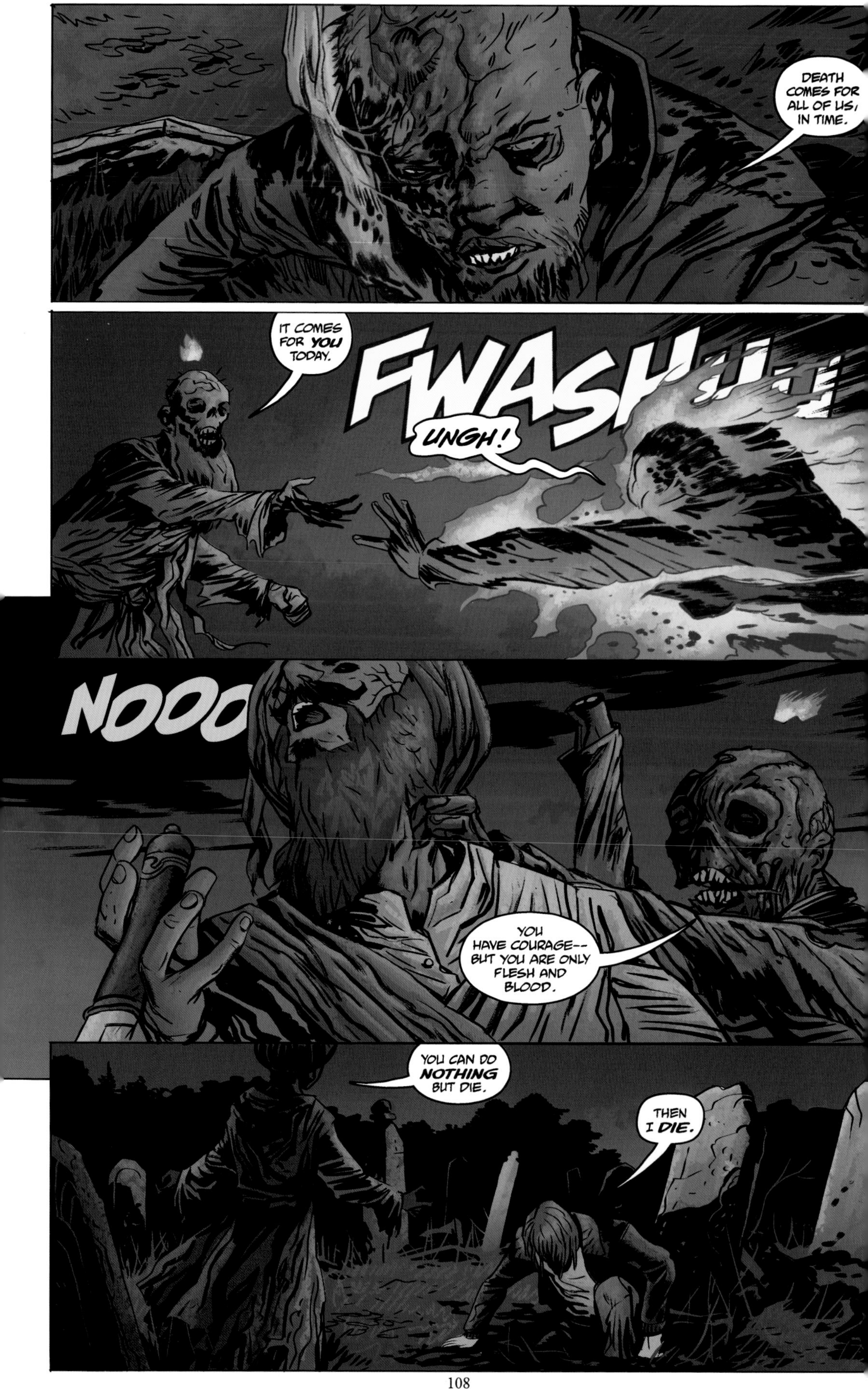
DEATH COMES FOR ALL OF US, IN TIME.
IT COMES FOR YOU TODAY.
FWASH
UNGH!
NOOO
YOU HAVE COURAGE-- BUT YOU ARE ONLY FLESH AND BLOOD.
YOU CAN DO NOTHING BUT DIE.
THEN I DIE.

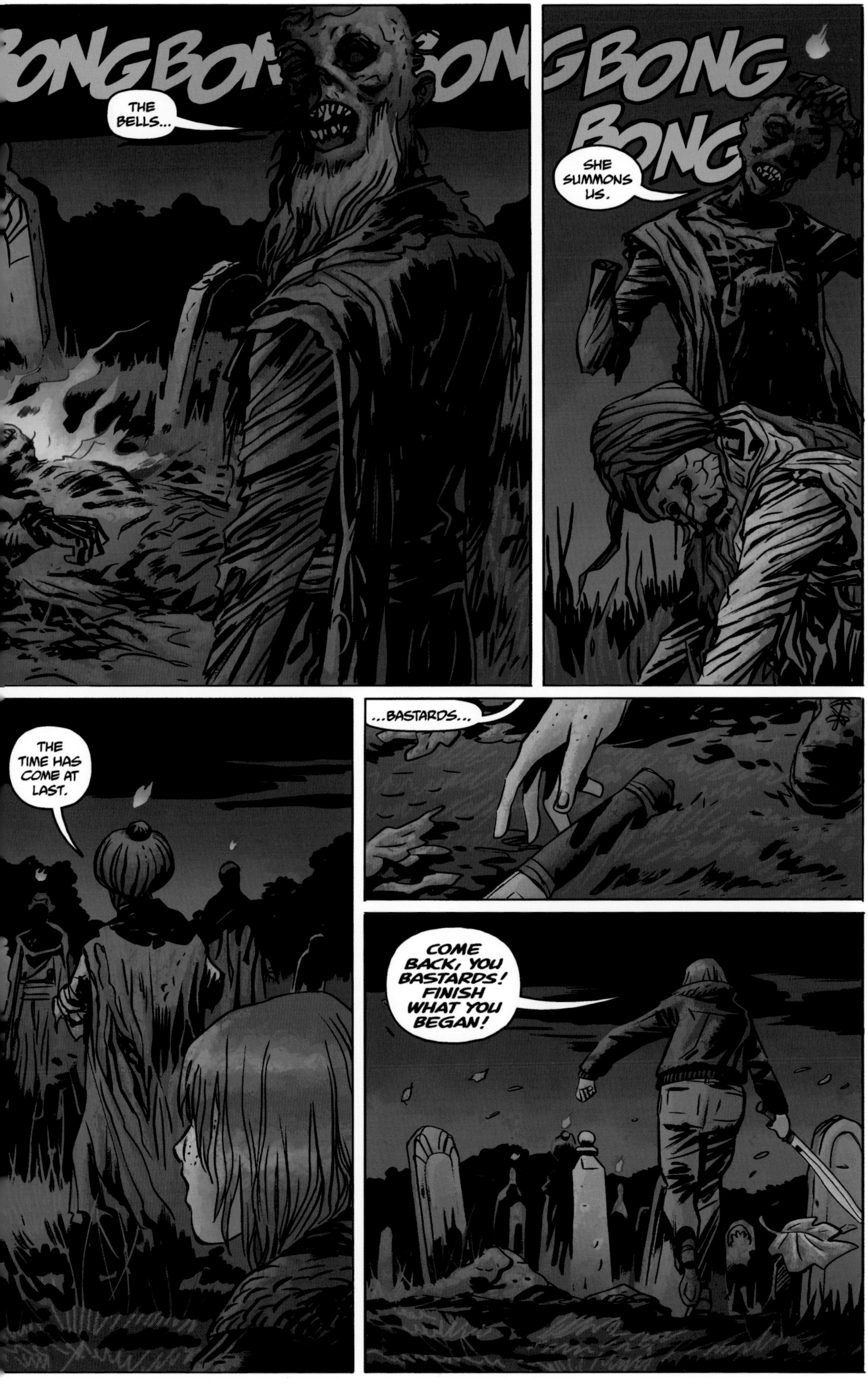
BONG BONG BONG BONG
THE BELLS...
BONG
SHE SUMMONS US.
THE TIME HAS COME AT LAST.
...BASTARDS...
COME BACK, YOU BASTARDS! FINISH WHAT YOU BEGAN!

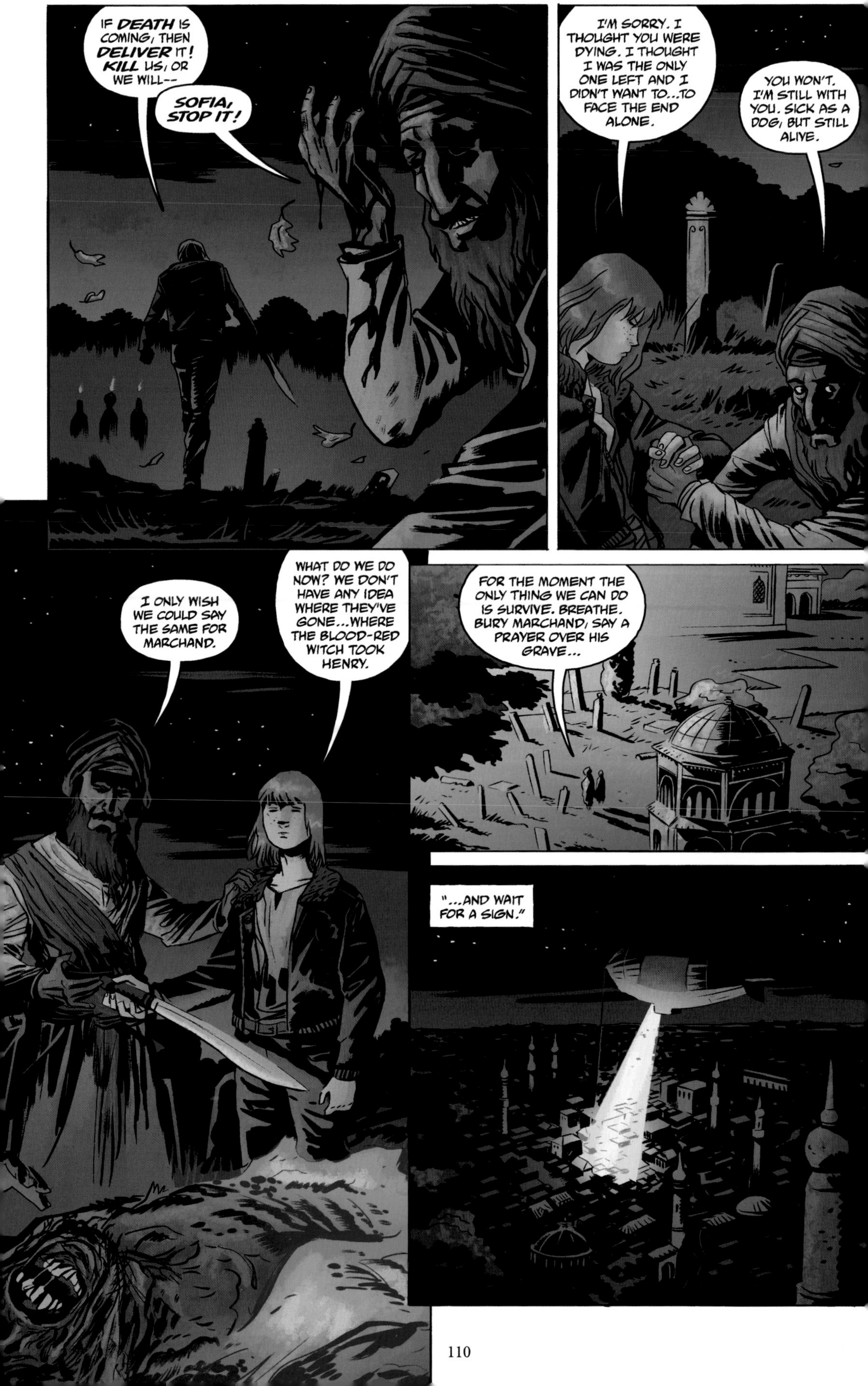
IF DEATH IS COMING, THEN DELIVER IT! KILL US, OR WE WILL--
SOFIA, STOP IT!
I'M SORRY. I THOUGHT YOU WERE DYING. I THOUGHT I WAS THE ONLY ONE LEFT AND I DIDN'T WANT TO...TO FACE THE END ALONE.
YOU WON'T. I'M STILL WITH YOU. SICK AS A DOG, BUT STILL ALIVE.
I ONLY WISH WE COULD SAY THE SAME FOR MARCHAND.
WHAT DO WE DO NOW? WE DON'T HAVE ANY IDEA WHERE THEY'VE GONE...WHERE THE BLOOD-RED WITCH TOOK HENRY.
FOR THE MOMENT THE ONLY THING WE CAN DO IS SURVIVE. BREATHE. BURY MARCHAND, SAY A PRAYER OVER HIS GRAVE...
"...AND WAIT FOR A SIGN."

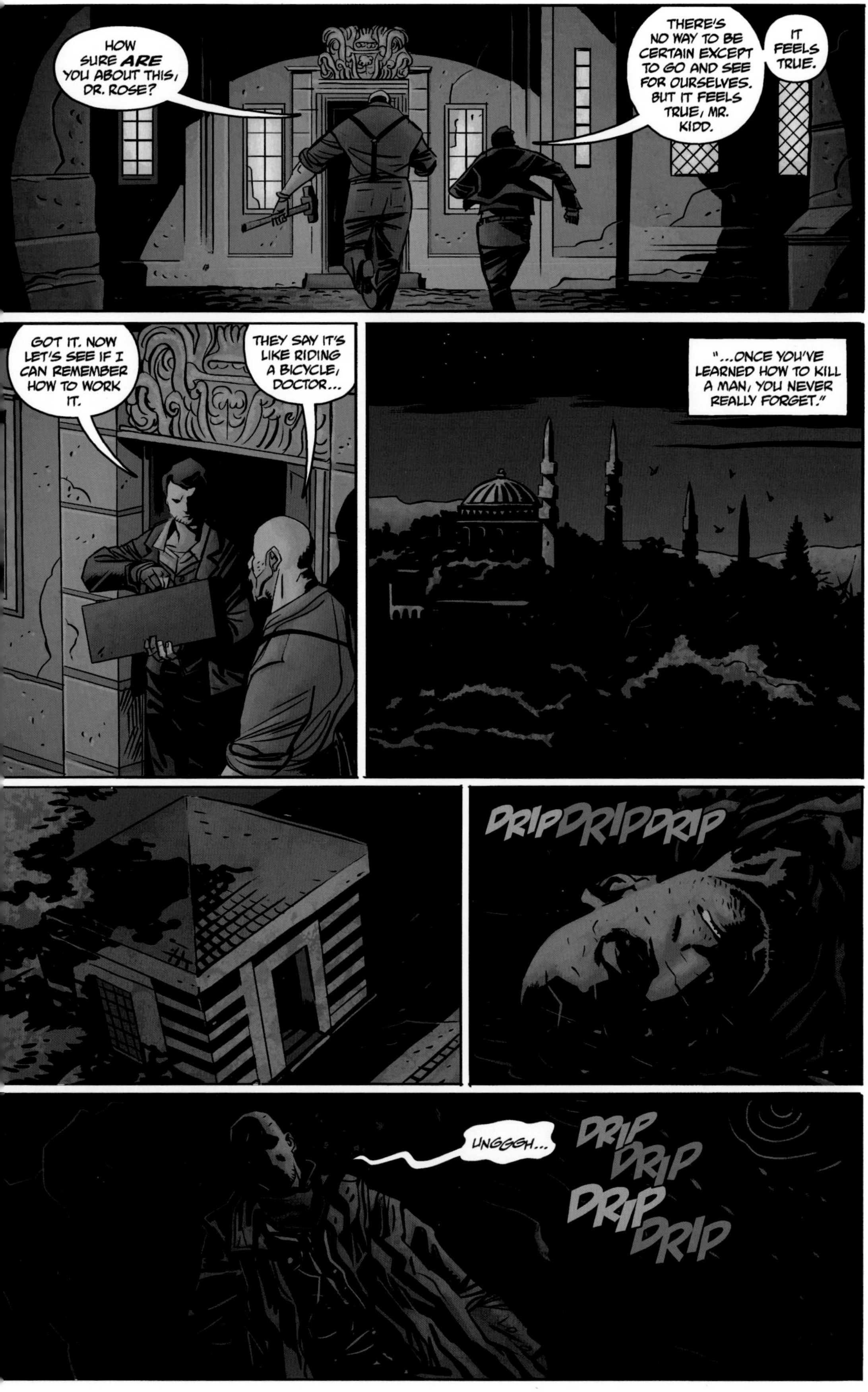
HOW SURE ARE YOU ABOUT THIS, DR. ROSE?
THERE'S NO WAY TO BE CERTAIN EXCEPT TO GO AND SEE FOR OURSELVES. BUT IT FEELS TRUE, MR. KIDD.
IT FEELS TRUE.
GOT IT. NOW LET'S SEE IF I CAN REMEMBER HOW TO WORK IT.
THEY SAY IT'S LIKE RIDING A BICYCLE, DOCTOR...
"...ONCE YOU'VE LEARNED HOW TO KILL A MAN, YOU NEVER REALLY FORGET."
DRIPDRIPDRIP
UNGGGH...
DRIP DRIP DRIP DRIP

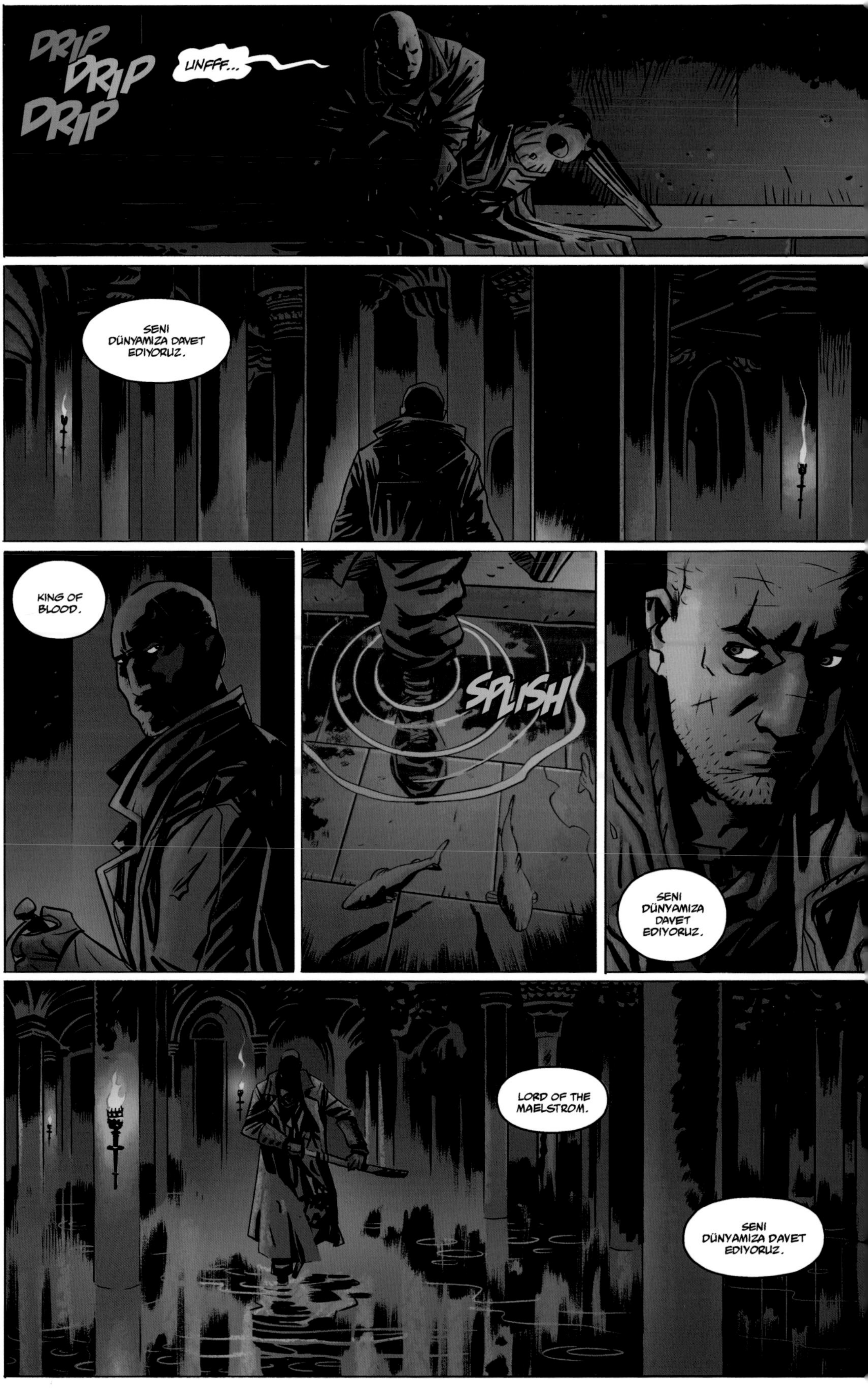
DRIP DRIP DRIP
UNFFF...
SENI DÜNYAMIZA DAVET EDIYORUZ.
KING OF BLOOD.
SPLISH
SENI DÜNYAMIZA DAVET EDIYORUZ.
LORD OF THE MAELSTROM.
SENI DÜNYAMIZA DAVET EDIYORUZ.

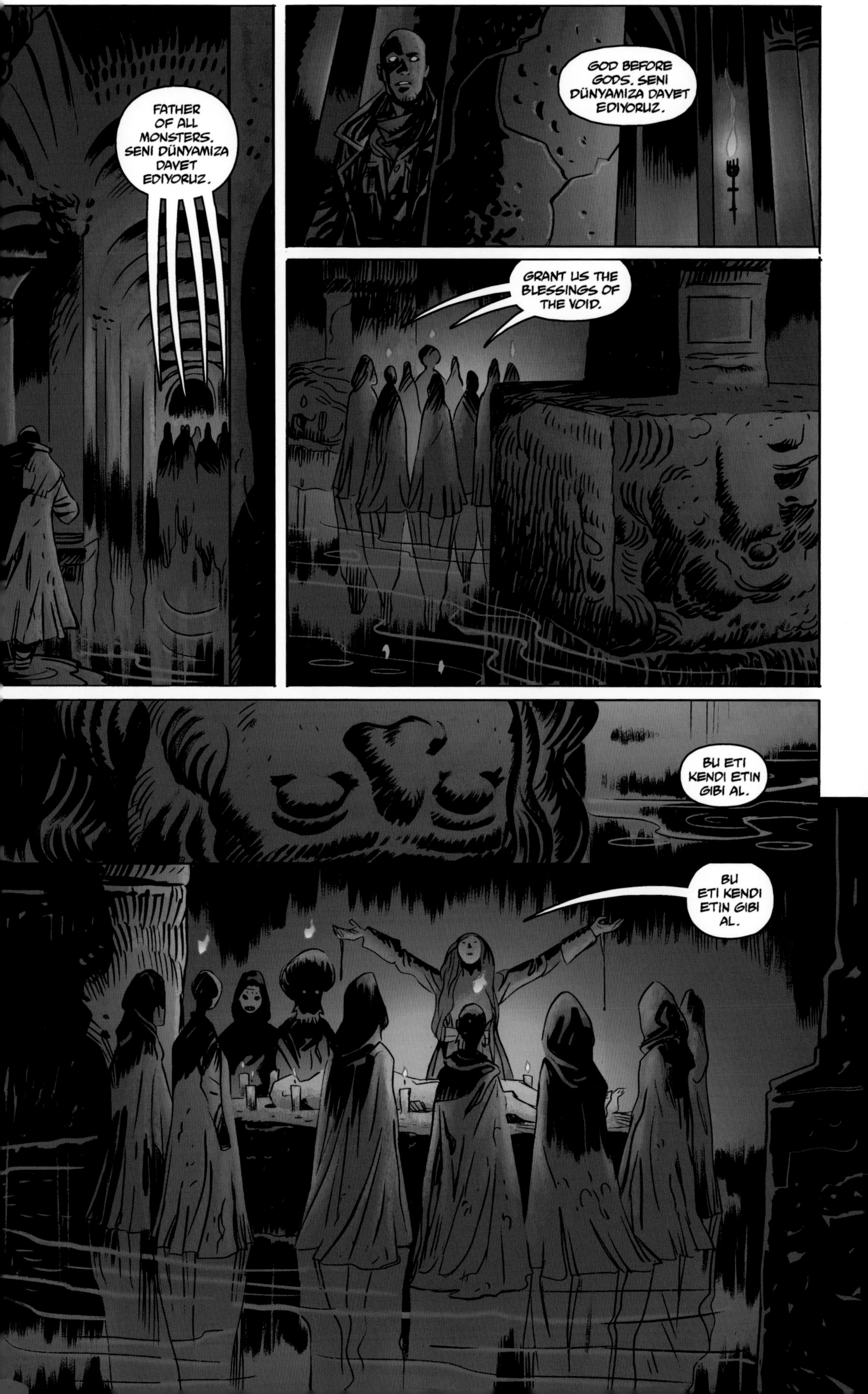
FATHER OF ALL MONSTERS. SENI DÜNYAMIZA DAVET EDIYORUZ.
GOD BEFORE GODS. SENI DÜNYAMIZA DAVET EDIYORUZ.
GRANT US THE BLESSINGS OF THE VOID.
BU ETI KENDI ETIN GIBI AL.
BU ETI KENDI ETIN GIBI AL.

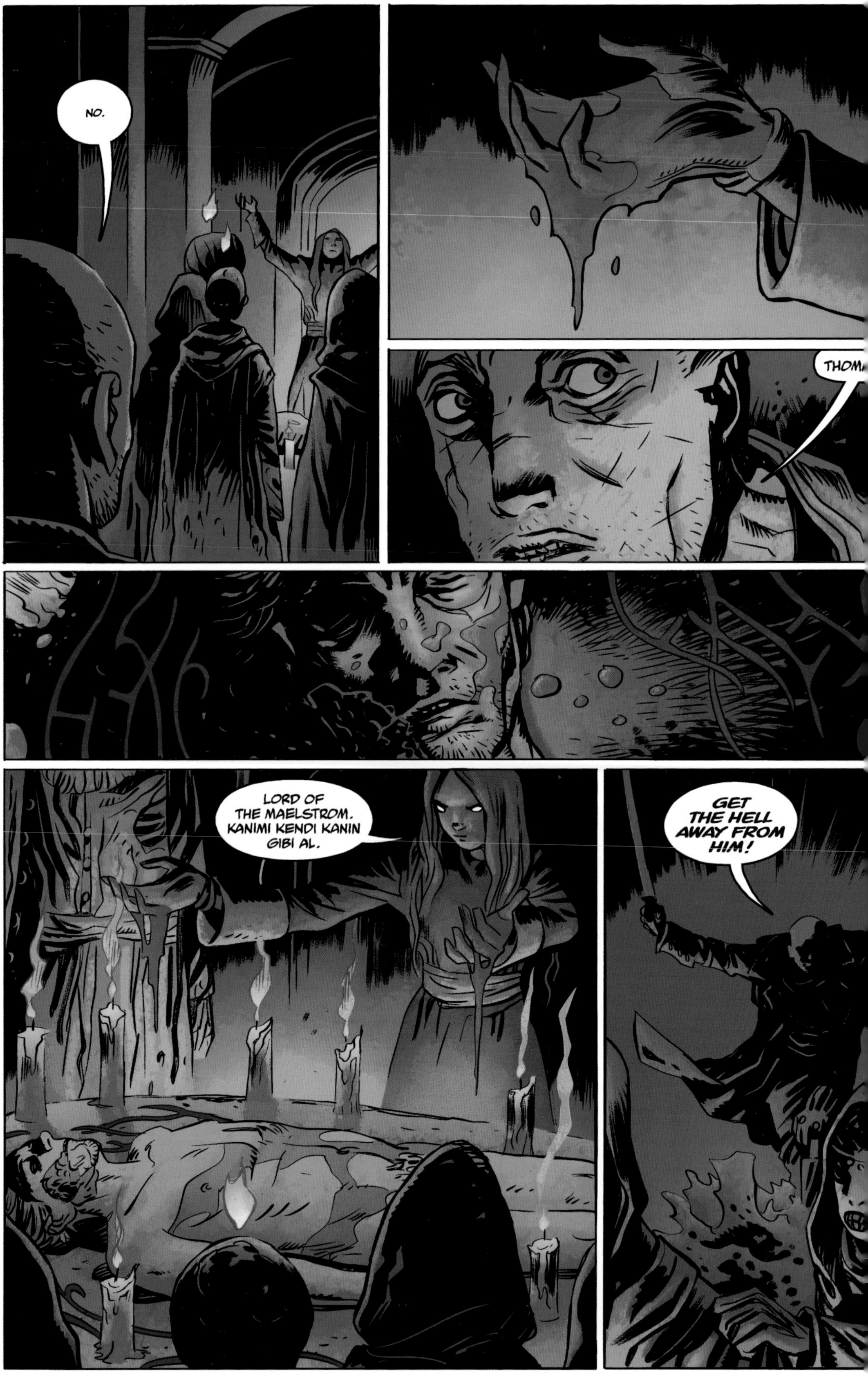
NO.
THOM
LORD OF THE MAELSTROM. KANIMI KENDI KANIN GIBI AL.
GET THE HELL AWAY FROM HIM!

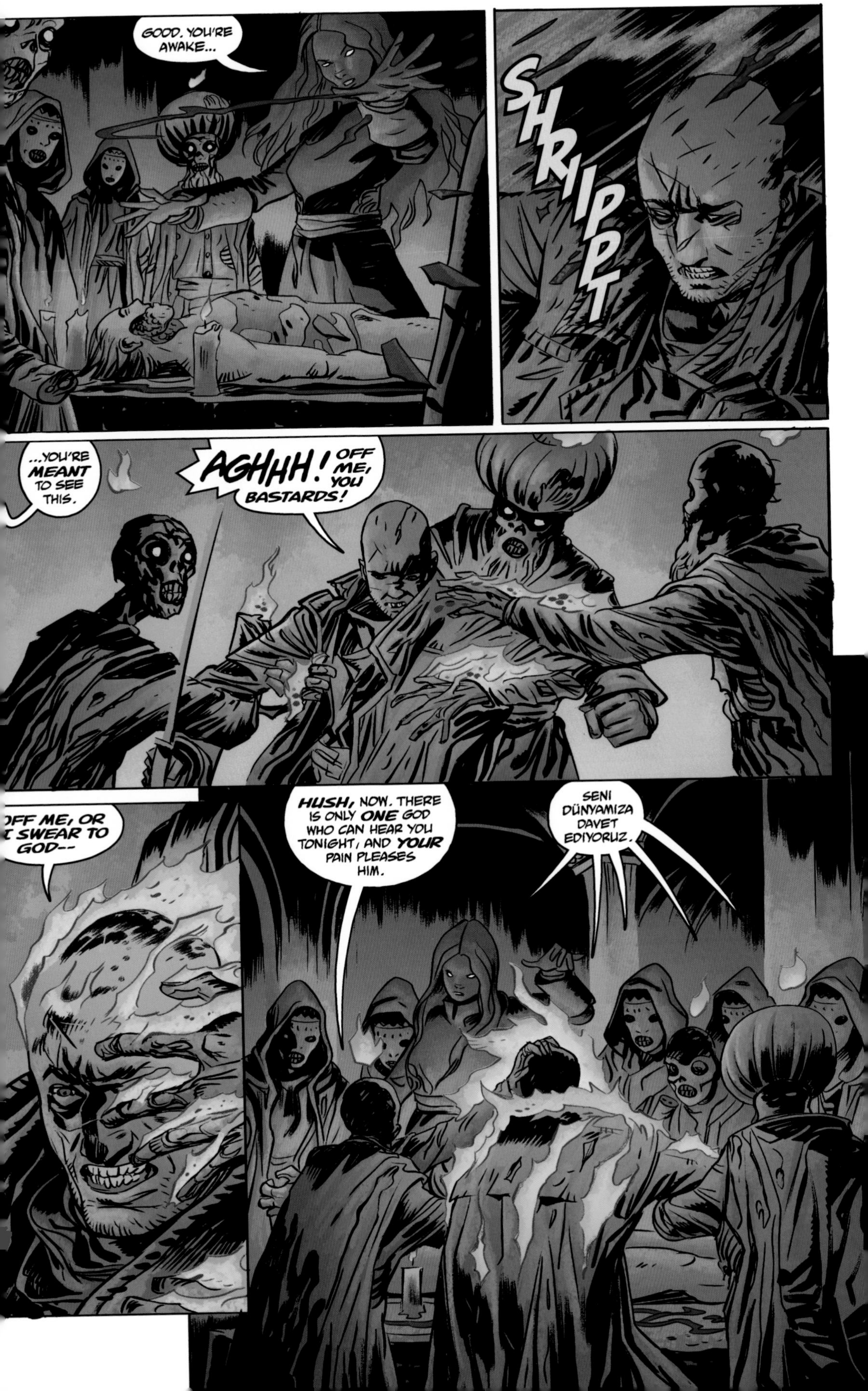
GOOD. YOU'RE AWAKE...
SHRIPPT
...YOU'RE MEANT TO SEE THIS.
AGHHH! OFF ME, YOU BASTARDS!
OFF ME, OR I SWEAR TO GOD--
HUSH, NOW. THERE IS ONLY ONE GOD WHO CAN HEAR YOU TONIGHT, AND YOUR PAIN PLEASES HIM.
SENI DÜNYAMIZA DAVET EDIYORUZ.

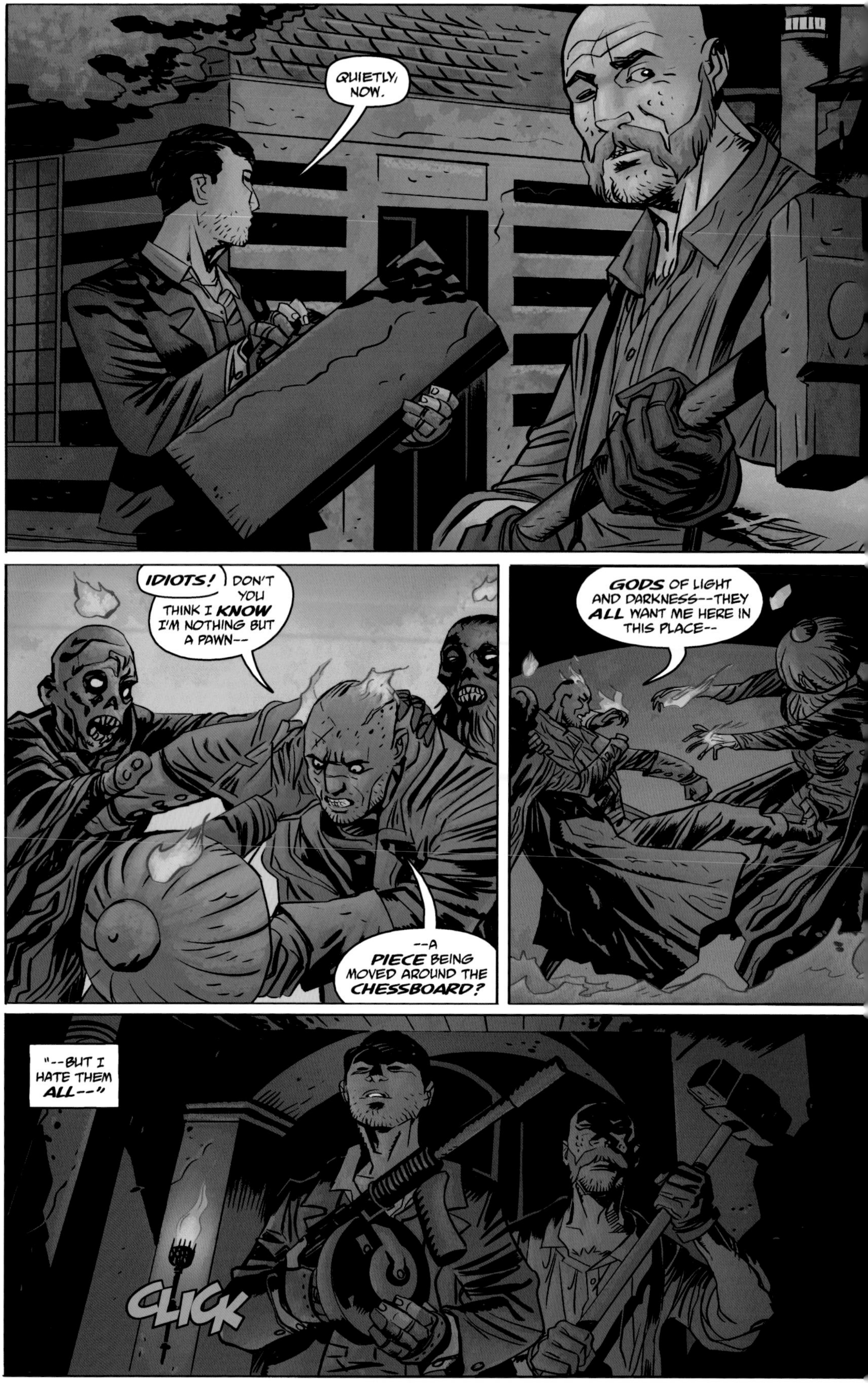

QUIETLY, NOW.
IDIOTS!
DON'T YOU THINK I KNOW I'M NOTHING BUT A PAWN--
--A PIECE BEING MOVED AROUND THE CHESSBOARD?
GODS OF LIGHT AND DARKNESS--THEY ALL WANT ME HERE IN THIS PLACE--
"--BUT I HATE THEM ALL--"
CLICK

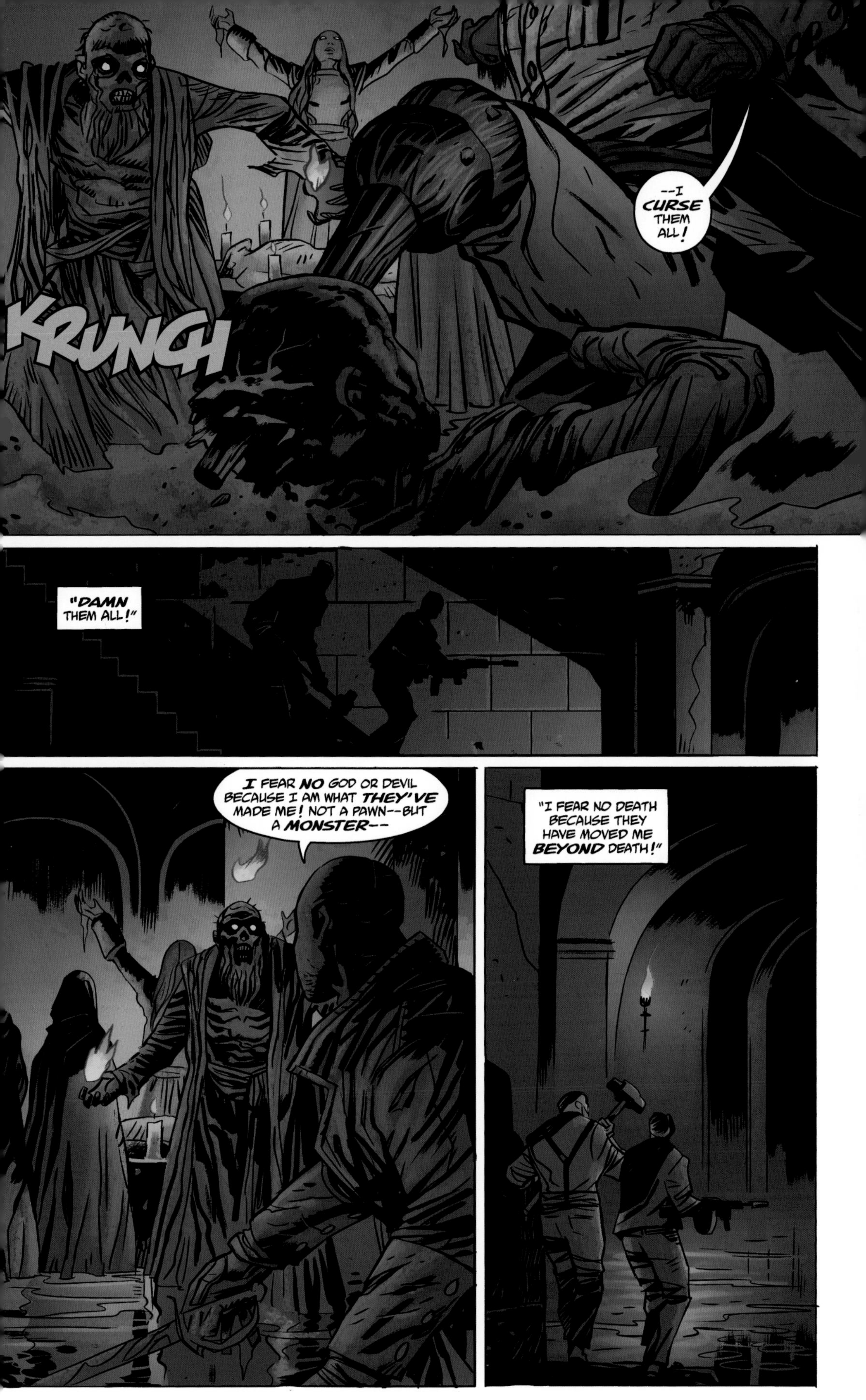
--I CURSE THEM ALL!
KRUNCH
"DAMN THEM ALL!"
I FEAR NO GOD OR DEVIL BECAUSE I AM WHAT THEY'VE MADE ME! NOT A PAWN--BUT A MONSTER--
"I FEAR NO DEATH BECAUSE THEY HAVE MOVED ME BEYOND DEATH!"

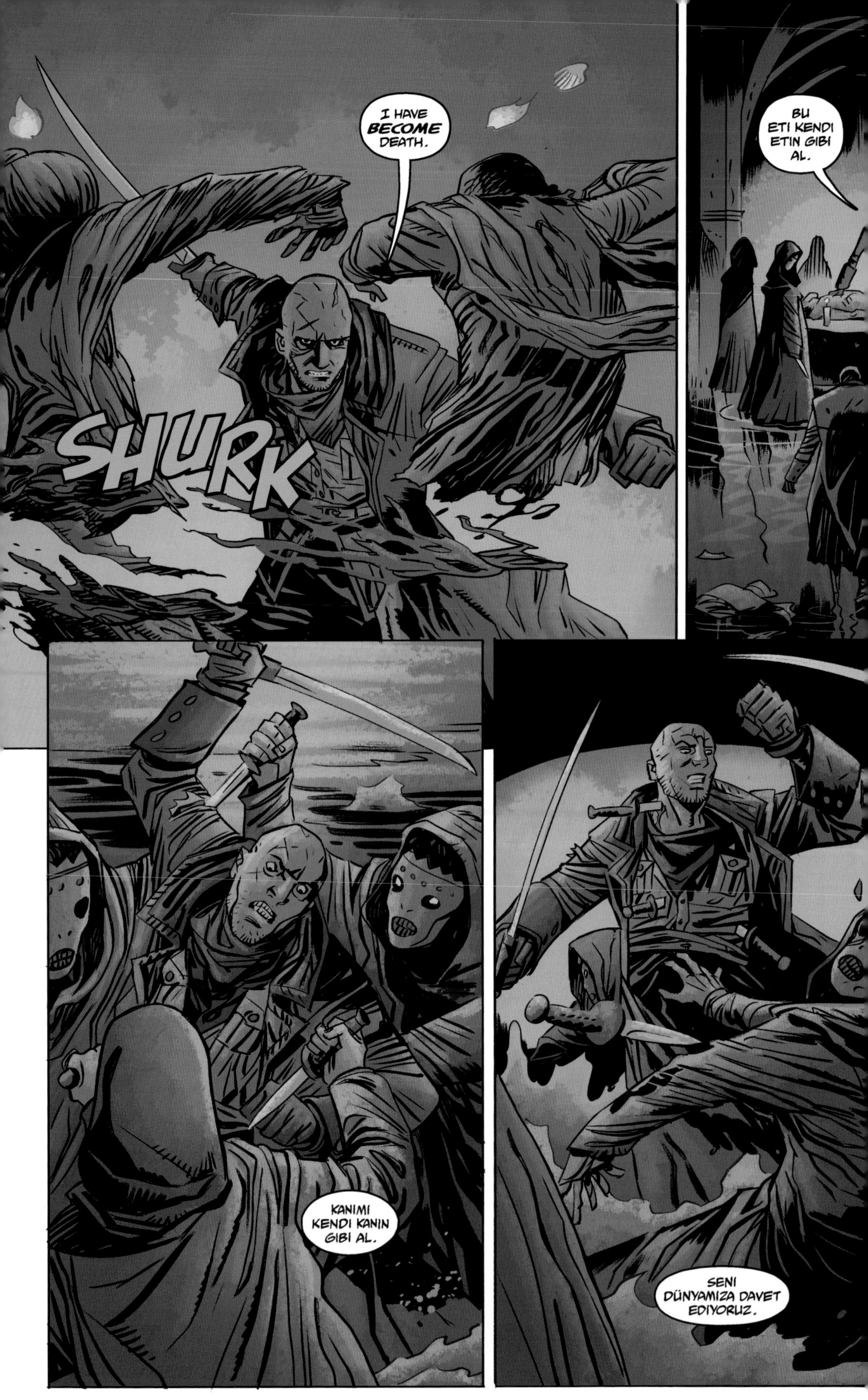
I HAVE BECOME DEATH.
SHURK
BU ETI KENDI ETIN GIBI AL.
KANIMI KENDI KANIN GIBI AL.
SENI DÜNYAMIZA DAVET EDIYORUZ.

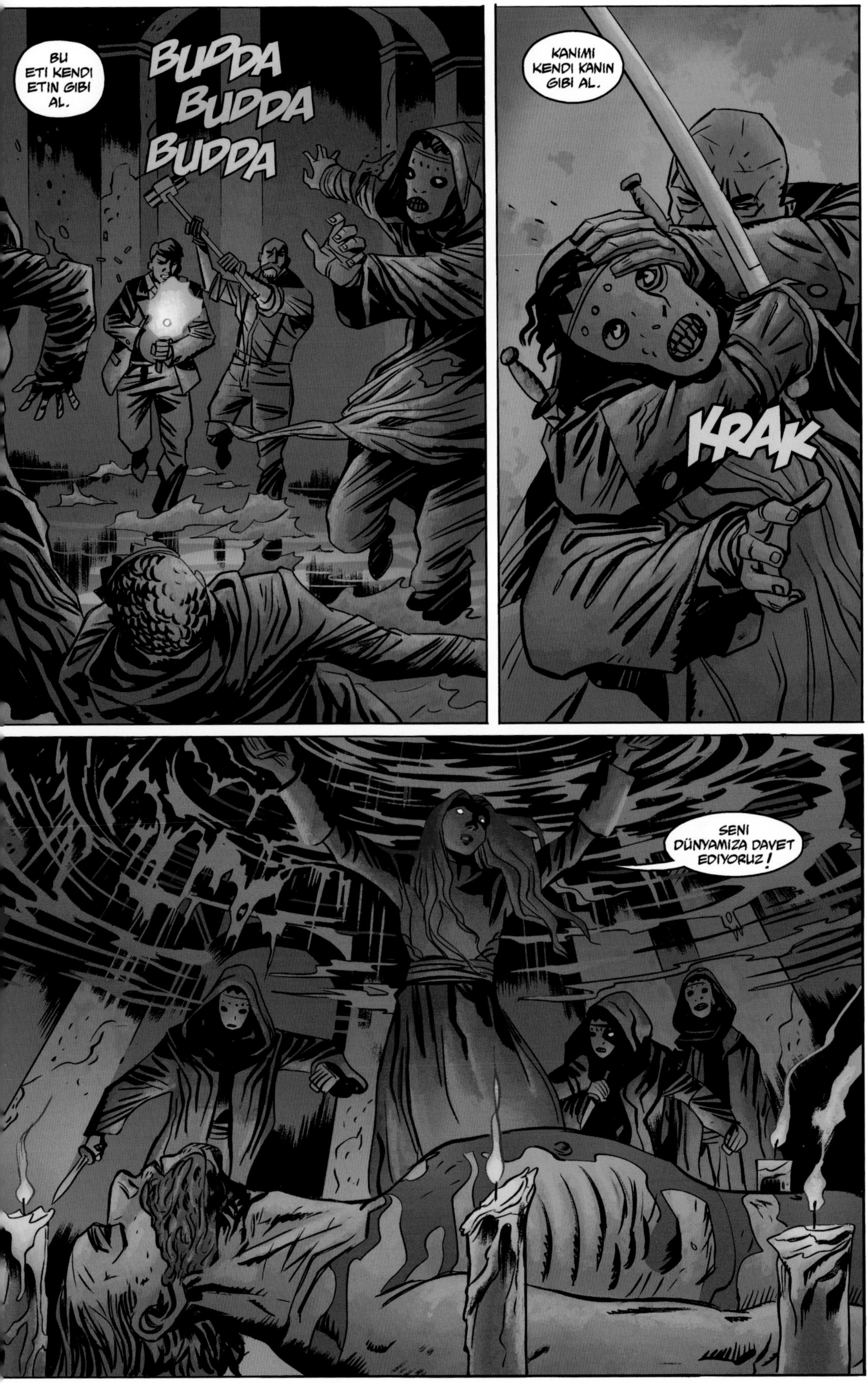
BU ETI KENDI ETIN GIBI AL.
BUDDA BUDDA BUDDA
KANIMI KENDI KANIN GIBI AL.
KRAK
SENI DÜNYAMIZA DAVET EDIYORUZ!

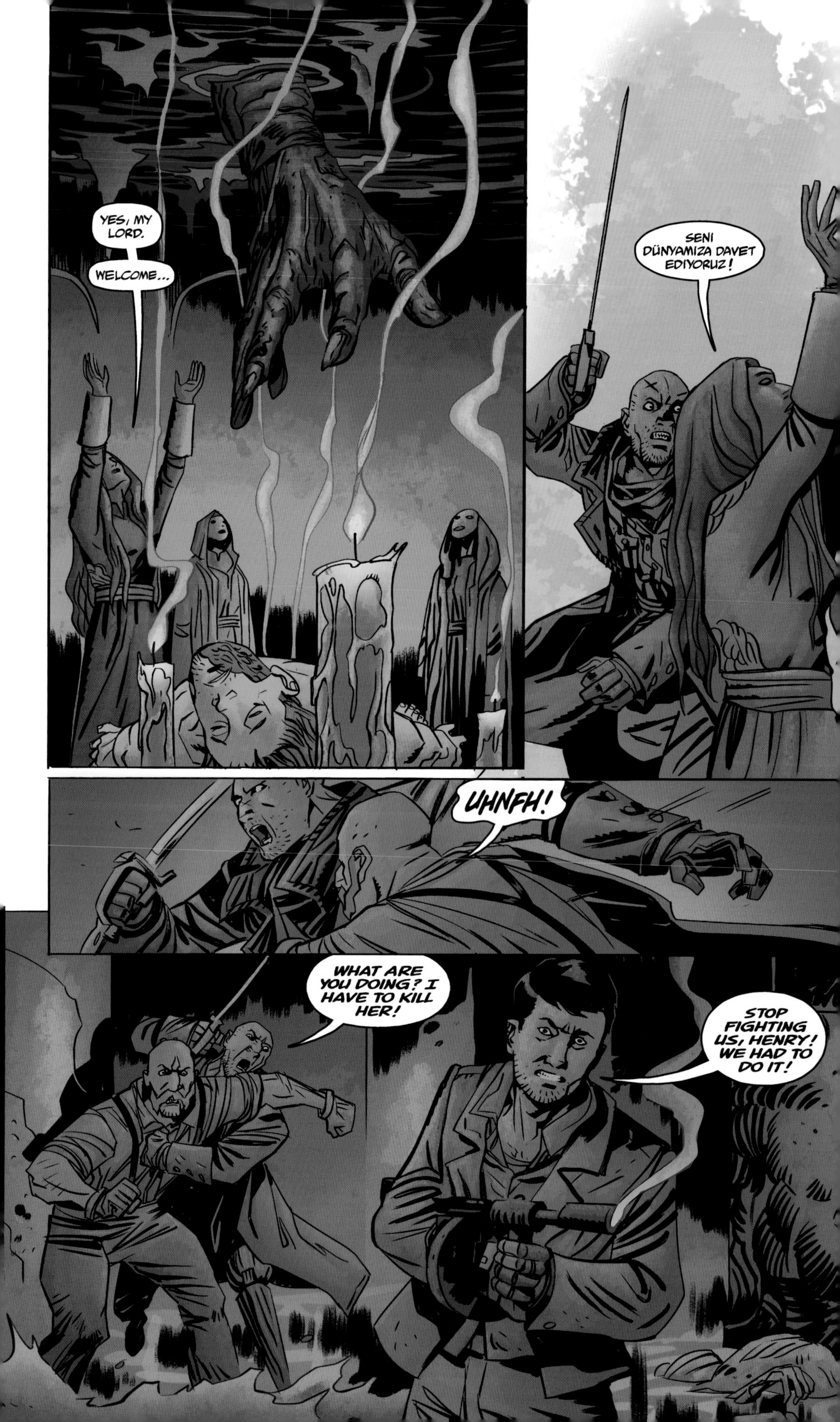
YES, MY LORD.
WELCOME...
SENI DÜNYAMIZA DAVET EDIYORUZ!
UHNFH!
WHAT ARE YOU DOING? I HAVE TO KILL HER!
STOP FIGHTING US, HENRY! WE HAD TO DO IT!

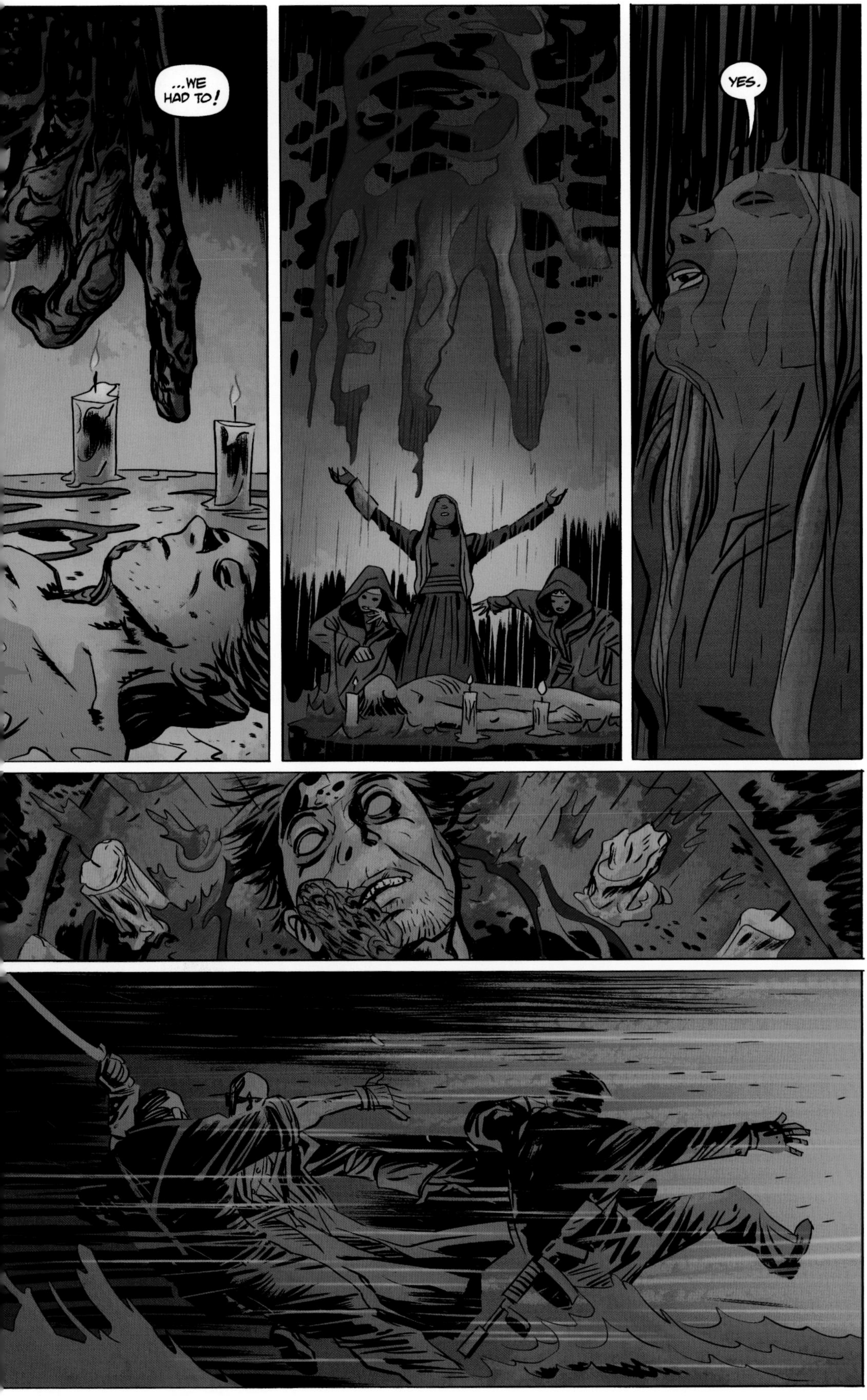
...WE HAD TO!
YES.

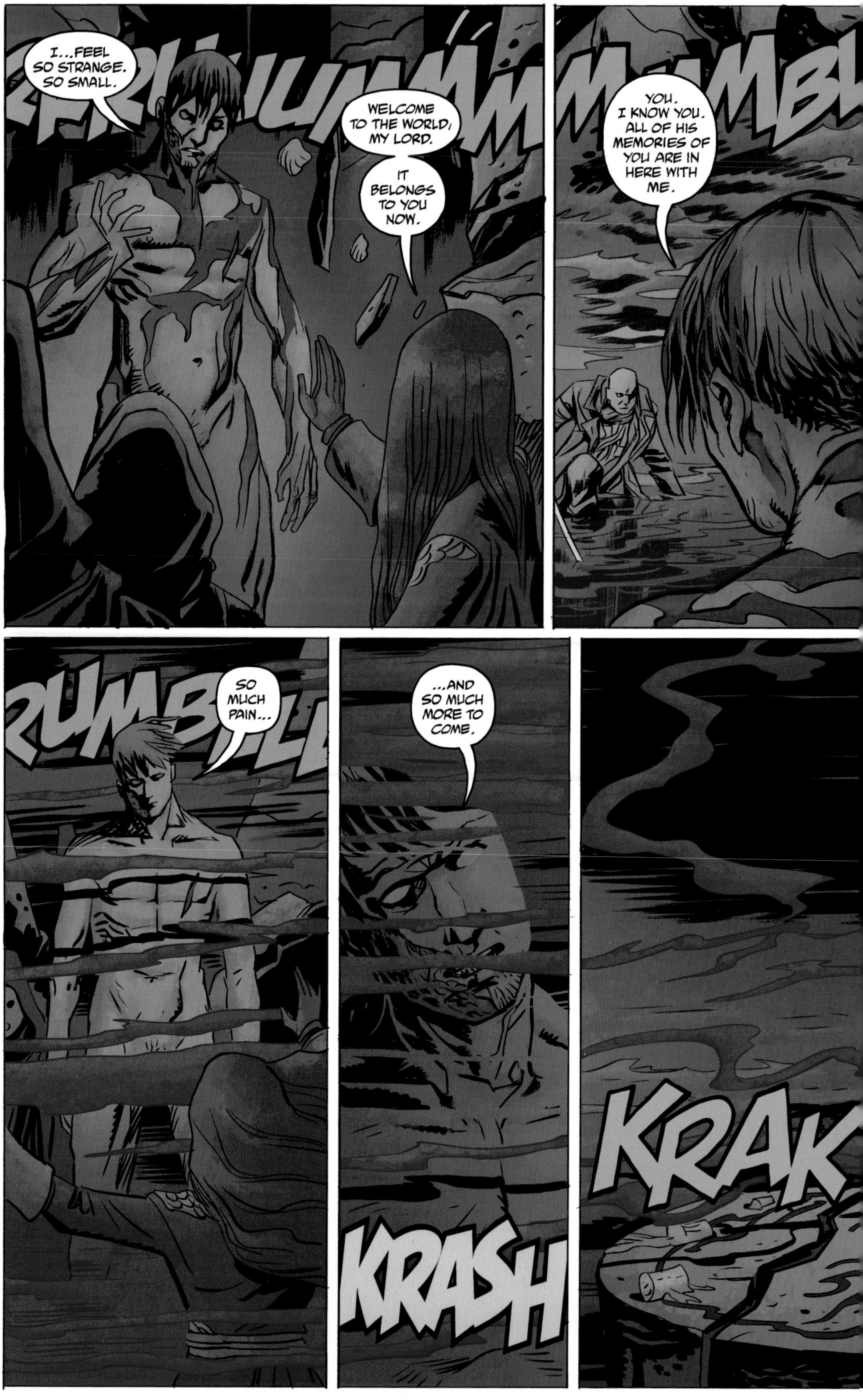
I...FEEL SO STRANGE. SO SMALL.
WELCOME TO THE WORLD, MY LORD.
IT BELONGS TO YOU NOW.
YOU. I KNOW YOU. ALL OF HIS MEMORIES OF YOU ARE IN HERE WITH ME.
SO MUCH PAIN...
...AND SO MUCH MORE TO COME.
KRASH
KRAK

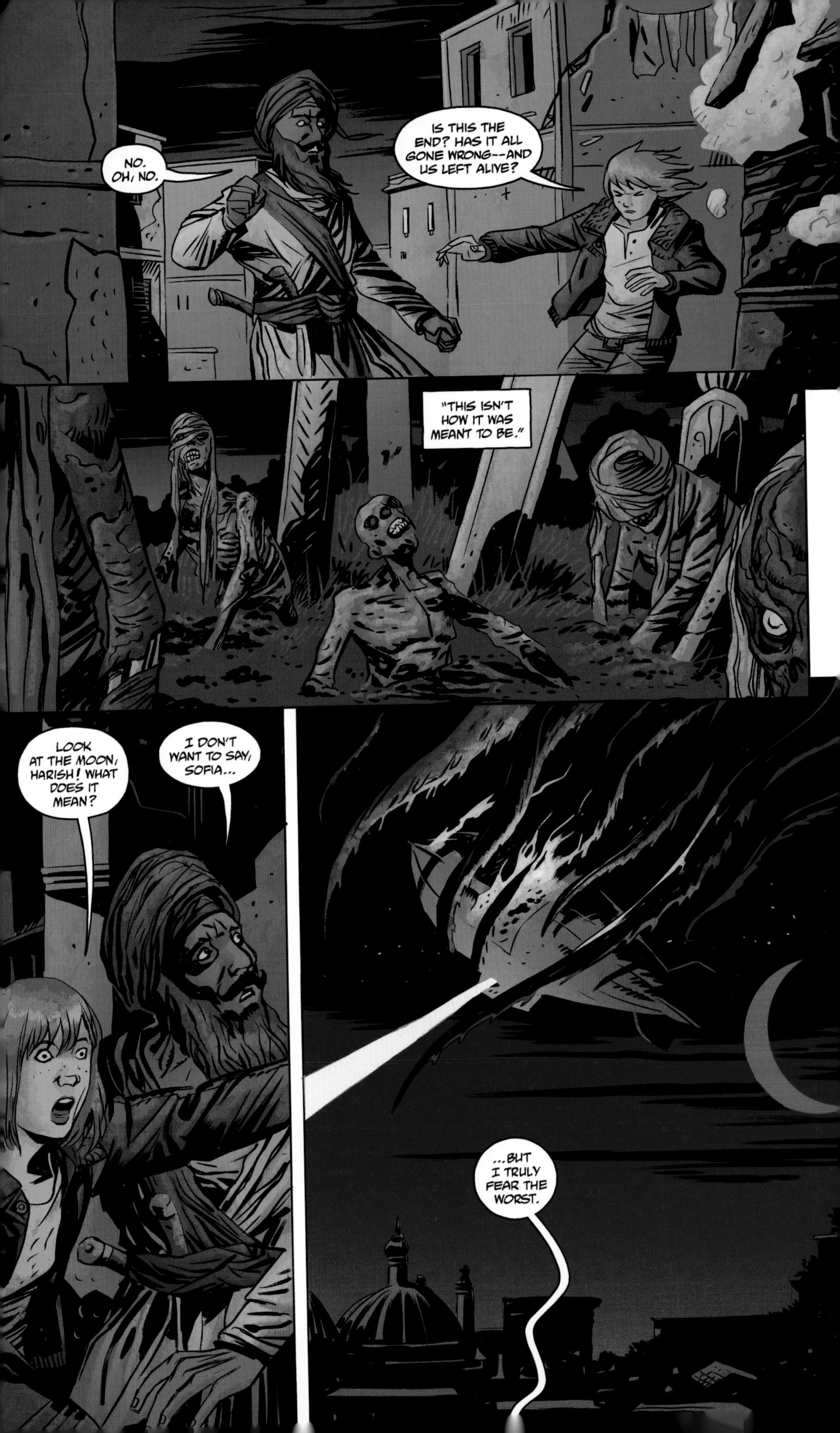
NO. OH, NO.
IS THIS THE END? HAS IT ALL GONE WRONG--AND US LEFT ALIVE?
"THIS ISN'T HOW IT WAS MEANT TO BE."
LOOK AT THE MOON, HARISH! WHAT DOES IT MEAN?
I DON'T WANT TO SAY, SOFIA...
...BUT I TRULY FEAR THE WORST.

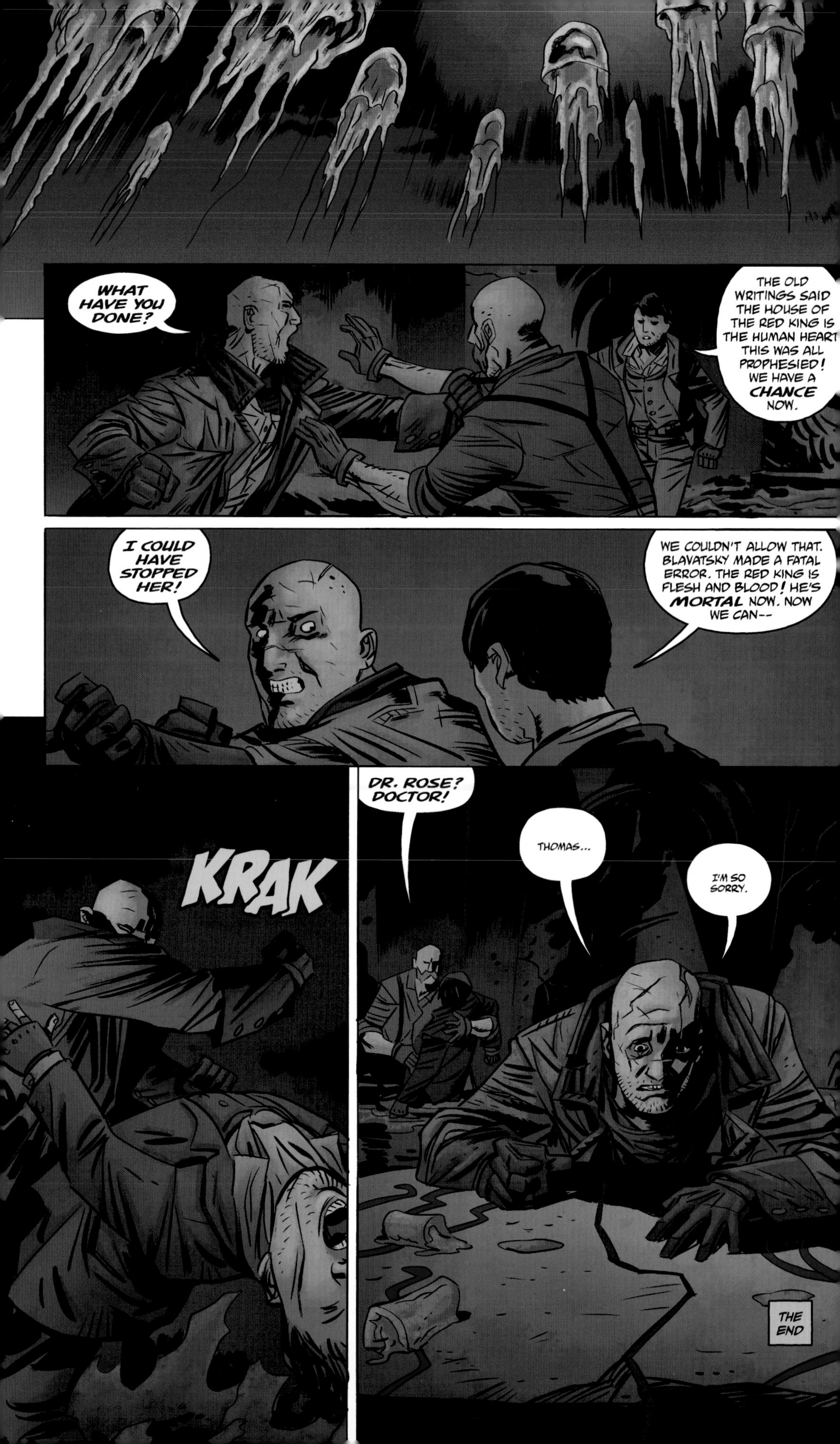
WHAT HAVE YOU DONE?
THE OLD WRITINGS SAID THE HOUSE OF THE RED KING IS THE HUMAN HEART THIS WAS ALL PROPHESIED! WE HAVE A CHANCE NOW.
I COULD HAVE STOPPED HER!
WE COULDN'T ALLOW THAT. BLAVATSKY MADE A FATAL ERROR. THE RED KING IS FLESH AND BLOOD! HE'S MORTAL NOW. NOW WE CAN--
KRAK
DR. ROSE? DOCTOR!
THOMAS...
I'M SO SORRY.
THE END

BALTIMORE™
EMPTY GRAVES

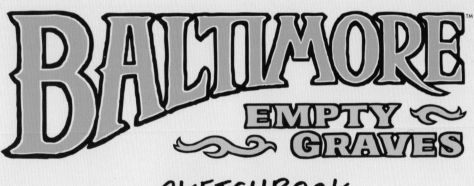

SKETCHBOOK

Notes by Peter Bergting and Ben Stenbeck

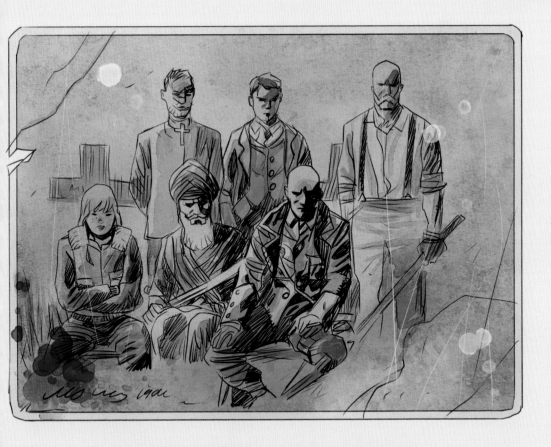

Peter Bergting: I thought it'd be a nice touch to have one of those classic group photos of our heroes, reminiscent of WWI soldiers gathered before that one final fight.

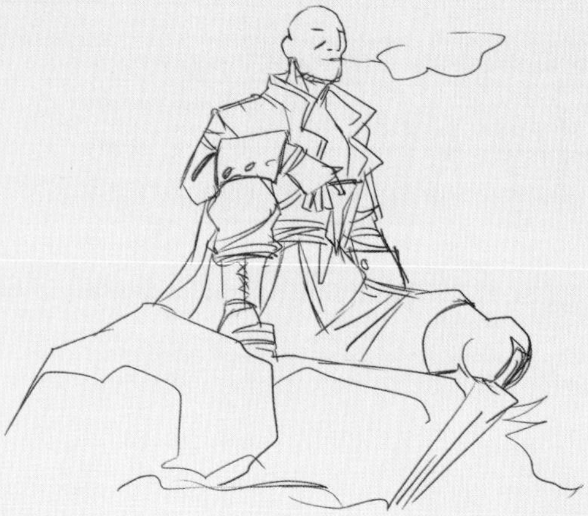

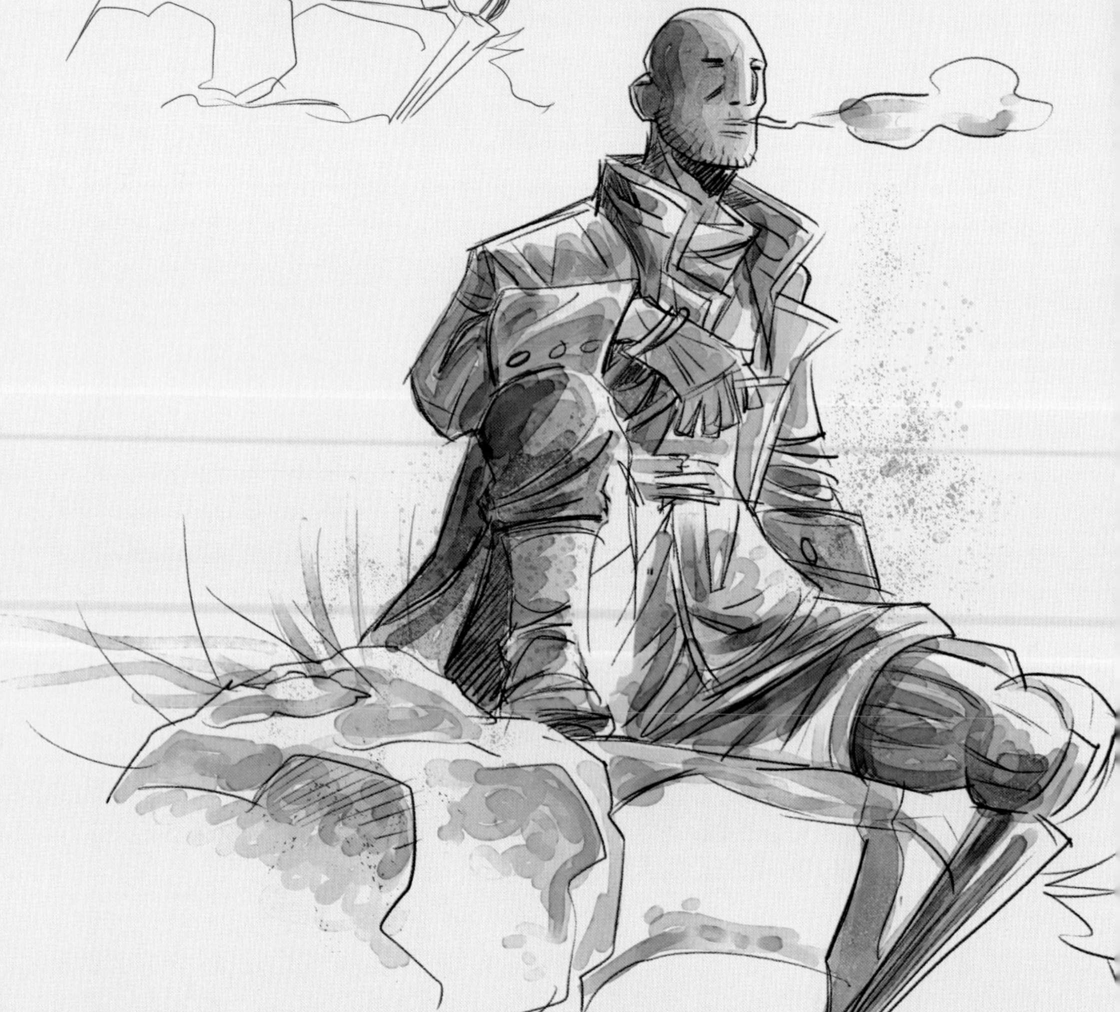

One of my favorite scenes from the book was Baltimore, just sitting there, looking out over the sea.

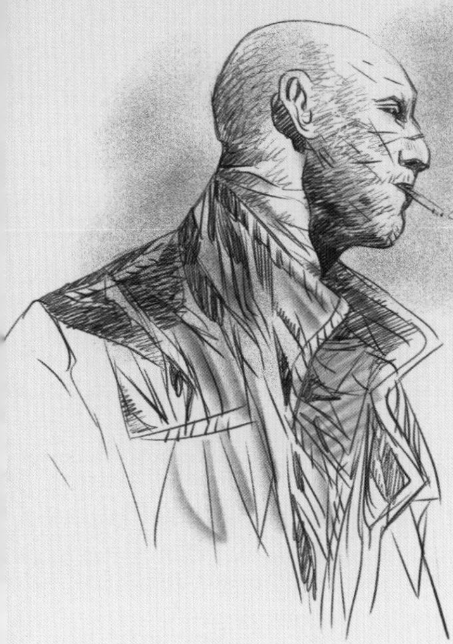

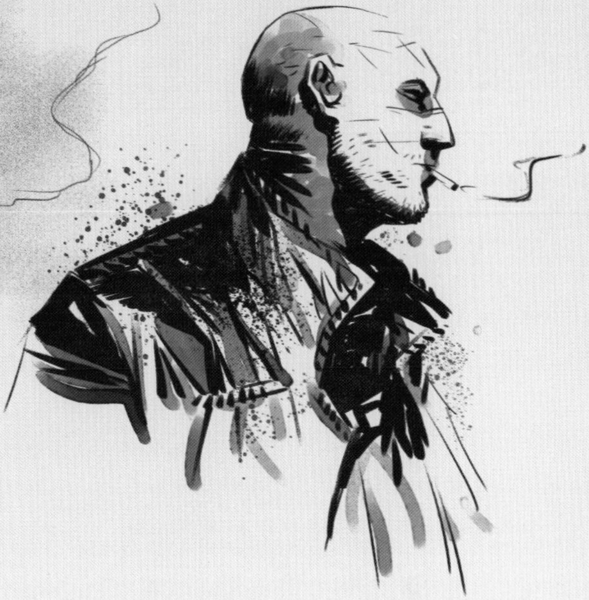

I have a neighbor that looks uncannily like Lord Henry. In fact they could probably be twins, and I can't stop thinking how awesome he'd look in a trench coat and wooden leg.

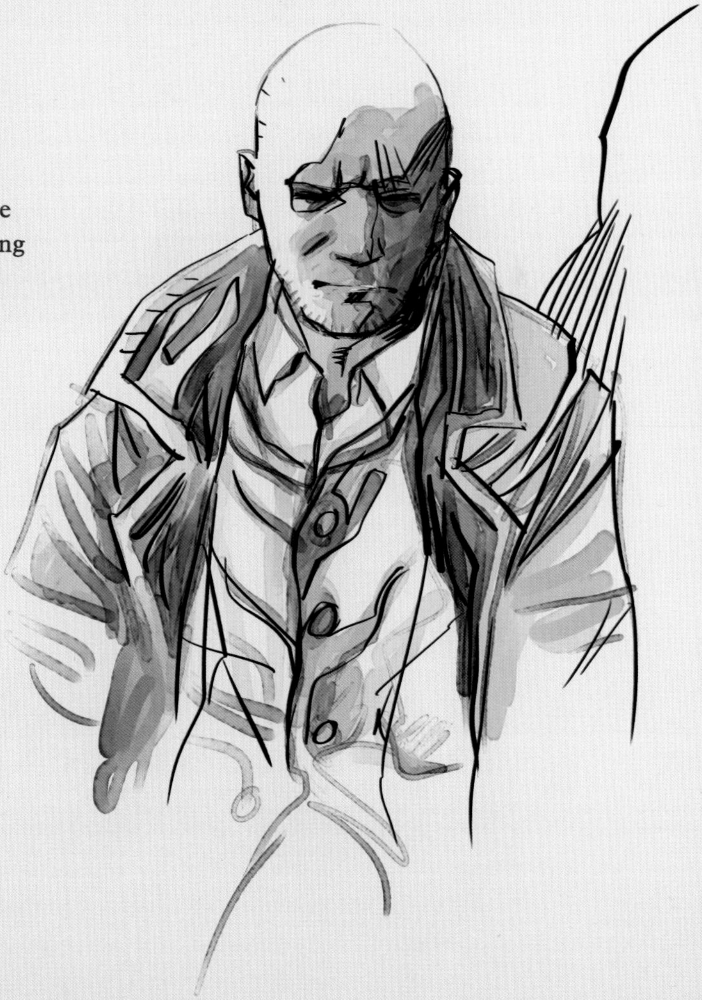

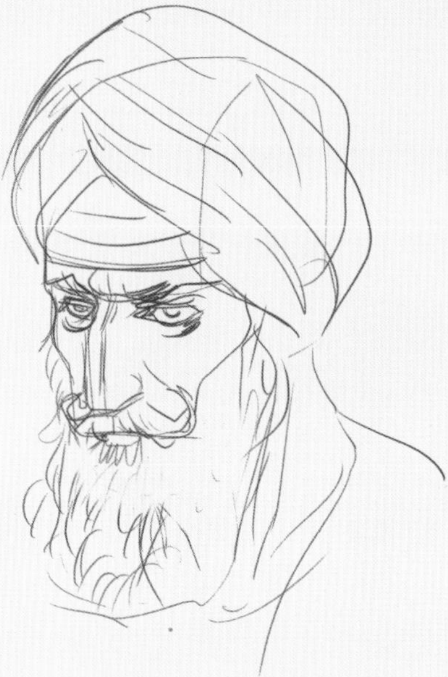

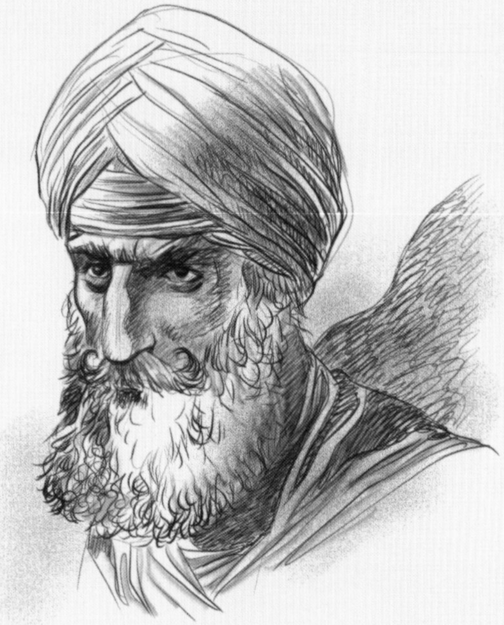

Harish is one of my favorite characters ever. I love how composed he is, never faltering. I don't like drawing his beard though. Any beard, really. And there are so many beards in this book.

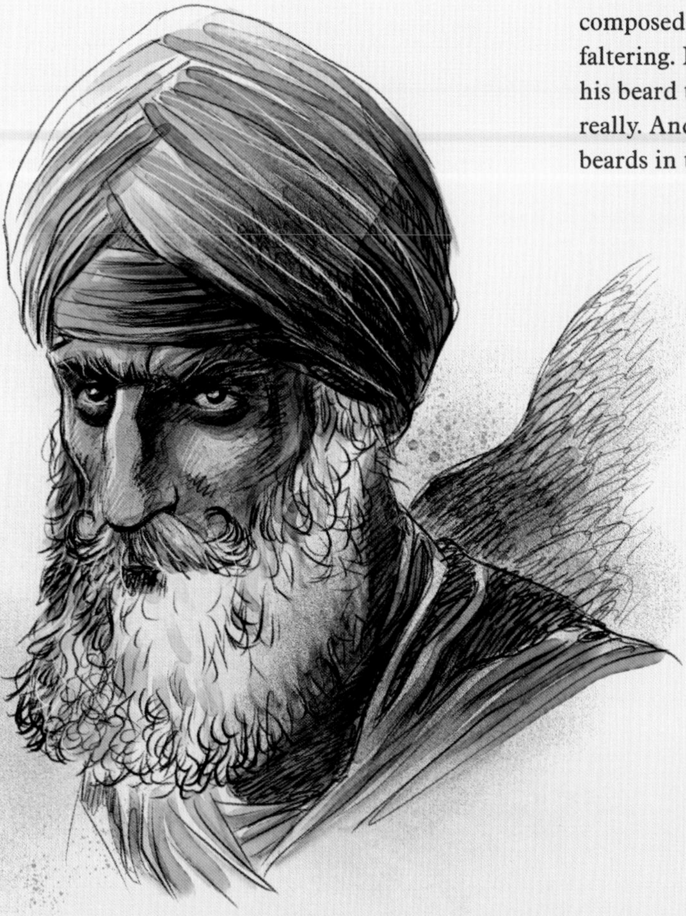

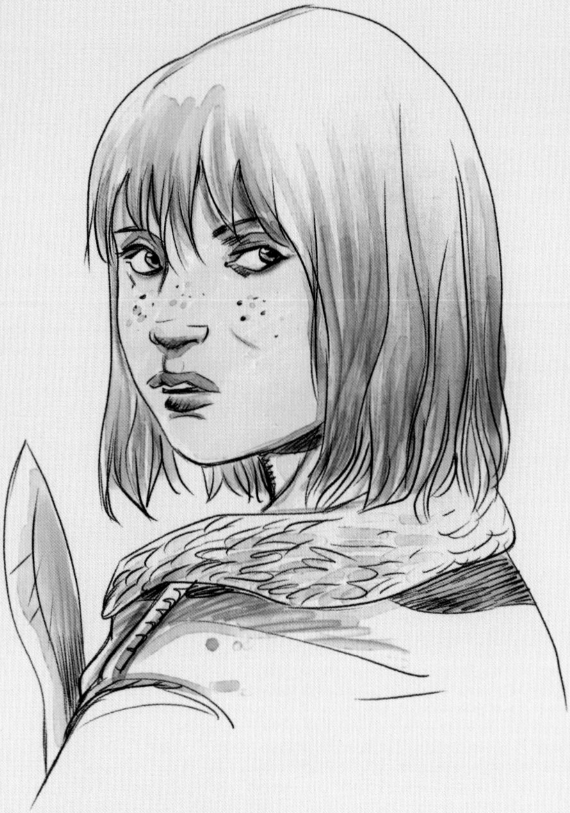

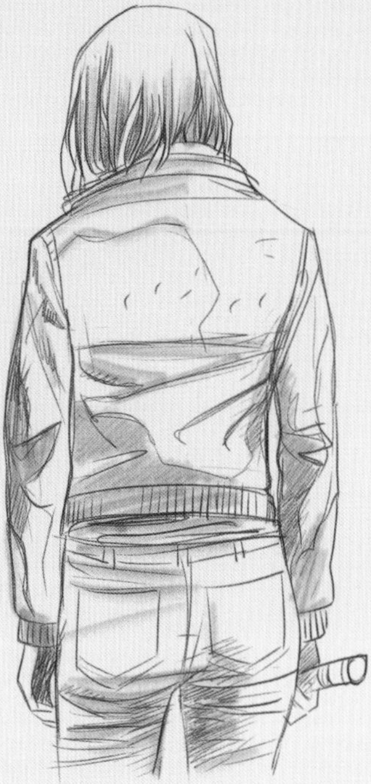

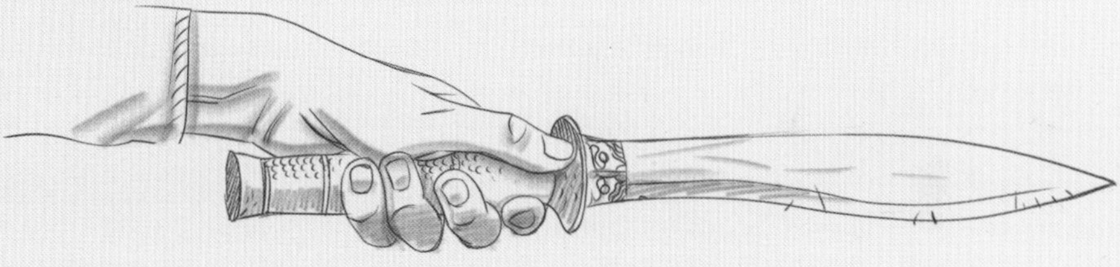

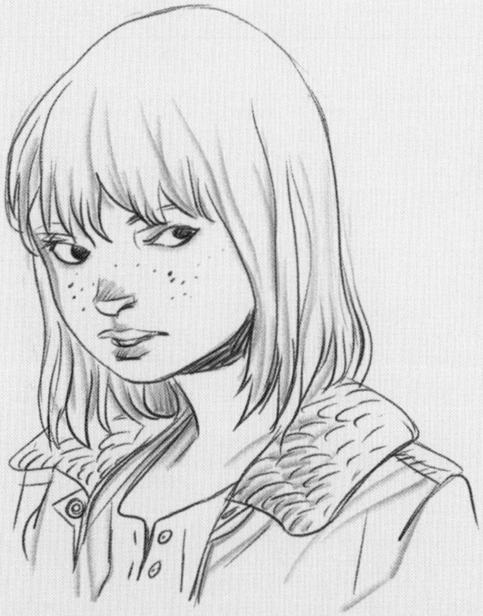

Sofia has gone through a couple of stages in the series. In the beginning I didn't really know where she'd end up, or even if she'd be a recurring character. She's just getting tougher and tougher. If Mike and Chris kill her in the next series, I will be very unhappy!

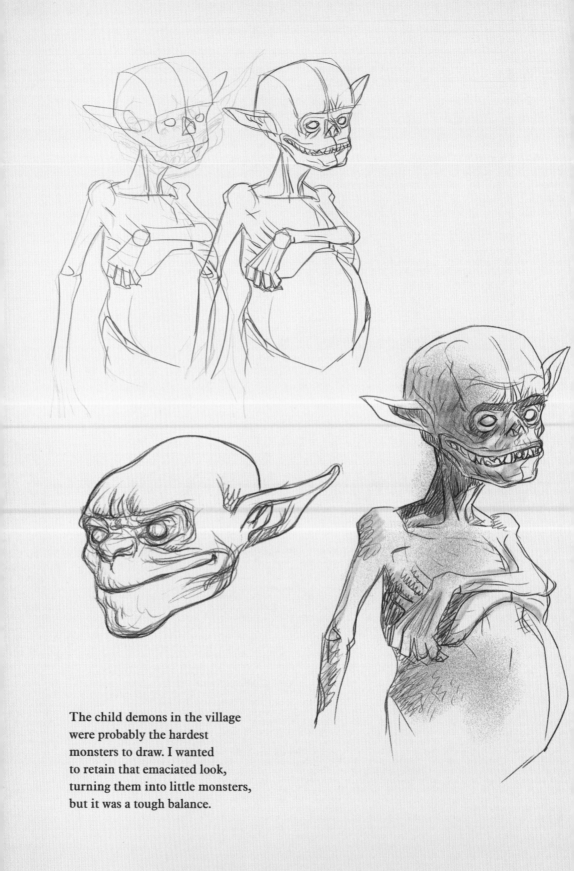

The child demons in the village
were probably the hardest
monsters to draw. I wanted
to retain that emaciated look,
turning them into little monsters,
but it was a tough balance.

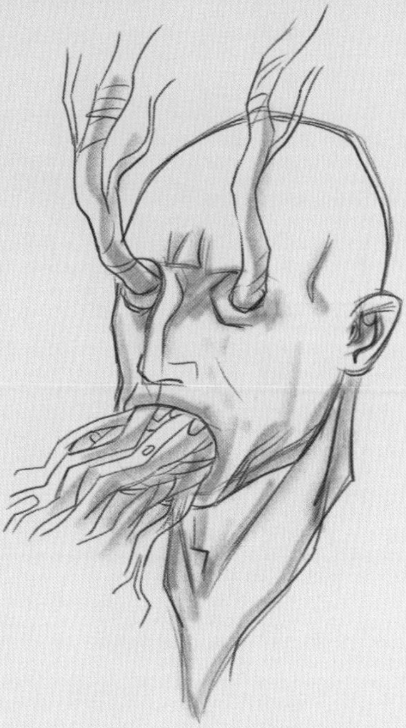

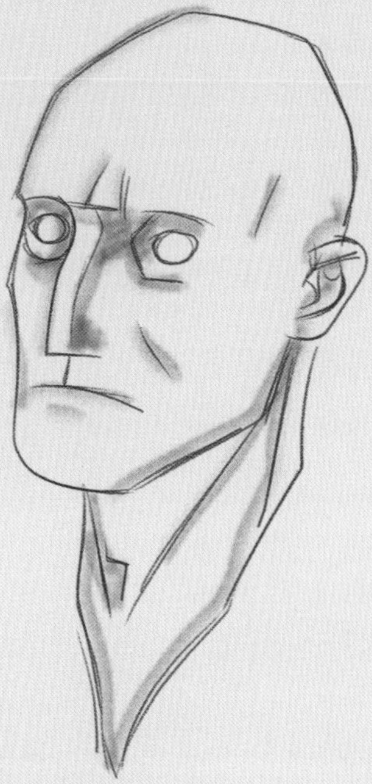

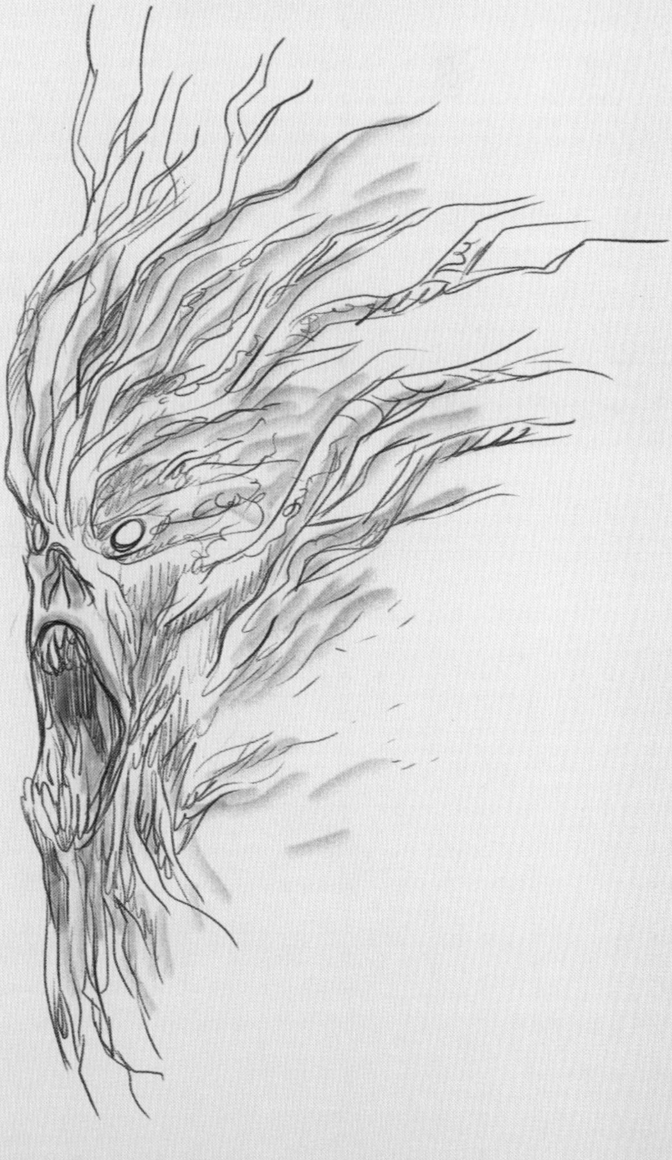

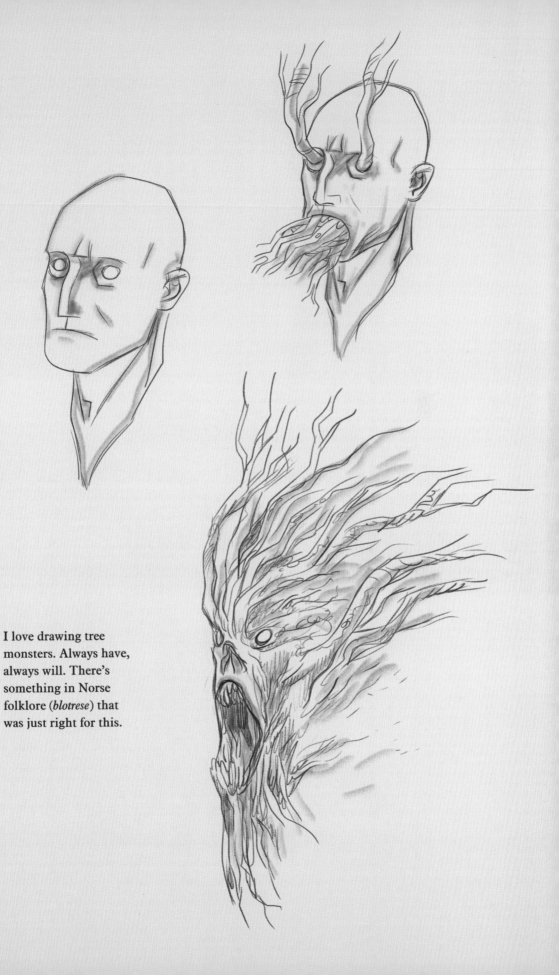

I love drawing tree monsters. Always have, always will. There's something in Norse folklore (*blotrese*) that was just right for this.

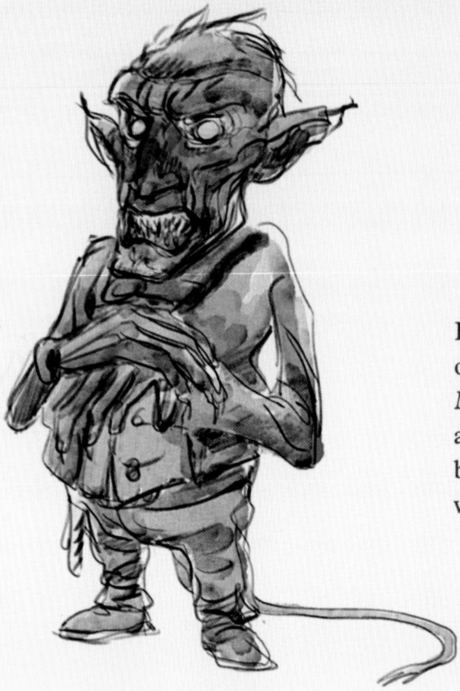

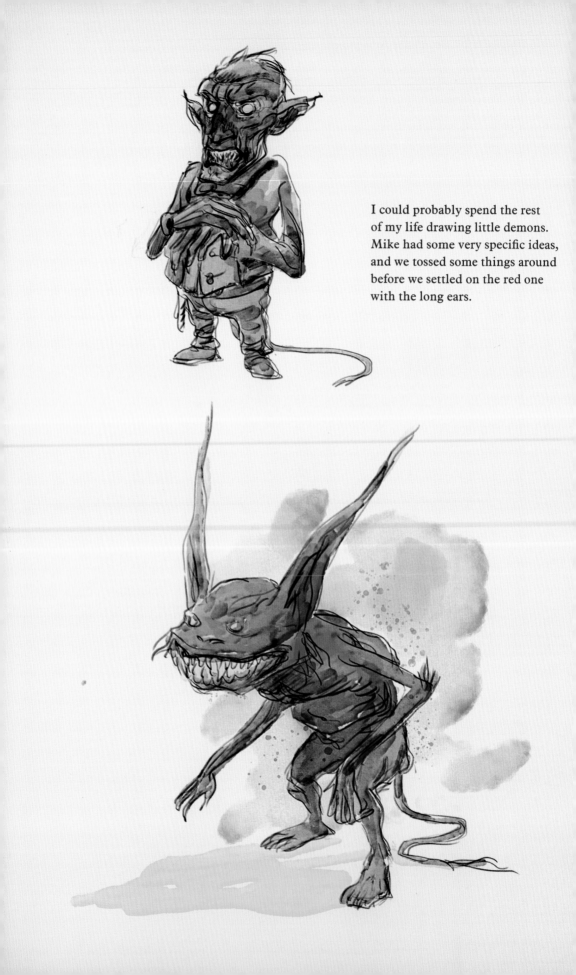

I could probably spend the rest of my life drawing little demons. Mike had some very specific ideas, and we tossed some things around before we settled on the red one with the long ears.

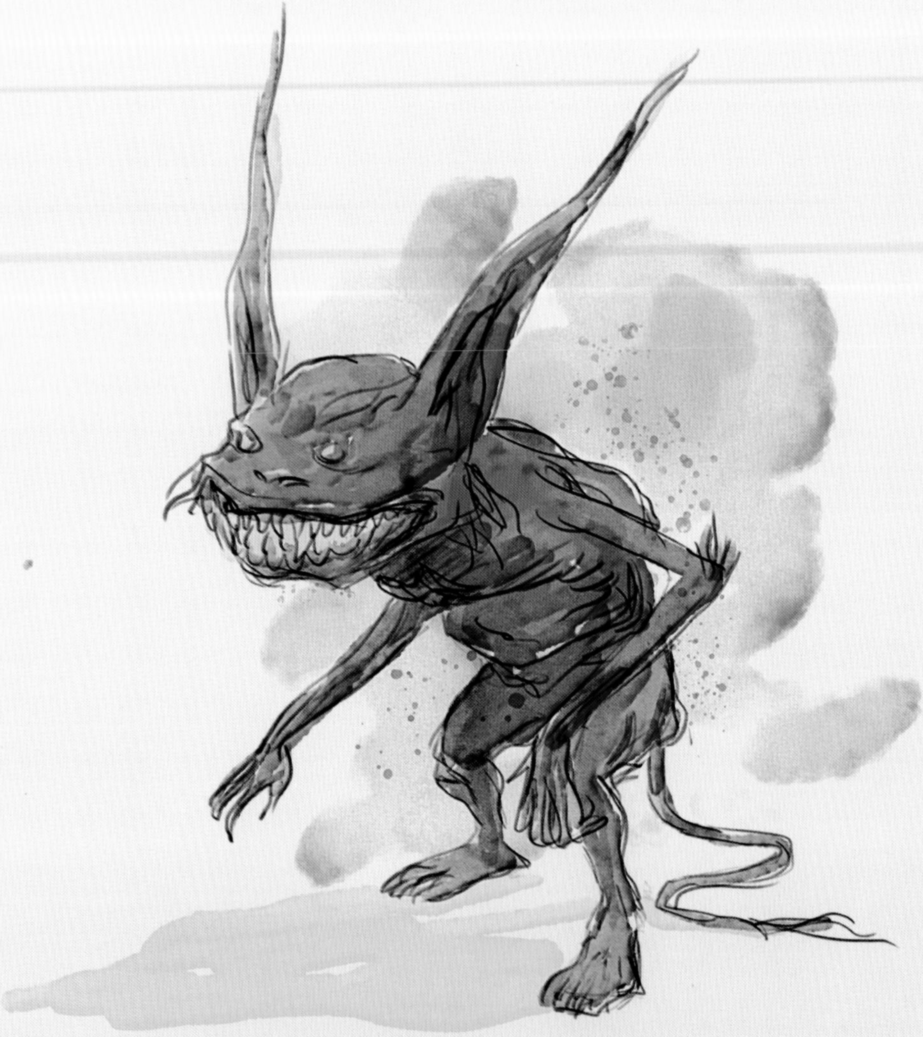

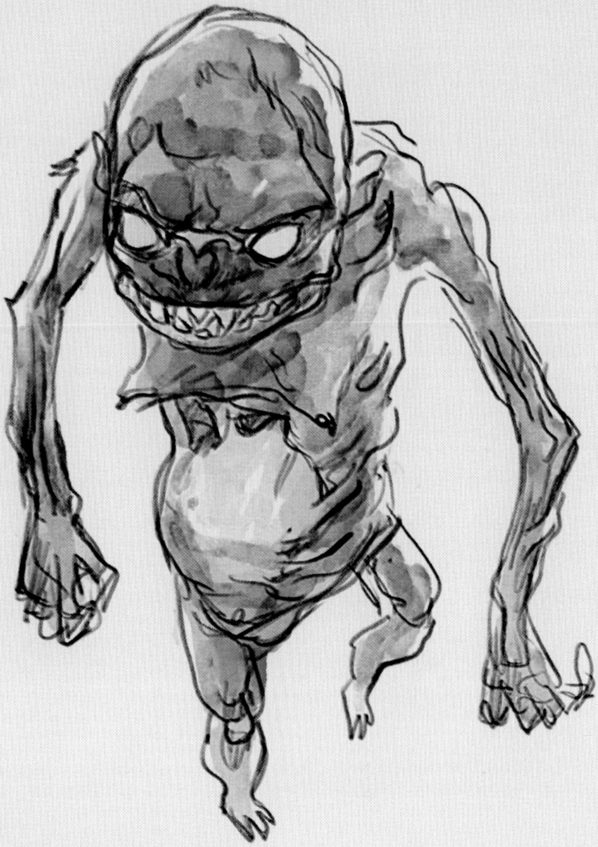

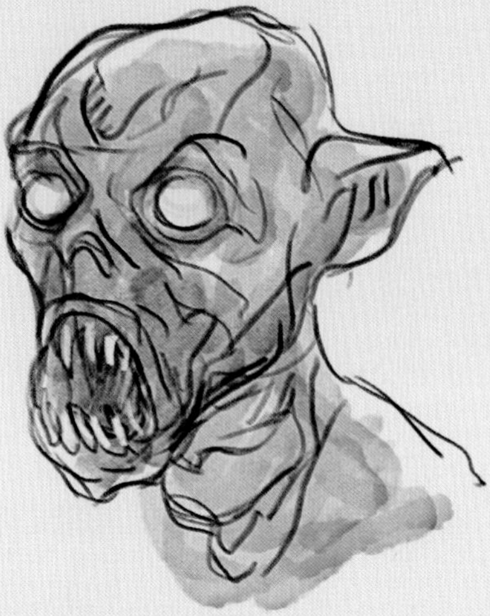

I did love this little guy in the oversized cloak with that weird mouth, though. Hope I can draw him in some other book one day.

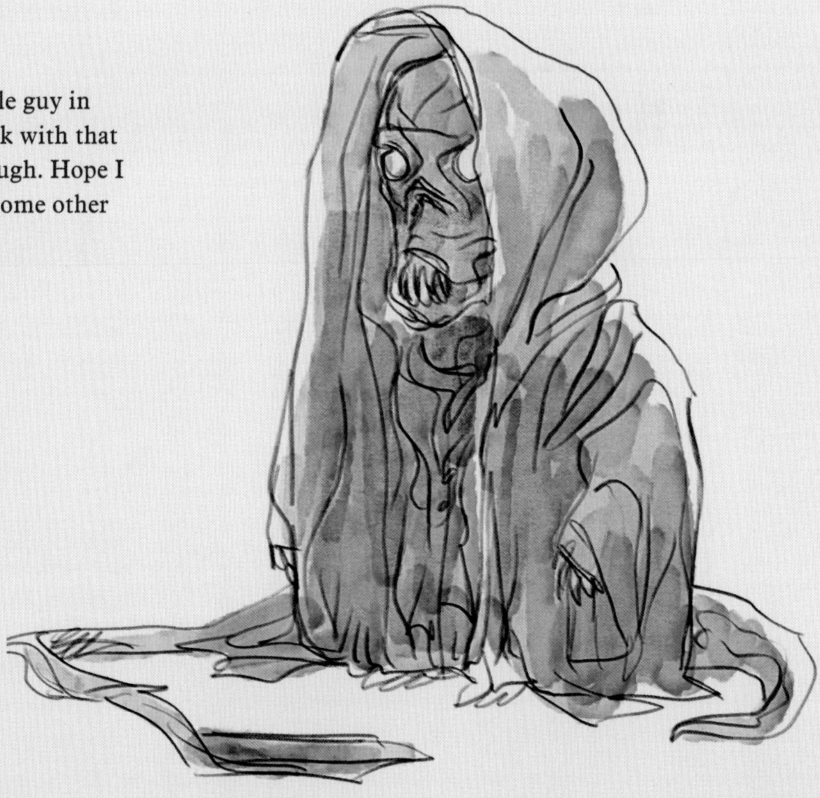

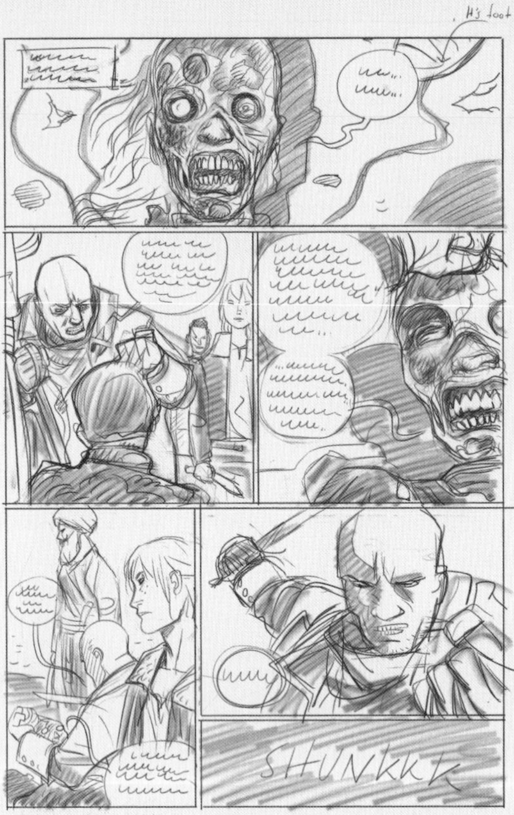
H's foot
SHUNKKK

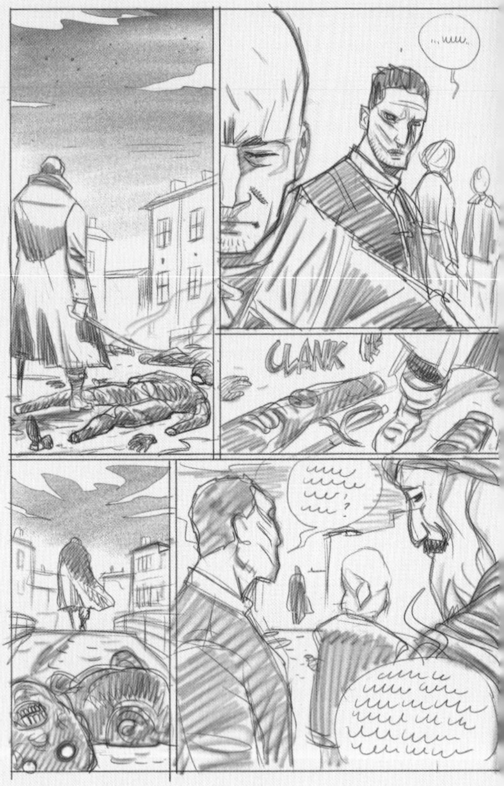
CLANK

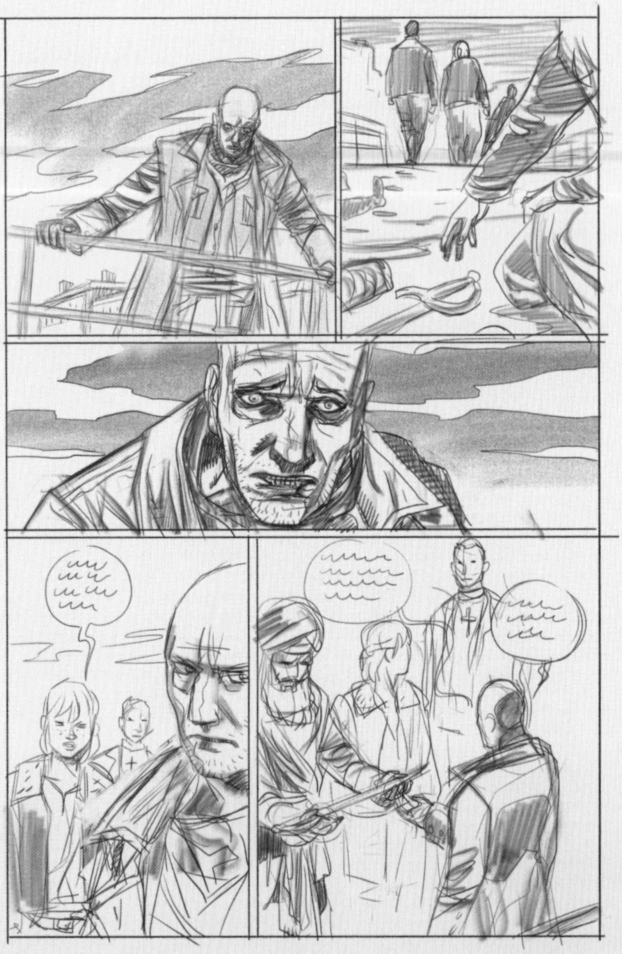

This was a fantastic scene to draw. So much emotion, but with most of it conveyed without words, I had to focus all that turmoil in Henry's face. I do have trouble providing clear penciled pages, even more than making thumbnails and layouts, since I know I will redraw the same details ten to twenty times while inking to get it right. If I had to pencil for someone else to ink my pencils, I would probably go mad. But this was one instance where I was actually pretty happy with the pencils.

I remember Scott commenting on Harish giving Baltimore the sword in the last panel, and Lord Henry reaching for the blade and not the grip.

had a bit of a problem drawing hese pages. Not so much rith the characters, but with he goblin. I did numerous evisions trying to make it look cary, but that grin just made it ook cheesy. And it was such a antastic idea in the script, like his big tick, perched on her ack sucking the life and sanity ut of poor Mr. Kidd's wife. 'he coloring really brought this ome, though.

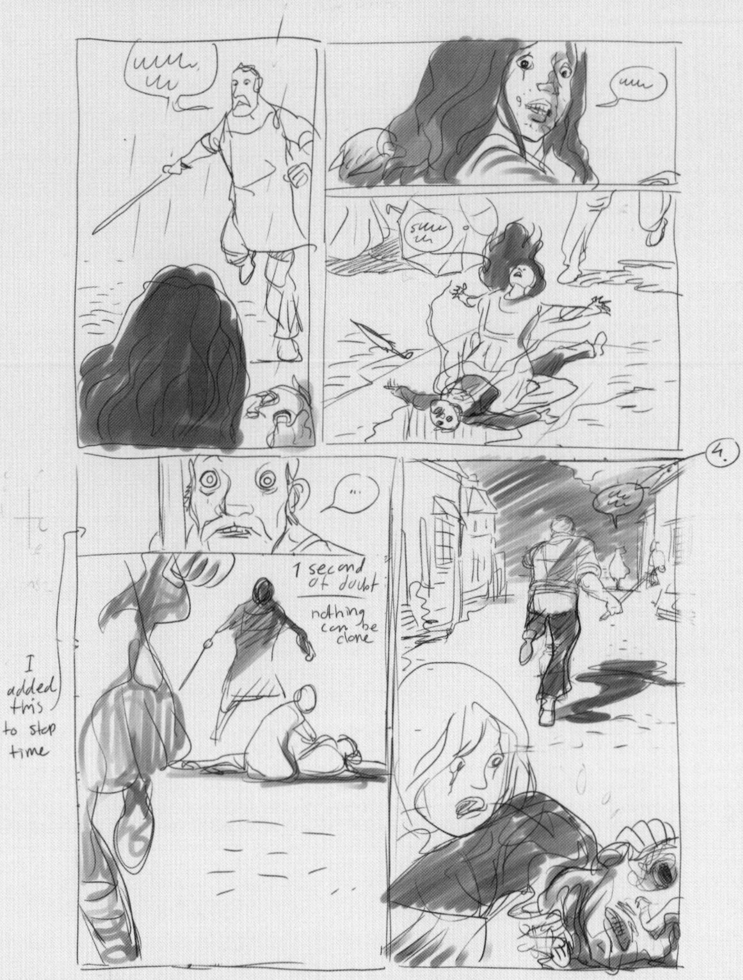
4.
1 second of doubt
nothing can be done
I added this to stop time

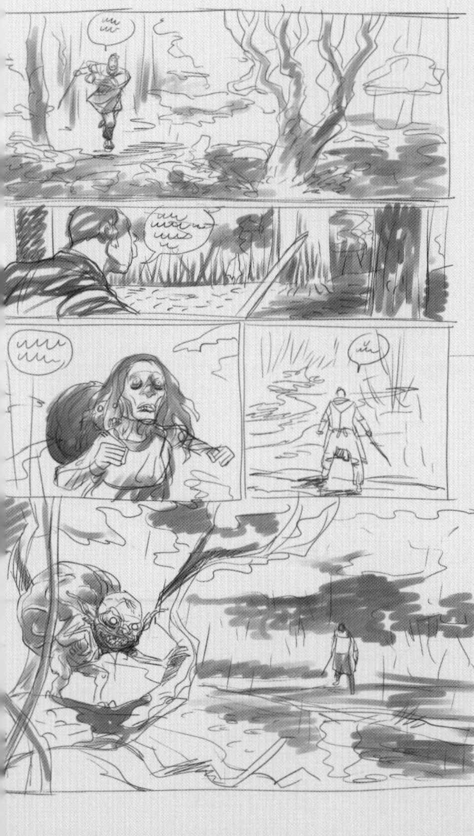

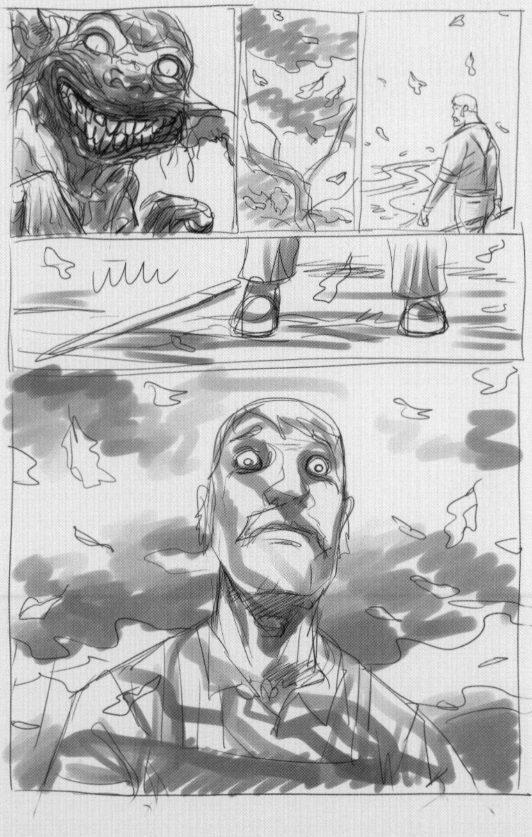

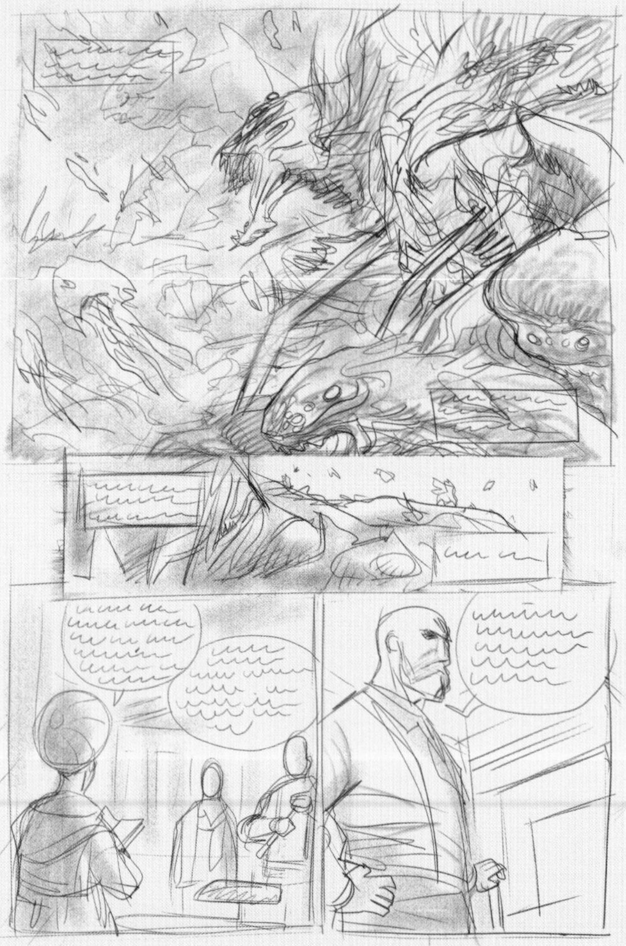

If there's a chance to draw big crazy monsters, I'm all in. And I think we reached peak crazy with this page (so far, at least). The hardest part isn't coming up with the monsters; it's finding the balance with all that action going on in the panel. It's the same with the rest of the pages. The craziness has to be balanced with real emotions. Scott and the gang keep me focused on the stuff I miss, like switching angles to make the action easier to read.

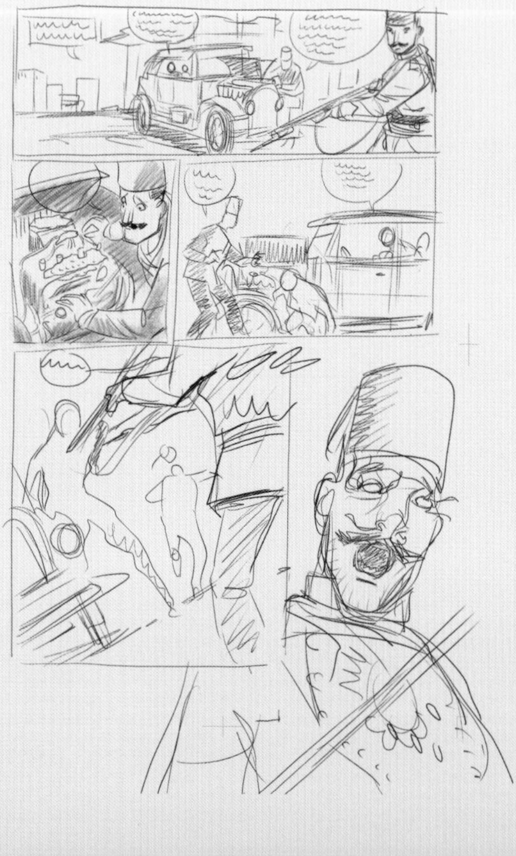

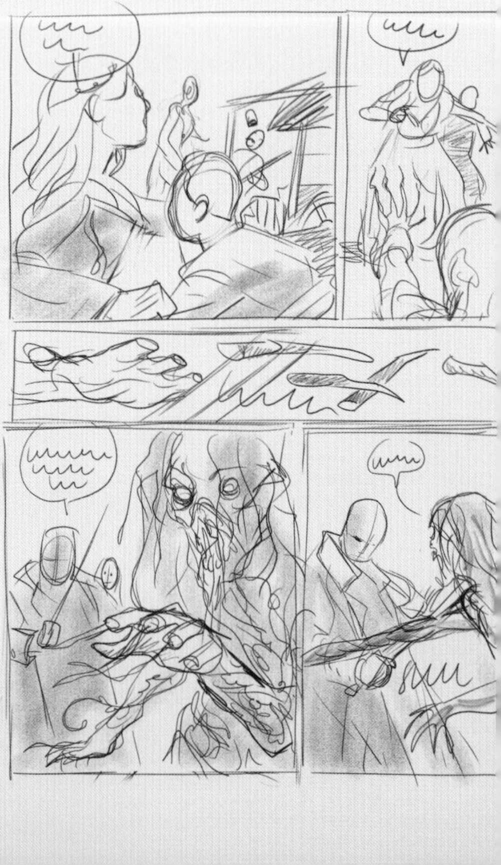

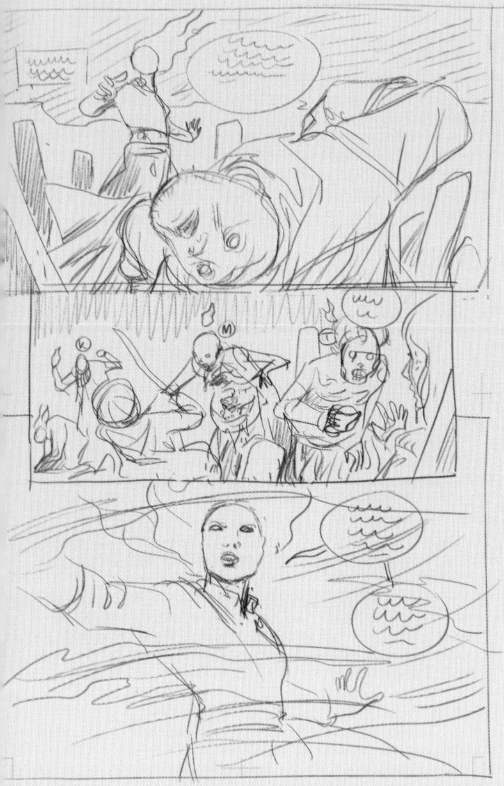

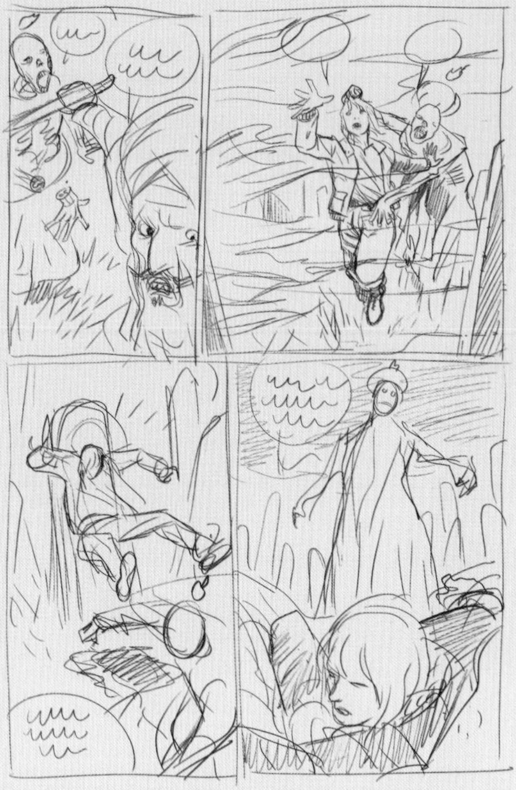

The cemetery scene was a blast to draw. The very specific design of the stones and the temple lent itself naturally to the Mignolaverse. I know I'm all over the map when inking, but I try to keep the style consistent unless the action takes me in a different direction. The only thing I really try to stay clear of is veering too close to Mike's style, and I kept redrawing to avoid that.

If there's one thing that bugged me, it's that the Sultans kept going through bodies as they were mowed down, and I had to make sure that they were at least somewhat recognizable as three specific individuals throughout the scenes.

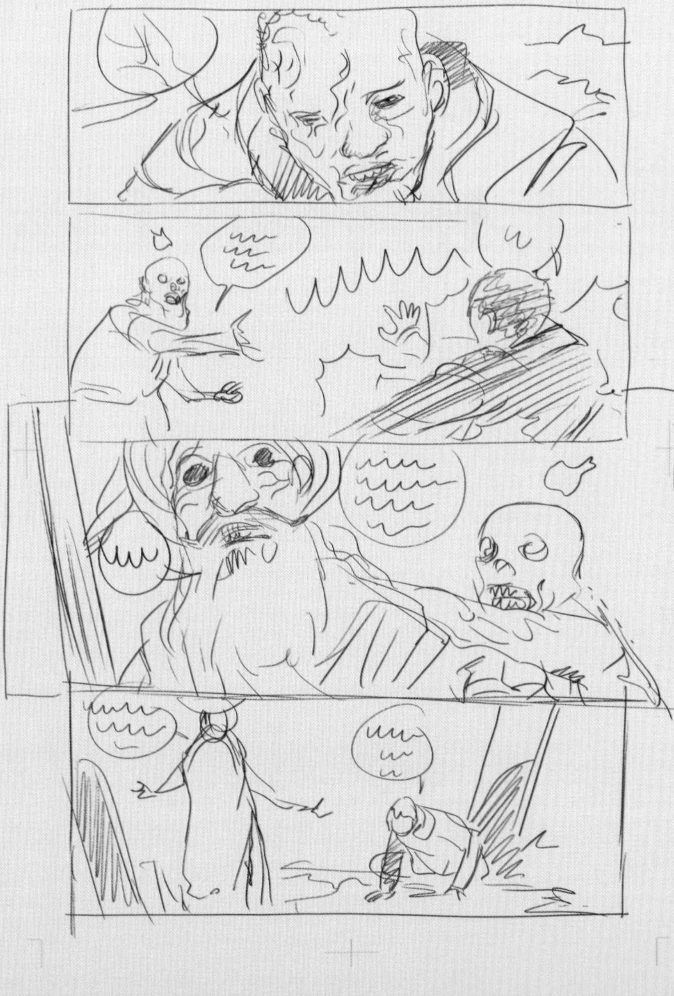

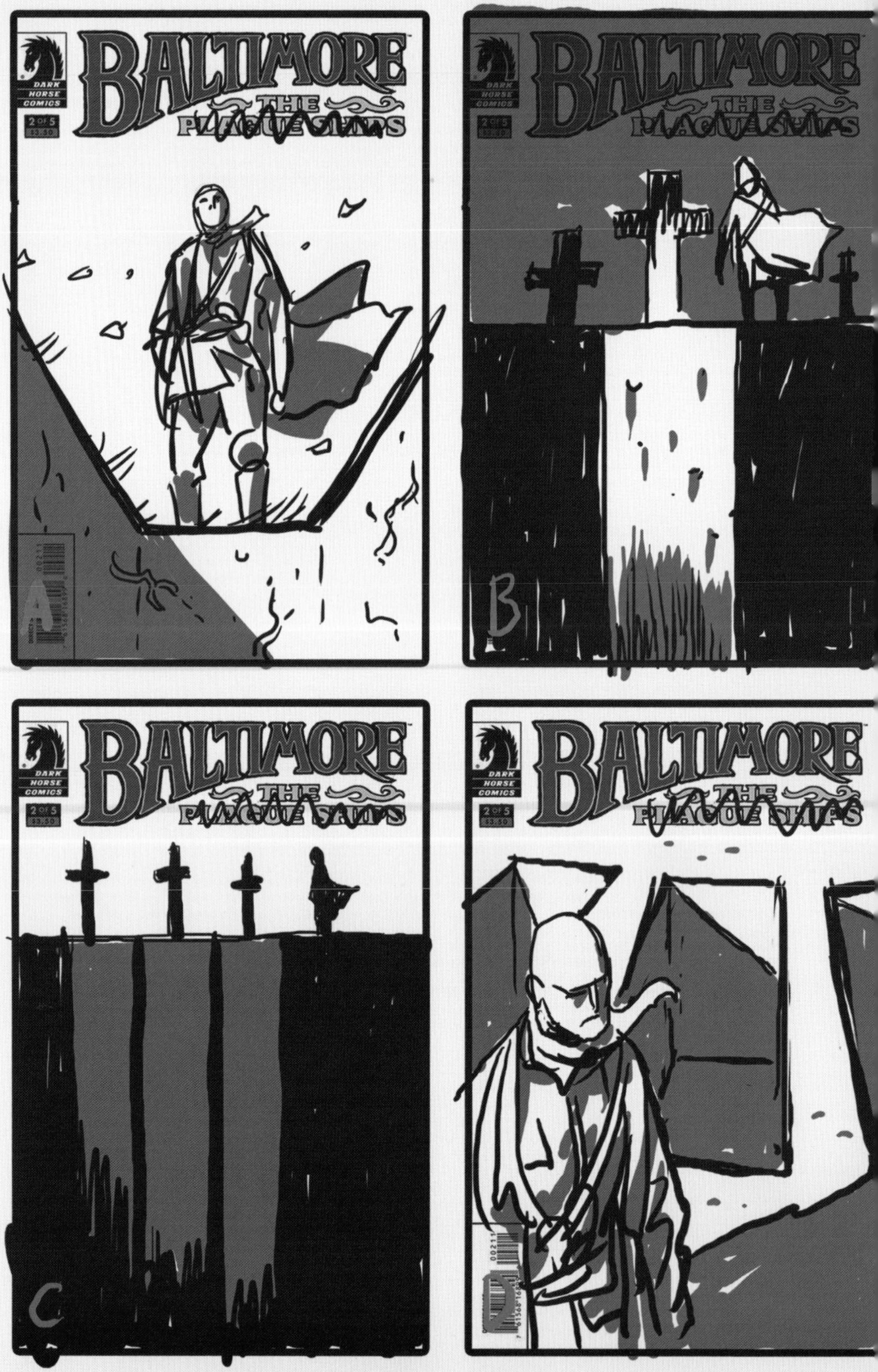
DARK HORSE COMICS
BALTIMORE
THE
2 OF 5
A
DARK HORSE COMICS
BALTIMORE
THE
2 OF 5
B
DARK HORSE COMICS
BALTIMORE
THE
2 OF 5
C
DARK HORSE COMICS
BALTIMORE
THE
2 OF 5
D

Ben Stenbeck: Thumbnails for the issue one cover . . .

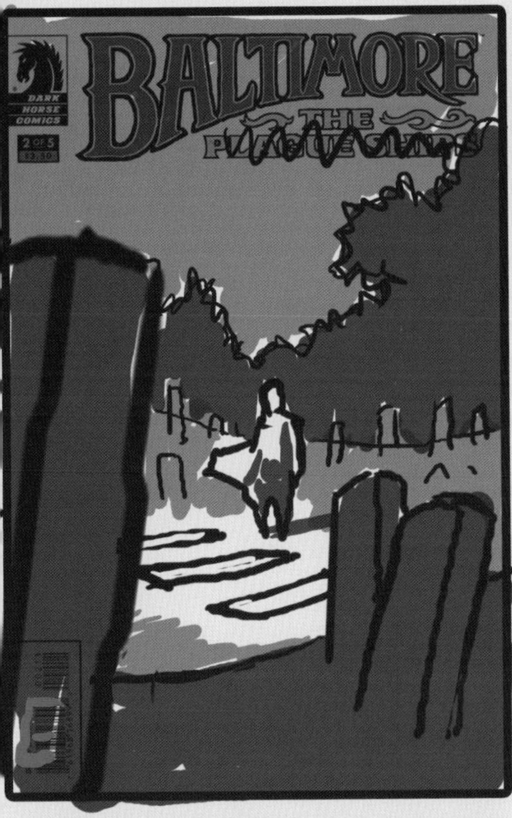
DARK HORSE COMICS
BALTIMORE
THE PLAGUE SHIPS
2 OF 5

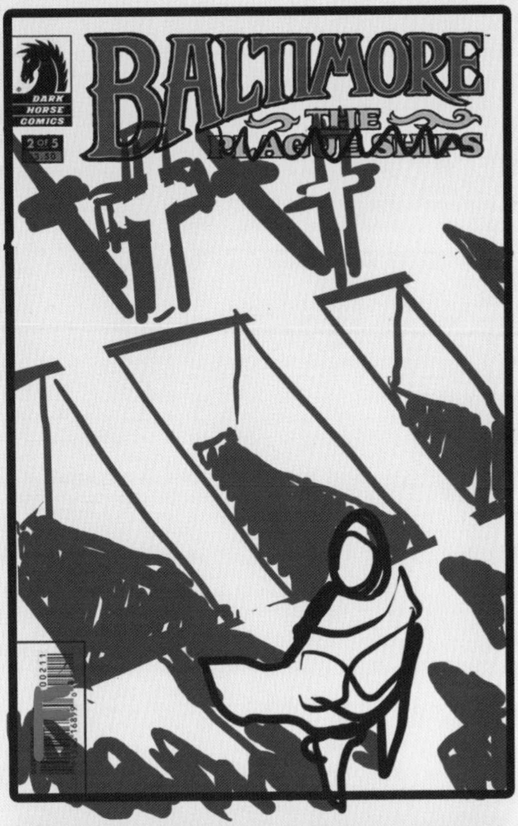
DARK HORSE COMICS
BALTIMORE
THE PLAGUE SHIPS
2 OF 5

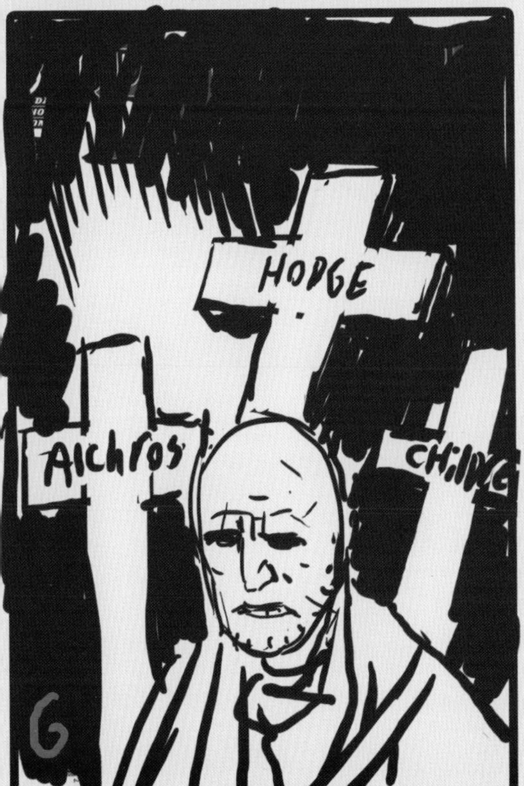
HODGE
Aichros
G

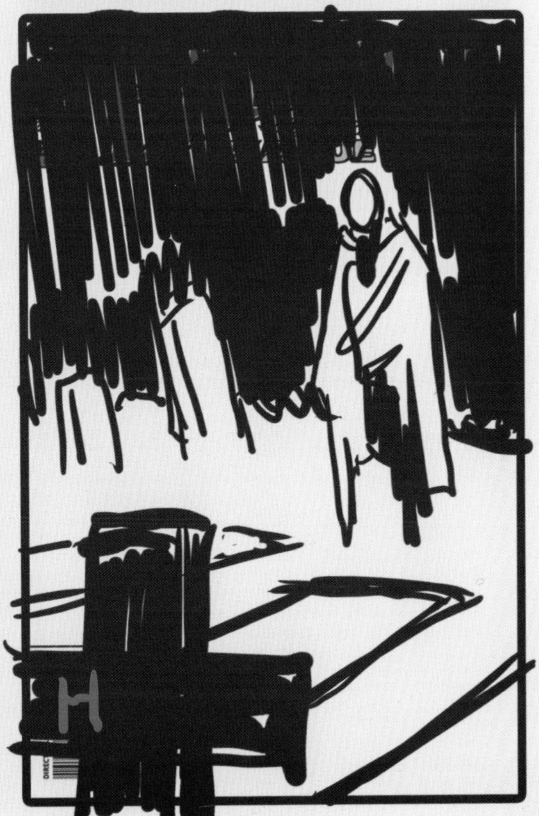
H

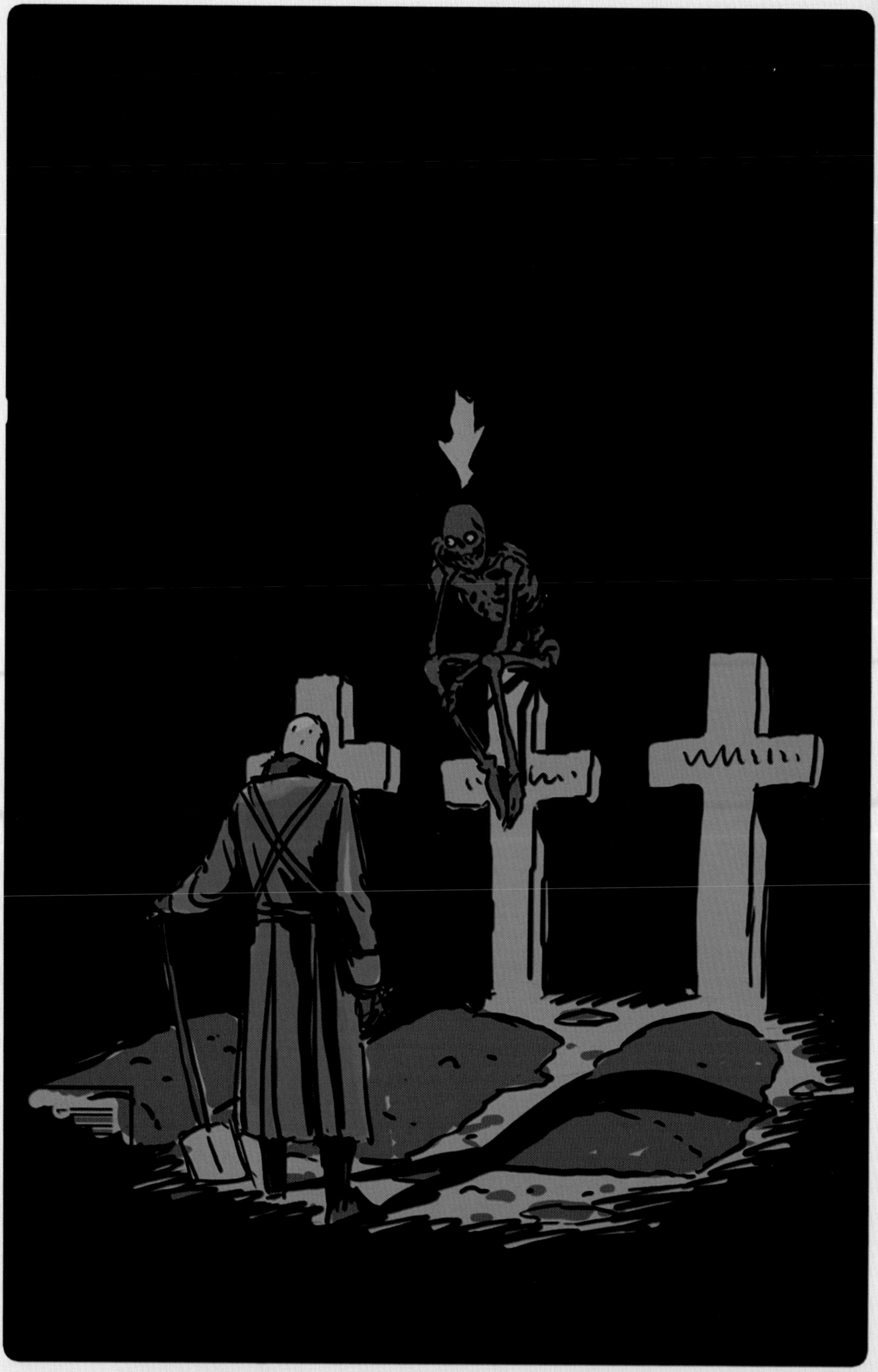

These aren't all the sketches I did for issue one, but it was taking a while, until I did *this* weird sketch. It just seemed strange enough to be interesting. Everyone agreed on it.

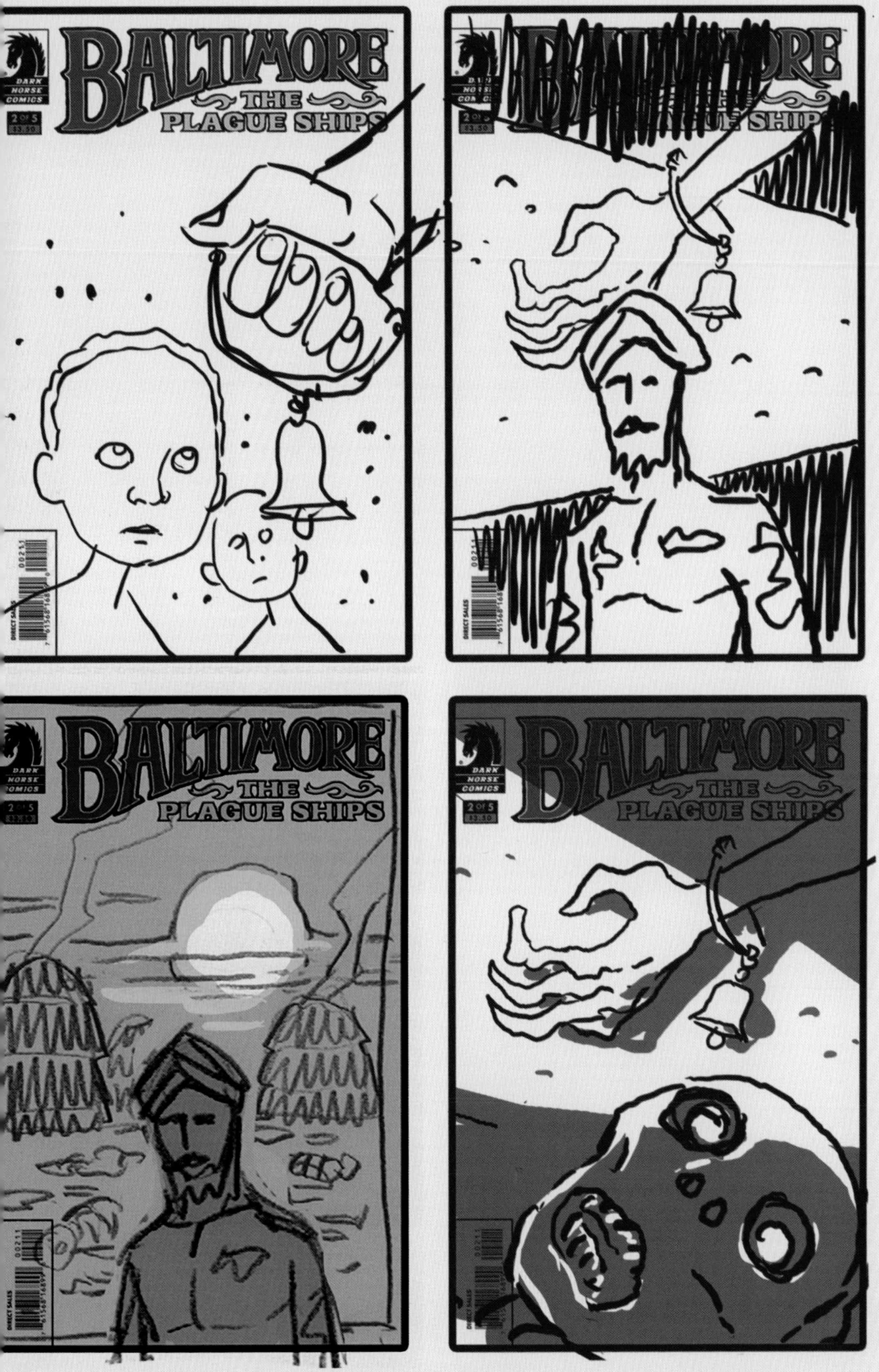
BALTIMORE
THE
PLAGUE SHIPS
DARK
HORSE
COMICS
2 OF 5
DIRECT SALES

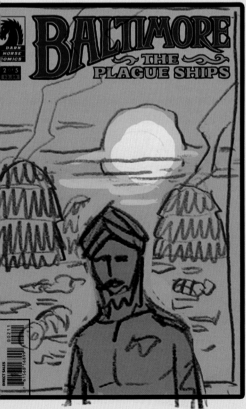

Thumbnails for issue two.

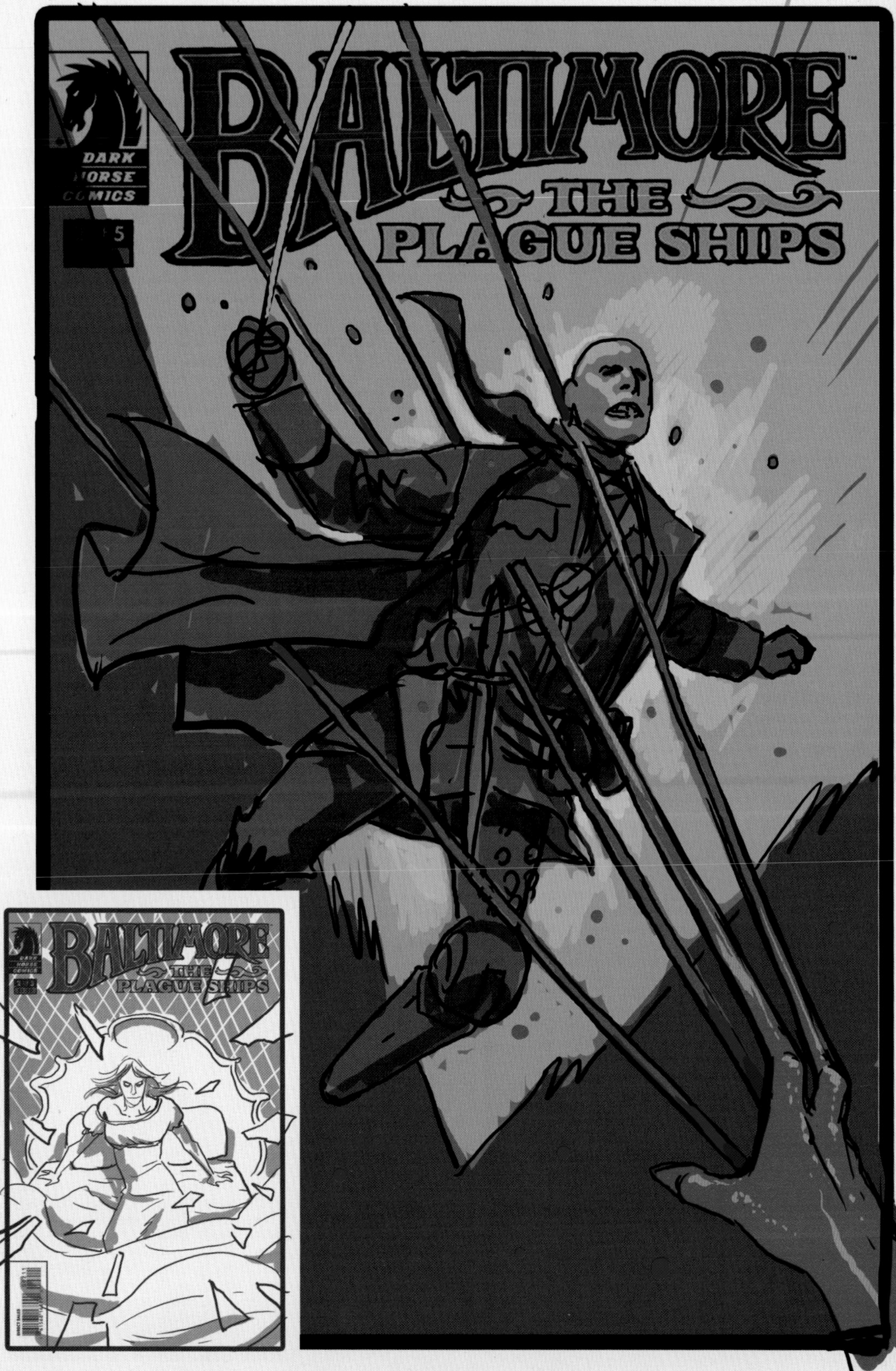
BALTIMORE
THE PLAGUE SHIPS
DARK HORSE COMICS
BALTIMORE
THE PLAGUE SHIPS

The green one was my initial idea for the issue four cover, but once I decided I wanted to do a "pincushion" Baltimore on the issue five cover, I thought something quieter would work better, and tried the shot of the witch on the bed. But then, because of the Blavatsky revelation in the issue, I made the issue four cover a bit of a nod to Mike's cover for *The Curse Bells* #5.

Also by MIKE MIGNOLA

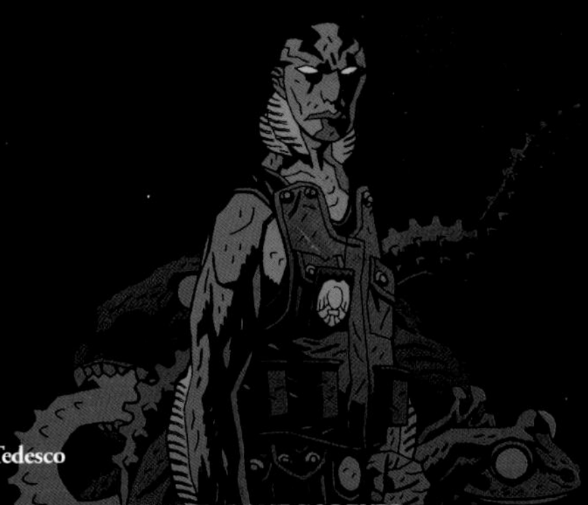

.R.D.

UE OF FROGS
ne 1
hris Golden, Guy Davis, and others
SBN 978-1-59582-609-1 | $34.99
ISBN 978-1-59582-675-6 | $19.99

ne 2
ohn Arcudi, Davis, and others
SBN 978-1-59582-672-5 | $34.99
ISBN 978-1-59582-676-3 | $24.99

ne 3
Arcudi and Davis
ISBN 978-1-59582-860-6 | $34.99
ISBN 978-1-61655-622-8 | $24.99

me 4
Arcudi and Davis
ISBN 978-1-59582-974-0 | $34.99
: ISBN 978-1-61655-641-9 | $24.99

–1948
Joshua Dysart, Paul Azaceta, Fábio Moon,
iel Bá, Max Fiumara, and Arcudi
N 978-1-61655-646-4 | $34.99

NG HUMAN
Scott Allie, Arcudi, Davis, and others
N 978-1-59582-756-2 | $17.99

IPIRE
Moon and Bá
N 978-1-61655-196-4 | $19.99

.R.D. HELL ON EARTH

W WORLD
Arcudi and Davis
N 978-1-59582-707-4 | $19.99

DS AND MONSTERS
h Arcudi, Davis, and Tyler Crook
BN 978-1-59582-822-4 | $19.99

SSIA
h Arcudi, Crook, and Duncan Fegredo
BN 978-1-59582-946-7 | $19.99

IE DEVIL'S ENGINE
D THE LONG DEATH
th Arcudi, Crook, and James Harren
BN 978-1-59582-981-8 | $19.99

IE PICKENS COUNTY
ORROR AND OTHERS
ith Allie, Jason Latour, Harren,
d Max Fiumara
BN 978-1-61655-140-7 | $19.99

IE RETURN OF THE MASTER
th Arcudi and Crook
BN 978-1-61655-193-3 | $19.99

COLD DAY IN HELL
ith Arcudi, Peter Snejbjerg, and
aurence Campbell
SBN 978-1-61655-199-5 | $19.99

HE REIGN
F THE BLACK FLAME
ith Arcudi and Harren
SBN 978-1-61655-471-2 | $19.99

HE DEVIL'S WINGS
vith Arcudi, Campbell,
oe Querio, and Crook
SBN 978-1-61655-617-4 | $19.99

LAKE OF FIRE
with Arcudi and Crook
ISBN 978-1-61655-402-6 | $19.99

FLESH AND STONE
with Arcudi and Harren
ISBN 978-1-61655-762-1 | $19.99

METAMORPHOSIS
with Arcudi, Snejbjerg, and Julián Totino Tedesco
ISBN 978-1-61655-794-2 | $19.99

END OF DAYS
with Arcudi and Campbell
ISBN 978-1-61655-910-6 | $19.99

THE EXORCIST
with Cameron Stewart, Chris Roberson, and Mike Norton
ISBN 978-1-50670-011-3 | $19.99

ABE SAPIEN

THE DROWNING
with Jason Shawn Alexander
ISBN 978-1-59582-185-0 | $17.99

THE DEVIL DOES NOT JEST AND OTHER STORIES
with Arcudi, Harren, and others
ISBN 978-1-59582-925-2 | $17.99

DARK AND TERRIBLE AND THE NEW RACE OF MAN
with Allie, Arcudi, Sebastián Fiumara, and Max Fiumara
ISBN 978-1-61655-284-8 | $19.99

THE SHAPE OF THINGS TO COME
with Allie, S. Fiumara, and M. Fiumara
ISBN 978-1-61655-443-9 | $19.99

SACRED PLACES
with Allie, S. Fiumara, and M. Fiumara
ISBN 978-1-61655-515-3 | $19.99

A DARKNESS SO GREAT
with Allie, S. Fiumara, and M. Fiumara
ISBN 978-1-61655-656-3 | $19.99

THE SECRET FIRE
with Allie, S. Fiumara, and M. Fiumara
ISBN 978-1-61655-891-8 | $19.99

LOBSTER JOHNSON

THE IRON PROMETHEUS
with Jason Armstrong
ISBN 978-1-59307-975-8 | $17.99

THE BURNING HAND
with Arcudi and Tonci Zonjic
ISBN 978-1-61655-031-8 | $17.99

SATAN SMELLS A RAT
with Arcudi, Fiumara, Querio, Wilfredo Torres, and Kevin Nowlan
ISBN 978-1-61655-203-9 | $18.99

GET THE LOBSTER
with Arcudi and Zonjic
ISBN 978-1-61655-505-4 | $19.99

WITCHFINDER

IN THE SERVICE OF ANGELS
with Ben Stenbeck
ISBN 978-1-59582-483-7 | $17.99

LOST AND GONE FOREVER
with Arcudi and John Severin
ISBN 978-1-59582-794-4 | $17.99

THE MYSTERIES OF UNLAND
with Kim Newman, Maura McHugh, and Crook
ISBN 978-1-61655-630-3 | $19.99

FRANKENSTEIN UNDERGROUND

with Stenbeck
ISBN 978-1-61655-782-9 | $19.99

JOE GOLEM: OCCULT DETECTIVE—THE RAT CATCHER & THE SUNKEN DEAD

with Golden and Patric Reynolds
ISBN 978-1-61655-964-9 | $24.99

THE AMAZING SCREW-ON HEAD AND OTHER CURIOUS OBJECTS

ISBN 978-1-59582-501-8 | $17.99

BALTIMORE

THE PLAGUE SHIPS
with Golden and Stenbeck
ISBN 978-1-59582-677-0 | $24.99

THE CURSE BELLS
with Golden and Stenbeck
ISBN 978-1-59582-674-9 | $24.99

A PASSING STRANGER AND OTHER STORIES
with Golden and Stenbeck
ISBN 978-1-61655-182-7 | $24.99

CHAPEL OF BONES
with Golden and Stenbeck
ISBN 978-1-61655-328-9 | $24.99

THE APOSTLE AND THE WITCH OF HARJU
with Golden, Stenbeck, and Peter Bergting
ISBN 978-1-61655-618-1 | $24.99

THE CULT OF THE RED KING
with Golden and Bergting
ISBN 978-1-61655-821-5 | $24.99

NOVELS

LOBSTER JOHNSON: THE SATAN FACTORY
with Thomas E. Sniegoski
ISBN 978-1-59582-203-1 | $12.95

JOE GOLEM AND THE DROWNING CITY
with Golden
ISBN 978-1-59582-971-9 | $99.99

BALTIMORE; OR, THE STEADFAST TIN SOLDIER & THE VAMPIRE
with Golden
ISBN 978-1-61655-803-1 | $12.99

AVAILABLE AT YOUR LOCAL COMICS SHOP OR BOOKSTORE! • To find a comics shop in your area, call 1-888-266-4226.
For more information or to order direct visit DarkHorse.com or call 1-800-862-0052 Mon.–Fri. 9 AM to 5 PM Pacific Time.
Prices and availability subject to change without notice.

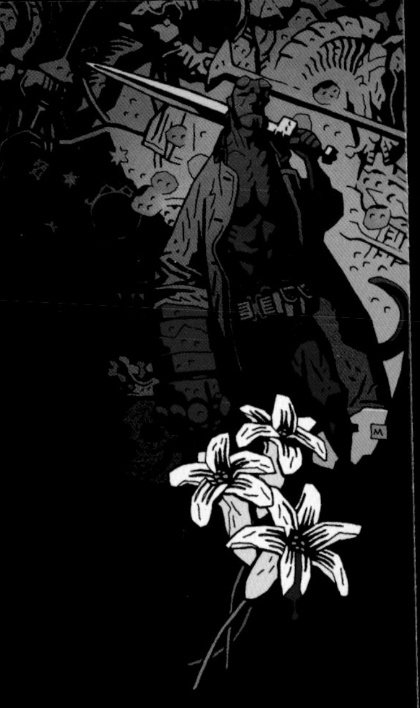

HELLBOY™

by MIKE MIGNOLA

HELLBOY LIBRARY EDITION VOLUME 1:
Seed of Destruction and Wake the Devil
ISBN 978-1-59307-910-9 | $49.99

HELLBOY LIBRARY EDITION VOLUME 2:
The Chained Coffin and The Right Hand of Doom
ISBN 978-1-59307-989-5 | $49.99

HELLBOY LIBRARY EDITION VOLUME 3:
Conqueror Worm and Strange Places
ISBN 978-1-59582-352-6 | $49.99

HELLBOY LIBRARY EDITION VOLUME 4:
The Crooked Man and the Troll Witch
with Richard Corben and others
ISBN 978-1-59582-658-9 | $49.99

HELLBOY LIBRARY EDITION VOLUME 5:
Darkness Calls and the Wild Hunt
with Duncan Fegredo
ISBN 978-1-59582-886-6 | $49.99

HELLBOY LIBRARY EDITION VOLUME 6:
The Storm and the Fury and The Bride of Hell
with Duncan Fegredo, Richard Corben, Kevin Nowlan, and Scott Hampton
ISBN 978-1-61655-133-9 | $49.99

SEED OF DESTRUCTION
with John Byrne
ISBN 978-1-59307-094-6 | $17.99

WAKE THE DEVIL
ISBN 978-1-59307-095-3 | $17.99

THE CHAINED COFFIN AND OTHERS
ISBN 978-1-59307-091-5 | $17.99

THE RIGHT HAND OF DOOM
ISBN 978-1-59307-093-9 | $17.99

CONQUEROR WORM
ISBN 978-1-59307-092-2 | $17.99

STRANGE PLACES
ISBN 978-1-59307-475-3 | $17.99

THE TROLL WITCH AND OTHERS
with Richard Corben and others
ISBN 978-1-59307-860-7 | $17.99

DARKNESS CALLS
with Duncan Fegredo
ISBN 978-1-59307-896-6 | $19.99

THE WILD HUNT
with Duncan Fegredo
ISBN 978-1-59582-431-8 | $19.99

THE CROOKED MAN AND OTHERS
with Richard Corben
ISBN 978-1-59582-477-6 | $17.99

THE BRIDE OF HELL AND OTHERS
with Richard Corben, Kevin Nowlan, and Scott Hampton
ISBN 978-1-59582-740-1 | $19.99

THE STORM AND THE FURY
with Duncan Fegredo
ISBN 978-1-59582-827-9 | $19.99

HOUSE OF THE LIVING DEAD
with Richard Corben
ISBN 978-1-59582-757-9 | $14.99

THE MIDNIGHT CIRCUS
with Duncan Fegredo
ISBN 978-1-61655-238-1 | $14.99

HELLBOY IN MEXICO
with Richard Corben, Fábio Moon, Gabriel Bá, and others
ISBN 978-1-61655-897-0 | $19.99

HELLBOY IN HELL VOLUME 1: THE DESCENT
ISBN 978-1-61655-444-6 | $17.99

HELLBOY IN HELL VOLUME 2: THE DEATH CARD
ISBN 978-1-50670-113-4 | $17.99

HELLBOY: THE FIRST 20 YEARS
ISBN 978-1-61655-353-1 | $19.99

THE ART OF HELLBOY
ISBN 978-1-59307-089-2 | $29.99

HELLBOY II: THE ART OF THE MOVIE
ISBN 978-1-59307-964-2 | $24.99

HELLBOY: THE COMPANION
ISBN 978-1-59307-655-9 | $14.99

HELLBOY: WEIRD TALES
ISBN 978-1-61655-510-8 | $24.99

HELLBOY: MASKS AND MONSTERS
with James Robinson and Scott Benefiel
ISBN 978-1-59582-567-4 | $17.99

HELLBOY AND THE B.P.R.D: 1952
with John Arcudi and Alex Maleev
ISBN 978-1-61655-660-0 | $19.99

HELLBOY AND THE B.P.R.D: 1953
with Chris Roberson, Ben Stenbeck, Paolo Rivera, and Joe Rivera
ISBN 978-1-61655-967-0 | $19.99

THE HELLBOY 100 PROJECT
TPB: ISBN 978-1-61655-932-8 | $12.99
HC: ISBN 978-1-61655-933-5 | $24.99

NOVELS

HELLBOY: EMERALD HELL
By Tom Piccirilli
ISBN 978-1-59582-141-6 | $12.99

HELLBOY: THE ALL-SEEING EYE
By Mark Morris
ISBN 978-1-59582-142-3 | $12.99

HELLBOY: THE FIRE WOLVES
By Tim Lebbon
ISBN 978-1-59582-204-8 | $12.99

HELLBOY: THE ICE WOLVES
By Mark Chadbourn
ISBN 978-1-59582-205-5 | $12.99

SHORT STORIES

Illustrated by Mike Mignola

HELLBOY: ODDER JOBS
By Frank Darabont, Charles de Lint, Guillermo del Toro, and others
ISBN 978-1-59307-226-1 | $14.99

HELLBOY: ODDEST JOBS
By Joe R. Lansdale, China Miéville, and others
ISBN 978-1-59307-944-4 | $14.99

AVAILABLE AT YOUR LOCAL COMICS SHOP OR BOOKSTORE! • To find a comics shop in your area, call 1-888-266-4226.
For more information or to order direct visit DarkHorse.com or call 1-800-862-0052 Mon.–Fri. 9 AM to 5 PM Pacific Time.
Prices and availability subject to change without notice.

DARK HORSE BOOKS
DarkHorse.com

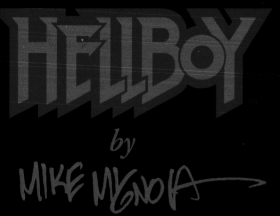